FINDING
Maggie

BY TERRY SYKES-BRADSHAW

ISBN 978-0-9822187-6-1

Library of Congress Control Number: 2016918039

Printed in U.S.A.

Published by Braughler Books LLC
braughlerbooks.com

Dedication

"Mom always liked you best."
Tommy Smothers

In loving memory of my brother Bill, aka Kayak Santa.
I'm sure Bill would have liked to dictate his own
dedication so I'll try my best to channel him --
To my brother who was smart, handsome,
hilarious and brave. Not to mention, a master craftsmen
making his own kayaks and a boater extraordinaire.

It was nice growing up with someone like you –
someone to lean on, someone to count on –
someone to tell on!

You should be here.
I miss you.

ACKNOWLEDGMENTS

I'm not sure why I thought the third time would be the charm. I should have known better. Publishing is NOT easy whether it's the first book or the third or the 300th. Although considering the amount of time it takes me to get a book published most of you will be sipping herbal tea at the old folks home before you see number four, let alone 300.

So if, as they say, it takes a village I'd say that mine is approaching the population of a megalopolis. The Mayor of my village is, of course, my sister Kathy Shimp without whom Maggie would still be lost. She has been my confidant and support through this lengthy passage and always has my back. *Te quiero.*

I wouldn't be here either without the Village Council, my book club, the Book Babes of Fort Myers who served as first readers, critics and wine connoisseurs. Everything goes better with wine, right? Especially this book. Thanks so much for your input.

I owe a lot to the rest of the village people (no, not *those* Village people). I'd like to thank —

- my brilliant and talented daughter and cover photographer, Kathy Bradshaw. You always make me look good.

- my mom who uses her red pen liberally and still supports me even when I (in her opinion) put in too many commas.

- my family — Chris, Helen, Alyssa and Kathy. You are the sunshine in my life. You make me smile. Most of the time.

- my friends Edie and Grace. I love you both for just being there for me.

- Pamela Fagan Hutchins for reading Maggie while she recuperated from surgery. Definitely above and beyond and her suggestions were right on target.

- Katrina Kittle for editing the final version and being a cheerleader as well as the adverb police. Even though I confess I didn't take all of them out. Seriously.

- David Braughler and Braughler Books for loving Maggie and finally getting her out there.

- my husband, Bill, who uses tough love to keep me on track. No wine until the day's work is done! Thank you for sticking with me through writers' block and crabby times. I love you always and all ways.

It does take a village. I'm grateful for mine. **You are the best.**

CHAPTER
One

Maggie Murphy teetered on the brink of the precipice – her toes curled over the rocky ledge to keep her balance. Her legs wobbled with fatigue. It had been a long climb to the summit but the view was definitely worth it. At the bottom of the steep ravine she could make out huge boulders tumbled along the bank of a rushing river. A gust of wind tousled her hair and a single drop of perspiration dripped from her forehead and down her cheek. A large bird swooped over her head nearly brushing her face with its wing. Maggie ducked.

She heard a branch snap as a shower of small pebbles exploded from the mountain path behind her and cascaded down the slope. Startled, Maggie's heart pounded. She wasn't alone? What was it? A bear? Was she about to be eaten by a bear? She lurched away from the drop off and whirled to confront the intruder. Not a bear but a man, dressed all in black – his eyes glaring and his face contorted with rage.

She inched backward as he advanced toward her. One step. Then another. She couldn't tear her gaze from his face, lost her footing and toppled over the edge of the cliff into the void.

Maggie opened her mouth to scream but the rushing wind tore the words from her lips as she plummeted toward the rocks far below. The sky and trees blurred as the boulders loomed closer and closer. She squinched her eyes closed and braced for the impact and – woke up in a cold sweat.

Heart racing, Maggie rolled over onto her back and yanked the covers up under her chin. She focused on the ceiling as she reentered the real world. Her breathing slowed and she used a corner of the sheet to wipe the perspiration from her forehead.

It wasn't the first time she'd had that dream -- no, nightmare -- and, she feared it wouldn't be the last. She turned onto her side and tried to forget it and the stomach-clenching plunge, but she couldn't escape the images no matter how hard she tried. She did her yoga breathing exercises in an attempt at sleep but it was no use. She gave up, shoved aside the tangled covers and stumbled out of bed and into the bathroom.

She didn't turn on the lights until after she used the toilet and was standing at the sink with cold -- damn the plumbing -- water running over her hands. She contemplated her image in the mirror. Then she dried her hands and ran her still damp fingers through her short blonde hair trying to fluff it back into something other than sleep-distorted disarray. She sighed. She looked exactly like she felt. Tired, disheveled and out of sorts.

She turned out the light and reached for the door into the bedroom -- illuminated by the neighbor's bright security lighting. She could see the lump in the bed that was her husband, Dwight. Oblivious to everything. Especially her. Her hand on the door, she stopped and, without actually thinking about it, stepped into her walk-in closet. She felt for the light switch, jamming her nail against the wall before she found it and flicked it on. And then, as if guided by some ethereal presence, she pulled on her favorite pair of jeans, a T-shirt and a sweater and grabbed her gym bag from the floor.

She tiptoed through the bedroom and paused by the bed to stare at Dwight. His snores were the only sound in the room. She shook her head and closed the door behind her, careful not to make a sound as she made her way downstairs and into the kitchen.

Coffee, she thought. I need coffee. She tiptoed across the room to get to the coffeemaker. It stood as a reproachful sign of the direction Maggie's life was taking, because at that moment she remembered that she had forgotten to buy coffee during her grocery-shopping trip the day before. Life without coffee in the morning was simply unacceptable.

Okay, then, I'll just go out and get a cup. She glanced at the clock on the stove. Not even five o'clock. Not much open, but maybe the gas station on the corner? Yes, of course, the gas station was open. She could get coffee there.

Maggie pulled on her tall boots and her leather jacket. She scooped her purse off the counter, threw it over her shoulder and started out the door. Then she turned back to the dry erase board hanging on the wall. Probably the majority of the communication between Dwight and her was done on that board. Snippets of information about comings and goings. That was about it these days. Still … she scrawled a quick message so that he wouldn't worry about her. *"Gone for coffee. And a drive. Talk later. M."*

She yanked open the back door to the garage and a puff of air blew a crumpled piece of lined note paper off the counter and onto the floor. Maggie stooped to retrieve it and recognized Dwight's precise handwriting. *"Maggie. Pick up my good suit at cleaners. Go to bank to pay mortgage. Buy beer."*

Maggie stared at the note. She was certain that if she'd looked in the mirror she would see smoke curling from her ears. *Seriously. What ever happened to please and thank-you? Buy beer? I don't even drink beer. Uh uh. No way.*

She snatched a pen from the counter and scratched her response. *"Do it yourself!"* Then anchoring the page under Dwight's car keys, she stalked out the door.

Maggie popped into her red VW bug, threw her gym bag into the back seat and had the music blaring before she was out of the driveway. She grinned as she pictured the disapproving faces of her son and daughter, James and Julie. They both acted like she was an outdated relic and her music only a step removed from natives beating on jungle drums. Ha, they weren't here now were they? Maggie turned the volume up and tapped her fingers to the beat on the steering wheel. Once she was on her way she drove still fuming over Dwight's assumption that she would just run any errands he dictated she should. She forgot for a moment that she was just going out for coffee. She steered through her silent neighborhood and reflected on how peaceful it was before the day's activities began in earnest. She noted the lights on at the Dillon place and wondered if Janet Dillon was practicing her Jazzercise routines before her 5:45 a.m. class. Now that was dedication. Maggie thought, maybe I should get certified and teach Jazzercise. It's not like *I* have anything important to do — besides run errands for King Dwight. She turned the corner and relegated Janet and her dance moves and Dwight and his bossiness to oblivion. Time to think about it later.

3

She drove without any particular destination in mind for some time, her thoughts skittering from worries over one child to worries over the other. Sometimes it felt like all she ever did was worry. Both of her offspring believed it was perfectly acceptable to dump all their problems on Maggie -- Julie's roommate was a party girl who invited her boyfriend to frequent overnights in their shared room. James changed his major on a daily basis and needed constant counseling on whether or not to transfer to a school less academically challenging. Both expected her to wave her magic Mom-wand and make everything okay again. Maybe Maggie believed she could do it too. The thing was, she realized, she didn't want to do it anymore. Being the emotional center of everyone's universe was exhausting. And, frankly, not that much fun. There used to be more to life.

She spotted a beat up red pickup truck with a license plate that read, *"Hot Shot"* and Maggie found herself following it onto the interstate and heading south. *All men are the same. Hot Shot, indeed. Maybe I'll just drive for a while and then I'll turn around. Maybe I'll stop at the outlet mall and do some shopping.* She pulled into the left lane and accelerated as she cranked up the music . "Save me San Francisco," warbled Train. "I've been yes but now it's hell no," Maggie sang along, changing the words to fit her mood.

She'd been driving for about an hour when she realized that she had never gotten her coffee. The longing for a fortifying hot cup nagged her until she took the next exit and pulled into a McDonald's. She was surprised at how busy it was. In her suburban isolation she hadn't been aware of how many people were up and out at this ungodly, at least to her, hour of the day. She parked her car, slid out and looked around assessing the other customers. It was still dark and a hazy moon floated just above the horizon. Tall spotlights lit up the parking lot and Maggie counted mostly trucks − stenciled on the side with various business names and logos -- and an occasional car. A chilly breeze ruffled her hair. She zipped her leather jacket to her chin and hurried toward the entrance

Inside the restaurant Maggie was greeted by the familiar aromas of coffee and baked goods. Her stomach rumbled and she considered whether or not to order an Egg McMuffin or some other calorie-and fat-laden breakfast item to go with the coffee. A good-looking man wearing a black leather jacket and a light blue crewneck sweater sat at a table by the window sipping coffee as he focused on his iPad. He looked up and smiled at her as she breezed by him. Maggie gulped. She had to admit that she was out of practice. Way out of practice. But if she wasn't mistaken that smile said, "Whoa. I think you're extremely attractive." Was he flirting with her? Suddenly Maggie found herself riveted by the contents of her purse. She dug around -- looking for what? Lip gloss? Seriously, she chastised herself, that cute guy is not flirting with a middle-aged wife and mother. Is he? She smiled back at him and hurried to the counter — her heart pounding just the tiniest bit and a tiny grin turning up the corners of her mouth. You really need to get out more, she thought.

A young woman and a little girl of about three stood in front of Maggie in line. The young woman was dressed in worn jeans and denim jacket. She had some bills crumpled in her hand and was debating the breakfast options with the little girl. The little girl's blonde curls made her think about her daughter Julie at about that age. The child clutched the leg of the young woman's jeans and looked up at her. "But I want ..."

"We'll see, Chloe," the young woman said as a look of sheer panic crossed her face.

Maggie looked over her shoulder following the woman's gaze and saw a pair of state troopers entering the restaurant. They appeared to be checking out the place, scanning the various customers. The young woman froze as it seemed that the troopers' eyes had landed on her.

Maggie made an impulsive decision. The little girl reminded her so much of Julie. Something about that determined little face tugged at her and she stooped so that she was eye level with her. "Chloe," she said, "do you want the pancakes or some scrambled eggs this morning? You know I promised whatever you wanted today."

Chloe's eyes grew round, but she was willing to play the game if she got her pancakes out of the deal. "Pancakes, please," she said.

The young woman turned, her back to the troopers, and mouthed, "Thank you," at Maggie.

"Not a problem, sweetie," Maggie said to the little girl, "Nanas are good for pancakes you know."

Maggie scooped up Chloe and breathed in that special little girl smell — a cross between crayons and baby shampoo. A Julie smell. Maggie whispered, "You know you should never, ever talk to a stranger, but since your mommy is here it's okay. Just this once."

"But she isn't my mommy."

Oh, God, Maggie thought, here I am aiding and abetting a kidnapper. What was I thinking? She was about to signal the troopers when Chloe said, "She's my big sister, April."

Maggie exhaled as the knot in her stomach eased and she placed the order for Chloe's pancakes and her own Egg McMuffin. She examined the face of Chloe's big sister more carefully. She couldn't have been older than 15 or 16. She turned to her and said, "Order whatever you want. It's on me."

The troopers, having found nothing of concern, were drinking their own cups of coffee and laughing with one of the clerks. Carrying a tray of food, Maggie led the two girls to a corner booth and set the food down on the slightly sticky laminate top. Maggie scrubbed at an orange juice spill with a napkin while Chloe dug into her pancakes as if she hadn't eaten in a month. Maggie leaned back and sipped her coffee and waited for the older girl to explain.

April? Was it? fiddled with her food and finally met Maggie's gaze. "Thank you so much for all of this. I have some money, but I have to make it last."

Maggie said nothing and picked at her muffin.

"I didn't commit any crime if that's what you're thinking," April continued. "Well, not really."

"What are you doing then?" Maggie asked. "You seemed pretty spooked by those troopers."

April scrutinized Maggie without speaking for a few seconds. Then said, "My mom died a few days ago. And all that's left for Chloe and me is my stepdad. He's never liked us. We were always too much trouble. As long as Mom was around it was okay. He wouldn't hurt us but now? I don't know -- I can't let Chloe stay in that house."

"So you grabbed your little sister and ran?"

"I'm not running really. I'm going to find my mom's sister. My Aunt Molly."

"And she's said she'll take you in?"

"No-o-o-o," April said. "Not yet. But she will."

Maggie sighed. She really should turn the girl over to the troopers, she really should, but something was holding her back. There was just something about the two girls made her want to make things right for them. Maybe it was as simple as that they needed her. Stupid as that might be.

"What makes you think that?" Maggie asked.

"Mom talked all the time about Aunt Molly and how close they were as kids. But Aunt Molly didn't like Kurt. That's my stepdad. Aunt Molly tried to talk Mom out of marrying him and Mom wouldn't listen. So Aunt Molly wouldn't talk to Mom anymore. But with Mom gone, maybe she'd want us." The girl's voice was hopeful.

"Are you sure she could she even afford to take you in?"

"Mom said Aunt Molly fell into a pot of money. Married a sweet rich guy who would give her the world. She said Aunt Molly had a big house and too much time on her hands. So-o-o ..." April spread her hands. "I know she'll take us."

"And where does this Aunt Molly live?"

April chewed her lower lip. "Not far. In Stallingsworth."

Maggie stared at her. "Not far? It's at least 200 miles. And you and Chloe are walking?"

April squirmed. "I -- um -- thought we could hitch."

Maggie's eyebrows shot up. "Hitch? You thought you'd hitch with a three year old in tow? April, that's totally out of the question."

April hung her head. "I guess. Are you going to turn us over to those troopers then?"

Maggie dared a quick glance at the troopers who, finished with their coffee, were heading for the door. And then she made a decision. "I might regret this. I probably will. But I'll take you to your Aunt Molly's."

April launched herself over the table at Maggie and flung her arms around her in a huge hug nearly upending a glass of orange juice. Laughing and crying, she said, "Oh, thank you. Thank you. I'll pay you. I have money. Oh, thank you."

Maggie held April for a moment before she disentangled herself from her arms. "Wait. There is a condition. I'll take you to your aunt's house, but if she can't or won't take you and your sister, I'm taking you back to your stepdad's house. That's the deal. Take it or leave it."

April frowned. "I don't know."

"I have to go potty, April," Chloe said. "Now."

"Okay, sweetie," April said to her and turned to Maggie. "It's a deal. I know Aunt Molly will want us. I just know it."

As Maggie watched the two girls head for the restroom, she had to wonder what she'd gotten into. Wasn't kidnapping punishable by death and dismemberment? Or maybe just life in prison? Without cute shoes and purses. Oh Good Lord. But she couldn't leave them on their own, could she? No way.

CHAPTER
Two

Chloe skipped ahead of Maggie and April as they left McDonald's. As they approached her red Bug, Chloe stopped in her tracks and whirled around to grab her big sister's arm. "Punch buggy," she cried.

Maggie and April laughed at her obvious delight.

"Haven't heard that one in a while," Maggie said.

Chloe's face lit up as she realized that not only was she seeing a "punch buggy," but also she would be riding in one. "This is your car?" she said. "I'm riding in this car?"

"It's mine all right," Maggie said. "Every last bit."

Maggie popped the trunk and took April's backpack from her. "Is this all you've got?" she asked. "Hardly seems like enough for the two of you."

"I didn't want Kurt to notice anything different so I couldn't pack an entire suitcase. Besides I have enough money to buy us what we need."

Maggie made a skeptical face. "I'm sure you do."

The three of them piled into Maggie's Bug, Chloe bouncing and giggling in the back seat. "Buckle up, back there," Maggie said. "I don't have a car seat for you."

Maggie turned to April. "Do you have an address for your Aunt Molly?"

April gave her the address and Maggie plugged it into her GPS. (She'd asked Dwight for a special necklace for Christmas last year and he responded with the GPS. Always a romantic.) "Okay, then," Maggie said. "Off we go."

As they pulled out of the parking lot and onto the interstate, Maggie debated again the wisdom of her decision to take the girls. She knew they were runaways. And maybe they had frantic parents searching for them. She probably should turn around and turn the girls in. That would be the responsible thing to do. Wouldn't it? But one look at April's face scrunched in concentration as she played with the radio, dialing in a Top 40 station, and she knew she was in for the duration. She couldn't abandon them. Her gut told her that she was doing the right thing, and so she squelched the suspicious voice in her head and just drove.

Several hours, one donut stop and two potty stops later, the GPS, affectionately called Betty, directed her into a quiet, tree-lined street in a pleasant, moderately upscale neighborhood in Stallingsworth. Chloe and April had lapsed into subdued silence and gazed with wide eyes at the well-tended homes.

"Oh, April," Chloe piped from the backseat. "Did you see? That house has a pool!"

"Shh-h," April said. "I'm concentrating." She gripped the piece of paper with the address on it with tense fingers.

Suddenly both "Betty" and April spotted their destination—2324 Flower Petal Lane. A two-story brick with a large front porch. Shrubs lining the front walkway and driveway. Large trees dotting the spacious lawn. It looked homey and welcoming. A basketball hoop stood guard next to the drive and a bike lay abandoned in the grass. A tan SUV with its doors wide open sat in front of the dark blue painted garage door. Maggie pulled into the driveway and sat with the engine idling, trying to decide what to do next. Before she could make a plan, the front door flew open and a woman about Maggie's age burst out. She wore skinny jeans tucked into riding boots and a long, grey tunic sweatshirt. Her dark hair was pulled back into a ponytail and huge sunglasses shaded her eyes.

"That's her," April said and bolted out of the car and raced toward the woman.

"Aunt Molly," she cried and flung her arms around the woman who, startled, took a step back.

"Whoa," she said and tried to extricate herself, but April hung on, sobbing.

The woman managed to loosen April's grip and held her at arm's length to get a better view of the clinging girl. Emotions crossed her face in rapid succession. Her annoyance at being accosted ebbed into shock and recognition and finally her face melted into tears.

"April?" she said. "Can it really be you? What are you doing here?"

Maggie turned off the engine and helped Chloe from the back seat of the car. The two of them stood watching the tearful reunion from a short distance. Chloe sucked on her thumb and used her other hand to clutch Maggie's. Her tiny fingers were icy.

"Aunt Molly?" she whispered.

Aunt Molly looked over April's head and spotted Maggie and Chloe. She broke free of April's grip and ran the short distance to squat on her heels in front of Chloe. For a moment, the two of them gazed at each other. Chloe appeared as confused and unsure as the woman herself seemed to be.

The silence stretched out until Aunt Molly reached forward and scooped Chloe up in her arms. "Baby doll. Oh, my sweet Lord, you've gotten so big."

Chloe squirmed to get down, but Aunt Molly held on tight and as April appeared at her side, she looped an arm around her shoulders and pulled her into a group hug. After a few moments the woman noticed Maggie standing to one side, shifting her weight from one foot to the other.

"Where's my sister? Where's Annie?" the woman asked.

"You don't know me," Maggie said. "And I don't know your sister. I just met April and Chloe this morning. It's a long story."

Molly, still holding her nieces, looked confused. "Then who are you?"

Maggie stuck out a hand. "I'm Maggie Murphy. Maybe I should let April explain."

The woman looked Maggie up and down and then shrugged. "I'm Molly Callahan. I guess we'd better go inside."

Molly led the way into the house and into the kitchen. She motioned the girls and Maggie to sit at the round wooden table while she started the coffeemaker and poured juice for April and Chloe. When everyone was settled, Molly shot Maggie a quizzical look. "Okay. I'm sure there's a perfectly good explanation for my nieces to show up on my doorstep at this time on a school day. And I want to hear it."

Maggie nodded at April. "Go ahead, honey. Tell your aunt what you told me."

April sucked in a huge breath. "We just couldn't stay with Kurt anymore, Aunt Molly. Not after Mom died. And so ... "

All the color drained from Molly's face. White-faced and shaking she dropped into a chair. "What? Annie dead? How? Why?"

"You didn't know?" April asked.

"My God. Of course, I didn't. I would have been there. Why didn't you call me?"

April stammered, "B-but K-kurt said he'd called you. And he s-aid that you were too busy with your k-kids to come to Mom's funeral."

Molly leaped to her feet and paced back and forth across the room. "That bastard," she said as her eyes filled with tears. "Oh, sorry, I shouldn't ... But, my God, what a liar. To keep me from my sister's funeral? I'll kill him."

Finally Molly calmed down enough to sit back down. She took both of April's hands in hers and said, "How did Annie -- your mom -- die? I didn't know she was sick. We haven't talked much in the last few years. Why didn't she call me? I could have helped."

"She wasn't sick, Aunt Molly. She was driving into town the other night and she got hit by a drunk driver."

"Oh, no! Not Annie! Was anyone else with her?"

"No," April said, "it was really late and Kurt wanted beer. And he was too drunk to drive himself so Mom went. I woke up when their voices got too loud and I heard them. Arguing. He was yelling and then he hit her."

"I will seriously kill the bastard." Molly put her hands over Chloe's ears. "What a monster."

Maggie felt uncomfortable and out of place. She would have preferred not to be involved, but felt maybe she should explain her part in the drama. "I happened to meet April and Chloe at the McDonald's on the interstate just outside of Clarksville and -- "

"The interstate?" Molly interrupted. "April, what were you and Chloe doing on the interstate?"

April refused to look at her aunt, staring into her juice glass. "I -- um -- was going to hitchhike here to talk to you and see if you could let us stay with you. Maggie bought us breakfast and offered to drive us."

Maggie was defensive. "I know I shouldn't have. And they shouldn't have trusted me, but ..." She spread her hands. "I didn't know what else to do."

Molly forced a grim half-smile. "It's okay, Maggie. I'm glad it was you who found them and not someone else."

Molly turned to April -- tears spilling down her cheeks. "You know better than to take a ride with a stranger, but -- this time you are forgiven."

Molly patted April's hand. "Why don't you take Chloe outside to get your stuff? I need to talk to Maggie alone for a minute."

When the girls left Molly scrubbed at her eyes with a napkin and said, "My sister married Kurt a few years ago when Chloe was a newborn. I never liked him and I knew he was bad news, but she was terrified to raise the girls alone after her first husband was killed in Iraq. So eyes wide open she walked into it. I tried to talk to her after the wedding, but every time I called Kurt would answer. He'd tell me that Annie was out or was busy with the girls. Always something. He said she'd call me back, but she never did. I managed to get her once or twice, but she was afraid he'd find out and wouldn't stay on the phone. Finally, I just gave up."

She slid her coffee mug around on the table, pushing it forward and back. "I'll take care of them now. I can't bring Annie back, but I can fix this with Kurt."

April and Chloe reappeared towing April's backpack.

"Kurt won't care, Aunt Molly," April said. "He always told Mom we were two big anchors that dragged them down. He hates us."

Molly narrowed her eyes. "Thank you, Maggie. I owe you everything. My husband and I will handle things. I can't tell you how grateful I am that you decided to have coffee at that McDonald's this morning."

She pushed back her chair. "Girls, let's take your bags upstairs and get you settled. I'll call your step -- um -- Kurt later."

The three of them walked Maggie outside to the Bug and she gave each girl a hug. "I think you'll be okay now," she said. "Your Aunt Molly will take care of you."

Wiping tears from her eyes April hugged Maggie back. "Thank you, Maggie. You rescued us."

They exchanged addresses, e-mails and phone numbers and Maggie climbed into her car. Molly had her arms around the girls as Maggie backed out of the driveway and headed for the highway. As she disappeared down the street, she could hear Chloe calling, "Bye, bye Maggie. Bye bye, Bug."

CHAPTER
Three

When Maggie was out of view, she pulled off the road and let her head fall back against the headrest. She finally was able to release the tears she had been holding in. She cried for a few minutes and then sat up and blew her nose. She wiped her eyes and dug a tissue out of her purse. *What was I thinking,* she wondered. *Who do I think I am, anyway? Super Maggie riding to the rescue of small children in distress astride a red VW Bug.* She shook her head. *I am crazy. I should just go home right now.* She checked her watch and did rapid calculations. If she left right now she could be home by early evening. She could make a late dinner for Dwight and -- There was something she needed to do first. Chloe's innocent little face and April's earnest one floated in front of her eyes. She picked up her cell phone and punched in Julie's number. Her daughter's voice would cheer her up. The phone rang and rang and Maggie was about to hang up when she heard Julie. "Hi, It's Julie. I can't take your call right now. I'm off finding a cure for the common cold. Leave your number and I'll get back to you when I've made the world safe for one and all."

Maggie grinned. Just like Julie. Couldn't leave an ordinary message. And she changed them at least once a week. Each message more outrageous than the last. She knew that her kids never listened to voicemail, but she needed to connect so she left a message for Julie. "Hi, babycakes. It's Mom. I just wanted to hear your voice. Call me when you cure the common cold. I love you. Bye."

Then Maggie heaved a sigh. Her cell phone languished on the passenger seat, a silent reproach to her thoughtlessness. Dwight must be mad with worry. Or more likely confused. She'd been gone since daybreak and hadn't called him. And that wasn't like her at all. To be honest, it had never even occurred to her to call. Now, though, before she got back on the road, she'd make that call.

She hit speed dial and waited for Dwight to answer. When he picked up after at least a million rings, he sounded breathless and his greeting was abrupt. "Yes?"

"Hey, it's me."

"Maggie?" His tone smoothed a bit. "Hey. I've been meaning to call but you know how it is. Hectic. I'm still at the office. Anyway, I won't be home until really late. Dinner with a client."

"You haven't tried to call me all day." Maggie said and allowed herself to be annoyed with him.

"No. Is there something I'm forgetting?"

Just me. "Not really. But I left before you were even up this morning and I thought you'd call."

Dwight sounded confused. "You weren't up when I left. You were still in bed."

He hadn't even noticed that she wasn't in bed. Nice! "I left you a note," she said. "Two actually."

"Didn't see any note. So, I'll see you at home later then. Gotta go."

"Wait," Maggie said, but she was too late. He'd disconnected.

So much for him worrying about her. She eased the car into gear and pulled back onto the road. As she neared the interstate she passed several large chain hotels and on impulse pulled into the parking lot of one of them. He'll never miss me she decided. And it's late and a long drive. *Maybe I'll just spend the night and drive home tomorrow. I'll call him later. Not that he'll even notice if I'm there or not.*

Maggie couldn't remember the last time she had stayed in a hotel room all by herself. All she knew for sure was that it felt decadent to have that king-sized bed, that king-sized bathroom, that tiny mini-bar, every square inch of territory, and not have to share a bit of it. She bounced on the bed aware that she was acting like a self-indulgent child. And she didn't care. She pushed the buttons on the remote control and tuned the television to the Lifetime Network where some sappy movie about unrequited love was playing. She wandered into the gleaming tiled bathroom and examined the lotions and potions provided there. Realizing that she'd left home before dawn, she knew that a shower would feel heavenly. What wouldn't feel heavenly, though, was putting on the same clothes she'd been in all day. Ugh. She checked the bedside clock and decided that she had enough time before dinner to run to the Target she'd seen close to the hotel. Grabbing her purse before she could have second thoughts, she hurried out of the room and downstairs to where she'd parked her car. If you're going to play hooky from your life, you might as well do it in fresh clothes.

An hour later Maggie was checking out of Target with considerably more than what she strictly speaking needed for her overnight adventure. She'd been in a shopping mood, though, and hadn't put up much resistance when something "spoke to her." She bought the necessities -- shampoo and conditioner, underwear, a pair of neon pink sleep pants and a matching tank top bedazzled with lime green sequins spelling out the word "Diva", as well as jeans, a couple of sweaters and the most adorable leopard print flat shoes she had ever seen. She added a bottle of wine and some chips to the basket and sighed in contentment. Now she was equipped for a great overnight.

She decided that she needed a wheeled bag to transport her loot and selected one of those. Then she detoured through the book department to pick up the newest paperback by her favorite author -- one she had been wanting to read for months. On her way to the front of the store to check out she cut through the stationery department and stopped dead in her tracks when she spotted a display of journals. Journaling, Maggie recalled, had always been something she really enjoyed. Back before life and children interfered. Back when she had thoughts that were worth writing down. So, hmmm. One journal in particular caught her attention -- on the cover was the Eiffel Tower decorated in multi-colored glitter. Maggie plucked it from the shelf and turned it over to examine it. Then, she shrugged and started to put it back. But what the heck? The Eiffel Tower brought back a myriad of memories -- maybe this was a sign. A sign of what she wasn't sure, but she tossed the journal in her cart and hastily headed for the check out lanes before she could find something else to buy.

She unloaded her purchases in her hotel room and took a long, luxurious shower before dressing for dinner. Clean clothes and hair improved her outlook and she felt upbeat as she entered the hotel dining room. It was only sparsely occupied and the maître d' ushered her to a table next to the window with a splendid view of the empty swimming pool. Maggie ordered a glass of wine and took her time reading the menu. She hadn't felt this relaxed and unhurried in a very long time. More to the point, she didn't miss Dwight. In fact, she was enjoying being alone. The solitude suited her just fine.

After the waiter took her order -- salmon and wild rice with braised veggies -- Maggie leaned back and sipped her wine as she gazed around the dining room. A youngish couple sat at a table close to her both absorbed, not in each other but in their respective phones. Texting or e-mailing or whatever. Maybe they weren't married, but certainly they had no particular interest in communicating. Other than by phone, of course. Maggie grimaced. *Reminds me of Dwight and his omnipresent iPhone.*

At another table an older couple leaned toward each other, laughing and talking. He said something and she threw her head back and peals of gaiety rang out and Maggie smiled at them. The woman noticed her and smiled back. Gave her a small wiggle of her fingers as if to say we're silly but we love it. Maggie thought about Dwight. *We used to be like that. When did we quit noticing each other?*

Maybe if she just made the effort. She dug in her purse and pulled out her cell phone and noticed that it was running low on battery. Naturally, she hadn't thought to pack up the charger in her rush to leave. She returned the phone to her bag. Save the battery and call him later.

The waiter served her dinner with a flourish and she ate it taking time to savor every bite. She didn't want this dinner to end so she prolonged it by ordering a decadent dessert and coffee. Finally, she couldn't eat or drink another thing and the dining room was nearly empty. Time to call it a night.

Maggie changed into her new pajamas and retrieved the bottle of wine from the mini-bar where she had left it chilling. Congratulating herself for remembering to buy a corkscrew, she struggled a bit, but managed to open the bottle. She smiled and poured wine into a drink glass, turned on the television and crawled into bed, propping herself up on a pile of pillows. Flipping through the channels, she sipped wine and munched chips. And -- Oh crap! She hated to interrupt her divine alone time, but one look at the clock told her that she had to call Dwight. Or not. How long would it take before he realized she wasn't there? It would serve him right if she didn't call. But her better instincts took over. And he probably would notice if she was AWOL all night. Probably.

She picked up her cell phone and called home. No answer. Damn Dwight anyway. Okay then, she'd leave a message on the machine. "Dwight, it's me. Maggie. I wanted to let you know that I won't be home tonight. I got tied up with something. I'm fine. You can call me if you feel like it. Love you, bye."

She disconnected and thought about it. Dwight typically ignored the answering machine and its little flashing light. Of course, any e-mail or text on his iPhone elicited his immediate attention. Maggie sighed and hit speed dial for Dwight's cell. She listened to it ring and ring and was composing a message in her head when he answered. Again, he was abrupt. "Dwight, here."

"Do you ever look at caller ID? It's I. Maggie."

"Oh, sorry babe. I should have called. I'll be late."

"Dwight, listen to me. I'm not home. I'm still in Stallingsworth."

There was dead silence and as the seconds ticked by Maggie thought he'd disconnected. Until, his voice harsh, Dwight said, "What the hell are you doing in Stallingsworth? Why aren't you home?"

Maggie blew out a sigh. "I got involved in something and I decided not to drive home tonight. I'm at a hotel."

"A hotel? By yourself? Honestly, Maggie, you're my wife. I thought -- I mean -- I need you to be home waiting for me."

Maggie's cheeks were hot and her heart pounded in her ears and any attempt to stay calm was shoved aside by righteous indignation. "You thought what? Waiting? I don't answer to you, Dwight Murphy. And I'll do what I damn well please. What are you? Some caveman?"

Dwight sounded apologetic when he answered. "Okay. That was a bit Neanderthal of me. But still -- I don't get it. You're in Stalling-sworth? When are you coming home?"

Maggie began to explain but then stopped. He wouldn't get it and she didn't feel like trying. "I'll be home -- " The phone went dead before she could finish her sentence.

"Tomorrow," she whispered to the empty room.

Maggie tossed the useless cell phone onto the bed and considered using the room phone to call him back. Then she gave an angry shake of her head. "Damn it. Let him stew."

She threw back the covers and launched herself out of bed. She snatched the wine bottle from the dresser and filled her glass to the top. Then she gulped most of it and refilled it before she settled back into the pillows. *To hell with Dwight. To hell with everything.* Maggie was exactly where she wanted to be and she was going to enjoy it if it killed her. She flipped channels until she found the Tonight Show and her anger fizzled away as she listened to Jay Leno joke with his guests. She opened the paperback she'd bought earlier and scrunched down so her head was supported by the pile of pillows. Reading in bed was a singular pleasure to Maggie but Dwight insisted on turning out the lights every night way before she was ready to put aside her book. Now, this, she told herself, was very nice. Maggie fell asleep with all the lights and the television still on and her book open on her chest, the dead cell phone nestled next to her.

Doors slamming and thudding footsteps in the hallway outside her door woke Maggie, and she was amazed to discover that it was morning. Her lips were glued to her teeth and her mouth tasted like garlic and old paste; a fragment of potato chip was stuck to her cheek from rolling over on the partially consumed bag; her eyelids were pasted to her eyes, but she felt surprisingly fantastic considering the half empty wine bottle leering at her from the desk. She had slept like she hadn't slept in weeks — barely moving, except, of course, to demolish the chip package.

Maggie stretched from the tip of her toes to the top of her matted hairdo. Hm-m-m. She sat up as she was struck by the realization that she hadn't had the dream of falling off the cliff that had been plaguing her for weeks. The one that, she concluded, was a metaphor for her entire life. She was being pushed over the edge and falling, falling, falling.

She punched up the pillows behind her head and channel surfed to find the Today Show. While Matt and Al kidded with each other Maggie contemplated the day ahead of her. When she thought about home, though, butterflies attacked her stomach and her body grew heavy with reluctance to abandon her little self-created cocoon right here in this lovely hotel.

Well, coffee would help, so she started the coffeemaker on the desk and waited for coffee to brew. The thought of eggs and pancakes and perhaps a muffin spurred her into action after she'd polished off the carafe of weak, bitter hotel coffee. Real coffee would be wonderful.

Maggie showered and climbed into some of her new clothes -- clean undies, jeans, a brightly striped pullover sweater -- and stood at the sink carefully applying make-up. She squinted at her reflection as she lined her eyes and brushed on mascara. She fluffed her hair and then dug through her gym bag for her flat iron. Good thinking, she complimented herself, bringing the gym bag. Lucky to have it stocked with make-up and hair necessities for after Jazzercise class.

When was the last time she'd spent so much time on her appearance? When had it mattered to her? She and Dwight had been married forever and he wouldn't have noticed if she'd painted her face like a mime and dyed her hair blue. So he wasn't a big inspiration. The kids weren't home anymore and even if they were they only saw Maggie as "good old mom" — always there for them no matter what. Maggie knew she was always in too much of a hurry to spend much time on her hair and make-up. She tended to race out the door, usually late for wherever she was heading, thrown together like a pile of castoffs, grabbing whatever was handy without any thought to fashion. Today, though, she was taking time. She deserved it, darn it.

When she finished, she stepped back to appraise herself. Not bad. Her short hair was stylishly cut, her eye make-up made her eyes look greener and larger, her tiny laugh-lines just gave her character. Her figure? Not bad either. All those hours at the gym or doing Jazzercise had been rewarded. What was there not to like?

"Looking, good, Maggie," she told her reflection. "Lookin' damn good."

When Maggie entered the dining room she was surprised to find it humming with activity. Nearly every table was filled and delicious aromas wafted on the air. She was instantly enveloped in the sound of convivial chatter and occasional laughter. A bright-eyed young hostess greeted her and escorted her to one of the few empty tables. Maggie sat down and looked around. She felt as if she were an island of solitude in the sea of activity. Rather than making her feel left out, though, she reveled in the idea that she was being swept along with the crowd toward someplace fun and festive.

As she drained her coffee cup and popped the last bit of English muffin into her mouth, an older woman at the next table leaned over. "Would you mind if I borrowed some of your Equal?" she said. "There isn't any on my table and I hate to bother my waitress."

"Of course," Maggie said as she handed her the bowl containing the sweeteners.

Maggie studied the woman as she stirred the sweetener into her coffee. Tiny with immaculately styled salt and pepper hair, the woman was well-dressed in a dark suit, bright jersey top and sleek black boots. A business woman Maggie guessed.

"Thank you so much, dear," the woman said as she returned the bowl. "It's busy here this morning isn't it?"

"It is," Maggie said. She angled her chair away from the woman and focused on the dinnerware.

But her neighbor wasn't going to be avoided. She pulled her own chair a bit closer to Maggie's table. Maggie could see that the woman was making herself comfortable.

"I'm Mary Lou Jennings," she said.

"Maggie Murphy."

"Nice to meet you, Maggie. Are you here for the conference?"

"Conference?"

"Yes, indeed, I'd say most of this crowd are here for it."

"Oh," Maggie said, not sure if she wanted to get involved or not.

"Get Your Groove On."

"Pardon me."

"The conference. It's called *Get Your Groove On*. For women trying to get a new start in life or restart an old one." Mary Lou Jennings considered Maggie for a moment. "You should come, my dear. I think you'd enjoy it. Charming women and a decent lunch."

Maggie looked around her at the other women in the dining room. There was a happy buzz of, perhaps, anticipation. The women seemed to have a purpose. At least, they were doing something for themselves if Mary Lou was correct. Getting their grooves on. Cool.

"But," Maggie said, "I'm not registered or anything. I don't have a spot."

"Registration at the door," Mary Lou said. She pointed. "Right over there."

"Well-l-l."

"Oh, come on," Mary Lou said, "what do you have to lose?"

Indeed! Maggie tossed her napkin onto the table. "Okay, Mary Lou, you got me. I'll do it."

The image of Dwight flickered in her mind. He'd definitely be annoyed. At least, she should call him, but her phone ... "I have to make a call first, though. Could I borrow your cell phone?"

"Of course, dear, but you need to hurry a bit. First session starts at nine." She handed Maggie her phone. "I have to get inside but you can give it to me later. Okay?"

"Thank you so much," Maggie said. "I'll hurry."

Maggie waited until Mary Lou dropped some bills on the table and hurried toward the ballroom where the conference was being held before she dialed Dwight's number. He answered on the first ring.

"Dwight here."

"It's me," Maggie said. Did he ever check caller ID? He should know who it was. Oh, well, it didn't matter. Did it?

"Maggie, thank God." The obvious concern in Dwight's voice nearly made Maggie change her mind.

Then she stiffened her back and pressed the cell phone against her ear. She took a deep breath. "I'm not coming home today after all. I'm going to attend a conference here in Stallingsworth and stay another night."

"But, Maggie," Dwight began, "you can't just ... "

Maggie knew she might relent if she talked to him much longer so she said, "Honey, I can't talk. First session is in 15 minutes and I have to register and get my room for another night. I'll call you later. Bye. Love you."

Maggie slumped in her chair. Whew. Had she made the right choice? Dwight had sounded alarmed. Maybe she should just go home after all. She was wrestling with her choice when Mary Lou reappeared.

"Come on, Maggie," she said. "Let's get you registered." She shepherded Maggie toward the registration table. Maggie's protest died before she could voice it.

"Lead me to it, Mary Lou," Maggie said. "I can't wait."

By the time Maggie completed her registration and arranged to have her room for another night, most of the other conference attendees had already assembled in the ballroom. She scanned the room looking for an empty seat and then, spotting one in the front of the room, made her way toward it. As she settled into the seat juggling her purse and the packet of conference information she'd been given, she heard someone introducing the first speaker and looked toward the stage. She was amazed to discover that it was her new friend Mary Lou Jennings being introduced. Apparently she was more than just another attendee. She was, in fact, the keynote speaker.

The audience grew quiet as Mary Lou began to speak. "I'd like to extend the warmest welcome to all of you women." She paused. "And the lone gentleman back there." All heads turned to focus on the single man in the group. Mary Lou continued. "I know it's been a long journey to get here today, but I hope that by the time you leave tonight you all will *Get Your Groove On.*"

Polite applause. Maggie applauded along with them.

"I am well aware," Mary Lou said, "that loss is not easy to deal with. No matter at what stage we are, we fear that loss. It changes us. It changes our lives."

Loss? Maggie observed her fellow participants. They looked like a typical gathering of women.

"After we lose someone dear to us," Mary Lou was saying, "we have a long journey until we are ready to resume our lives. Or start entirely new ones. The choice is ours."

Someone dear to us? Maggie cut her eyes to the woman next to her. A single tear ran down the woman's cheek. What on earth?

"We are here today to put aside our grief. To rise up from mourning. To begin anew. *To Get Our Groove On.*"

Applause again. Louder this time. And Maggie shot to attention as it dawned on her. Grief? Mourning? Loss? Oh, God, it was a gathering of widows — and, of course, the single widower. She certainly did not belong in this particular crowd. She started to edge out of her seat but her seatmate tugged on her arm. "Dear," she said. "It's all right. Don't be afraid. We all must face our lives as they are now. We can't run away."

"No," Maggie tried to explain, "I'm not ... "

"I know, dear," the woman said, "you don't think you're ready. But you are. Take it from me. After Stan died, I didn't think I'd ever be able to move on, but here I am."

"You don't understand," Maggie said, but the woman was no longer interested in Maggie. She had refocused her attention on Mary Lou behind the speaker's podium.

"So, in conclusion," Mary Lou said, "we'll reconvene after a short break for coffee and pastries. Look over your packets and you will see that we have four sessions scheduled. You can choose a workshop for each session. And, of course, a wonderful lunch will be provided. Thank you all for coming and let's say it together."

"Get Our Grooves On," the crowd chorused.

Oh, Lord, Maggie thought. I've got to get out of here. She started for the exit, but her path was blocked by groups of women gathering their things and chatting about which of the workshops each planned to attend. Before she could escape, she spotted Mary Lou bulldozing her way toward her.

"Maggie," Mary Lou said. "I'm so glad you decided to stay. Let me introduce you to one of the coordinators of this year's event. This is Clara Smythe. One of my dearest friends."

Maggie shook hands with Clara, a large woman dressed in a pant-suit and sensible shoes.

"Delighted to meet you, my dear," Clara said. "I'd recommend the workshop on restarting one's career for someone as young and pretty as you. That would be a good place to start."

"There's been a mistake," Maggie began, "I'm not … "

But Clara had turned to welcome another woman and then put her hand on Maggie's shoulder. "This is Sarah Duvall. She's going to the workshop. Why don't you two go in together?"

Sarah was younger than the other two, dressed in skinny jeans like Maggie's and boots. Her red hair was cut in a bob that swung over her eye as she grinned at Maggie. "Guess it's you and me, then. What's your name again?"

"It's Maggie. Maggie Murphy."

"Maggie, then, let me guess. You were a successful career woman before you married. And yes --" She shrugged. "You can be one again."

Maggie eyed Sarah and was about to make another denial. But then what the hell? Maybe she'd learn something and all the women she'd met so far had been so warm and welcoming. So what if Dwight wasn't exactly dead, their relationship sure was in need of mouth-to-mouth resuscitation.

"Okay, Sarah, let's go get some coffee and one of those fattening pastries."

Over the next few hours Maggie learned how to jumpstart an old career or jump into a new one (as close as she could remember her writing career died about the same time she gave birth to her first child); she got tips on how to dress for success (right up Maggie's alley) and how to plan for a secure financial future (Dwight handled all their finances — maybe it was time for her to learn the difference between stocks and bonds and mutual funds).

At first Maggie felt like a fraud. Dwight, although a bit of a jerk, was still very much alive. She had no business at a conference for widows, for heaven's sake. These courageous women were funny and smart and put Maggie to shame. She should absolutely not be complaining about her situation. Still, as she met more women and heard their stories, she began to be accepted into the group.

There was Ann (Richard— prostate cancer) and Donna (Max— heart) and Carol (Ron—plane crash) and of course, Clara (Ed—complications after surgery) and Mary Lou (Fred—stroke) and, saddest of all, she thought, Sarah (Brian—Land mine in Afghanistan). As she listened to the stories her admiration for these brave women grew. And whenever one of them asked about her dearly departed, Maggie squirmed and changed the subject.

Over lunch Maggie deflected all the inquiries with stammers and evasion, but finally as she was listening to Mary Lou's funny stories about her Fred and Clara's about her Ed, Maggie made a decision. These lovely people were opening their hearts and their lives to poor widowed Maggie. She couldn't let them down. The very next chance she got she was going to have to kill Dwight off. Nothing gory, she decided, but definitely fatal. She let her mind roam over the possibilities as the other women chatted about the morning.

Her opportunity arose more quickly than she anticipated. The women were discussing the choices of afternoon workshops and Sarah nudged Maggie and winked. "I'm thinking we should go to the one on getting back into the game."

"Game?" Maggie said.

Sarah made a comical face and winked again. "You know -- dating, romance, sex. Getting *that* groove on."

"Why not?" Maggie laughed. "Our sex life could certainly." She realized her mistake and hurried to cover her error. "I mean, our sex life could have used a boost." She stammered a bit. "I mean, while Dwight was alive that is."

There she'd done it. She'd killed him. Sorry Dwight. Let the games begin.

She had their attention now. Mary Lou set her coffee cup on the table and twisted to face Maggie. She put a hand on Maggie's arm and said, "Why, Maggie, dear, that's the first you've mentioned Dwight — was it?"

"Yes," said Clara. "Has he been gone long?"

Only a few minutes. "Not long," Maggie said. She forced a mournful look.

"Oh, my, " Ann said. "I knew it must be a recent death because you clammed up whenever we asked about him." She got up to come around the table to hug Maggie.

In turn each of her luncheon companions hugged Maggie and offered her tissues and condolences. Feeling even more a charlatan than before, Maggie tried to answer their well-meaning questions. Most were easy. She could tell a million stories about Dwight, but when the question she had been dreading came, she was not prepared.

"So, if you don't mind telling us," Sarah said, "how did he die? You're so young and all."

Taken aback at the directness of it, Maggie blurted the first thing that came into her mind. "It was murder."

Oh, God, now what had she done? The women's faces grew ashen with shock and horror. Maggie's words hung in the air like a storm cloud. Before this lie could go much further, Maggie had to fix it. "No, not really," she said. "I mean ..." What did she mean? *Think, Maggie, think.* "It was in a bank robbery." *Oh, much better.* "He was at the bank and bam." *Honestly. You could have just said it was cancer and been home free,* she chided herself as she watched the other women.

Stop it now. Tell them the truth. You are no more a widow than you are a runway model. You're a big fat liar. Tell them now. But the words stuck in her throat as the other women pummeled her with condolences.

"Oh, you poor thing."

"I think I heard about that."

"It must have been awful for you."

"So young. How sad."

Poor Dwight. Well, at least he died a hero. Maggie did that much for him. "It was terrible," she said, "but he tried to stop the robbery and..." She let the sentence dangle and allowed them to come to their own conclusions.

Maggie was saved from further fiction by the time. Afternoon sessions were about to begin and the group broke up, planning to meet again at the dinner.

As Sarah and Maggie walked together toward the session on igniting a love life, Sarah tugged Maggie into a corner and blocked her way as Maggie tried to edge past. Her eyes twinkling, Sarah grinned as she inspected Maggie's face. "Hey, girlfriend," she said, "your husband didn't die in a bank robbery did he?"

Maggie fumbled with the zipper on her jacket. She knew she was blushing and couldn't quite meet Sarah's eye. "I don't want to talk about it," Maggie said.

Sarah laughed. "I knew it." She took Maggie's arm. "Come on, let's go get our grooves on. You can tell me the rest later."

At dinner that night the luncheon companions gossiped about the workshops each had attended. Sarah regaled the group with stories about the workshop on dating and sex. "So," she said. "There was this one woman." She turned to Maggie. "How old would you say she was, Maggie?"

Maggie giggled. "Oh, about 80 give or take a decade."

"And she," Sarah continued, "asked so many questions. You could almost see the veins in the leader's neck. She was so exasperated, but trying to be kind."

"And then," Maggie prompted, "tell them what happened."

Sarah was chuckling even before she spoke. "This woman asks, all serious and straight-faced, what type of birth control she should use." Sarah hooted. "Birth control? Seriously?"

The rest burst into laughter. When she regained her composure, Mary Lou wiped her eyes on her napkin. "I'll bet that was Helen. She's a pistol. Attends every one of these things."

"It was hilarious," Maggie said. "At least she didn't ask what positions to try."

Sarah choked on her wine and Maggie pounded her on the back while their companions smiled and waited for the two to recover.

Fortunately for Maggie, two other bereaved people joined their dinner table. Their new companions were Marilyn (Douglas -- suicide) and Roger (Alice -- breast cancer), and they drew the focus of the sympathies of the others. Now that they knew that Dwight had "died of a gunshot" in a bank robbery, they were inclined to leave Maggie to her sorrow and not grill her. Sarah, though, kept flashing ironic looks at Maggie and murmuring, "Must have been awful for you," while Maggie scowled at her.

Over dry chicken and overcooked vegetables, Mary Lou entertained them with reminiscences about her hometown, Sweet River, South Carolina. According to Mary Lou it was the best place to live in the entire world. "The people in Sweet River are just about the most caring on earth," she drawled -- her accent getting thicker with each glass of wine. "Y'all would just not believe how they rallied around me when Fred died." Her voice trailed away and a faraway look crossed her face.

Clara leaned across the table and poked Mary Lou. "Hey, come back."

"So, how did y'all manage?" Mary Lou addressed everyone. "What got you through?"

"Facebook," Sarah said.

"Facebook?" Clara asked. "How did that work for you?"

As Sarah explained how Facebook helped her work through her grief, Maggie allowed her thoughts to drift back to her own life. She felt guilty sitting here with these people pretending to be something she wasn't. Here she was surrounded by people who had lost their true loves while she was simply running away from hers. Life wasn't fair. She was leaving behind what they had lost.

At last the meal ended and Maggie could escape with her guilt and remorse. Everyone drifted off to his or her room except Sarah who apparently had no intention of leaving Maggie to her unhappy thoughts. "Hey, Maggie," she said, "Want to get a drink in the bar? I could use some girl talk."

Now how on earth could Maggie say no to that? Poor young widow needs to talk. Maggie sighed and followed Sarah into the bar. Soon they were seated at a table sipping margaritas.

"So," Sarah said and put her elbows on the table and rested her chin on her hands. "Give it up, girl. Tell me."

"I'm sure I have no idea what you're talking about." Maggie sucked margarita through her straw.

"Right. I'll spell it out for you. You aren't a widow, are you? Your husband is not dead."

Maggie gulped. She guessed she wasn't as good an actress as she hoped to be. Sarah was on to her. "What makes you say that?"

"My awesome powers of perception," Sarah said. "Whenever you talk about him, the look on your face is annoyance, not grief. It's as simple as that."

"You are totally crazy," Maggie said.

"Uh huh. I'll tell you something. I came out of this whole mourning process with one thing. And that is I can smell a rat from a mile away." She smiled to soften her harsh words, but Maggie was stung.

Maggie hung her head. "Well, when you put it that way."

"I do. So give a poor grieving widow some dirt."

Maggie narrowed her eyes. "Not dirt exactly, but you're right. Dwight is very much alive and well."

"Ah, ha. I knew it."

"What made you so sure? I thought I was pretty convincing."

"Maybe," Sarah said with a chuckle, "but you should have seen your face when you told us that Dwight had been murdered. I thought you were going to pass out."

Maggie folded her hands behind her head and gazed at the ceiling. "Yeah, that wasn't my finest moment. I don't know what made me say that. It just came out."

"Then when you tried to change it? Oh, God." Sarah giggled.

"I thought it made him sound kind of noble."

"Maybe next time you should share with the widows that he died rescuing a small child from a burning building. You'll really get them with that."

Maggie examined Sarah's face. "Are you really this cynical?"

Sarah shook her head. "Not at all. It's my coping mechanism. Didn't you learn a thing about grieving today?"

"Way more than I wanted," Maggie said. "Want another?" She indicated her margarita glass. Sarah nodded and Maggie signaled their waitress. "It made me sad."

"Death is sad. Take it from me," Sarah said. "But life is not. So go live it. If you can't live with him, live without him. Just don't let your life slip away. I'm not going to and you aren't either."

By the time they finished their second drinks, Maggie and Sarah had forged a friendship that they knew would last far beyond the conference. They promised to stay in touch and sealed the deal with a third drink. And then coffee with Bailey's. Finally, they left the bar and took the elevator to their rooms. As Maggie got off at her floor she turned back and said, "Breakfast?"

"Can't," Sarah said. "My in-laws have the baby and I'm leaving early. But I'll call and e-mail and text and, oh yeah, Facebook."

"It's a deal."

They hugged and Maggie wandered down the hall and slipped into her room. Unbelievable. What a day.

CHAPTER
Four

Maggie overslept the next morning and by the time she got to the dining room, it was nearly empty. None of her friends from the conference were there, so she let the hostess lead her across the room to an unoccupied table set for one. Before she reached it, though, a woman seated by herself snagged her leg. Maggie stopped and found she had been waylaid by none other than Helen, the sex-crazed octogenarian.

"Weren't you at the *Get Your Groove On Conference* yesterday?" Helen asked.

"I was."

"Please join me," Helen said. "I hate to eat alone."

Maggie swung her head from side to side and, seeing no gracious way to decline, took the unoccupied chair at Helen's table. "Maggie Murphy," she said holding out her hand.

Helen shook it with a firm grasp. "Helen Potter."

Maggie waited for the waitress to pour her coffee and take their orders. As she watched the waitress cross the room, Maggie said, "So, did you enjoy the conference?"

Helen patted her perfectly coiffed hair. "I did. I come every year and I always learn something new."

I'll bet, thought Maggie. "It was informative," she said.

"Oh, yes," Helen agreed. "Didn't I see you at the workshop on sex?"

Maggie choked on her coffee. "Um, yes. You did."

"What did you think? I thought it was good as far as it went."

"Hmm-m." Maggie murmured.

Helen leaned across the table her blue eyes gleaming. "There was something I wanted to find out about and maybe you know."

Maggie squirmed in her chair, one foot jitterbugging under the table. "Hmm-m?"

Helen pulled her chair closer to the table and looked to make sure no one could overhear them before she whispered, "What do you know about a bikini wax?"

"B-b-bikini wax?" Maggie stammered. Her face was hot and she prayed for the floor to open up and swallow her. Then the absurd image of Helen getting a bikini wax floated into her mind and she had to bite her cheek to keep from laughing. Wait until she told Sarah about this one.

After that, Maggie figured she'd heard it all and managed to fend off Helen's questions with noncommittal answers and was amazed at how much she enjoyed her breakfast with the woman. She discovered that Helen was feisty and entertaining with a quirky sense of humor. She laughed more in an hour with Helen than she had in a month of breakfasts with Dwight.

Maggie was in an upbeat mood as she left the hotel thinking about her breakfast exchange. She tossed her bags in the back of her Bug and hopped in the front. She started the engine, put the car in gear and backed out of the parking space. As she was about to exit the lot she saw the big green signs above the highway directing the traffic. Pick one -- North toward home and Dwight. Or South toward the unknown. Maggie pulled into a vacant spot and turned off the engine.

She didn't know which direction she wanted to go.

Guilt swamped her as she thought of her conference friends. They couldn't choose to go home to the loved ones they had lost. She should go back to Dwight. That was the right thing, the responsible thing, to do. She loved him. Or she had loved him. Hadn't she? Yes, she had. But now? They weren't connecting on any level. Not even a sexual one. She thought of Helen. It wouldn't be fair to Helen to abandon her marriage. Go home to Dwight for Helen's sake? That made no sense.

A vision of Sarah's laughing face and sparkling eyes came to Maggie. Sarah told her to live her life. No one else's. Live for Maggie. Not for Helen or Dwight or even for Sarah. Okay. Then that's what she'd do. Have an adventure. Go South. Be a road warrior. Okay then. But what about the kids? They'd think Mom had gone over the edge.

Then it hit Maggie. Over the edge, indeed. Just like in her dream. She was shoved over the edge and she fell down and down spiraling out of control. Until she hit rock bottom. Or, in the case of her dream, woke up in time to avoid hitting rock bottom, which is exactly what she was going to do this very second. Avoid hitting bottom. Go back to the top of the cliff and try her wings. Soar. Go South.

She put the Bug in gear and accelerated onto the interstate — south-bound.

CHAPTER
Five

An hour later, Maggie was whizzing down the interstate, sunroof open, belting songs along with Tim McGraw as the CD player cranked them out. "Li-ve like you are flying," Maggie sang at the top of her voice, thinking of Julie as a little girl chirping those words from her carseat in back. Flying, indeed, was what the *Get Your Groove On* gang was doing.

It was one of those days when the sky was a brilliant cloudless blue and the sun shimmered overhead. Maggie enjoyed the freedom of being on her own. No one expected her anyplace in particular. No one could reach her on her dormant cell phone. She wouldn't allow her thoughts to stray to Dwight and the kids. Today was for her. Until, that is, she flew by the sign announcing that the next rest area wasn't for 70 miles and she glanced at the fuel indicator. Oops. Should have filled up before she hit the road. The low fuel light was gleaming an ominous orange and Maggie knew from experience that she didn't have 70 miles of gas left in the tank.

That wasn't a problem. A few miles further she spotted an exit sign and another sign listing the gas stations. Okay, then. She could use a break anyway. Buy some gas. Stretch her legs. Get coffee.

Just off the highway she wheeled into the nearest gas station and stood, hands pressed into the small of her back, staring up into the sky as the gas sloshed into the tank. When she was in motion, she hadn't let herself dwell on anything even remotely unpleasant. Now, however, she found herself worrying about Dwight. She had said she'd be home today and if she didn't show up he might freak out. Call the cops even to report a missing wife. At the very least be more than a little ticked off. She should call.

Serendipity. Maggie remembered passing a Verizon store close to the exit from the interstate. She'd stop there and buy a charger for her phone. She couldn't be out of touch forever even if conversation with Dwight held no appeal at the moment.

Tank filled and coffee stashed in the cup holder, Maggie drove the short distance to the store and went inside. About half an hour later she emerged the proud owner of not a charger, but rather a brand new, high tech, smart phone. One with all the bells and whistles. The charming young man at Verizon had convinced her, without too much trouble, that her phone was inadequate. An embarrassment. Not even as smart as a fifth grader. Equipped with all the accessories and a fully charged phone, Maggie had just blundered into the 21st Century.

Seriously. What was I thinking? Maggie looked with trepidation at the spanking new phone now riding shotgun in the Bug. She wasn't sure she could even make a phone call on the dang thing, let alone use all the marvelous features that had so enchanted her in the store.

Well, no time like the present. Maggie pulled off the highway at the next rest area and, clutching her new toy, found a quiet spot at a picnic table outside. She sucked in a deep breath and punched buttons. Then she put the phone to her ear and waited.

"Dwight, here."

Maggie waited a second for him to actually look at the caller ID. Then -- "Maggie! I've been going crazy! When will you be home? You can't just drive all over creation." Worry and annoyance fought for supremacy in his words.

If Maggie had any doubts before, his parental tone cleared them away. She said, "Dwight, listen to me. I can and will drive all over creation as you put it. I need some space to figure things out. I'll be home when I have done that and not a single second before."

"But you can't -- " he began and then paused. "Just a minute Maggie, I have to take care of something here. Don't hang up."

She heard him giving instructions to someone. His secretary? She didn't know and she didn't care. She drummed her fingers on the picnic table as she waited for him to conclude his business and nearly hung up.

"Okay. I'm back. And I was saying you can't do that. I want -- Oh, damn, wait a second. Listen I have things here I have to do. I can't talk now. We can talk about this tonight. When you get home!"

"Dwight, listen, I won't be -- "

But she was talking to empty space. Dwight had disconnected. Maggie held her phone at arm's length and glared at it. "Smart phone, indeed. If you are so damn smart, maybe you can tell me what I'm supposed to do about my jerkface husband."

She obviously didn't expect an answer and glowered at the phone awhile longer before pitching it into her purse and marching back to the Bug. She slid inside and slammed the door with such force that coffee slopped out of the cup. She grabbed a wad of napkins from the glove compartment and mopped the spill -- her movements jerky and short. Furious tears blurred her vision. She fished into her purse to find a tissue and blew her nose. "Idiot," she fumed. "Jerk. Moron." Venting made her feel more human, so she shifted the car into gear and pulled back onto the interstate. "Creep. Dumb ass. Big, stupid cretin."

Maggie drove for the next couple of hours oblivious to everything except the black strip of highway as first Tim McGraw and then Keith Urban and then Jimmy Buffet serenaded her. She replayed Dwight's words over and over, each time getting more incensed with his dictatorial attitude. Finally she concluded that this could only lead to insanity. She needed something else to think about. She spotted a Target sign in the distance at the next exit. Well, that would do. She exited and headed for the store. Before she reached it, she stopped at a red light and studied the green signs directing travelers to various destinations.

Columbia—50 miles. Furwell — 102 miles. Sweet River — 214 miles.

Sweet River? Why did that ring a bell? Then Maggie remembered Mary Lou's voice at dinner. "The folks in Sweet River wrapped their arms around me and got me through my grief. They are the givingest people in the world."

Well, why not? Sweet River was as good a destination as any. She could abandon the boredom of the interstate for a route that would take her through small towns and farmland and see where she ended up. She pulled over and plugged Sweet River into her GPS, sending a silent thank you to Dwight for his practical gift. He'd certainly never dreamed that the gift would help his wife to run away. Served him right.

Scooting past cows grazing in fields, along narrow winding roads, and through small towns with a single stoplight, Maggie reveled in her trip. She was seeing the real America, not the sanitized interstate version. She turned off the CD player and let the sunny silence seep into her consciousness. She let her anger drain away and replaced it with contentment. Probably wouldn't last, but great for the moment.

Maggie stopped for a diet-soda at a grocery store in one of the small towns she passed through. The clerk greeted her with a "howdy do" as she entered and gossiped with her as if he had all the time in the world as she checked out. Not exactly the same experience as at one of the giant food emporiums at home.

It took much longer than it would have on the interstate, but finally she saw the sign proclaiming that she had arrived -- "Welcome to Sweet River, South Carolina, Home of the Walruses." Although Maggie was travel weary and a bit stiff, she was eager to explore the town that Mary Lou had raved about.

As she followed the signs directing her to Sweet River village center, she drove past lovely old homes. They were mostly two-story and sided with white clapboards and many had spacious attached front porches with large rockers sitting on them. The streets were lined with huge trees just beginning to bud. The yards were green and well-tended, often decorated with large flower pots and small statues. At home in Ohio it was too early to feel spring in the air, but here it was all around.

Maggie crept through the village enjoying the scenery. Children played in yards or rode bikes along the sidewalk. She passed a jogger or two and was rewarded with a wave when she slowed to let them pass. The street she was on dead-ended at the village green and at the end of the space she spotted a white-painted latticed gazebo. Trees dotted the green area and small shrubs were spaced among them.

Across from the green Maggie could see shops and pedestrians. She circled twice before she found a parking spot a few blocks from the activity. She parked and locked the car and took a minute to survey her surroundings. If it hadn't been for the modern cars, she might have thought she had stepped back in time to another, less stressful era. If a woman in a hoopskirt had come out of one of the homes, Maggie wouldn't have blinked.

Maggie strolled down the sidewalk enjoying the remainder of the day. The late afternoon sun was still warm enough that Maggie shed her sweater and tied it around her waist. As she approached the shopping area she remembered Mary Lou saying, *"Agnes' Sweet River Café and Sweet Shop* is the best place in town to get breakfast or lunch. That Agnes makes the best apple pie that y'all will ever have."

Maggie's stomach grumbled. She hadn't thought about eating and breakfast had been a long time ago. Pie sounded wonderful. She found *Agnes' Café* with no problem. It was sandwiched between a jewelry store and a gallery with a collection of paintings in the window. *Agnes'* had cheery red and white curtains in the windows and a big screen door. Hunger spurred Maggie forward and she hurried toward the café. Just as she reached the door two women, perhaps mother and daughter, and a small girl were leaving. The older woman held the door for Maggie and said, "Try the tomato basil soup. Agnes has outdone herself today."

If Maggie had been hungry before, she was starving now. Agnes had her at tomato basil. Maggie stepped inside -- surprised at how busy it was for this late in the afternoon. She loitered by the case of baked goods in the front of the store, trying to decide if she should seat herself or not and a large woman wearing an apron hurried over to her. "I'm sorry you had to wait," she said. "It's a zoo in here today."

"Am I too late for lunch?" Maggie asked.

"Oh, my no," the woman said. "It's never too late for a hungry customer."

She steered Maggie to a table next to the window and handed her a menu. "I'm Agnes, by the way. And you are?"

"I'm Maggie. Maggie Murphy. Mary Lou Jennings sent me."

Agnes' face lit up, her blue eyes sparkled. "Mary Lou! I haven't seen her in ages. I miss her. How on earth is she?"

"I think she's doing well. I met her at a conference yesterday and she raved about your place and your pie. I thought I should check it out for myself."

"You are more than welcome. Can I start you off with something to drink? Coffee, tea, soda pop?" Agnes leaned down and said conspiratorially, "Or I could scrounge up a glass of wine if you'd like." She winked.

Maggie grinned. "Now that would be perfect. White, if you have it."

"Be back in a jiff."

Maggie studied Agnes as she bustled away and decided that she looked comfortable. Agnes was round and large-bosomed with hair the color of *café au lait* piled haphazardly on her head, a pencil stuck through it. She paused at each table to speak to customers, laughing and teasing. She did seem like someone who would pass out hugs the way she passed out coffee and pie.

"There you go," Agnes said as she placed a glass of white wine in front of Maggie. "Have you decided what you would like?"

"I knew before I came inside. I'll have the tomato basil soup. And a salad if you've got it."

"Perfect. I have a feta, tomato and tossed green salad that I recommend."

Maggie nodded agreement and sipped her wine as she waited for Agnes to return with her food. Agnes' café was warm and cozy. A bar stretched across the back of the restaurant and tables were scattered around the open space. Each table was decorated with a vase of fresh flowers. Maggie sniffed to make sure. Yes. Definitely fresh.

At a large table near the bar a group of six older women -- purses and coats slung over the backs of their chairs -- chattered and laughed. As Agnes returned to Maggie's table with the bowl of steaming soup, a burst of laughter echoed through the room. "They seem to be having fun," Maggie said nodding at the women.

Agnes placed her soup in front of her and followed it with a basket of fresh bread and the salad. She glanced over her shoulder and grinned. "That would be Verdie Cranford and her gang. Just back from their annual spring shopping spree to Charleston."

Maggie noted the shopping bags cluttering the floor around their table. "Looks like a successful trip."

Agnes nodded and started away and then turned back to add an aside. "Yep. If you want to know anything at all about Sweet River or any of our citizens, just ask Verdie. She's a virtual encyclopedia of all things Sweet River. There are no secrets she doesn't know. And she loves to share." Agnes winked.

"I'll keep that in mind," Maggie said.

The tomato basil soup was amazing and the salad delicious. Maggie devoured her food with gusto, hungrier than she had realized. As she was finishing the last crumb of the homemade wheat bread that had been served with her meal, Agnes came back to her table.

"Would you care for dessert, Maggie? I have pie that will make your taste-buds leap up and say howdy."

"No thanks, Agnes. I'm stuffed. I'll have to try it another day." Maggie was shocked at her own words. She hadn't known until that second that she planned to stick around. "Can I ask you a question?"

Agnes paused in clearing the table. "Anything."

"Do you know of someplace I could spend the night? It's getting late and I don't want to drive anymore today."

"I sure do. That would be Gladys Tomlinson's B & B. Let me clear these dishes and I'll give you directions. It's walking distance from here."

CHAPTER
Six

Maggie left Agnes and the Sweet River Café with promises to return and directions to Gladys' B & B in hand. She wandered down the street peeking in store windows and noting restaurants that looked inviting. The people on the street smiled at her and wished her a good evening. Maggie blew out a happy sigh. It was peaceful in this quaint village and the citizenry was sure friendly. A tiny bubble of happiness tickled her brain and she smiled to herself. Main Street was only a few blocks long and Maggie turned the corner following Agnes' directions to the B&B. The street sign announced that Maggie was now on Cranberry Lane and she checked the directions Agnes had written to find the number -- 1512 Cranberry Lane. She meandered down the street checking out the big, mostly 19th century homes lining the street. Huge old trees with gnarled branches hung over the lawns.

The few people outside greeted her warmly as she passed. Only a short distance from Gladys' place, Maggie passed the lone single-story house on the street. It sat a bit back from the sidewalk and the late day sunlight reflected on the faded yellow siding giving it a pleasant glow. A weather-beaten For Sale sign listed to one side in front. Maggie walked past and then stopped. Something about the little yellow cottage was calling to her. She reversed direction and stood contemplating it.

Maggie swung her head from side to side. There was no one around. So what could be the harm in taking a closer look? She picked her way across the unkempt lawn stepping over branches dropped in some long ago storm. On the front porch she noticed that the siding was faded and peeling. She ducked to avoid a loose shutter hanging precariously by one corner and edged up to the front window. She cupped her hands around her eyes to peer inside through a broken window. All that was visible was a single room with a faded sofa and an old-fashioned rocking chair. Suddenly the chair began to rock back and forth as if pushed by an invisible hand. Maggie blinked and rubbed her eyes. No way. That chair did not move by itself. Must have been a gust of wind blowing through the broken windowpane. She blinked again and squinted so that she could see more clearly. Nothing. A silent room. Nothing moving.

Maggie shook her head and wandered to the back of the house and tried to check out the inside but the windows were grimy and dirty streaks obliterated most of the view. She sighed. What was she doing? Seeing ghosts in an abandoned house, that's what. I'm a nutcase, she thought -- and one with an overactive imagination.

She shrugged, wiped her fingers on the seat of her jeans, double-checked the address on the paper in her hand and backed down the cracked and weedy driveway eyeing the house as if a white-sheeted spirit might chase her. She tripped over a hunk of displaced concrete, caught her balance and hurried toward *Gladys' B&B*.

Ghosts indeed!

Maggie had to knock three times before a mid-thirtyish woman wearing ripped jeans and a paint-stained and oversized flannel shirt came to the door with a paintbrush in one hand. "Are you Maggie?" she asked, waving her paintbrush.

"How did you know?" Maggie said.

"Agnes called me to make sure I had a room for you." The woman waved her paintbrush. "I sort of accidentally decided to paint the kitchen."

Not sure what response was called for, Maggie stammered a reply. "Ag-agnes said you had a room?"

The woman put down her paintbrush and wiped her hand on the jeans before she stuck out a hand. "Sorry. I'm being rude. I'm Gladys Tomlinson. Come on in."

Maggie stepped into the foyer and looked around. An inviting living room to her left and a dining room papered with big red and yellow flowers opposite had hardwood floors with braided rugs. Both rooms had tables scattered throughout with vases full of flowers topping them. Maggie sniffed and smelled twin aromas of fresh paint and cinnamon.

"This is so cute." Maggie smiled at Gladys who beamed back.

"Let me show you the room."

Gladys led the way to the top floor and opened the door to a tiny room with a slanted ceiling nestled under the eaves. A cheerful flowered comforter topped the queen-sized bed and soft lighting glowed from the bedside lamps. Maggie sighed. "This is adorable. I love it."

Gladys opened a door to reveal the tiny bathroom with a pedestal sink and white lace curtains fluttering at the open window over the claw-footed tub. Maggie sighed again and Gladys laughed. "I take it you approve."

"Approve? It's more than that. Something about this room makes me happy. I may never leave."

Gladys chuckled. "And I'm glad to have you."

Having found a "home" for the night, Maggie headed back to retrieve her car and her luggage. She started out the door and then paused, hand on the doorknob. "Can I ask you something about the neighborhood?"

"Fire away," Gladys said.

"I noticed a cute yellow bungalow a couple of doors down the street. What do you know about it?"

"Oh, that's part of the old Edison estate. Did you notice the mansion behind it? Well, the yellow place was the carriage house back in the day."

"Edison? As in Thomas?"

"Well, not Thomas, but some shirttail relation. Anyway, the carriage house hasn't been occupied for at least a couple of years. Kind of an eyesore, but it's been saved a million times from demolition because it's a historical preservation site."

"There's a For Sale sign in front. But do you think it's available to rent?" Maggie wanted to know.

"Frankly, I think the owners would jump at the chance and probably cut you a deal. And the neighbors would throw you a huge welcome party. Are you interested?"

Maggie shrugged. "I just might be."

As Maggie passed the bungalow on her way back to get her car, she copied down the realtor's phone number from the sign posted in front. Then she fished her new smart phone out of her purse and shot pictures from various angles. As she strolled toward her car, she let herself imagine what the yellow cottage could look like if it was given a little loving care. Pipe dreams, of course, she told herself. *I'm totally going back home tomorrow. Or maybe the day after. Or surely by the end of the week. Definitely.*

When Maggie let herself back in to the B&B, Gladys was nowhere around. Thumps and clanging noises echoed from the kitchen so Maggie assumed she was busy with her painting project. Not wanting to interrupt Maggie hauled her collection of bags up the steps to her top floor room pausing at the first floor landing to catch her breath. *I'm ridiculously out of shape,* she huffed. *Need to get back to Jazzercise. When I go home. Soon, right?*

She used the big old-fashioned brass key Gladys had given her to unlock the door to her attic loft and dragged herself and her possessions inside. She dropped everything just inside the door and collapsed on the bed. Whew.

The silence enveloped her and she felt the weariness of the long day seep away. She'd been worrying, during her drive, about Chloe and April. She pictured them with their Aunt Molly. Laughing. Or alternately -- crying and miserable. It was time to find out. She dug in her purse to find the slip of paper on which she'd written Molly's information and punched the cell phone number into her phone.

The phone rang and rang and Maggie was about to give up when the ringing stopped. A thudding noise replaced the ringing and she could hear sounds of a scuffle. "Mine," she heard a tiny voice say. "My turn. Stop it, April."

And then, "Aunt Molly's phone. This is Chloe."

"Chloe. It's Maggie. How are you, sweetie?"

"Maggie!" Chloe shrieked. "Where are you? In the Bug? Are you coming to visit?"

Maggie laughed. "No, sweetie, I'm not. I'm in a B&B and --"

"What's a B plus B? Another car?"

"Whoa. I'm staying at a nice -- um -- inn. I called to see how you and April are? Is everything okay with Aunt Molly?"

"It's a - ma- zing! They have a dog. Well, a puppy really. It licks my face." There was a pause. "No, April, don't. I'm talking to Maggie. I want --"

April took over. "Hi Maggie. Chloe can be such a pain sometimes. I'm so glad you called."

"How are you? Are you okay?'

"Super. Seriously. Aunt Molly is great. Oh, wait, she wants to talk to you."

Maggie grinned. It sounded like a mad house but in the best possible way.

"Maggie?" Aunt Molly said. "I'm so relieved to hear from you. I lost your number or I would have called." She went on to tell Maggie that everything was working out perfectly. "Kurt was more than willing to have the girls stay with us. He isn't their father and never adopted them, so he has no rights."

Maggie said, "I'm relieved too. I hoped that he wouldn't be a problem. And I'm glad that I didn't do the wrong thing by bringing the girls to you."

"Absolutely, not. It will be a bit tight here but the kids are doubling up with mine and having them here makes up somehow for the years I didn't see my sister. I see her in them so much it breaks my heart." Molly sniffed.

"Thank goodness," Maggie said. And by the time they hung up Maggie's mood had lifted. She had done the right thing. Thank you very much. Alleluia. Now here she was in this adorable room about to figure out her own life. She stood up and began to pull clothing out of her bags.

Maggie had just arranged the last of her things when there was a knock on the door. She opened it to find Gladys on her doorstep, dressed in leggings, high boots and a long sweater, hair still damp from a shower. "Hey," Maggie said.

Gladys peered around Maggie into room. "Are you settled in okay? Do you need anything at all?"

Maggie shook her head. "Nope. I'm fine."

Gladys fumbled with a thread on her sweater before she said, "I was wondering if you might like to go out and catch some dinner. I can't take the paint smell in the kitchen tonight and I would love the company." She hesitated. "That is, of course, if you don't have other plans."

Maggie opened the door wider. "Come in and sit down for a sec. I'll put on some lipstick and grab a jacket."

"You're sure I'm not interrupting?"

"Oh, yeah, you are. I was totally going to read my paperback book and paint my nails. Big plans. Actually I'd love to go out with you."

Gladys (please, call me Gladdie) beamed. "I have just the place in mind."

The two women walked down the street doing the getting-to-know-you chat until Gladdie stopped in front of a shabby storefront on a side street not far from *Agnes' Sweet River Café.* "Here we are," she said.

Maggie hitched her purse up on her shoulder and surveyed the building. "Here?"

The gold lettering on the plate glass window was cracked and faded. Maggie had to strain to make it out. *"Sweet River Books. Where your reading begins."*

"A bookstore?"

Gladdie tugged the heavy door open and held it for Maggie. "Well, it used to be. But now... "

Maggie spun in a circle taking in the largish room. Three of the walls were lined with bookshelves filled with dog-eared paperback books. Along the fourth was a heavy dark wood bar. Tables of the same wood as the bar were scattered about, all of them lighted by old-fashioned desk lamps. The place was crowded, most of the tables filled. Overhead were open scaffolding and beams from which hung tiny spotlights making the lighting dim and shadowy.

"This is so cool," she said.

A tall, slender guy of about 35 with the scruffy day-old-beard-look hurried over to the two women. He swept Gladdie off her feet and planted a kiss on her cheek. Laughing, she struggled to get away. "Chad. Put me down, you big jerk."

She grinned up at him and Maggie sensed something going on between the two. Chad dropped Gladdie to the ground and patted her behind. Uh huh. Definitely something going on.

"Maggie, this is my –- er -- friend, Chad," Gladdie said. "He owns this place."

"It's great. Do you sell books too?" Maggie asked.

"We used to, but not anymore. Now it's mostly burgers and beer. The true book lover crowd is probably scarfing lobster at *Mirabelle's.*"

"Mirabelle's is an upscale seafood place on Main Street," Gladdie

explained. "Maybe another night."

"Maybe," Maggie said with doubt creeping in. "I'm not sure how long I'll be here."

Chad seated them at a round table near the front window and Gladdie ordered a beer and Maggie a glass of white wine. While they waited for their drinks, they perused the menu cleverly attached to old book covers and Gladdie told Maggie more about the bookstore/bar.

"Chad inherited this place from his Aunt Harriet. It really was a bookstore back then. He tried to make a go of it as a bookstore, but the big chains moved in and killed his business. But Chad is pretty stubborn and he loves the place. So ..." Gladdie swept an arm around.

"It's great. So he doesn't sell books?"

"He would if you asked, but mostly it's a great place for a book exchange. You know. Bring one in. Take one home."

Chad returned with their drinks. "What'll it be, ladies?"

Both ordered burgers, Maggie's a turkey burger and Gladdie's a rare beef, with fries. The two chatted as they waited for the food. Finally, curiosity won out, and Maggie had to know. "So, are you and Chad dating? Or something?"

"Mostly, 'or something'." Gladdie's gaze followed Chad as he scurried around taking orders and refilling drinks. "We've known each other since we were in elementary school." She sighed. "I used to have a major crush on him."

"Looks to me like you still do."

"Yeah. Maybe. It's a small town. Not so many options."

"And he's very cute."

"There is that!"

Chad reappeared with their food and hung around, kidding with them for a few minutes. "What brings you to Sweet River, Maggie?" he asked.

"Pure luck. And curiosity. And Mary Lou Jennings."

Chad and Gladdie said in unison, "You know Mary Lou?"

"That would be an exaggeration. I kind of met her yesterday at a conference."

"Oh, my God. *Get Your Grove On*," Gladdie said. "You're a widow? I'm so sorry."

"I'm not really -- " Maggie began but Gladdie wasn't listening.

"Here I've been going on and on," Gladdie said, "and you're mourning."

"I'm really not -- " Maggie tried again.

Chad placed a sympathetic hand on Maggie's shoulder. "Dinner's on me."

"No, no, I couldn't," Maggie protested. "I really should tell you."

Chad shook his head. "I won't hear a word of it. Dinner's on me." He turned his back and made his way across the crowded room, stopping to chat with his customers, back to the bar.

"I should tell you -- " Maggie began, but Gladdie cut her off.

"It's not necessary," Gladdie said. "I know how you must feel."

Maggie rolled her eyes. Poor Dwight. She'd killed him again. Well, in all fairness, this time she hadn't intentionally murdered him. It was more of an accidental death. She couldn't be blamed for that. Could she?

Over dinner Maggie and Gladdie swapped life stories and found that they had a lot in common. Both were only children raised by parents who adored them and each other. Both were English majors at small liberal arts colleges. Both had married young and lost their husbands — Maggie's to a faux death and Gladdie's to divorce. And both had not-quite-grown children who ignored their mothers until they needed a mommy's shoulder to weep on.

As they lingered over a second drink, Gladdie complained about her ex's bad habit of spending exorbitant amounts of money on his new girlfriend and his stinginess when it came to child support. In turn, Maggie wanted to share "Dwight stories", but was too guilt-stricken by his "death" at her own hands to say a negative word. "Dead" Dwight was a paragon in every way. Maggie really wanted to confess to Gladdie that she was a big fat liar, but something held her back. She wasn't sure what, but Dwight stayed dead. Rest his soul.

As the two strolled back to the B&B, Maggie pulled Gladdie to a halt in front of the yellow bungalow. "Have you ever been inside?" she asked her.

"Sure. It's been a long time, though. It's a wreck now, but it used to be cute."

"Hmm-m. Maybe it could be again."

"Sounds like you really are interested. Tell you what -- I'll call my friend, Azalea Williams. She's the one handling the listing. I'm sure she'd love to show you around."

"That would be awesome. I'm dying to see the inside. It was a guest cottage? Tell me everything you know."

"Well, it was owned by some cousin of Thomas Edison, as I told you earlier and..."

Maggie listened enthralled to Gladdie's stories of owners past and present. Something about the rundown yellow cottage spoke to her and she was inclined to listen -- in spite of the mysterious rocking chair episode.

During the night it started to rain and the patter of drops on the tin roof outside her window lulled Maggie into a dream where she lived in the yellow cottage with her dozens of cats. The fact that Maggie abhorred cats apparently hadn't sunk into her unconscious mind, but when she woke up, she shivered. Ugh. Maybe the dream was trying to tell her something. Be careful what you wish for or you might end up with cats. Something like that.

CHAPTER
Seven

Breakfast the next morning was so amazing that Maggie would have liked to lick her plate. A fresh fruit cup with real whipped cream was followed by a selection of homemade muffins and rolls and an egg white frittata that melted in her mouth. The coffee was perfect and Maggie almost groaned with pleasure as she devoured her food.

Finally, too stuffed to take another bite, she leaned back in her chair and cradled her coffee mug in her hands as she gazed out the window at the trees swaying in the breeze. The rain had let up, but it was grey outside and the ominous sound of thunder grumbled in the distance.

Coffee pot in hand, her face flushed from cooking in the warm kitchen, Gladdie glided up to Maggie and pressed a business card into her hand. "This is Azalea's card. I called her and she was absolutely thrilled. She asked me to tell you that she'll meet you at Agnes' at ten this morning. She'll give you the lowdown on the place and if you still want to see it, she'll give you the grand tour."

"I think I'd like to hug you," Maggie said.

Gladdie grinned. "Feel free anytime. But maybe you should wait until you see the place. It really is a disaster."

"It can't be that bad, can it?"

Gladdie did an exaggerated eye-roll. "You tell me after your visit."

Five minutes before her ten o'clock appointment Maggie was waiting for Azalea at Agnes' Café. She had gotten caught in a sudden downpour on her way to the café and was wet and bedraggled. Her shoes squished and her sopping jeans clung to her thighs and slapped against her ankles with each step, but nothing could spoil her anticipation. She was blotting the water out of her hair with a napkin when a stunning African American woman burst into the restaurant. She was at least six-feet tall with a Victoria's Secret model's figure and mocha skin that glowed with health and TLC. Her black hair was pulled into a chignon and shoulder length silver earrings dangled from her perfectly formed ears.

"Dang, girl," she said to Agnes as she shook out her umbrella. "It's a monsoon out there." Her laugh was silvery and low. She murmured something to Agnes who pointed at Maggie's table.

The woman swept across the room and held out her hand to Maggie. "Hey. I'm Azalea Williams. You must be Maggie."

"Pleased to meet you," Maggie said. "I've heard so much about you from Gladdie."

Azalea's throaty chuckle told Maggie that she hadn't heard everything about this gorgeous woman. Azalea dropped into a chair across from Maggie and draped her raincoat over the back. She motioned to Agnes for coffee and positioned her briefcase on the table in front of her. All business now, she leaned toward Maggie. "So you're interested in the old Edison place, are you? Let's get down to business."

Two hours later Maggie waved with one hand as Azalea drove off in her silver Beemer. In the other hand she clutched the signed rental agreement for the yellow carriage house. What can I possibly be thinking? Maggie wondered as she stood on the sidewalk, rain pelting her already soaked hair. What on earth am I going to tell very-much-alive Dwight? That was a conversation she did not want to have, but she couldn't avoid it much longer. She slunk back to the B&B, letting the rain drench her as anxiety curled in her stomach.

Maggie showered and changed into dry clothes and then sat cross-legged in the middle of the bed, her phone a silent reprimand by her side. She picked it up and stared at it and then let it fall back onto the pillows as she leaped up to make coffee in the small room coffeemaker. She paced back and forth as she waited for the coffee to perk and then took her time putting in just the right amount of creamer. If she'd had a sock drawer to organize rather than call Dwight, she would have done it. But she was out of excuses so she picked up the phone and punched in his number. Maybe he wouldn't answer and she could leave a message. Yeah, right. That'd be great. "Hi Honey. I've rented a house and

I won't be home. Like ever. Love you, bye."

But -- "Dwight, here!"

She gulped. "Hi."

He sounded happy to hear her voice. Oh, damn. "Hi, Maggie. Tell me you're on your way home."

"Not exactly."

"Not exactly? Not exactly!" He exploded. "When are you coming home, Maggie? I'm tired of this crap. I want you home."

Now that was more like the Dwight she knew and, damn it, loved. But they couldn't go on this way and she had found a solution. Maybe.

"Listen to me, Dwight. I need you to listen."

He cleared his throat but said nothing. Maggie waited. The silence hummed with an almost tangible disapproval. At last he said, "I'm listening."

Maggie gulped a huge mouthful of coffee, burning her tongue. "Damn."

"What?"

"Not you, Dwight. I burned my tongue. So, hear me out. We haven't been really happy in a long time."

"Speak for yourself," he interrupted her. "I'm perfectly happy." He paused to consider. "You aren't?" He sounded surprised.

"No. I'd have to say not. We don't talk. You're way too busy with work to spend time with me. I can't blame you. I know you love your job. But what about me? The kids are out of the house. I haven't really worked in ages. Frankly, I'm bored to tears." The words tumbled out. "I didn't mean to run away. It kind of just happened. But I need to do this. Really. Trust me. I'm not leaving you."

He interrupted again. "Oh, seriously you're not? I don't believe I saw you in the kitchen this morning." His words were mild but his tone was hostile. "Or in the bedroom last night."

"Don't even go there, Dwight. We haven't had sex in God knows how long. You are always out with customers or working on your laptop until early morning."

His voice calmer but ice cold, he said. "Then what are you doing? And when might I expect to resume this marriage?"

"We need to spend some time apart. I need to. Then we can talk and see where we are." She heard herself pleading. "Please, Dwight. Don't make this any harder than it has to be. It'll be better for both of us in the long run."

His next words were a knife to her heart. "Do what you need to do. I'll do what I need to do. We'll see how it works out."

Had she gone too far? "Please, Dwight, don't be mad. I need to figure things out."

Icicles dripped off his words. "Fine. Let me know how it goes. And, oh, by the way, how to get in touch with you. And what to tell your friends who keep calling."

Maggie tried to explain about the yellow cottage, but Dwight wasn't listening. She had done the unthinkable, at least to him. She'd left him and his pride was far too mangled for him to listen to any explanation or defense. Finally, they hung up. Both angry. And, at least one of them, unwilling and unable to discuss the issues.

Butterflies fluttered in her stomach. Maggie didn't know how this would turn out, but in spite of her anxiety she felt a curious optimism. Things would work out. She knew it.

Maggie reached for the Eiffel Tower journal that sat on the bedside table. She cracked it open and balanced it on her knees and began to write.

Maggie's Journal
Day One

I think I've run away from home. And Dwight is really pissed about it. I, on the other hand, feel oddly happy. And relieved. In spite of everything. Go figure.

CHAPTER
Eight

Maggie teetered on the stepladder peeling strips of mildewed wallpaper from the wall of the yellow bungalow. At the same time she supervised the cleaning crew she had hired to remove years' accumulation of dirt, bugs and dead creatures. As horrible the condition of the house was, though, Maggie was excited. The place had so much potential — once the grime was scraped away.

The cottage consisted of a single large room with high-beamed ceilings and a crumbling brick fireplace against the side wall. A tiny kitchen opened off the rear of the main room and Maggie was almost afraid to tackle it. The appliances — if you could even call them that — were ancient and covered with grease. The kitchen sink was cracked and rust-stained, the single center faucet hanging loose.

Azalea said it had been a few years since anyone had occupied the house? More like a few decades. Still, as the cleaning crew hauled and scrubbed and sanitized, Maggie created pretty pictures in her mind of how the place could look. She was entertaining herself with daydreams about being interviewed by one of those home magazines when she glanced out the grimy front window and saw Gladdie striding up the front walk.

Maggie scrambled down the ladder and threw open the door to let her in. "Thought you might need some nourishment," Gladdie said as she set a large thermos of coffee and a bakery box on the rickety wooden table in one corner. She opened the box with a flourish to reveal an assortment of freshly baked muffins. "Voila."

"Gladdie, you're a saint," Maggie said. And the cleaning crew fell on the goodies as if they were famished.

"How's it going?" Gladdie asked.

"A century's worth of dirt cannot be expunged in a single day," Maggie said drawing herself up in a haughty posture. Then she laughed. "Let me tell you how it's going to look. When we're both very aged crones."

Gladdie oohed and aahed as Maggie described her visions. After a few moments, Gladdie looked around. "I don't mean to be a wet blanket," she said, "but I don't see a bedroom. Where are you going to sleep?"

"That's the best part," Maggie said. "Come over here." Maggie tugged Gladdie to the very back corner of the room and shoved aside a tarp hanging from the beams. "Look."

"Oh, wow," Gladdie purred when she saw the circular stairway leading to a tiny sleeping loft. "Now that is cool. My kid would go nuts for it."

"Mine too," Maggie said. "I think that's what sold me. My daughter Julie has a thing for lofts."

"And the bathroom is where? Out back?"

"Don't be silly." Maggie led Gladdie through the kitchen to show her the surprisingly modern bathroom.

"Now that's a pleasant surprise," Gladdie said.

"According to Azalea," Maggie told her, "an artist was using it as his studio and put in the bathroom. I have him to thank for it."

Her box of baked goods demolished and the thermos empty, Gladdie gathered up her things while the crew went back to work. Maggie stood in the doorway chatting with her. "Hey, I'm meeting Azalea for lunch at Agnes'. Why don't you join us? One o'clock?"

"Sounds good, but I have to go out to the Farmer's Market right now and buy some fresh produce for the B&B. I might be a bit late," Gladdie said.

"Me too," Maggie said. "I have to wait 'til the workers finish for the morning."

As it turned out, the crew broke sooner than expected for lunch -- needing to replenish not just their energy, but also their cleaning supplies. Making the yellow bungalow habitable was a daunting task. Maggie closed the door after them and then changed her mind and followed behind them. She had plenty of time before her lunch appointment with Azalea so she meandered down the street to *Gladys' B&B* hoping to persuade Gladys to walk downtown with her. Gladys was nowhere to be found, however. Only Caitlyn, Gladys' second in command, was at home. She was vacuuming the living room, her iPod plugged into her ears, her hips in her tight jeans wiggling suggestively to the music. She never even heard Maggie come in. Maggie climbed the stairs to her third floor room and stripped off her dirt and sweat-stained T-shirt. She scrubbed her hands and face with almond scented bath soap and pulled on her last clean T-shirt. She slapped on some make-up, slicked on lip gloss, shrugged into her denim jacket and made her way back to the sidewalk in record time.

Maggie breathed deeply and inspected her surroundings. The street was quiet — only a few cars and fewer pedestrians disturbed the tranquility. Maggie heard birds chirping and a train whistle hooted in the distance. As she strolled down the street she had the oddest sensation that she had lived here all her life. Not rational, of course, but all she knew for sure was that she was filled with a happiness and expectation that she hadn't felt in a very long time.

As she rounded the corner onto Main Street she found it bustling with activity. Almost every parking space around the green was filled and pedestrians dotted the sidewalk. A group of grade-school children followed like ducklings a young woman carrying a clipboard. The woman, probably a teacher, kept turning to count heads — making sure the ducklings were all accounted for.

Maggie explored some of the shops, checking out the inventory and debating buying some new clothes to add to her small wardrobe. She decided to come back and do some serious shopping another day when she wasn't grubby and tired. As she approached *Agnes' Sweet River Café* she passed the jewelry store that she had noticed on her first afternoon in town. Never one to resist jewelry, Maggie stared through the window and then gave in to her curiosity and hauled the door open. She paused as she read the gold lettering and grinned at the name — *"Jewelicious. Baubles for Me and You"*.

Inside Maggie found a treasure trove of sparkling, colorful and totally enticing jewelry. She wandered through the aisles picking up bracelets, sliding rings onto her fingers, holding earrings up next to her head. She slipped on a bracelet made of graduated blue stones giving it an ombre effect. She was in heaven trolling through the eclectic collection of traditional styles and extremely modern ones

She was so absorbed that she jumped when a store clerk appeared and asked, "Is there anything I can do for you?"

Maggie smiled at the petite dark-haired woman. "Not really. I'm just browsing, but you have fantastic things in here. I don't know what to buy, but I'm sure I have to have something."

"Thank you," the clerk said. "I appreciate that. I'm the owner and I make a lot of the stuff myself."

Maggie fingered a bracelet made of glimmering blue stones of different shades. "Well, this is awesome. You're a genius."

The woman quirked an eyebrow at her. "Thanks again. Are you just passing through our little village?"

"Actually, I just rented a place here. The yellow bungalow on Cranberry Lane?"

"So, you'd be Maggie then."

"Wow. News travels fast in Sweet River. I just signed the papers."

The clerk grinned. "Verdie Cranford stopped by earlier. She's the town crier."

Maggie shook her head. "So I've heard."

"Excuse me, I should introduce myself," the woman said. "I'm Jewel." She smiled a rueful smile. "Jewel Boxer."

Maggie chuckled. "Seriously? Jewel Boxer?" Then she realized that she was being rude. "Oh, I'm sorry. I shouldn't laugh. I'm sure you've heard it all before. I'm Maggie Murphy."

Jewel grinned. "I have. What else could I do with a name like that?"

"I love *Jewelicious*. It's awesome. I have a lunch date at Agnes' right now," Maggie said, "but I'll be back to do some shopping."

"Anytime. I'm always here. If I'm not selling, I'm creating in the back room."

Maggie checked her watch and saw that it was nearly time to meet Azalea and hurried to the door. As she left the shop she noticed a small Help Wanted sign posted in the window and she made a mental note to ask Jewel about it the next time she was in.

As she entered the café next door Agnes, herself, greeted Maggie and pointed a red-lacquered fingertip toward the back. "Azalea's already here."

Sure enough, Azalea had set up camp at a round table in the rear of the restaurant. She had her phone clamped to her ear, her laptop open in front of her and papers spread all over the surface of the table. When she saw Maggie, she fluttered her fingers at her and mouthed, "Sorry."

Maggie hung her jacket over the back of the chair and remained standing, shifting her weight from one foot to the other as she watched Azalea with awe. The woman was a tornado — scribbling on scraps of paper, tapping the keyboard of her laptop, talking into the phone. Finally, Azalea disconnected and slumped in her chair. "I am so sorry, Maggie. But it was about your place so I hope you won't mind."

"My place?"

"Yep. I got some painters to come by and spruce things up. And electricians and the phone and cable company too. We'll have you set up and comfy in no time flat."

"That's amazing. I thought I'd have to arrange all that myself."

"If you needed a brass band, we'd probably do it. We're so thrilled to have that eyesore -- I mean, your house -- occupied again."

House? Her house? First realization and then panic washed over her. How could she afford all of this? In the beginning it hadn't bothered Maggie to charge her expenses on the credit card she shared with Dwight. She was simply taking a few days off. A sabbatical if you will. She fully intended to return to her real life in Ohio. But after she signed the rental agreement for the yellow bungalow, she didn't want to continue using that credit card. After all, asserting her independence was meaningless if she was spending Dwight's money to do it. Not that, to be fair, he would have a problem with it. He had never been that kind of a guy. But still … So she called her bank in Winslow and arranged for them to transfer the funds in her savings account to the Sweet River Bank and Trust. Maggie's grandmother had left her some money when she died and combined with the small salary Maggie earned freelancing part-time for the local newspaper she had accumulated a nice nest egg. But she was spending Nana Belle's money much more rapidly than she had anticipated. Her heart pounded with apprehension. At this rate she'd be broke before she finished fixing up the bungalow. And she couldn't -- no, wouldn't -- ask Dwight for help.

"How can I pay for all these repairs?" Maggie had to ask.

"Don't worry about it. The owners are glad to do it. Besides it's part of the rental agreement," Azalea said.

Maggie sagged into the chair with relief. The owners. Thank goodness. And if she got a job soon, she could make it. She could do this.

Before Maggie had a chance to say anything else, the door to the café was thrown open and Gladdie burst inside. Flushed from exertion, her coat flying open, Gladdie crossed the room. She scooped up an armful of papers from a chair and plopped down. "Whew," she huffed. "Sorry to be late."

Azalea gazed at her with a questioning look until Maggie said, "I invited Gladdie to join us. Hope you don't mind."

The realtor chortled. "Mind? Not a chance. I'm always delighted to spend time with my very first client."

Gladdie nodded and explained to Maggie. "'Zalea was a newbie. Just got her license. I came home a sad and pathetic divorcee. She found me the B&B and we scored me a sweet deal on it. Right 'Zalea?"

Azalea buffed her nails on the sleeve of her jacket. "Whoop tee doo, Miss Gladdie and I won her the jackpot."

The two beamed at each other while Maggie looked on in amusement.

A little blonde with a perky attitude appeared to take their orders and when she left, Maggie told them about her visit to *Jewelicious* next door. "And," she finished, "I have never seen jewelry like that before. That Jewel is an artist."

"That she is," Gladdie agreed. She looked thoughtful. "I don't know how you'll feel about this, but I have an idea for you, Maggie."

Maggie waited for her to go on.

"I know Jewel is swamped, particularly when tourists are in town. She can't make the jewelry fast enough. Since she is the only one who works in the store, she has to make her jewelry at night. I'd say she hasn't had more than a couple hours sleep a night for months. If you wanted a job, Maggie ... " She trailed off.

Maggie tapped a fingernail against her front teeth. Maybe this was the life preserver she needed. "I saw a Help Wanted sign in the store. When I get my house shaped up, I might just see if Jewel would want me. I really should bring in some cash."

Azalea snatched her laptop and her fingers flew over the keyboard.

"What are you up to, 'Zalea?" Gladdie asked.

"Sending an e-mail to Jewel. Tellin' her we killed two birds with one stone. Maggie needs a job. And Jewel needs help." She stopped typing.

"Ta da."

Maggie was overwhelmed. One day she was going out for coffee at home and a week later she was living and working in Sweet River and having lunch with two new friends. Whew. Things were moving way too fast. And, as usual, her thoughts flew to Dwight. How would he take this latest development? She started to protest. To tell Gladdie and Azalea that she wasn't going to stay after all. But when she opened her mouth, the words that came out were not what she had planned.

"Oh, Lord," she said. "I think I'd love a job at *Jewelicious*. I never met a jewel I didn't like."

It was settled shortly after that when Maggie stopped to see Jewel on her way back to her little yellow bungalow. Jewel was delighted to have her and more than willing to wait until she was settled for her to start work. Maggie walked back to the cottage, her head swirling and her feet dancing.

CHAPTER
Nine

Maggie spent the rest of the day peeling long strips of wallpaper and collecting bags of trash. She was on her knees pulling old books from the shelves next to the fireplace and stacking them in a box when she unearthed something unexpected. An old newspaper was wedged into the corner of the bottom shelf. Maggie stuck a fingernail -- already bemoaning her manicure -- under the edge and pulled. The pages shredded as she tugged. Her back stiff, her joints screaming for relief, she was about to leave the paper where it was jammed when her nail caught on something. Maggie leaned as far into the opening as possible and spied what seemed to be a slit in the back of the shelf. She scrubbed at it with a tissue and was astounded when she realized she had uncovered a loose brick eight inches long built horizontally into the wall at the back of the cupboard. She grabbed a screwdriver and pushed the edge of it into the crumbling mortar and wiggled it until the brick finally fell out. Maggie thrust her hand into the opening and probed with the tips of her fingers, terrified that she might find a dead rat or something equally unsavory. Finally, though, she managed to pull a wad of papers free. She held her breath as she examined the now unburied treasure. And exhaled in surprise when she realized she hadn't found just some scraps of debris. No. She had what appeared to be a very old diary. She sat back on her heels and opened the book with great care. The pages were thin and the edges were crumbling, but she could read the words on the title page. *"My Diary by Margaret Booth Edison."*

Margaret Booth Edison? And this was the carriage house from the Edison estate? Whoa. This was definitely an intriguing find.

Maggie carried the book closer to the window so she could see it better, but the ink was faded and almost illegible. She'd need to examine it in better light. Too excited to continue cleaning, Maggie wrapped the diary in the napkins that Gladdie had left behind. Then she tucked it into a trash bag and clutching it in one filthy hand, Maggie closed the door to the yellow bungalow and raced back to the B&B.

Maggie was dying to show the diary to Gladdie, but she wasn't home. So Maggie climbed the stairs to her room and set the diary, still wrapped in its trash bag, on the dresser. Then she stripped off her work clothes and turned the shower on full blast. She eyed the diary as she waited for the water to get warm. She could hardly stand the wait to read the book, but was enjoying the anticipation too. She sudsed her hair and body as she tried to imagine what was written inside. Probably nothing earth shattering, but it was a message from the past and she was overwhelmed by curiosity. What mysterious secrets might be revealed? She flashed back to the rocking chair on her first day in Sweet River.

She stepped out of the shower and wrapped a towel around her wet hair and another around her body. Then, unable to stand it another second, she peeled the garbage bag away and placed the diary on the bedspread. She fingered the leather cover. It wasn't as large as she had first thought. Maybe seven by nine inches. Actually, when she looked at it more closely, it was more of a sketchbook than a diary. Using just her fingertips she opened the cover and read, for the second time, *My Diary by Margaret Booth Edison*. She turned the page and saw the first entry was dated May 11, 1899.

Before she could read further her phone trilled. She thought of ignoring it, but when the caller ID said it was Dwight, she sighed and swiped it on. Their conversations hadn't been that satisfying the last few days, but Maggie was excited and, in spite of the continuing estrangement, wanted to share her discovery with him.

Before he could say a word, Maggie blurted, "Dwight. You'll never guess what I just found."

Dwight chuckled the old Dwight chuckle. "A plane ticket home," he suggested.

"Don't be silly. This is way more exciting than that."

A chilly note crept into Dwight's voice, but he was trying. She'd have to give him that. "Okay, Mags. What did you find?"

"Oh my God, this is so cool. I was digging in the fireplace at my — um — the house and I found a secret door and guess what was in it?"

She knew mentioning the house was a mistake. The chill in his voice deepened. "The house, huh? Okay, I'll bite. What did you find? I hope it was something good. Like jewels or money left there after a bank heist."

"Don't be dumb. It was a diary. Written by someone named Margaret Booth Edison. How cool is that?"

"Oh, very cool. That and a buck won't get you a cup of coffee."

"You know I'm not in it for the money," Maggie said. And the conversation disintegrated from there.

"Yeah," Dwight said. "What are you in it for? For us? I don't think so."

"It's just. It's just. It's so old and what if there's some big revelation or something."

Dwight snorted. "Same old Mags. Always the romantic. Listen, I just called to let you know that I'll be out of the country for a week or so. I let the kids know, but you should call. Quite frankly, they think their mother has lost her mind."

Maggie's feelings were hurt. She knew they shouldn't be, but she couldn't help it. Why was he always so damn mean about anything she got excited about? A million years ago, he might have been as intrigued as she was, but now only business kept his interest. She agreed to phone the kids and he agreed to text her his itinerary and they hung up. She gazed at her prize. It was mangled and dirty. Pages coming loose from the binding. Dwight's attitude kind of ruined it for her. I should just toss it in the trash, she told herself. But she knew she wouldn't. I'll look at it later. Maybe Gladdie will be excited. Someone had better be.

Maggie offered to buy Gladdie dinner if she'd go to Chad's Bookstore with her. She really needed the company and she wanted to show Gladdie her diary. Gladdie didn't hesitate. "It doesn't take bribery to get me to go Chad's, you know." She snickered. "There's just something about a good — um — burger!"

Maggie waited until they had ordered and were sipping red wine before she asked the question that she'd been dying to ask. "What do you know about someone named Margaret Booth Edison?"

Gladdie played with her napkin, folding it into an accordion and then unfolding it. She sipped wine and looked around the room. "Um

-- why do you ask?"

Maggie went on high alert. There was something that Gladdie didn't want to tell her about this Margaret person. "Gladdie, you're stalling. What is it?"

Gladdie tapped a nail against the table in kind of a Morse codish tapping. Long, long, short.

"Gladdie," Maggie warned.

"Oh, all right. How superstitious are you?"

"Moderately. Why?"

"Because Margaret Booth Edison was murdered."

"Murdered?"

"Yes. In the bungalow."

"Oh, my goodness. Really?"

Somberly Gladdie looked Maggie in the eye. "There's more. Supposedly she was murdered in the house. Her body was found in her bed there. And folks around here claim the house is haunted."

"Haunted?"

"Stop repeating everything I say. Yes, haunted. And that's why no one wants to live there. The few people who have tried haven't lasted long. They left claiming they'd heard noises or seen curtains moving. One woman claimed she'd seen a ghost pacing back and forth."

Maggie shivered. The rocking chair? Had she seen the same ghost? It wasn't her imagination after all? She'd thought she was crazy but maybe this Margaret really was haunting her house. She wasn't sure whether to be terrified or fascinated. Should she tell Gladdie? Of course, she should. Or maybe not.

"Well, why didn't you tell me this before? Maybe I wouldn't have rented it."

Gladdie hung her head. "I know I should have, but I really wanted to have you as my neighbor. It's been kind of lonely for me and we hit it off so well and...."

Maggie patted her hand. "It's okay. I'm not afraid of ghosts. Not much anyway."

Their dinners were served and Maggie ate a few bites before she put down her fork and leaned across the table. "Here's the thing. And now it's even more interesting. You'll never guess what I found in the fireplace this afternoon."

Mouth full, Gladdie stopped chewing and shook her head. She swallowed and said, "Not old bones, I hope."

"No, not bones. I found an old diary. Once upon a time it belonged to Margaret Booth Edison."

Later, Gladdie cracked a new bottle of red wine and the two women settled on the couch in front of the fire at the B&B to pore over the diary of Margaret Booth Edison.

May 11, 1899

Daniel is coming home tomorrow and I am not sure whether I am excited or frightened. So much has happened since he went away. I am not the same woman, not the same wife, as the one he left behind. I was just a newlywed. I was so shy and so afraid to have left the house of my father to move into Daniel's house. I was a little mouse. So quiet. Afraid to upset Daniel with my silly ways.

But, most of all, and I must say it to you, Dear Diary, I was afraid to enter the marriage bed. I feared and dreaded it before our marriage. Even after our marriage when the fear went away, I still was only able to endure his attentions, not crave them. Not as I have learned is possible.

I am ashamed and not ashamed in the slightest. I will have to confess all to Daniel. I do not know what he will do when he learns. I fear he will be disgusted. Perhaps he will throw me to the street. I cannot say.

Daniel returns tomorrow. I must wait and see.

Maggie stared at Gladdie. "Daniel killed her. I know he did."

Gladdie's eyes were round. "The stories must be true. They say they found her murdered in her bed. Daniel did it."

Maggie swallowed more wine and let her hand rest on the diary. She riffled the pages. "But, Gladdie, look. This is just the first entry. He obviously didn't kill her right away."

Gladdie stoked the fire and sat back down, curling her feet under her. "Read the next entry, Maggie. I'm dying here."

May 14, 1899

Daniel has been home for two days now and he is much changed. His experiences in the war have damaged him. He is impatient and angry. The servants are afraid to come near him and, of course, I, too, am walking very carefully around him.

I dare not confess to him for fear of setting off his new and violent temper. He was never thus before. Indeed, he was never a cheerful man, but he was patient with me and kind. I do not care much for this new husband.

I had planned to confess all to him, but now I do not know. Perhaps I should simply slip away. It might be for the best. I could easily escape if I so desired. I am torn.

"Maybe she ran away," Maggie said. "Daniel doesn't sound like much fun."

"Sounds to me like she had someone else," Gladdie suggested. "Maybe she cheated on him while he was gone."

"Well, that would sure explain a lot, wouldn't it?"

May 15, 1899

Connor has come back to Sweet River once again. He is waiting for me at the Inn. It is only two doors away but it is as far as if he was across the sea. I cannot bear it. I cannot. I must go to him.

He says he will wait, but I don't believe he will. Connor is impatient. He doesn't like to put off his satisfaction for very long. He wants me. But for how long? I do not know.

"The Inn?" Gladdie squeaked. "This B&B was the old Sweet River Inn. Her lover was here. Maybe right in this room. Oh, God. This is so exciting."

Maggie poured more wine in their glasses. "And Connor is a bit of a jerk as well if you ask me." She made her voice sing song. "He won't put off his satisfaction. The nerve. Just like a man."

"Too true," Gladdie said. "Read the next entry."

May 16, 1899

I remember the night that I went to Connor and we consummated our love. I could not resist. When he put his lips upon mine, I melted into his arms. It was but moments before we were unclothed and rolling on the bed. It was ecstasy, but then I was stricken with so much guilt I could do nothing but weep uncontrollably. Connor held me while I wept. He dried my tears. And told me I must leave Daniel and come to him. I must or he will leave the Inn and Sweet River forever.

From the moment we first saw each other – when I attended my dear-

est friend Glenda Carlson's lawn party with my parents – I was smitten. Connor, so tall and handsome and elegant striding toward me in his riding jacket, tight breeches and tall black boots. Just remembering it my breath catches in my throat, how he bowed and took my hand. "I am Connor. And you are?"

How his dark eyes never left mine and my voice trembled as I answered. "I am Margaret."

How after that we met whenever we could, the cemetery, the garden, his room in the inn where we first made love, anywhere to be away from the prying eyes of the citizenry.

And now he threatens to abandon me if I don't agree to run away with him immediately? How can he say this to me? He knows I love him more than anything. And does he not love me enough to wait? I cannot hurt Daniel, but I cannot bear to lose Connor. What shall I do? Oh, God help me, what shall I do?

"You see," Gladdie said. "Typical. And I bet she told Daniel about Connor and Daniel went wild and killed her."

"I know you said they found her in her bed. Who found her?"

"As the story goes, the servants found her. But not in her bed in the big house. They found her in the carriage house." She looked at Maggie fearfully. "In your house."

"Hold it," Maggie said. "This is new information. I thought she lived in the bungalow."

"Uh uh. She lived in the big house with her husband. But wait, maybe she told Daniel about Connor and he threw her out and she moved into the bungalow. That sounds reasonable."

May 19, 1889

I will be cursed by the Lord. I cannot stay away from my wonderful Connor. He is my one true love. My soulmate. My world would be desolate without him. I have tried to resist him, but I cannot. He says that he has needs and I must not deny him. His needs are strong and so are mine. I am cursed. Oh, Lord, I am cursed.

Gladdie jerked her feet out from under her and planted them on the floor. Her brown eyes flashed in the fire lit room. "Needs? Needs! Good God Almighty what is it with a man and his fricking needs.

Some things never change. Poor stupid Margaret."

Maggie threw her head against the back of the couch and rested her feet on the coffee table. She couldn't help thinking about Dwight. Did he have so-called "needs" that she wasn't filling? And was he looking for someone else to fill them? He wouldn't. Would he? She shoved aside those disturbing thoughts and poked Gladdie in the ribs and laughed. "Take it easy. This was a long time ago and we didn't even know these people."

"I know that." Gladys was indignant. "But we're part of their lives whether we want to be or not. I live in the Inn where Connor did her wrong. And you live in the house where she lived in shame after Daniel tossed her out."

"We don't know that's what happened."

"Yes, we do. Read the next entry."

Maggie turned the page. Then she turned it back. She skimmed through the diary anxiously. "Pages are missing, Gladdie. The next entry is July 4."

July 4, 1899

Today is the big Sweet River Fourth of July celebration. It is being held, as it always is, on the green. The band will play from the gazebo and fireworks will be lit when it darkens. I am not attending though. I have been feeling unwell and I cannot endure crowds.

I have been too unwell of late to even write in my dear diary. It is almost too wearying to pick up my pen and put ink to the page. I nap every day and seem to have no energy.

As I feared, my dear Connor has left Sweet River. He left me a note. He did not even tell me himself. He could not wait for me any longer, he said, and when he delivered an ultimatum, I could not leave Daniel. For he is ill. He has developed a terrible cough and a shaking of the hands. He is often fevered and cannot take any nourishment. How was I to abandon my ailing husband? Even for the joy of being with Connor. My joy would have been tarnished by thoughts and fears for Daniel.

And so I am in bed while the celebration goes on. I am suffering as much as Daniel. I cannot eat. I cannot sleep. Food is of no interest and if I do eat, it comes back up.

Where is my dear Connor? Will he return as he has promised?

Gladdie threw her head back and groaned. "I can't take it anymore, Maggie. That stupid wench is pregnant, isn't she? And doesn't even know it."

"Well, she didn't have the benefit of having watched Lifetime Network and reading romance novels like we have. Relying on her intuition probably wouldn't have gotten her far. She hadn't a clue."

Maggie thought about Julie. What would she do if Julie got herself pregnant? Julie was smarter than that, wasn't she? She wasn't as clueless as poor Margaret. Still -- some things never change. I'll drive myself nuts if I keep this up, she thought. She held her glass out to Gladdie.

Gladdie emptied the remainder of the wine into their glasses and took a swig. "Let's stop for tonight. I won't sleep as it is."

"I was kind of into it."

"No. Let's save it. Promise me."

Reluctantly, because she really wanted to read more, Maggie agreed and rewrapped the diary in its trash bag. The diary spent the night on Maggie's bedside table while Maggie looked at it with longing every time she opened her eyes. She wanted to solve this mystery, but she'd made a promise so she didn't touch the book.

Over the next week Gladdie and Maggie fell into a nightly ritual -- wine, a fire, and the next installment of Margaret's diary or The Margaret Chronicles as they began calling it. Maggie spent her days working on the restoration of the yellow bungalow and Gladdie kept her B&B guests comfortable, but evenings found them poring over the diary.

It would have been tempting to devour the entire diary in one sitting, but they preferred to nibble at it bit by bit — reading a section and then talking. They discussed Margaret, of course, but they also talked about themselves and their lives. Margaret, who had been dead longer than either of them had been alive, created a bond between them closer any living person could have.

Each night Maggie set the diary on her dresser—now tucked away in its own plastic container borrowed from Gladdie's kitchen. Margaret's diary had become something of a good luck charm for Maggie. Call her crazy but she felt good vibes emanating from it. Okay, yeah, that was a bit over the edge. Each night she closed it with regret and longing and each day she eagerly awaited the next installment.

July 6, 1899

I have written to Connor and now I wait for his response. I am hoping that he will forgive me once he sees my letter. I have begged for his forgiveness and pledged my undying and eternal love. How can he turn his back on that? I know that he cannot.

I have only just posted the letter to him so I will have to endure the next few days without knowing what he will say or do. I still cannot believe that he did not come to me before he left nor offer me one last chance to go away with him. I pray that he will recognize his error and come back to me.

"Let me say this," Gladdie said as she put her wine glass on the coffee table, "Margaret is starting to get on my nerves. I mean, what kind of simpleton just hangs out waiting for her one true love to come back."

Maggie stretched her toes toward the crackling flames and heaved a sigh. "We-l-l-l ... it wasn't like she could hop into her red Bug and book out of town. How was she supposed to chase Connor down?"

"I suppose," Gladdie said in a grumpy voice. "But, what a wimp!"

July 10, 1899

Still no word from Connor. Time is passing so slowly.

Daniel is better. His fever and chills have passed, but he is weak and frail yet. His mood has improved as well. He is able to sit in the sun for an hour each day and his appetite is improving as well. It would make me happy to have him recover if only I would hear from my dear love.

I am still unwell, particularly in the mornings. I am beginning to have a fear that I might be with child. I pray it is not true for it could only be Connor's child and not that of my husband, Daniel. It is too soon to be sure. I must go to church and pray to God for my monthly.

Gladdie banged her glass down on the table. "Dear Lord, the woman is an imbecile."

Maggie laughed at the look on Gladdie's face. "Calm down, my dear. People back then couldn't Google the answers to their questions. And besides, pregnancy, particularly with someone other than a husband, was definitely not cocktail party chatter."

"Probably didn't have cocktail parties either. I doubt that gloomy

Daniel would have liked that."

"That's a pity," Maggie said. "A party would have done both of them a world of good."

It dawned on Maggie that both she and Gladdie were becoming very attached to poor Margaret. Maybe even an unhealthy attachment? Nah. They cared -- about a dead person. That's all it was.

CHAPTER
Ten

Work on the yellow bungalow was progressing well. The cleaning crew completed its work and was replaced with a gang of electricians and carpenters who made the necessary repairs to bring the cottage up to 21st century standards. The great room was whitewashed and the beams stained a deep brown; the brick façade of the fireplace had been cleaned and restored; the hardwood floors were polished so that they gleamed. The circular stairway leading to the sleep loft had been reinforced and the loft itself rebuilt.

One day Maggie and Gladdie borrowed Chad's pick-up and scoured the Sweet River Flea Market for glassware and dishes. Another day they trekked to the outlet mall and bought towels and bedding at bargain prices. Maggie decided to try to use the furnishings already in the cottage. Everything was in a bit of disrepair but she knew she couldn't make the bungalow into the show place she dreamed it could be overnight. Some things would have to wait.

The bed, though, couldn't wait. Maggie and Gladdie had crawled up the spiral steps to the loft to check out the repair work and Maggie noticed the ancient mattress for the first time. Stained and ripped, it was not a pretty sight.

Maggie gagged. "Gladdie. Look at this mattress. It's so gross. It goes."

Gladdie poked at it with the toe of her sneaker. "Careful. I bet it is home to an entire family of disgusting little creatures."

"Argh. Help me pitch it over the side and then we can drag it outside."

"I'm not touching that thing," Gladdie said. "I'll bet it's the very mattress that Margaret was lying on when Daniel offed her."

"Oh, sure. I'm positive we wouldn't find Margaret's DNA on it, but I shudder to think of what else might have happened on it."

"Good point."

The two struggled as the mattress buckled. Finally they were able to maneuver it over the edge of the loft and outside.

Maggie wiped her hands on her jeans. "I feel better just getting rid of that. Let's go buy a new one."

On the way to the *Fancy Furnishings Furniture Emporium* on the edge of town, Maggie and Gladdie drove by a busy mall. Maggie wheeled the Bug into the parking lot. "I've been living in the same clothes for weeks. I'm in desperate need of a shopping fix."

"I never say no to shopping," Gladdie said, "particularly if it's with someone else's money."

"What on earth will Dwight say when he gets the bills?"

Gladdie stopped in her tracks. She whirled to face Maggie. "Dwight? But he's dead." Her face was a question mark. "Isn't he?"

It had to happen, of course, and here it was. Sooner or later Maggie had to tell Gladdie the truth. They'd become too close for her to keep up the pretense of being a pathetic, dejected widow. Not that she was doing a very convincing job playing the dejected part. And she didn't do *pathetic* at all. Frankly, she was tired of make-believe and preferred Gladdie be a confidant not a shoulder to pretend-cry on. So, Maggie sighed and tried to gather her thoughts before speaking. She refused to look at Gladdie as she fumbled in her purse, her head down. She nearly walked into a light post before she met her friend's eyes and blurted, "True confession time. You caught me. Dwight is about as dead as I am."

"But. But. But," Gladdie stammered. "W-why?"

"Long story," Maggie said, "but basically it was easier to let everyone at the *Get Your Groove On Conference* think he was one of the dearly departed. I accidentally got into the conference and everyone just assumed that I was a widow." Maggie lifted one shoulder in a what-the-hell shrug. "And I let them. I felt guilty, but that didn't stop me."

"No one guessed?"

"My friend Sarah did -- I've told you about her, right? -- but she thought it was hysterical and she just went along."

Gladdie shook her head and started walking. "The things you learn about people you thought you knew. Humpf."

"Are you mad?"

A grin split Gladdie's face. "Hell, no. Personally I would have killed Randy off if I thought I could get away with it. Figuratively, of course."

A wave of relief washed over Maggie. "Virtual death is much less messy than real death. I mean, look at poor Margaret."

"You're telling me."

Giggling, the two women headed for the mall.

As Maggie unpacked her new clothes in her room that evening, she was struck suddenly with the urge to tell Dwight about her new life in Sweet River. It was an old habit to dissect every single event of every single day with him and she missed it. Even though they had stopped talking long before she left home, she never gave up thinking that things might change. Maybe they could talk now. Time and distance being what they were.

Maggie propped pillows behind her and leaned against the headboard, legs stretched the length of the bed. She punched Dwight's speed dial into the new phone. Yes, she had learned to take advantage of some of its myriad features. As it rang Maggie realized that she didn't even know if Dwight was back after his trip. How long had it been since they'd talked anyway? She'd been so busy at the house, she'd lost track. She had managed to talk to the kids, though. However, those conversations weren't very satisfactory, to be honest. Both James and Julie were determined to play the guilt card.

Julie confided to her that, "Daddy is miserable. He misses you so much. How long are you going to torture the poor man?"

"The house is a mess," James wanted her to know. "Dad never does the dishes or picks up anything. Poor Dad. He doesn't know what to do."

Oh, right. Poor Dwight indeed. But the kids were pros at this guilt-inducing thing and their tag team attack was beginning to wear her down. No matter how hard Maggie tried to explain to them that she needed to figure out where she wanted her life to go, they tried even harder to convince her to come home. Now. They wanted the status quo back. She didn't blame them. Divorce they understood. This so-called abandonment of her life, they couldn't comprehend at all. Maybe I should throw in the towel and go home after all. No one was happy with things the way they were.

She'd almost given up on Dwight when he picked up.

"Dwight here." The tone abrupt and businesslike.

"Maggie here."

His voice softened. "Ah, Maggie May, I've been thinking about you."

Maggie caught a breath and her heart lurched. Maggie May? That was his pet name for her and she hadn't heard it in forever. "You have? That's nice."

"And I missed you too."

"You did? That's even nicer. Why?"

"Hang on a sec, Mags, I just got in and I want to get comfortable. I have stuff to tell you." A couple of moments passed while Maggie picked at the bedspread and stared at Margaret's diary on the dresser.

"I'm back," Dwight said. "That's better." She heard him take a gulp of something and heard ice cubes tinkle.

"So, you're home," Maggie said. Brilliant deduction.

"Yep. And the thing is, I really missed you. I missed us."

"You did?" Was she ever going to say anything sensible?

"I was in Paris as you know. And every place I went I remembered our honeymoon there. I saw us at every tourist spot, walking down the Champs Elyseés, at the Eiffel Tower. You know."

Tears came to Maggie's eyes and she sniffed. "Um, I don't..." She sniffed again.

"Aw, geez," Dwight said, "I didn't mean to make you cry."

"You didn't. I mean, I am but. No, that's okay. Oh, Dwight, do you remember when I wanted to go up in the Eiffel Tower but it was so crowded?"

"And you got hysterical," he said, "and wouldn't even look out."

"And you were so sweet and let me bury my face in your jacket. And you weren't even embarrassed."

He cleared his throat. "Ah hem. Well, in the interest of complete disclosure, I actually was kind of embarrassed, but you were so damn cute and clingy I couldn't tell you."

They both laughed. And then silence. Neither of them spoke. The ticking of Maggie's travel alarm seemed to reverberate throughout the room.

Finally, Dwight said, "So-o-o. Are you coming home soon then?"

The knot in Maggie's stomach tightened. "I can't. Not yet. I can't. I told you about my – um -- the house. I have a lease."

"Break it." Dwight's voice was harsh.

"Dwight. I can't. I wish I could explain it better but all I know is that there is something here I need to finish. It sounds stupid, I know."

Silence dragged out. Then, his words ragged and stiff, Dwight said, "Then we don't have much to talk about do we? I thought, well, never mind what I thought. We can talk some other time. Good night, Maggie."

"Dwight? Honey, listen. I can..." But it was no use, he had disconnected and she was talking to empty air.

Maggie turned her phone over and over in her hand before she dropped it onto the bed next to her. Why was this so hard? She wanted to share things with Dwight. How excited she was about the house. Margaret. The diary. All of it. He wouldn't listen. Maybe couldn't. He wanted things the way they had been forever and she just wouldn't do that anymore. How could she get him to understand?

July 16, 1899

I have written to Connor every day. I fear that he has not received my letters or surely he would respond. I dare not post them myself so I have relied upon my maid, Birdie, to do the job for me. I have questioned her and I find her answers to be truthful. She swears she has done as I asked.

I have sent the letters to Connor's home in North Carolina, The Singing Winds Estate. Perhaps he has not gone there. Perhaps he is still traveling. Or, my heart breaks at the thought, he has forgotten me and found another.

Mother has noticed my malaise and has made an appointment for me to see Doctor Cardwell. I know she suspects, as I do, that I am with child. I pray that it is not so. I don't believe that Daniel would be willing to raise another man's child and he will know that it cannot be his.

Oh, Connor, where are you?

Daniel is much improved. He is in good spirits and full of energy. After his illness following Connor's departure, it is a relief to see him bounding about the estate as if he was never ill at all.

Gladdie stopped reading and leaned back against the arm of the couch. Margaret's diary open on her lap, she held her wine glass up to the light and rotated it. The glass reflected flames from the fire, sending a play of light over the wall. She studied her glass as if it might speak.

Her gaze on the flickering flames, she murmured, "This is crazy, but I have a theory about what happened. Margaret says that Daniel got sick at the same time Connor disappeared. Coincidence or something else? I wonder."

Maggie was hypnotized by the fire. Hazy images of Dwight and Connor and Daniel floated through her mind She sipped her wine only half listening to Gladdie, her thoughts far away. "Hmm-m-m," she murmured.

Gladdie put her glass on the table and twisted so that she could see Maggie's face. "Maggie? Hey. You aren't even listening to me."

"Yes, I am. Really."

"Then what did I say?"

"You said..." Maggie wrinkled her nose. "You said. Oh, okay, you got me. I wasn't really paying attention."

Gladdie cut her eyes to her friend. "Duh. What's going on? Is there something the matter?"

Maggie shook her head. "I talked to Dwight."

"And?"

"It was good. We reminisced about our honeymoon in Paris. Happy memories."

Gladdie sat up and leaned her elbows on her knees, gazing at the fire. "Go on," she prodded Maggie. "And?"

"He said he missed me. He called me Maggie May. It was almost like old times."

"Ah," Gladdie said. "I see."

"No, you don't. He asked when I was coming home and I told him I couldn't do that yet. There's the house and my job at *Jewelicious* and my friends here and everything." Maggie paused to catch her breath. "And he hung up on me," she wailed. "Just when we were having such an agreeable conversation."

"It'll all work out," Gladdie assured her.

"I don't know, Gladdie. I just don't. Anyway, what were you saying about Connor and Daniel? Distract me."

Gladdie closed the cover of the diary. "I was saying," she went on, "that maybe it wasn't such a big coincidence that Daniel got sick at the exact same time that Connor took off."

"I don't see what you're getting at."

"Okay, here goes -- maybe Daniel found out about Margaret's affair with Connor and killed her lover." Gladdie put her hand to her heart and sat up straight. "And it quite literally made him sick with regret or something else."

"Well-l-l." Maggie was unconvinced but willing to consider Gladdie's theory. "It's not like we can solve this mystery, but it's interesting to try. Is there another entry?"

"Just a few more," Gladdie said. "Read it or call it a night?"

"One more," said Maggie. "Let me read."

July 30,1899

Dear Diary, I have just come from seeing Doctor Cardwell and he has confirmed what I already knew. I am with child. Connor's child. I know that I should not feel the way I do. I know that a woman in this condition and these circumstances should feel fear and concern and regret, but I do not. From the first moment that I heard the words "with child", I have felt only joy. At first, it was just a tiny bubble, but now my entire being is filled with happiness. A baby. I have dreamed of a baby my entire life.

It would be perfect if only Connor was here to share my joy, but he has abandoned me and I have heard nothing from him in all these many weeks since he left Sweet River. My joy, though, is only slightly diminished by his absence and I have made a decision about what is best for me and for my baby.

I cannot ask Daniel to raise another man's child. I will not. I have thought of not revealing the truth to him, but Daniel is not a fool. He can do the math that proves I became with child while he was still serving our country. Once he understood that it was not his child Daniel would never agree to raise it and would become angry and distant with me. Life would be unendurable. So, dear diary, I am going to raise this child on my own. I am a modern woman and these are modern times far different from even my mother's day. It will not be easy, but I must do it.

Mother has agreed to help me as much as she can, but she doesn't approve. When she heard Doctor Cardwell's words, she turned pale and could not speak. I fear I will be a disgrace to her, but Mother is a strong woman. She says I may come to live with her and my father if I would like. If Daniel will not have me.

I am not going to accept her offer as much as I love her for making it. No, I have decided to move to the little yellow bungalow on the estate. It is a perfect place to raise a child. The estate belongs to me, after all. Daniel does not own it. I won't evict him from the mansion. I don't want to cause him more hurt than I already will. But I won't live with him either. I am going to do this on my own. I pray that I can manage. I have education and courage and I am going to test that now.

I will confess everything to Daniel tonight and move into the yellow bungalow tomorrow.

Gladdie leapt from the couch and whooped, "Atta girl, Margaret!" She yanked Maggie to her feet and the two danced a happy jig around the room, laughing and hugging each other in glee. Finally, breathless the pair collapsed on the couch.

"She finally showed some gumption, after all," Gladdie said. "You gotta love a modern woman."

Maggie's face fell. "Geez, Gladdie. That gumption must have led to her demise. Daniel got pissed off when he found out she was pregnant and moving out. Women didn't do stuff like that back then."

"You're right. Damn." Gladdie looked bemused. "I can't remember when it was that she was murdered. Do you think Daniel would be so evil as to kill a pregnant woman?"

"In the heat of passion maybe," Maggie suggested.

"We need to do some research," Gladdie said. "I'm going to the library tomorrow."

CHAPTER
Eleven

A few days later Maggie's new bed was delivered and the little yellow bungalow was finally ready to be occupied. She hummed along with the music blaring from her new iPod speakers as she stuffed the last of her things into the new bag she bought to accommodate her growing wardrobe. All that was left to do was roll the bag down the street and into her new house. She was bubbling with excitement. Maggie hadn't lived on her own in, well, she'd never actually lived completely on her own. She'd lived with roommates and a husband and kids, but never in a place totally hers. There, that does it. She zipped the bag, set it on the floor and went to say good-bye to Gladdie.

Maggie was torn between being sad and ecstatic about that. She knew that she'd miss the comfortable companionship that they had developed over the few weeks they'd known each other. But it wasn't as if she was moving back to Ohio or anything. That thought brought her down the tiniest bit. Ohio. Dwight. The kids. Damn. Why did she have to think about that right now? She wasn't going to let those thoughts spoil her day. She clomped downstairs and found Gladdie up to her elbows in flour and apples.

"Yum," Maggie said. "Apple pie."

"I'm baking it for you. As a housewarming present."

"Come over tonight and I'll make dinner," Maggie said. "Pie a la mode for dessert."

"I'll do better than that," Gladdie said brushing her hair off her face and dusting flour over her hair. "I'll make dinner."

"No," Maggie protested. "You've done enough. Let me cook."

"Sweetie," Gladdie said. "You don't even have a stove yet."

"I have a microwave. Tell you what. You cook here and I'll warm it up in my brand new microwave. Please. I want to have my first dinner in my new home with my closest friend in Sweet River."

Gladdie stuck out a flour-coated hand and Maggie took it. "Deal," Gladdie said. "I'll help you move the last of your things down there."

Maggie unlocked the door and stood back to let Gladdie enter the yellow bungalow ahead of her and beamed with anticipation. Gladdie didn't let her down. "Oh, my God. It's so adorable. You've really done a lot in the last couple days. I love it."

Maggie followed Gladdie into the house and gazed around with satisfaction at what she had accomplished. The single room radiated warmth -- the old furniture covered with an eclectic collection of blankets and scarves in a rainbow of colors. Maggie had painted the scarred dining table and chairs a shiny white and placed a bright red vase full of spring flowers in the center. Upstairs, the impressionist-like print of the comforter was just barely visible. The curtains that fluttered at the now gleaming windows were the same swirl of color as the comforter upstairs. The cottage was enchanting and bright and inviting and Maggie couldn't believe it was hers. Well, hers as much as a rental and weeks of slave labor could make it.

She hauled her luggage into the center of the room and sank onto the couch absorbing the fact that she was home. Gladdie squeezed in next to her and nudged her with her hip to get her to move over. Then, still wearing their jackets, Maggie and Gladdie simply sat unmoving and breathed the aroma of fresh paint and fresh flowers.

"Awesome," Maggie said.

"Totally," Gladdie agreed.

A few minutes ticked off the antique cuckoo clock and then Gladdie wiggled her toes, drawing lazy circles in the air. "Hmm-mm," she said.

"My, but you're talented." Maggie chuckled as she watched Gladdie make toe figure eights. "You oughta take your show on the road."

Gladdie pushed herself to a sitting position. "My talented toes and I really should hit that road if we're going to have any chance of dinner."

"Gladdie, I can -- " Maggie began.

But Gladdie interrupted. "You are not going to lift a finger. Your housewarming dinner is on me. Your mission, should you choose to accept it, is to provide the wine."

Maggie drew her knees to her chest and hugged them and then uncurled and arched her back. "That sounds great. I hadn't realized how tired I am until just this minute."

Gladdie hopped to her feet and hands on hips looked down at Maggie. "What do you say to making it a real party? I was thinking I could call Azalea and Jewel and see if they wanted to join us."

"That would be awesome. Do you think they'd be available?" Maggie couldn't stop smiling. Having Azalea and Jewel there would make it a true housewarming celebration.

"It's Sunday. I'll bet they'll jump at the invitation." Gladdie paused with her hand on the door. "Eight o'clock?"

"Perfect," Maggie said and closed the door and leaned against it. She surveyed her new living quarters and was delighted with it all -- from the lumpy couch to the three-legged armchair to the rag rugs scattered over the floor, she loved everything. She wandered through the living area trailing her hand over the woodwork and patting pillows into a more pleasing shape. Home sweet home.

As she lugged her bags up the spiral staircase to the sleeping loft, she banged her elbow and knee on the wall. Cursing under her breath she staggered to her bed and collapsed. Hands tucked behind her head she breathed in and out listening to the sound of a lawnmower outside. She rubbed her sore elbow and went out like a fat kid trying to steal second. Half an hour later the sound of a motorcycle on the street outside woke her and she struggled to a sitting position and reached for her cell phone. Dwight. She had to share this moment with him.

He answered on the first ring. "Babe."

"Hi."

"Speak. You called me, you know."

"I know, but now I'm wondering if I should have bothered you."

Dwight answered in an injured tone. "Since when have you bothered me?"

Maggie couldn't tell him how many times in the last few years that she absolutely had bothered him. Interfered with his thinking about something much more important than her petty problems. She couldn't tell him that and still have the civil conversation she wanted to have. So she said instead, "I have something to tell you."

He'd learned his lesson over the last few weeks and didn't bother to ask her when she was coming home. "Okay. I'm listening. On the edge of my seat actually."

"Sarcasm is not necessary. I moved into the house today. In fact, I'm lying on my brand new bed right this very second. Birds chirping. Bees buzzing."

"Aw, Maggie May, you're killing me here," Dwight said. His mournful voice made her wince.

"Be happy for me," Maggie pleaded. "Please."

"I am happy for you. Here's an idea. What do you say I drive down there and get a tour of this new mansion of yours? Maybe christen that new bed?" He tried a suggestive chuckle but it fell short.

Maggie squiggled into a more comfortable position and her eyes fell on the diary propped on the floor next to the bed. She and Margaret were quite the femme fatales, weren't they? Making the men they loved suffer. At least she hadn't cheated on Dwight. She asked herself if he had cheated on her, but then dismissed the idea as not likely. She hoped.

"Honey," she said, "I'd love for you to see the bungalow. It's so cute. I need some time to myself before that happens, though. I need to figure some things out."

"Don't take too long, Mags," Dwight said. "I'm only human."

Maggie thought of Connor and his "needs" and heaved a huge sigh. "I promise it will be soon."

"Give me a call," Dwight said his voice cracking just a bit, "when you find yourself."

Maggie grabbed her purse and flew down the stairs and out the door to find wine and fresh air. A short time later she was jogging down Main Street toward the *Un-Whined Wine Shop*. Her sprint cleared her head and she was in better spirits by the time she bought wine, fancy crackers and a wheel of brie and toted it all back home. She dropped her bags in the kitchen and started to set her newly painted table. Having a party always cheered her up and Dwight's warning wasn't going to ruin it for her. Not a chance.

When she heard the thump of her brand new brass doorknocker at precisely eight o' clock that evening, Maggie was showered and dressed in velvet jeans and a sparkly top. The table was set with her new dishes and candles glowed from every empty surface. Maggie gave the room a once over and pronounced it ready for guests. She flung open the door and found Azalea and Jewel on the doorstep — each holding a serving dish. Gladdie brought up the rear towing a cooler on wheels. Maggie stepped back to usher them into her new home. "Welcome," she said. "I'm so glad you could make it. It was kind of last minute."

Azalea rocked skinny jeans and had wrapped her head with a colorful turban in the same colors as her bright silk shirt. Her caramel skin glowed with health and spoke to the benefits of great genes or maybe an expensive skin care program. In her four-inch stilettos she stood more than six feet tall and towered over Jewel who, although she claimed to be five feet tall, probably fell just short. Maggie was struck by Jewel's necklace of colorful stones that coordinated with, but did not match, her earrings and bracelet. Jewel dressed simply, letting her jewelry make a statement against a plain black silk top and slacks. Gladdie, too, had dressed up for the occasion in leggings and a long, clinging sweater top in deep burgundy.

Maggie held her breath as she waited for their reaction as they took in every detail. Azalea was the first to first to speak. "Maggie, this is amazing. You've done a phenomenal job with the place."

Maggie let out the breath she'd been holding. She hadn't realized how much she was hoping for their approval until that moment. "Thanks, Azalea," she said. "I couldn't have done it without your help in finding the right people to work on it."

"That's my job," Azalea said. "You've done me proud."

Gladdie poked Jewel's arm. "You're awfully quiet," Gladdie said. "What do you say?"

"I say it's beautiful."

Maggie's grin widened until she thought her face would break. "Then let the party begin. Wine anyone?"

Maggie poured wine and Gladdie set up the food buffet style on Maggie's freshly restored dining table. The four women loaded their plates with Gladdie's home cooked lasagna, warm garlic bread and Caesar salad and settled around the faux fire glowing in the fireplace. An instant camaraderie sprang up between them and they talked as thought they had been friends for years. The four were at different stages of a woman's life and each brought her own unique perspective to the newly created friendship. And, as it often does among women friends, the talk turned to men.

Azalea had been married for going on twenty years to her insanely gorgeous ex-NBA player husband, Jermaine. She and "Jer" were such a striking couple that they were often mistaken for celebrities. "Don't even start with the 'he was a pro basketball player so he must be famous,'" Azalea told them. "Jer was never a super star. Well, at least not on the courts." She winked and leered. Their two sons followed in the father's size 15 footsteps and were completely obsessed and possessed with basketball.

"Our house is as close to being a gym as they can make it. You should see the mound of dirty socks I have to wade through every day." The look on her face said that she didn't mind at all.

Gladdie had been divorced from her ex, Randy, for nearly five years. It had been a struggle at first, she said, "But when I bought the B&B, I knew that I was exactly where I needed to be. Sweet River is home."

Happily single, Jewel had been involved in several serious relationships, but for one reason or another nothing led to marriage. "I have given up wishing for that particular institution, I guess," she told them. "My business is going well and I have an occasional date. If it happens, it happens."

It was Maggie's turn. The other three sipped their wine and the air hummed with anticipation. Her friends eyed her as she considered how much to tell them. Somehow she just wasn't ready to have the debacle of her marriage the subject of any discussion. Why spoil the party when it was going so well? So, telegraphing a silent apology to poor Dwight, she murdered him yet again. "I'm a widow," she said pulling a mournful face.

Gladdie raised an eyebrow and popped a bite of garlic bread in her mouth observing Maggie as she chewed. "Go on," she urged Maggie. "I can't wait to hear the story."

Maggie scowled at her, but continued her sad tale. "It hasn't been that long," she said. "And I kind of needed to get away from everything. I decided to pack up and find a new spot to settle down." Oh, yes, she'd packed up all right. And run like a bunny being chased by a barking dog.

Jewel studied the flames. "Hmm-mm. But why pick Sweet River? I mean, there are zillions of more exciting places to live."

At least, Maggie didn't have to stray too far from the truth in explaining that particular decision and she told them about *Get Your Groove On* and Mary Lou Jennings. How she'd seen the sign for Sweet River and came to see if what Mary Lou had said about the town was true and stayed because it was. True, that is.

As the first wine bottle was consumed and the second nearly gone, the women settled back and conversation flowed as easily as the wine. Gladdie and Maggie brought coffee and apple pie from the kitchen and they dug in with more appetite than one would have imagined considering how much dinner that had all packed away.

Finally, Jewel groaned and pushed her plate away. "Good Lord, I haven't eaten like that in I can't remember how long. It's the gym for me tomorrow."

"I should probably get going," Azalea said but she didn't budge. "Jer just got home from a business trip and you know what that means." Her exaggerated wink was comical.

"Whatever does that mean?" Jewel teased.

Azalea straightened the turban and grinned. "The man has needs."

"Needs?" Maggie and Gladdie burst out laughing. "Just like Connor," Maggie said.

Azalea looked offended. "Who's Connor?"

"Well-l-l," Maggie said, not sure whether to explain or not. Gladdie quirked an eyebrow and rolled one shoulder. Then she nodded.

Maggie went to the bookshelves on either side of the fireplace and plucked *"The Margaret Chronicles"* from its resting place. She carried it to the coffee table in front of the couch and gently put it down. Jewel and Azalea leaned forward to see what she had placed there. Maggie patted the diary with two fingers. "It's a diary."

"A diary?" Jewel asked. "Yours?"

"Don't be silly, Jewel," Azalea said. "Look at it. It's ancient and falling apart."

Maggie lifted the diary and cradled it in her hands. She stroked the cover with her forefinger. "I found it."

"Found it?" Jewel asked.

"I was cleaning the bookshelves by the fireplace one day and discovered a secret door behind a loose brick in the wall. I pried it open and there it was. *The Diary of Margaret Booth Edison.*"

"Margaret Booth Edison? Wasn't she the one who -- " Azalea said.

" -- was found murdered in her bed, according to local legend,"

Gladdie finished. "Yep. The same one."

"Wow," Jewel said reaching for the diary and then falling back. "That's amazing."

"What's even more amazing," Azalea said, "is that Margaret was found dead in her bed in this very house. And no one ever was ever arrested or charged for the murder. Or alleged murder."

"Spooky, huh," said Gladdie. "So Maggie and I have been reading excerpts from it every night. It's fascinating."

Azalea scooped the nearly empty bottle of wine from the table and emptied it into her glass. She twirled it between her fingers and then plonked it on the table. "What's really fascinating," she said, "is that Margaret's ghost has supposedly been haunting this bungalow for the last century."

Maggie frowned. "So I keep hearing! I'm sort of kidding but I think I might be psychic."

"What? Why? Have you seen her?" Azalea asked.

"Not exactly."

"What do you mean, not exactly?" Gladdie wanted to know.

"Well," Maggie said, "On my first day in town. On my way to your house, Gladdie, I stopped by the house and looked in the window."

"And you saw Margaret's ghost?" Jewel asked.

"No, but I saw the rocking chair. That one over there." Maggie pointed across the room at the freshly painted rocking chair piled with colorful pillows. "And all of a sudden it started rocking. It was probably the wind. I'm not sure. And as suddenly as it started, it stopped."

"Do you think it was Margaret?" Jewel said.

"I don't know. There wasn't any ghost or anything. And I haven't had any -- um -- sightings since. This will be my first night here. I'll let you know in the morning if Margaret stops by."

"Hang on," Jewel interrupted them. "I want to know more about the diary. What it said. Can I read it?"

"We're nearly finished," Gladdie said. "We could finish it tonight."

"Then you can go back and read the beginning if you want," Maggie offered. "With one condition. It doesn't leave my house."

"I accept," Jewel said. "Read."

Maggie looked at Gladdie. "You or me?"

"You," Gladdie said.

And Maggie began to read --

August 3, 1899

Dearest Diary… Daniel has been away in Columbia on business and I haven't been able to speak with him about my baby and my move to the cottage. Birdie and Mother helped me move all my things to the yellow bungalow while Daniel is gone. When he returns he will find me absent from the big house. I can't imagine his reaction. Will he be angry or hurt or will he not even notice my absence?

Daniel is a very different man from the one I married five years ago. When we met I loved him for his strength, his calm, his acceptance of everyone around him. He was such a comfort to me when Father was so ill. I have to confess, though, that I never felt the same passion for Daniel that I feel for Connor. But I was content. My life was good.

Then Daniel went to war, The Spanish-American War. He returned a much damaged man. He is impatient and intolerant of those of us who continued our innocent lives here in Sweet River while he witnessed the horrors of war. He was on the battlefield where blood and death and soldiers losing their limbs were an everyday occurrence. This new Daniel can be so hard and cold and his eyes often burn with hatred for the world.

And Connor? He has such a joy for living. He teased me and made me laugh. Where Daniel was black, Connor was the brightest of light. I tried but I could not resist his charms. And where is he now? He has left me to deal with the fallout of our passion.

The baby. Oh, how I love this baby. She, I am sure it is a girl, will be my miracle.

Yet, how can I be this happy when I have abandoned my husband and fled to my special refuge—my little yellow cottage?

Maggie stopped reading and marked the spot with her finger. She stared into the fire, images of the past and the present swirling in her mind. The circumstances were very different, but both she and Margaret had fled their marriages for the comfort of the yellow bungalow. A century apart yet barely a second in the universal plan. And Margaret ended up dead. Not a good omen.

"Maggie?" Gladdie said. "Hey, are you okay?"

"Oops, sorry," Maggie said. "I got distracted."

"I feel like I'm in an Alfred Hitchcock movie," Azalea said. "What happens next?"

"Maggie," Gladdie said, "Do you want me to read it?"

Maggie nodded and handed the diary to Gladdie.

August 4, 1899

I am so incensed, Dear Diary, that I fear my brain might explode. My anger has overwhelmed me and I have no idea what to do. It's a very good thing that Daniel is not here for if he were I might harm him in some physical way.

I must back up and relate what I discovered today. Daniel is still in Columbia and I am happily living in the little yellow cottage. I went to Daniel's study this afternoon to retrieve some legal papers attesting to my ownership of the estate. I know that Daniel keeps all of his papers in a locked file in his bureau, but I have the combination to the lock. It is our wedding date. How very romantic of him. I unlocked the file and found the papers that I need and was about to secure the file, when I found something that made my heart stop and my face flush with fury. My letters to Connor. The letters I sent to my true love. It came to me as a crushing blow. My letters had never been sent. Connor never read the outpouring of my heart.

I will have this out with Daniel upon his return.

Gladdie pressed the diary closed and lifted her head. "Wow," she said. "Just wow."

"That bastard," Azalea said.

Jewel raked her fingers through her hair. "He kept her letters to Connor? That's so bad."

"There must be more to the story," Maggie said. "Is there another entry?"

Gladdie flipped a few pages of the diary. "Yes, but it's pretty short."

Maggie reached out a hand to take the book and Gladdie handed it to her. "Okay, let's see what happens," she said.

August 5, 1899

Daniel got home last night. I am going up to the big house to confront him soon. I must know what he has done. My letters to Connor were never sent. Daniel must know about our love. He cannot know about the baby, but I will tell him. Then I will seek out Connor to deliver our wonderful news.

My new life—and the life of my baby—will begin on this day. I am nervous and excited all at one time, dear diary.

"Is this for real?" Azalea jumped to her feet and paced around the room. "Seriously? Or are you two playing games with us?"

Gladdie tapped the tips of her fingers on the cover of Margaret's diary. "How can we be certain of anything, 'Zalea? The only way we could know if it's authentic is to take it to the Historical Society and let them do whatever they do to verify things."

"Maybe we should do that," Jewel said.

"Not yet," Maggie said. "I can't explain it, but something tells me I need to hang onto it awhile longer." She took the diary out of Gladdie's hands and replaced it on the bookshelf next to the fire. "I'll take care of it until the time comes. Okay?"

No one uttered a sound as the four considered the options. Azalea stopped pacing and stood facing the rest, her back to the imitation flames. Her skin glowed in the firelight. "I don't know about y'all, but this is one of the most exciting things I've seen or heard in forever. We are witnesses to history and maybe a better understanding of the ghost who haunts Maggie's bungalow. I say we keep it to ourselves."

The other women nodded agreement. Azalea plucked the tattered book from the shelf and laid in on the coffee table. Then placing her hand on the diary, she said, "Come on y'all. Put your hands on the diary and swear that we won't reveal its contents to anyone. It will be our secret."

"That's silly," Jewel began.

Maggie reached forward and covered Azalea's hand with her own and, after a moment's hesitation, Gladdie and Jewel did the same. "We solemnly swear," each said in turn. A sheepish grin crossed Maggie's face.

"I guess that makes the four of us The Secret Society of Protectors of the Margaret Chronicles. Do we need to prick our fingers and share blood?"

"That will not be necessary," Azalea said. "But, on second thought…"

"Yuck," Gladdie said with a grimace. "I'll go to the library tomorrow and see if I can learn anymore about Margaret's death. Because if that was the last entry, Daniel must have killed her that very night."

"Maybe," Maggie said but she wasn't convinced. "I still think there's more to the story."

CHAPTER
Twelve

After Maggie said good-bye to her dinner guests, she set up her iPod on its speakers and sang along at the top of her voice to her favorite songs as she washed and dried the dishes and straightened up the cottage. She emptied the remnants of the last bottle of wine into her glass and sank onto the couch to enjoy the solitude. It was intoxicating and, oh, okay, she had to admit, a bit lonely as well. This solitary stuff would take some adjusting to, but she would figure it out. It was glorious to be on her own and answerable to no one. She wondered if Dwight was lonely too. So shoot her, she kind of hoped so.

She opened the new paperback she'd been saving to read, but her eyelids kept sliding to half-mast. Finally, she gave up the effort, closed the book and hoisted herself to her feet. She washed her wine glass in the sink, left it in the drainer and went into the bathroom to brush her teeth and pull on her PJs. Toothbrush still in hand she checked the locks on the doors and turned out all the lights except a small table lamp in one corner. Then, satisfied that she was safely tucked in for the night, she dragged herself up the circular staircase and fell into bed. She barely had time for a single toss and half a turn before her eyes slammed shut and she sank into a deep sleep.

After a couple hours of sound sleep, Maggie was caught up again in The Dream. She was once again on the edge of the same cliff peering down the steep ravine to the huge boulders below. She heard the same menacing footsteps behind her. Took the same fearful step backward and toppled into the abyss. There the dream changed. This time the scream that the wind ripped from her lips was not one of fear but rather one of exhilaration. The same exhilaration one might feel when riding in the front of the rollercoaster. More *woo hoo* than *aieeeee*. As she plunged downward she observed the trees, the flowers, even a baby fawn, with a lazy detachment. Near the bottom her fall changed from a plummet to a float and she touched down with the grace of a gymnast who had just successfully completed a vault. She raised her arms over her head in the classic gymnastic pose and listened to the crowd cheering. Tens across the board.

Maggie woke feeling pleased and proud of the accomplishment unlike the heart pounding terror the dream usually induced. She rolled over on her back and laced her fingers behind her head, blew out a blissful sigh, and enjoyed the sound of the applause.

She tugged the covers up to her chin and snuggled in trying to re-enter the pleasant dream, but the crowd noise was keeping her awake. Why wouldn't they stop the foot stomping? And then she came wide-awake with a lurch of her heart. The noises she heard weren't coming from her dream. They were coming from downstairs. She sat up with a jerk taking the covers with her. Someone was in the cottage. She heard footsteps under her head. Then she recognized the squeak of the antique rocking chair she had rescued from the cottage's debris.

Careful not to make a sound she rolled out of the bed and onto the floor. On hands and knees she crept toward the edge of the sleeping platform and stared into the room below. The table lamp glowed in the corner casting shadows into the inky blackness. Her eyes unaccustomed to the dark, Maggie squinted until -- she saw her. A woman was rocking in the old rocking chair -- back and forth, back and forth. *Scr -- eech, Scr -- eech.* Maggie blinked and rubbed her eyes. She could barely breathe.

The woman wore a long, high-necked dress, with long sleeves that puffed at the shoulders. A dress that might have been worn at the turn of the century -- and not the 21st. Suddenly the woman looked up and Maggie stumbled back a step still keeping her eyes on the rocking woman. As Maggie watched, the woman tilted her head and raised a hand in a silent salute. Maggie let out the breath she hadn't known she was holding with a whoosh. It must be, it had to be... Then the woman rose from the rocker and turned toward the door. It was Margaret. Maggie was positive, for when Maggie saw her in profile, she recognized the woman's baby bump. Pregnant. As Maggie huddled frozen the woman glided across the room and through *(seriously right through)* the locked and dead-bolted front door and vanished. *Through the door? Who does that?* A ghost, Maggie answered herself.

The ghost of Margaret Booth Edison.

Hands shaking and heart thumping Maggie crawled back into bed and pulled the covers over her head. Breathe, Maggie, breathe, she told herself. A dream. Obviously the product of too much food and too much wine. She didn't believe in ghosts. Did she? Ghosts didn't exist. Not really. Maybe at Disneyworld, but in real life, in Maggie's own living room? Not so much.

Maggie checked the bedside clock. Three o'clock. She wanted, no she needed, to call someone. She needed to share this. Gladdie? No, she couldn't wake her at this hour. Or Azalea or Jewel. That left only Dwight. He must be sound asleep. He wouldn't like to be awakened. Tough. She needed to talk.

Dwight's voice was froggy with sleep. "H-h-hello?"

"Honey?"

"Maggie?" And then more alert. "Maggie. What's wrong? Are you okay? Are you sick?"

The concern in Dwight's voice brought tears to her eyes. "I'm sorry. I shouldn't have woken you up. Go back to sleep. I'll call you tomorrow."

"Like hell you will. You call me in the middle of the night and expect me to just forget it? Sorry, babe. Tell me what's up?"

"You'll think I'm crazy."

"Maggie!" He sounded impatient.

Maggie sucked in some air. "I saw a ghost."

His chuckle accelerated into hoots of laughter. "You saw a what? Did I hear you right? A ghost?"

Maggie had to smile in spite of herself. "Stop laughing," she huffed. "I'm serious."

Maggie and Dwight talked for at least an hour. She pictured him lying in their bed, pillows punched up behind his head, his thick dark hair messy and his eyes blind without his contacts. She missed him, she realized, more than she thought she would. She missed this Dwight, though, not the workaholic, humorless drone he had become. Finally, Maggie's phone beeped insistently that its battery was about to die so she whispered a reluctant goodnight and disconnected. But not before Dwight said, "When, my Maggie May? When?"

And she answered, "Soon."

CHAPTER
Thirteen

From the very first minute, Maggie loved working at *Jewelicious*. She loved the bright, open shelves; the colorful display of jewelry sparkling in the sunlight; she loved helping the customers pick out just the right piece for that special someone; she loved working with Jewel to select stones and create designs, but most of all she loved getting up each morning filled with energy and anticipation, knowing that she was needed.

Jewel insisted on presenting pieces of jewelry to Maggie. At first, Maggie protested. "I can't take that without paying for it. Even though I'm tempted."

Jewel just laughed, a delightful girlish sound. "Don't be silly, Maggie. You'll be a walking advertisement for *Jewelicious*. All you have to do is tell anyone who asks where you got it."

Maggie gazed with longing at the jewelry displays. Jewel's pieces were unique and beautiful. True art. Maggie sighed. "Okay, Jewel. You got me. I've never met a piece of jewelry I didn't covet since I was three and slipped my first silver gilded Cracker Jack ring on my chubby finger. I'll joyously be your billboard." She slipped a multicolored stone ring on her middle finger and held up her hand to admire it. "You are an artist."

The two women became more than co-workers -- they enjoyed each other's company. Jewel approached each day with a smile and a twinkle in her eye and from the first moment they met an instant rapport had sprung up. The laughter in the shop was infectious and customers lingered to chat and drink the coffee that Jewel brought over from Agnes' next door. Sometimes Maggie felt like it was party time all day long. Of course, work got done, but it was almost an afterthought.

One morning soon after she started working Maggie was whistling as she polished the glass display cases, stopping to take an occasional sip from the *Agnes' Sweet River Café* coffee mug that held her morning mocha latte. It was too early for most customers so Maggie had the music turned up and she didn't hear the tinkling sound that announced a customer.

"Hey, Maggie," Gladdie said.

Maggie jumped and dropped the bottle of glass cleaner on the floor, where it began creating a puddle. Maggie grabbed a wad of paper towels and squatted to soak up the mess. From her position below the display case she tilted her head to look up at Gladdie. "You scared me," she said in a mock accusatory voice.

"Sorry," Gladdie said. "Where were you?"

Maggie lifted one shoulder. "Don't know. In the iPod zone, I guess. What brings you in this fine morning?"

Gladdie strolled around the store peering into the display cases, trying on pieces that were in counter displays. "Hm-m-m," she said as she slid a bracelet on her wrist. "Oh, sorry, I got sidetracked."

Maggie unfolded from her crouch with the wet paper towels in her hand and waved them at Gladdie. "Easy to do in here. So, you were saying?"

Still wearing the bracelet, Gladdie spun so she could see Maggie's face. "I finally got around to doing some research on our friend Margaret. I just came from the library and I wanted to tell you..."

Gladdie was interrupted by a noisy group of customers crowding through the door. Laughing and calling gaily to each other, the women dispersed throughout the store. "Oops, tour bus at twelve hundred," Gladdie said.

Maggie's froze as she kept an eye on the horde. "There are so many of them at one time."

"You'll be fine," Gladdie said. "Tour groups are typically really laid back. And also typically quick to part with large sums of cash."

A large woman appeared next to Maggie. "How much is this, dear?" she asked holding out one of the most expensive pieces on display.

Before Maggie could form an answer, Gladdie slipped the bracelet she was wearing off and handed it to Maggie. "Take care of business, kiddo. Can you meet me for lunch at Agnes'? I can tell you what I found out then."

"One o' clock?" Maggie asked. "I have something to tell you too."

Gladdie was waiting for her when the last of the tour crowd faded away and Maggie was able to take her lunch break. Face flushed, Maggie breezed into Agnes' trailing apologies. "I'm really sorry, Gladdie. It was a zoo all morning. Jewel just got back from seeing her supplier so I could cut out."

"No problem, Maggie. Let's order first and then I'll spill all."

Maggie sank into an empty chair and shed her jacket at the same time. "Whew. Feels good to sit down."

Agnes took their orders and brought their drinks and then Gladdie took a deep breath and put both hands on the table in front of her. "Okay. Are you ready for this?"

"Shoot."

"It seems that the rumors about Margaret Booth Edison and her untimely death are true."

"Okay. So she died in my bungalow then. And that last diary entry was written just before she died."

"Not exactly. Here's where it gets interesting. According to Harriet Beecher…"

"Harriet Beecher?" Maggie asked.

"Yeah. Head of the *Sweet River Historical Society*. Do you want to hear this or not?"

"I do. Sorry, but Harriet Beecher? Go ahead, Gladdie, I'll be good," Maggie said with a grin.

"Okay, then. According to Harriet Beecher, Margaret died in your house, all right, but not until nearly a year later. In March of 1900, in fact."

"But that means…" Maggie let her words hang in the air.

"You got it, girlfriend," Gladdie said with glee, punching a fist in the air, "she had the baby."

"So then she and Daniel? Divorced?"

"Maybe, maybe not. Harriet said that the town records show the birth of a baby girl on February 14, 1900. But only one parent was listed —Margaret Rose Booth. No father's name appeared on any document."

Agnes breezed out of the kitchen with a tray of food and Maggie waited, impatient to hear what else Gladdie had learned, while she served their lunch. When Agnes finished and headed to the front of the café to greet new arrivals Maggie said, "That must mean that she and Daniel were no longer married. And she was living in the yellow bungalow."

Gladdie shook her head. "I checked with Harriet to see if there were records of things like divorces that far back. She dug around in some old files that had been saved to microfiche. And according to what we could find out, there was no official divorce on record. But it appears that they weren't living together. Here's where it gets even more fascinating. Apparently Margaret did own the estate, but her will listed Daniel as only heir."

Maggie caught her breath. "So there's the motive for killing her. We thought it was because she was pregnant, but maybe that wasn't it. Or only a part of it."

Gladdie nibbled at her wrap sandwich before she spoke. She wiped her fingers on her napkin and fished some papers out of her bag. "Harriet made me copies of everything we could find about either Margaret or Daniel or even Baby Rose Dawn. There's a lot here, but it boils down to the fact that we don't really know for sure if he killed her. I believe that no charges were filed against him. Or there aren't any on record. No indictments. Nothing." Gladdie paused. "Harriet and I didn't have time to sift through all of this. I'm sure there's a lot more information in these papers. You can read them for yourself."

Maggie tilted her chair back and inspected the ceiling. "So-o," she said after a few moments, "ancient history and possibly missing records. But we do know that Margaret had a child."

"Yep, it would seem so."

"Definitely, intriguing."

The two women tackled their lunches and gossiped about not much of anything for a while. Finally, Gladdie tossed the last bite of wrap in her mouth and washed it down with a swallow of sweetened ice tea. "What did you have to tell me?"

Maggie checked her watch. "Oh, jeez, this needs more time than I have right now. I have to get back so Jewel can do some creating. Come over for dinner and I'll tell you my tale then."

"A ghost? No way." Gladdie plunked her wine glass down on Maggie's coffee table and shot to her feet. She burst into the kitchen and returned a second later with the wine bottle in her hand. She thunked it on the table next to a stack of paperback books. "We're going to need the whole bottle before I get to the bottom of this," she said.

"You saw a ghost and you didn't think to tell me! Or Jewel? Or Azalea?" Gladdie's voice came out a high squeak. "Maggie, come on."

Maggie stared out the window at the deepening dusk. "I was going to, but..."

"No buts, Maggie," Gladdie tried an offended tone, but came off sounding eager. "Tell me about the ghost. It was Margaret wasn't it? What did she do?"

"I'm pretty sure it was. I mean, how many ghosts could be haunting my house?"

Gladdie paused, her wine glass halfway to her mouth. "Good point. Then definitely Margaret. What was she doing?"

"Well," Maggie said, "the first time I saw her -- "

"The first time!" Gladdie's voice was shocked. "You've seen her. You've seen Margaret more than once."

"Uh, huh." And Maggie went on to tell Gladdie about Margaret's first appearance on the night of the housewarming dinner party. "That was her star performance. The other times I've heard the rocker and then just caught a glimpse of her skirt or a sleeve."

"Spooky," Gladdie said. "Weren't you scared?"

"Not after the first time. Actually, she's kind of comforting."

"Does she – um – haunt you every night?" Gladdie bounced on the couch in excitement. "I want to see her. I mean it. I'm gonna come over and spend the night."

Maggie ran her hands through her short blonde hair making it stand up in tufts on top. She took her time answering, considering Gladdie's proposal. Well, why not? If Gladdie saw Margaret too, she'd know she wasn't losing her mind. "Sure, Gladdie. I'd love a slumber party. But what about your guests?"

"I can be home in time to feed them breakfast. Tonight?"

Maggie nodded and beamed. "Who ya gonna call? Ghostbusters."

Gladdie flew out the door and was back with her overnight bag before Maggie could reconsider. The two concocted a dinner out of the skimpy contents of Maggie's refrigerator and killed another bottle of wine in anticipation of bedtime and a visit from Margaret.

"The couch downstairs or share my bed?" Maggie asked when it was time go to bed.

Gladdie let out a squeal. "Down here? I don't think so. Margaret might comfort you, but I think she'd scare me to death."

"Do you snore?" Maggie wanted to know.

"Not tonight," Gladdie answered. "Don't think I'll sleep a wink."

The pair climbed up the stairway to the loft and slithered under the covers. And waited. And waited. And waited. And woke up as daylight shimmered in through the cracks in the curtains on the windows.

Gladdie sat up in bed and rubbed her eyes. "Did Margaret show up?"

"Not that I noticed," Maggie said. "I fell asleep. Maybe she was here and we missed her."

"Just my luck," Gladdie said with a groan. "I always miss the good stuff."

"Sorry. You can come back tonight," Maggie offered.

Gladdie stretched her arms over her head and swung her head from side to side. "Thanks, Maggie, but I'll pass. Your bed might be comfy for one, but I'm as stiff as a drink at a dive bar in Key West. I'll stick to my own bed from now on."

"You'll be the first to know if she shows up again," Maggie said.

"Pinky swear," Gladdie said offering Maggie her pinky.

Maggie linked her own pinky finger with Gladdie's. "Pinky swear," she said.

CHAPTER
Fourteen

Maggie's life settled into a comfortable routine. Mornings she ran (or strolled or staggered or limped) two miles and did her 150 crunches before she showered in her tiny, but nicely refurbished shower and grabbed something from the fridge to eat at *Jewelicious*. Most days she bought two mocha lattes at Agnes', one for her and one for Jewel. She usually ate her lunch with Jewel in the back of the store, but some days she lunched with Gladdie or even Azalea at Agnes' or at *Chad's Bookstore and Bar.*

When she got home from work, Maggie spent her evenings working on the refurbishing of her house or, when she was too tired for home improvement, she lay on the couch reading one after another the pile of paperbacks she had collected. Ones she had always wanted to read. She had decided against buying a television and missed it only the tiniest bit. She did wonder about the reality shows she was addicted to, but other than missing the crowning of the latest American Idol or Dancing with the Stars winner, she found she could do without it quite nicely. Television no longer was necessary to fill the holes in her life and for this alone she was grateful.

About once a week Maggie would call Sarah or vice versa. The two of them discovered that they could tell each other anything. Maggie could confide to Sarah that she felt guilty about Dwight's "death" at her own hands and how she had conversations with a ghost. Real conversations, thank you very much. And Sarah, in turn, entertained Maggie with tales about her baby daughter and her few feeble attempts at dating.

"Getting your groove on, are you?" Maggie asked.

"Well," Sarah said laughing, "if Helen can do it, I guess I'd better give it a try."

Maggie always hung up smiling.

On nights when solitude seemed more lonely than peaceful, Maggie would invite one of her new friends to dinner at the cottage or at one of the quaint eateries that Maggie discovered. She kept herself busy, but no matter how busy she was, eventually it would be time for bed. She would delay the moment for as long as possible, but then when fatigue was too much to bear, she would climb the circular stairway to the sleep loft and crawl into her bed and ... wait. Hands behind her head, eyes wide-open, she would lie with the covers pulled up to her chin, straining to hear any tiny thump or bump from the room below. Or the telltale squeak of the rocking chair. Most nights she would drift off to sleep without hearing a single sound and wake from a deep sleep a few hours later when some noise would pierce her consciousness and she would sit up in her bed. And rubbing her eyes she would creep to the edge of the platform and peer into the shadows below. Some nights she would only see the rocker gliding back and forth as if a body had just risen from it. Other nights she would catch a glimpse of a white skirt or sleeve disappearing as quickly as it appeared. But some lucky nights Maggie would hover on her perch and see her as clear as day. Margaret! Wearing the same old-fashioned empire-waisted dress. Trailing around the room as if she was hunting for something -- something lost to her. Something of importance.

Oh, okay, Maggie couldn't know absolutely what it was that Margaret might be doing, but she liked to weave a story around the ghostly apparition and her nightly visits. She supposed it really didn't matter, though, because Margaret was there in her living room. Maggie's very own personal and private ghost.

And Maggie intended to keep her that way. Gladdie had stayed over on a couple of occasions, but Margaret never showed up so even Gladdie began to doubt that Maggie had seen her. When Maggie would mention Margaret to Jewel or Azalea, they gave her the tolerant look of someone humoring a crazy person. So she kept her sightings to herself. Hugged the secret to her with a smile.

And Dwight? After the first night when he really seemed to suspend his skepticism and agree that Margaret was possible, he grew impatient with any mention of her.

"Come on, Mags," he said one night, "get over yourself. You're just using this make-believe as an excuse not to come back to me and the real world."

"No, Dwight," she'd protested, feeling protective of Margaret, "she's real. I do see her and I don't care whether you believe me or not. Margaret lived in this house. That's a fact. I think she's looking for something here? Why can't you put aside your stupid preconceived notions and give magic a chance?"

"Magic is it? Dead woman walking? Ghosts? Next thing you'll be telling me you're sprinkling pixie dust or holding séances to speak with the spirit world. Hey what about the Ouija board? Have you tried that?" Maggie could hear the impatience and frustration laced through his words. Maybe she didn't even blame him. Would she believe him if he started telling her ghost stories? Not that dead serious Dwight would ever spin a fairy tale.

"Don't be sarcastic," Maggie said. A definite edge in her voice. "If you're going to be that way, we won't discuss it."

"Fine," he said and slammed the phone down.

"Fine," she said to the humming silence at the other end of the line. "Be that way."

The more she thought about it -- and, of course, she thought about it a lot -- she could understand Dwight's attitude. He had been remarkably patient with what he could only feel was her abandonment of him and their marriage. She'd run away, after all. Who does that? When she spoke to either of the kids, they sided with Dwight. Mothers, in James and Julie's opinion, don't run away. And she sensed, as time dragged on and she showed no inclination to return to their life together, that Dwight's well of patience was drying up. She had to address the issue. And soon. But what did she want to do and how did she want to do it? Very good questions both of them. The answer came to her unexpectedly.

One evening she had a particularly contentious phone call with Dwight in which he told her she was acting like a selfish bitch and she, in turn, called him an insensitive bastard. Definitely not their finest hour. After the call ended in mutual hostility, Maggie leaped to her feet to pour herself a restorative glass of wine and tripped over the stack of papers Gladdie had been given by Harriet Beecher at the Historical Society. Maggie had been working her way through the pages but, as

Gladdie said, there was a lot there -- much of it dry and boring. It was a tedious process. She kept the pile on the floor next to the couch so she could wade through it a bit at a time. Now, though, the accumulation went flying in every direction and, cursing under her breath, Maggie bent to retrieve them. A copy of an old newspaper article caught her eye. *"Born to Mrs. Daniel Edison, a baby girl, Rose Dawn, 7 lbs. 8 oz., February 14."* A Valentine baby. Rose Dawn. Margaret's little girl. Maggie put the clipping on the coffee table and sifted through the other papers. Fascinated, she fetched her wine and sipping it began to read.

Several hours and at least two glasses of wine later, Maggie yawned and stretched and neatened the stack of papers as she set it on the coffee table. If the papers had ever been in order, she had certainly made a mess of them when she spilled them all over the floor. So, she read them in a scattershot manner, picking out and digesting whatever interested her -- discarding what didn't. It was fascinating reading but she really hadn't gathered any new evidence on the case. She riffled through the papers again looking for something -- anything -- that would break the case wide open. She drained her wine glass and slammed it on the table in frustration. Enough of this. Detecting is such drudgery. Time for sleep, perchance to dream. Thank you, Shakespeare. Maggie started to stand up and a piece of paper fluttered to the floor. She scooped it up and her heart started to dance faster. Where it had been a mere waltz seconds before now it was beating like a hard rock band playing the last few bars. She was clutching a copy of a newspaper article dated March 28, 1900. Headline — *SOCIALITE MISSING AND PRESUMED DEAD. Police Search for the Body of Margaret Booth Edison.*

Margaret Booth Edison, 32, wife of Daniel Keyes Edison, fifth cousin of Thomas Alva Edison, is missing and presumed to be dead after her maid, Birdie Byrne, was found slain in Mrs. Edison's bed with the bedding soaked in blood. No one has any information about the whereabouts of her employer. "She must be dead," a neighbor told the Sweet River Times reporter. "She would never have left Baby Rose Dawn alone if she could have helped it."

The police received an anonymous phone call regarding the death of Miss Bryne. When the police arrived at the Edison estate they spoke immediately with Mr. Edison. He was alone in the large mansion, but directed the police to the estate's guest home where he claimed his wife and baby had been residing. The infant was found with her grandmother, Mrs. Edison's mother, Mrs. Eliza Booth, at her home. The baby was unhurt.

Police reported that Mr. Edison's shirt was stained with blood. He explained that he had been slaughtering pigs when the police arrived to tell him that his wife was missing.

Mrs. Edison had no known enemies according to her husband. Police are working on the assumption that an intruder broke into the guesthouse and Miss Byrne caught him in the act of burgling her employer's home. They believe that Mrs. Edison may have returned home and surprised the intruder in the act of killing her maid. They believe he then may have panicked and killed Mrs. Edison and decided to dispose of her body.

No weapons have been found. The police are still searching for any evidence that could lead them to Mrs. Edison. Police Captain Neil Goodwell asks that anyone with any information about this case to please step forward.

The victim's mother, Eliza Booth, told police, "I'm not letting him near this baby." Mrs. Booth would not elaborate further on her statement. Mrs. Booth plans to relocate with the baby. "My daughter would not want Rose Dawn raised in Sweet River. I will take the baby to live with relatives in Drunken Hills, North Carolina, until my daughter is found. Dead or alive."

Maggie paced across the room her thoughts tumbling over each other like a pair of rambunctious puppies. Local legend had it that Margaret had been found dead in her bed in the yellow bungalow. But according to this newspaper account, she wasn't found dead at all. No. It was Birdie Byrne. So what happened to Margaret? Where did she disappear to? There could be some explanation. Like what? Daniel was covered in blood too? Pigs' blood? Not a chance. So he did do it. But there's no body. At least not Margaret's body.

Maggie sank onto the couch. Her thoughts tangled. She heaved a huge sigh. What happened here? What was Margaret's ghost doing? A simple haunting or something way more sinister? Perhaps avenging a murder?

Maggie climbed the stairs to the loft still trying out theories and finding them lacking. She woke the next morning still weary and crabby from lack of sleep. The insistent clanging of her alarm did little to improve her mood. And her mood slid even further into the black depths when she realized that Margaret had failed to appear. Crap.

Inspiration struck on her morning run. Dwight. She'd ask him to meet her in Drunken Hills for a weekend getaway. Oh, and, by the way, chase down Margaret's relatives. Brilliant.

CHAPTER
Fifteen

"I'll have a beer," Azalea said. "Bud Lite if you have it."

The burly waiter, sporting a full grizzled grey beard and a skintight T-shirt with "Big Sugar's Sweet River Bar" in block letters across the front, muttered under his breath as he scribbled on his pad.

Maggie whispered to Jewel, "What'd he say?"

"Sounded like girly beer," Jewel whispered back with a grin. "Don't suppose he thinks much of lite beers."

Gladdie and Jewel both ordered lite beers as well to the obvious consternation of their waiter. He turned to Maggie and said, "The same for you, little lady?"

Maggie squirmed. "Uh, no," she said, "I'd like a glass of Pinot Grigio." One look at the waiter's face and she added, "Please."

"Pinot what?" he said. His forehead wrinkled with obvious confusion.

"Pinot Grigio," Maggie said. "You know. Wine?"

The waiter's face cleared. "I know that. We don't get much call for that fancy stuff here, Missy." He jerked his head in the direction of a rowdy group of patrons, drinking beer and hollering at the television screen. "Them guys wouldn't know what to do with a Pinot Whatever. I'll see what we've got in stock."

"Whatever you have that's white will be fine." Maggie wanted to placate him.

As the waiter strode away toward the bar, Maggie said to her friends, "What do you think he'd have done if I'd ordered a Cosmo?"

"Probably would have choked on his chewin' tobacco," Jewel said. "This is definitely not a Cosmo kind of a place."

Swiveling her head to see the entire room Maggie checked out *Big*

Sugar's Sweet River Bar. Definitely not a spot to order a girly drink. Big Sugar's was more a peanut shells on the floor, beer drinking, pool shooting kind of a place. The testosterone level was off the charts and the noise level was as well. Flannel and ripped denim seemed to be the predominant wardrobe choice. Since the clientele was mostly male, Maggie and her friends were attracting a fair amount of attention from the other patrons. Especially Azalea -- who wore skintight jeans and a white shirt under her sequin-studded denim jacket and towered over her friends and most of the men in the bar in her cowboy boots with four-inch heels. The men at the table next to them gawked with naked admiration.

Azalea leaned back in her chair gesturing with one red polished nail as she entertained her friends with an anecdote about one of her clients. She seemed oblivious to the commotion she was creating among the bar patrons until one of the men from the other table scooted his chair across the floor and planted himself next to Azalea. "'Scuse me, Miss," he said. His words were somewhat slurred. "My friends and I wondered if you might wanna join ush for a little drink. We'd be honored."

Azalea slid her chair a few inches away from him and gave him a sideways glance. "Why, that's real sweet of you, but my friends and I are kind of busy with something here." She turned her back to him and tried to continue her story.

"A course we'd be honored if all of you join ush," he said and nearly fell off his chair as he slid it closer to Azalea again.

Azalea gave him a piercing look. "No thank you." Her voice was as sweet as frosting, but underneath was an ice cream cake frozen solid.

His friends hooted. "Now, Dave, leave the little ladies alone." But Dave didn't budge.

Just then the waiter reappeared with the beers and one jelly jar of a clear liquid that might or might not be wine. He put his meaty hand on Dave's shoulder and squeezed. "You heard the boys, Dave. Go on back to your table and leave the ladies be."

Disappointed, Dave slumped in his chair for a second before he lurched to his feet and staggered in the direction of the restrooms.

Gladdie leaned close to Maggie. "It's always an adventure being out with Azalea," she whispered in her ear. "Aren't you glad you came after all?"

"Truthfully," Maggie said, "I am."

When Gladdie had called earlier to invite Maggie to go out to Big Sugar's for a girls' night out, Maggie had refused saying she had too much work to do on the bungalow. But Gladdie persisted, telling her that all work and no play made Maggie a very boring friend. Eventually, Gladdie wore her down and Maggie agreed to come along. She hadn't been outside of Sweet River much since she arrived and a trip to Big Sugar's was a chance to explore a new part of the village.

Big Sugar's was on the outskirts of town on a two-lane road surrounded by vacant land. It was a big, rundown building with grey clapboard siding and a beat up sign with some of the lights burned out. *Big Suga weet iver Bar* blinked off and on. Inside it was loud, music blared from the jukebox and the smell of burgers and fries permeated the air.

"Thanks for asking me," Maggie said. "I'm having fun." She nodded her head at their waiter who was setting the beers on the table. "Is he Big Sugar?"

Gladdie shook her head. "Nah, Big Sugar is over there. Behind the bar." She nodded in that direction.

Maggie twisted in her chair so she could see who Gladdie was indicating and gulped. A mammoth man wearing a Big Sugar T-shirt was tending bar. He was perhaps six feet seven or eight and Maggie guessed he weighed in the neighborhood of 350 pounds. Not a bit of flab. All muscle. His neck was the size of a tree trunk and his biceps reminded her of bowling balls. His frizzy grey hair was tied back in a ponytail and he kept flipping it back as he poured drinks, opened beers and chatted up the drinkers on the bar stools.

"Oh, my God," Maggie said. "That's Big Sugar? Why do they call him that anyway? He looks the farthest thing from sugar that I can imagine. His T-shirt is the same size as the fitted sheet on my bed."

Gladdie hopped to her feet and loped across the room to the bar. Maggie could see her leaning on the bar talking non-stop to the giant and pointing in the direction of their table. Within a few seconds the giant discarded his apron and came out from behind the bar. He and Gladdie made their way back to the table.

"Maggie," Gladdie said, "I'd like you to meet Big Sugar." She paused. "And Sugar I'd like to introduce you to my friend, Maggie Murphy."

The giant extended his hand to Maggie and when she took it her hand disappeared in his grasp. "Nice to meet you, Miz Maggie," he said. "You must be the widow woman what's sprucing up the old Edison bungalow."

Maggie blushed. Widow woman. How was she ever going to explain her way out of that one? Gladdie had the cat-who-swallowed-the-canary smirk on her face, so Maggie knew that she wasn't going to be any help. Well, now was not the time to confess.

"Pleasure to meet you too, Mr. Sugar. Yes, I am renting the yellow bungalow." True as far as it went. Dwight's untimely demise and her unfortunate widowhood could be explored some other time. Say, three weeks from never.

Big Sugar pulled a chair up to the table and perched on the edge. Maggie wondered how long it would take for the chair to simply collapse under his weight. The chair squeaked in protest and Sugar shifted his weight. "I've been meaning to come around to your place and offer any help you might need in hauling things out of the house or to the dump. That place must be chock full of debris by now. It's been years since anyone, well anyone alive, has lived there."

Did Big Sugar know something about her ghost? About Margaret? Maggie had to find out. So softly that Sugar had to bend to hear her, Maggie asked, "People keep telling me that the bungalow is haunted. What do you think?"

She held her breath waiting for his reply.

Sugar rolled his eyes toward the ceiling and tilted back his chair so far that Maggie expected it to tip over. Then he lowered it and sat forward, elbows on knees. "I don't rightly know about ghosts, Miss Maggie, but I sure enough think it's possible. People say that Miss Margaret Booth Edison was murdered in her bed. That'd sure be good enough reason for me if I was lookin' to haunt someplace. That's all I can say."

Maggie leaned close and whispered, "What would you say if I told you I'd seen her? Margaret."

Sugar squinted at her and then his face broke into a huge smile. "I'd say, Miss Maggie, that we sure need to talk. When my girl, Nancy Beth, was little she used to play at the bungalow. No matter how we tried to keep her away she always was there. She told me that it was safe for her there because the nice lady watched over her."

Maggie's heart beat a little faster. "I'd love to talk more with you, Mr. Sugar. I want to learn all I can about Margaret."

"I got to go back to the bar now, Miss Maggie," Big Sugar said, "but I'll come by tomorrow about five to haul away some of your trash. If you happen to be there, maybe we'll just happen to talk."

"That's a deal."

As Big Sugar walked away, Gladdie said, "And that's why he's called Big Sugar. He's a real sweetie."

"Hm-m-m," Maggie said. She picked up the jelly jar and tipped a bit into her mouth. She grimaced and she wrinkled her nose as she swirled the contents of the jar. "What on earth is this?" She took another swallow. "Tastes like pond water laced with olive oil."

Jewel laughed. "We told you this wasn't a place for fancy drinks. I'll get you a beer." She started to signal their waiter.

Maggie put her hand on her arm. "No, that's okay, Jewel." She put her glass to her lips and took a cautious sip. "This stuff kind of grows on you. And beer and I don't do well together."

Maggie flashed back to her college days and her college sweetheart, DJ. Beer had been their drink of choice and it had led to some unfortunate situations. Ones she'd probably rather not dwell on. Especially DJ. Whatever had happened to the boy?

She dragged her attention back to her friends who had spotted four guys at a table far across the room. Better dressed and better behaved than the ones at the table next to them, they were completely absorbed in a baseball game on the jumbo television. "Now that's what I'm talkin' about," Azalea said. "Maggie should go over and get to know them."

"'Zalea," Maggie began. "You know I'm..."

What? Married? Separated from the Undead? Maggie wasn't up to confessing, but Gladdie was enjoying her discomfort way too much.

"Oh, go on," Gladdie said. She gave her a shove. "You being a widow and all. It's time you met a cute guy."

Rattled, Maggie looked around for their waiter and then signaled him to bring her another glass of pond water. "No, thanks," she said. "I'm good. I'm enjoying your company. No need for anyone else."

Jewel and Azalea teased her but Maggie refused to budge. A huge moan went up from the television watchers and there was head-shaking and losers reaching into their wallets to pay winners. With the game over and no longer requiring their undivided attention, the four guys slumped in their chairs and scanned the bar. One of them noticed Maggie and her friends and uncoiled from his seat and strolled over. He stopped behind Gladdie and hands on the arms of her chair bent and kissed the top of her head. She grinned up at him. "Hey, I wondered how long it would take for you to realize that we were here. Game was intense, huh?"

Chad snagged a chair from the table next to us and pulled it over. The drunk who'd tried to pick up Azalea snarled at him. "The ladeesh don't want co-company, buddy. Move along."

Chad gave him a manly pat on the back. Gentle but with the promise of more pressure if necessary. "This lady." He put an arm across the back of Gladdie's chair. "Is with me."

Muttering to his drinking buddies, the drunk slugged down the rest of his beer, and turned his back.

"So," Chad said, "what brings you classy women to a joint like this? 'Of all the gin joints in all the world, she walks into mine.'"

"Not only good looking but he watches old movies too," Gladdie said. Her smile widening. "What a catch."

"'Here's looking at you kid.'" Chad chuckled and hoisted Gladdie's beer and chugged.

Gladdie whispered in his ear and Chad unfolded himself from his chair and crossed the room to his table with long legged strides. He returned with one of the other guys. Taller than Chad at maybe six feet two and clean-shaven with a mop of thick, unruly brown hair, he sported horn-rimmed glasses and a pleasant smile that revealed straight white teeth. Maggie was immediately drawn to him. Down girl, she told herself, you're married even if no one else knows it. Flirting is not acceptable. But she couldn't take her eyes off him. He was hot.

Chad introduced him as Mac. Or was it Jack? With the bar noise, Maggie wasn't sure. "Mac(or Jack), you know Jewel and Azalea. And this is Maggie Murphy. She's new in town. Lives in the yellow bungalow on Cranberry Lane."

Mac caught Maggie's eye and Maggie couldn't look away. "Pleased to meetcha, Maggie. Would you care to dance? The Bad Boys are pretty good and they'll start playing in about five minutes."

Maggie hadn't noticed but a band was setting up on a platform at the back of the bar. The squeal of a microphone and the sounds of instruments being tuned had been drowned out by the jukebox and the general crowd noise, but now Maggie realized that a live band was next on the program.

"Oh, I couldn't," she said to Mac. "It's late and we've got to go…"

"Oh, no we don't," Jewel said. She settled into her chair as if she was planning to spend the night. "I'm having another beer." She raised her eyebrows at Azalea and Gladdie. "And they are too. So, Maggie, there's no hurry. Go on and dance."

Maggie tried to wiggle out of it, but her friends were determined and, if she was honest, dancing sounded fun. She hadn't danced in ages. Not really. Unless you counted bopping around the house with her iPod on. And that didn't count. Back in college. In the days of DJ and beer, she was quite the dancer. But she and Dwight never danced. Never.

"Okay," Maggie said and took Mac's hand. "Let's rock and roll."

By the time the Bad Boys were playing their last song and Big Sugar was announcing last call at the bar, Maggie was exhilarated, sweaty and bleary-eyed. *How much of that godawful wine had she consumed anyway?* It was hot and she and Mac danced almost every dance and she lost count of her drinks hours ago.

Maggie had really enjoyed herself. Mac (or was it Jack?) was a fantastic dancer and it was a challenge for her to keep up. But, in spite of being out of practice, keep up she did. Jack (or was it Mac?) and she didn't talk much. With the loud music and dancing, they didn't have much opportunity for intimate conversation. When the band did take a break and they could hear each other talk, they did the basic cocktail party chatter thing. Name, rank, serial number and, of course, her story of the sad and premature death of her beloved husband, Dwight. At some point the next day, she realized that she hadn't really learned much about Mac but that night it didn't seem to matter.

Her friends were long gone before Mac or Jack and Maggie closed down the bar. Since Chad vouched for Mac, Maggie wasn't worried about letting him drive her home. By the time Jack (or Mac) was pouring her into his Miata, she wasn't worried about anything at all. As the two of them left the bar, Maggie stumbled and then clung to Mac's arm as they picked their way across the parking lot. The tall lamps guarding the parking lot sent out a blurry glow and the sky rolled like the deck of a ship as Maggie lowered herself into the car. Oops. She hadn't been this drunk since the days of DJ and beer.

Either Mac could hold his liquor better than she or he hadn't had as much to drink, because he seemed to be sober. Or at least sober enough to drive. Then Maggie concluded that she didn't have a choice in the matter and closed her eyes. When she opened them again, Mac *(or was it Jack? Really must find out the guy's name)* was hauling her out of the car and steering her toward the front door of the yellow bungalow.

"Keys," he said. "In your purse?"

"Rightio," Maggie said and fumbled in her bag and dropped it on the ground.

Mac recovered her bag and dug in it until he found her keys. He unlocked the door and with one arm supporting her, maneuvered her inside and lowered her onto the couch. "Okay," he said, "I'll take off. It's been fun."

Maggie didn't want the night -- early morning -- to end. "Stay," she pleaded, "Have a glass of wine with me."

He grinned at her and patted her head. "Maggie, you've had enough. You need to sleep it off."

"I'm not drunk," she protested. "Only a little tipsy."

"Ah," he said, "Maggie May."

Maggie May? Maggie stared at him from her reclining position on the couch. His face was blurry and wavered in the dim light. But she knew him. It was Dwight. He had come to find her after all. Thank God. She'd missed him so much. Maggie lurched to her feet and threw herself into his arms. He felt so good. So strong. Maggie pulled his face down to hers and kissed him, refusing to let him back away even though he tried at first. She deepened the kiss, forced her tongue between his reluctant lips and was rewarded when he kissed her back. She pulled him down onto the couch and snuggled against him, tugging at the buttons on his shirt and kissing him at the same time. He responded by fumbling with the buttons on her shirt, finally getting it open and revealing her lacy bra underneath. She moaned and he pushed her down. It had been so long. Maggie's breath was ragged and her heart pounded. "Oh, Dwight, I've missed you."

He rolled off her and banged his hip on the coffee table as he extricated himself. He zipped his jeans and grabbed for his jacket in a single motion. "Oh, God, Maggie, I'm not who you think I am."

Maggie reached for him, catching his leg. "Yes, you are. You came back."

"I'm not Dwight. I'm not your dead husband." He stared at her as she tried to hold onto him.

Dead? Okay, now's the time to tell him the truth. "You're not dead," Maggie said. "Silly. How can you be dead if you're here?"

He sighed and sat down and wrapped her in his arms. "I know you miss him. It must be awful." And he held her as she woozily drifted off.

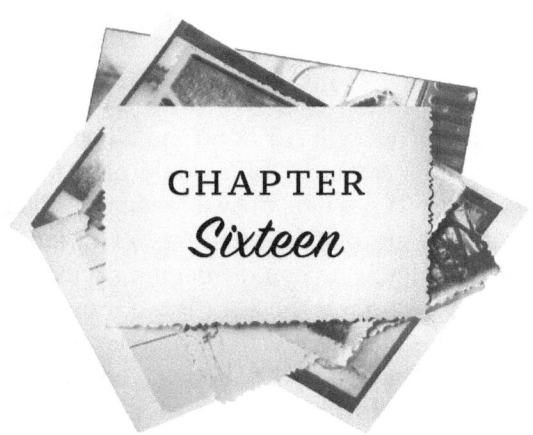

CHAPTER
Sixteen

Bright sunlight slanting through the porthole window above the sleeping loft woke Maggie the next morning. She rolled over and stretched to relieve the stiffness in her back and legs until -- Oh, my God -- she realized with shock that she was wearing only the denim shirt she'd worn to the bar. Her shoes were missing and she was appalled to discover her shirt was unbuttoned and her bra was unhooked, one bare breast exposed to the chilly morning air. And, oh no, her jeans were tossed in a heap beside her bed, and she was wearing only her panties. She sat up and ran her fingers through her hair struggling to remember how she got here. The last she could recall she'd been dancing with Mac at the bar.

She sank back onto the pillows and tried to reconstruct the previous evening but her head pounded like the bass on a souped up hot rod and when she tried to get up her stomach clenched and her mouth watered. Do not. Do not. Do not. She chanted to herself as she swallowed and waited for the nausea to subside.

Try as she might, though, she couldn't remember a thing. She'd been dancing with Jack? and Gladdie and Chad and Jewel and Azalea left without her. He must have driven her home and put her to bed. But if that's all that happened why were her clothes only half on? Had they? No, that's ridiculous. She wouldn't.

She had a fuzzy memory of Dwight being there too. And an even fuzzier memory of being totally turned on and wanting Dwight so bad. So bad, that….Oh, my God. What on earth had she done?

She rolled over on her stomach and pulled the pillow over her head. She groaned and pounded the bed with her fists. *No, no, no. I didn't have sex with some guy I picked up in a bar. Did I?* Even in the days after

DJ vanished she would never have done that. There is obviously an explanation. A perfectly good one. She would have to find it. But the how was the tough part. If she never saw Mac (or Jack?) again, it would be just fine. It would be beyond humiliating to run into him at Home Depot or someplace. "Hey," she could imagine saying to him, "where are the hammers? And, oh, by the way, speaking of hammers, did I have sex with you the other night when I was hammered?"

Maggie could hear the muffled sound of her cell phone ringing. Must still be in her purse downstairs. She tossed the pillow aside and looked at her bedside clock. Oh, no. Not only was she hung-over, she was hung-over and late for work. Must be Jewel calling to check on her. Maggie staggered out of bed and fought down the urge to throw up as she clung to the stair railing and tiptoed down the steps. In the bathroom, she inspected her mirror image with horror. She looked like a month of sleepless nights. Hair wild, eye makeup smeared, bags the size of the Hindenburg blimp under her eyes. Before she could do anything to repair the damage, she heard her the insistent banging of her front door knocker. Was it him? She couldn't face him this morning. Or ever. She grabbed her robe from the back of the door and pulled it on as she crept without making a sound into the living room to peer out the side window.

Gladdie! Bearing a thermos and a basket. Thank heavens. Maggie really needed a friend at the moment. And coffee. Please let Gladdie have coffee in the thermos.

Maggie yanked the door open and hauled Gladdie into the living room. "Boy, am I glad to see you," Maggie said.

Gladdie took a step back and eyed Maggie. "Lovely look," she said. "What happened to you? Wait. Don't answer that. I'll be back." Gladdie vanished into the kitchen and returned a minute later with two mugs of coffee. She handed one to Maggie. "Now talk."

Maggie buried her nose in the mug inhaling the fresh coffee aroma. "I love you, Gladdie." She took a swallow of coffee and leaned her head against the back of the couch -- eyes closed.

"You look like Hell," Gladdie observed without rancor. "Rough night?"

Maggie sat up and set her mug on the table in front of her. Her expression was doleful. "That's the thing. I don't know."

"What don't you know? You seemed to be having a great time when we left the bar."

"Too good, possibly," Maggie said with a sigh. "I really don't remember."

"Ah," Gladdie said. "Drinker's remorse."

Maggie covered her face with her hands. "More than that. I think I might have – um – "

"Might have what?"

"Had sex with a guy I picked up in a bar," Maggie wailed.

"Why would you think that?" Gladdie asked, "Is that something you usually do?"

"Of course, not, but look -- " Maggie stood up and untied the belt of her bathrobe and spread the robe open. "This is what I was wearing when I woke up."

Gladdie's eyes widened until they seemed to take up her entire face. She stared at her friend who wore only her bra -- unhooked at that -- and panties and an unbuttoned shirt. "Oh."

Maggie retied her robe and sank onto the couch. "As if that isn't bad enough, I don't remember a thing after you guys left the bar. It's all a big blank until I woke up this morning. Dressed -- or should I say -- undressed like this."

"Oops," Gladdie said.

Maggie cradled her mug between her hands, staring at its contents as if she could find an answer there. "I don't even know his name. Mac or Jack, I think."

"It's Mac. Mac McDougal. He's a good guy. Friend of Chad's. I don't think he'd ever sleep with a married woman, so you're probably okay."

Maggie felt ill. "That's the thing, Gladdie. He thinks I'm a widow. Fair game."

Gladdie shook her head. "Uh uh. He's a good guy. Not a player. He wouldn't take advantage of a woman. Particularly one who'd been drinking."

"Maybe I attacked him. It's been months since Dwight and I – you know – and even then it was pretty ho hum. What if I did?"

"Okay, Maggie," Gladdie said, "calm down. We'll get to the bottom of this somehow."

"How? I can't call him up and ask him. I never want to see him again. I'm so embarrassed whether we had sex or didn't. He'll think I'm a slut. Oh, God, I am a slut."

Maggie spent the rest of the day alternating between despair and prayer. Please God, she'd think, I'm a good person. Don't let me have done something incredibly stupid. And then her mood would drop into the black depths. *How could I have done it? I cheated on Dwight. I'm a bad person. He'll never forgive me.* She wasn't getting anything done and she was scaring off the customers with her gloomy aura, so Jewel sent her home early. "Get out of here, Maggie. Go home and take a nap. Come back tomorrow in a better mood. Please."

Maggie dragged herself out the door and down the street. Her head ached and she felt as if it was twice its size. She couldn't look at her reflection in the shop windows -- it made her sick. *I'm a bad person. A bad person. A very bad person.* The refrain pounded in her brain.

When she rounded the corner onto Cranberry Lane, she spotted a pick-up truck parked in front of the bungalow. He'd come back. To finish what they'd started? Oh, God. She stumbled to a stop and nearly reversed direction to go back the way she had come. Then she took a breath and decided that she'd have to confront him sooner or later. Better sooner. Her legs weighed a ton apiece as she trudged toward her house. When she reached the cottage, however, she realized with relief that it wasn't Mac after all. It was Big Sugar. She'd completely forgotten that she had agreed to meet him. She knocked on the window of his truck and he lumbered out of the cab, pulling on his work gloves. "We'll get this yard cleaned up in no time, Miss Maggie," he said. "I'll get started right now."

"Give me a few minutes to change into jeans," Maggie said. "We can do it together."

CHAPTER
Seventeen

Maggie and Big Sugar worked together as if they had been a team for years. To Maggie's amazement Sugar sang old show tunes under his breath in a deep smooth-as-chocolate syrup baritone as he labored. She couldn't help joining in when she knew the words. By the time they threw the last of the accumulated debris into the back of Sugar's truck they were belting out a mostly harmonious rendition of the chorus of Oklahoma.

"Wow," Maggie said. She slapped Sugar's hand in a high five. "You have a beautiful voice. Where'd you learn to sing like that?"

"Shucks, Miss Maggie," Sugar said. "I been singing all my life. Church choir and an occasional musical at the local theater."

"So that's why they call you Sugar. Your voice is that sweet. I could listen to you all day," Maggie said. And Sugar blushed -- his cheeks pink above his grizzled beard.

Blushed? A lesson to be learned here, Maggie. You certainly can never tell an album by its cover. You think you're going to hear country and Broadway comes out.

Sugar hauled out the ancient stained and mildewed carpet that Maggie had ripped up and stuffed that in the truck bed as well. And when Maggie mentioned a drippy faucet, he fetched his toolbox and, although it was a tight squeeze, wedged himself under the sink and fixed it.

Finally, with no other tasks that he could perform, Maggie offered him a beer or a soda. She was shocked when Sugar said he would prefer tea if she had it. Somehow he didn't seem like the type to drink tea – especially from Maggie's tiny bone china cups – a serendipitous thrift store find.

Big Sugar perched on the edge of Maggie's couch, his cup balanced on his knee. Maggie sat opposite him in Margaret's rocker, one foot keeping it in motion. Big Sugar took up most of the space in the small room -- the couch appeared tiny under his bulk. He was surprisingly graceful, though, as he added at least five spoonfuls of sugar to his cup, made a show of stirring it in and then hoisted it to his lips to take a demure sip. Maggie studied him while racking her brain for the right words to begin what she hoped would be a useful conversation.

Big Sugar looked around absorbing all the details. "Miss Maggie, you've shore done a mighty fine job on this old place," he said. "It's a sight for sore eyes."

"Thank you, Sugar," Maggie said. "It really means a lot to me. I have worked hard. There was just something about this place that spoke to me. You know?"

Sugar nodded. "I shore do. My Nancy Beth felt that exact same way. Why, me and my wife couldn't keep her away. She was always over here playing."

"You mentioned that the other day. But no one lived here?"

"Nope. Not anyone with breath in their body. But Nancy Beth always talked about the Lady in White. Said she lived here."

"Lady in White?"

"Nancy Beth said she wore a white dress and sometimes she sat in the rocker -- the one you're in right now, must be -- or drifted around the house."

"We worried all the time was it safe for Nancy Beth to be here. The place was abandoned and we thought maybe a homeless person would find hisself a dry place here." Sugar stopped. "Are you sure you want to hear all this, Miss Maggie?"

"Absolutely. Please go on, Sugar. Last night you led me to believe that you might know something about my ghost. About Margaret?"

"This is gonna make me sound crazy, but I and Minnie, that's my wife, wouldn't have Nancy Beth today if it wasn't for Margaret." He drained his teacup, deposited it on the coffee table and leaned toward Maggie. The couch wobbled and she held her breath, expecting it to splinter under his weight, but it held steady.

Maggie could hardly wait to hear Sugar's explanation. He studied her with narrowed eyes and finally said, "I'll just tell it and you can decide for yourself."

"Go on." Maggie was impatient, but willed herself to stay silent. She hurried into the kitchen and brought back fresh cups of tea.

Sugar settled himself on the couch, stirring his tea and stared out the window, his face devoid of emotion. Finally, when Maggie thought she'd have to shake it out of him, Sugar began his story.

"Nancy Beth, like I told you, was an independent little thing. We told and told her to stay away from this here bungalow, but she wouldn't listen. We told her we'd take away TV or her visits to her friends, but still she came. When she was seven we found a puppy that somebody left in a box on the road and we brought him home for Nancy Beth. Frizzles, she named him. Well, Frizzles and Nancy Beth were inseparable after that. Never saw one without the other 'cept when she was in school."

"One day Nancy Beth was late getting home from school. Minnie didn't think too much about it since she knew sometimes Nancy Beth would stop at a friend's house and lose track of time. But it got later and later and then it got dark. And still no Nancy Beth. Minnie called me and we both went out looking. Couldn't find her anywhere. Called all her friends. Checked every place. Still no Nancy Beth."

"Then we noticed that Frizzles was missing from his house in the yard. I called and called and no Frizzles."

"Now we were really scared. Nancy Beth was brave, but she wouldn't have stayed out past dark. That was one rule she never broke. She was kind of afraid of the dark, to tell the truth."

"We called the police. They put out one of them Amber Alert things. Nothing. That was the longest night of my entire life, I'll tell you. It was bitter cold, maybe about zero, and Minnie said Nancy Beth wasn't wearing nothing but her lightweight jacket."

Sugar took a swallow of tea and shifted his bulk so that he was more comfortable. Maggie waited.

"Anyhow. Morning come and still no Nancy Beth. I had been to the yellow bungalow at least three times knowin' how she loved the place, but she wasn't there. I figured I'd give it one more shot. Something told me. So I went back over there. Looked inside and in the yard and I was gonna give up when I saw the Lady in White. Plain as the nose on your face. She was sitting on the back porch when I come out and she motioned me to follow her. I was plumb taken aback but follow her I did. Clear to the very back of the yard. And I heard Frizzles barking. Real muffled like. Now I was crazy excited and sure enough the Lady in White had led me right to a place where there used to be a big well. Been covered for years with dirt and grass and no one knowed it was there. When I was right on top I could see the ground was mussed up and I took out my cell phone and called the police."

"Long story, short. Nancy Beth and Frizzles were right there. Buried about twenty feet down. Stuck in the old well shaft. Like to frozen to death they was too. We dug them up and, praise the Lord, both were alive and well. Bumps and bruises and Nancy Beth had a concussion, but alive."

"Nancy Beth told her mama and me that she wasn't scared because she had Frizzles with her. And that the Lady in White stayed with them all night and wrapped them in her dress to keep them warm and safe."

"Whew," Maggie said when Sugar paused for breath. "That's quite a story. So you and Nancy Beth both saw Margaret?"

"Well," Sugar said. He contemplated his teacup for a moment. "I can't say for sure if it was Margaret. But I can't explain it otherwise. Let's just say that I don't know that much about ghosts, but a feller can make a good guess. Minnie told me that ghosts attach themselves to places and things. That sometimes they have issues to solve before they can go to their rest. I dunno. Sounds off the rails to me, but I sure know that I saw the lady and I know Margaret died here so…."

"Did Nancy Beth ever tell you how she ended up in the well?"

Sugar scratched his head. "Yep. Said she was nearly home when Frizzles come barking to meet her. They were just in front of this here bungalow and he went all yippie and ran into the backyard. They had this game where he ran and she chased him. Well, she was running after Frizzles and splat -- one minute she was in the yard, the next down the well. And Frizzles jumped in too. Probably didn't want to leave her there alone. She called and called, she said, until the lady came and Nancy Beth fell asleep. Next thing she knew men and equipment were digging her up."

"Wow," Maggie murmured.

"Nancy Beth goes to college in Charleston if you want to talk to her," Sugar offered. "I could give you her number."

"That would be awesome," Maggie said. "I don't know why I'm so obsessed with Margaret, but I am. Do you think she'd mind me asking her about it?"

Sugar shook his head. "Nothing she'd like better, I guess, than talking about the lady. She thinks of her as her own personal angel." He paused to snug up his ponytail. "And me too."

After Big Sugar left with a promise to come back to help out with any repairs Maggie might have, she puttered around the bungalow, rinsing the tea things, straightening magazines, plumping and patting the couch cushions. She'd never really given ghosts much thought before this, but she was becoming a big time believer now. She made herself some scrambled eggs and toast and made more tea. The thought of wine made her stomach roll and, besides, she wanted an unfogged mind to puzzle out the Margaret thing.

After she'd eaten her dinner and washed and put away the dishes, she'd come to the conclusion that there was no answer. Ghosts are not something that can be clinically defined or put under a microscope. You either believe or you don't. And Maggie did. Now she just wanted to find out how Margaret had died. Was it Daniel who killed her and got away with it? Or someone else entirely? An intruder like Daniel told the police? Or was it something completely different?

Maggie settled on the couch with a fuzzy afghan pulled over her and gazed into the faux flames in her fireplace as she thought about her inspiration. What the heck did she have to lose anyway? Combine business with pleasure, so to speak.

She shuffled through the sheaf of papers from the Historical Society and finally found the clipping she wanted. Drunken Hills, North Carolina, That's where Margaret's mother said she was taking Baby Rose Dawn.

She picked up her cell phone and punched in the speed dial number. When he answered she said, "Dwight? Hey. How would you like to meet me in Drunken Hills, North Carolina? I've got the best idea."

CHAPTER
Eighteen

Maggie was fuming as she punched keys on her new laptop computer. Why on earth do they have to make things so complicated? Technology is supposed to help make life easier not cause nervous breakdowns. What was she doing wrong? It had seemed crystal clear when the helpful young geek at Best Buy explained everything to her. But now....

Agnes, being the modern woman that she was, had installed free WiFi at the café so Maggie was taking advantage of it. Camped out at a table near the window, she had her brand-new laptop open in front of her as she attempted to become familiar with all its features.

The night that Maggie had her brilliant idea to check things out in Drunken Hills, it also occurred to her that she could use Professor Google to aid her investigation as well. Her ancient laptop was at home in Winslow, Ohio, probably being ignored by Dwight and doing nothing more than collecting dust. Undoubtedly the entire house was collecting dust.

Maggie needed to be able to get online so she hopped in her Bug and found her way to the nearest Best Buy where she let the accommodating geek persuade her to buy this fancy schmancy laptop. The same one now defeating her most valiant efforts to set it up.

She was muttering curses under her breath, oblivious to everything except the images on the laptop screen, when a male voice said, "Hi, Maggie. Anything I can do to help you out with that?"

Startled out of her funk, Maggie jerked her head up and met the eyes of -- she'd hoped she'd never run into him again ever -- Mac McDougal. He was grinning as if he was amazed at his good fortune in running into her. Dressed in a navy peacoat with his horn-rimmed glasses shoved into his dark hair, he was every bit as hot as he'd seemed the night at the bar. Oh, God, Maggie groaned inwardly. That night. The one she didn't remember. *Was that a grin or an I've-seen-you-without-your-clothes-on smirk?* It was obvious that he wasn't going to go away and leave her to her misery, so she tried to formulate an intelligent comment and stammered, "Oh, er, um, hi. No. I mean. Yes. I mean." What *did* she mean?

Mac shifted the armload of books he was carrying. He smiled. *No that was a smirk. Definitely a smirk. Damn it, make him go away.* Or, better yet, Maggie prayed that the floor would open up and swallow her.

"I'm pretty good with computers," he said. "Mind if I join you? Maybe I can help."

He seemed sincere and, what the heck, it would be rude to refuse his help. *Wouldn't it? Not to mention, he was hot.* Undeniably hot. Damn. Maggie was positive that she must have slept with him. How, in her drunken state, could she have resisted? "Uh, sure. I'd love the help," she said. She cleared a chair. "Please do join me."

He shrugged out of his peacoat, dropped his armload of books on the floor, and sank into the chair across the table from Maggie. "Outstanding computer," he said. "New? Having problems?"

"Nah," Maggie said, "this look of total frustration and annoyance is my usual expression when I work on a computer." She stabbed at the keyboard with her manicured fingernail. "I love computers."

Mac tipped his chair back, nearly sending it over backward. "I can tell."

Maggie poked at the keyboard. "I don't get it. It looked so easy in the store. Why can't I get to my e-mails? What am I doing wrong?" She slumped in her chair and put her head in her hands. Then she gave Mac a long, assessing look. "I give new meaning to the word dummy."

Mac laughed as he got up to stand behind her and peer over her shoulder at the screen. "You aren't necessarily a dummy," he said. "We could order some lunch and I could stick around and we could figure it out together." He hesitated. "That is, if you would like me too."

He sounded almost shy. *Not a player. Please, not a player.* Maggie couldn't decide how she felt about him, but if he wanted to slap her laptop into submission, who was she to look a gift geek in the mouth?

"Absolutely," she said. "I always think best over a tuna sandwich."

Mac raised his eyebrows and then winked. "My favorite."

Two hours later Maggie and Mac were finishing their second -- or was it third? -- cups of coffee. They'd polished off tuna sandwiches and Mac, as promised, had slapped her laptop into submission. Now they had lapsed into the casual, getting-to-know-you, conversation that had been impossible in Sugar's noisy bar. Mac entertained Maggie with tales of his students at Sweet River University where he was, of all things, a history professor. "So," Mac was saying, "this one kid turns in this totally brilliant paper on the ethics of women serving in the Civil War. I was blown away."

"So, did you give him an A?" Maggie asked.

Mac chuckled. Low and throaty and infectious. "Nope."

"Why not? If it was so brilliant?"

He shook his head. "Well, I figured if I didn't get an A on it when I wrote it, why should he?"

"You wrote it?" Maggie giggled.

"Yep. Sure did. My Senior Thesis." Mac said. "And this bozo pulls it off the internet and tries to sell it as his own. Only he has the bad luck to try to sell it in my class."

"Not the crispest chip in the bag," Maggie said with a smile. "What did you do?"

"What could I do? I called him in, congratulated him on his excellent taste in authors and flunked him. Turned him in to the dean. Poor schmuck."

Their laughter died out and subsided into an uncomfortable silence. It hung between them like a damp fog. Maggie knew she wouldn't rest until she found out, so she blurted, "About the other night."

At the same time Mac began, "About the other night, I'm so --"

Uneasy laughter and then Mac said, "You first."

Maggie couldn't look at him. She stared over his head at Agnes chatting with customers on the other side of the café. "I don't know how to say this so I'll just say it flat out. I was -- um -- tipsy. And I never drink like that-- or I wouldn't have…." She shrugged. "You know."

A mischievous look crossed Mac's face. "You wouldn't have what? Danced? Let me drive you home?"

Too embarrassed to sit still, Maggie fidgeted with her napkin, ripping it to shreds. "You know. Kissed you. And the -- " She paused and then blurted, "I'm married."

"Married? You mean you were married. What's that got to do with it? I'm just sorry I nearly took advantage of a grieving widow. And I am so so sorry. I'm not that kind of a guy."

"I'm the one who should be sorry," Maggie said. Then his words sunk in. "Nearly? Nearly took advantage? You mean we didn't?"

Mac's grinned and heaved a huge sigh. "You don't remember? You thought we slept together? No, Maggie, no matter how much I wanted to. And I did. And do. We didn't do anything beyond kissing."

A bubble of relief started in Maggie's stomach and drifted to her brain. Tears came to her eyes. "We didn't? Oh, thank God. When I woke up, I was –- er – not totally dressed and I was sure. But we didn't?"

"You don't have to be quite so relieved. I've been told I'm not half bad in bed." His tone was teasing but he wasn't smiling.

"Oh." Maggie reached over to take his hand. "I'm sure you are. Oh, God."

"It's just when you thought I was your dead husband, I couldn't do it. I want you to know it's me when we do make love." He was dead serious, his stare unblinking. "If we do."

Maggie's heart lurched like a horse going over a jump. He was hot. Adorable and hot. And not Dwight, she reminded herself, not her very much still alive husband. Crap.

"But, but," she stammered. "I was only half dressed when I woke up in the loft. My jeans --"

"Wait," Mac interrupted her. "In the loft? When I left you were asleep on the couch and completely -- well, mostly –- dressed. You most definitely had your pants on."

"I did? But how did I get up to the loft. I must have been really out of it."

"You were," Mac said, "but I would have thought you'd remember going upstairs. You weren't that out of it."

Somewhere in the back of Maggie's brain, a memory was emerging from the fog. Dwight. She'd thought Dwight was there, kissing her, taking off her clothes and then leaving. But later, someone helped her up to the loft. Could it be that she had repressed that memory until now? Because she could see in her mind a woman in a white dress guiding her up the steps and tugging off her tight jeans and laying her in the bed and covering her with her quilt. Margaret? Yes, it must have been. The words floated back to her. "Sleep well, Maggie. I'll be here for you as long as you need me."

Wow. What had been in that wine anyway? She was either hallucinating or hobnobbing with ghosts in her sleep. Whichever it was, it
couldn't be good. Maybe she should seek therapy.

Mac stared at her as if he didn't know what to make of her, so she
made an effort to drag her attention back to him, but her head was
spinning. Did she seriously believe that she had been seeing a ghost?
And that ghost in fact spoke to her? And put her to bed? She was totally losing it. But Big Sugar believed that Margaret was real and he
didn't look like the kind of guy who had imaginary friends. He said
he'd seen her too. And Nancy Beth? Well, obviously Maggie needed
to talk to the girl. Because otherwise she could only conclude she had
one foot firmly planted in the loony bin. And was teetering on the
edge with the other.

Mac cleared his throat. "Ah hem. Maggie? Where'd you go?"

"I'm right here. Just trying to remember that night a little more
clearly."

"Not real flattering if you ask me," Mac said with a rueful smile.
"The lady can't remember our evening. Tell you what, in the future I'll
try to be more memorable. Deal?"

Tell him, Maggie, she thought. Tell him you're still married. Tell
him you can't make memories with him. But she didn't say a word.
Something was holding her back. And not just his hotness either.

Shortly after that Mac pulled on his jacket, scooped his armload of
books off the floor, dropped a kiss on the top of her head and started
toward the door. He turned and called over his shoulder as he tugged
on the handle, "Don't forget, Maggie. Next time it will be me and only
me. We'll see how that works for you." He waggled his fingers in a half
wave and shoved through the door to the sidewalk, pausing at the
window next to her table to smile at her. Maggie could feel the heat
stinging her cheeks. Honestly.

After Mac left Maggie refilled her coffee cup and attempted to re-
focus her attention on her now perfectly behaved laptop. Before she
could make much progress on her research, though, a pair of young
girls – probably students at Sweet River U – came in, dumped their
books on the floor and settled with their cups of latte at a table adjoin-
ing hers. Maggie took note of their attire – shorts much too short for
the chilly weather and sweatshirts displaying a sorority insignia. *Aren't*

they freezing? Maggie recognized that she was probably jealous. But not of their long tanned legs and beautiful faces, as one might expect. No. She was jealous because they were in school. *Hmm.*

One of them tossed her long blonde hair over her shoulder and whispered to her friend. Then both erupted in hoots of laughter. The blonde's friend, with an auburn pixie cut, glanced over at Maggie and mouthed an apology. Maggie waved a hand. "No problem," she said and pretended to be engrossed in her laptop screen.

Since she'd started journaling again she had rekindled her fascination with the art of eavesdropping and now she engaged in it shamelessly. In her college days she was a pro at it – saving up clever expressions and anecdotes to use in the stories she loved to write. And it was also handy, like now, for information gathering.

The blonde was saying to her friend, "That was Professor MacDougal who just left. He is so hot. I think I'm going to switch my major to History."

"He is hot," the other girl agreed, "but I doubt you could pass his classes. I hear he's pretty tough."

The blonde giggled. "I'd let him mess with my grade point any day."

Maggie chuckled under her breath. *So I'm not the only one.* She forced herself to stop eavesdropping on the giggling coeds and turned her attention to the computer screen. She googled Sweet River University and started to read through the list of classes offered the next semester.

She spent the rest of the afternoon at *Agnes' Cafe* working on her laptop trying to find all she could about the mysterious Margaret Booth Edison and her life and death. There wasn't much written about her. Obviously, an unsolved murder in 1900 wasn't top news in 2010. Maggie did learn that Drunken Hills, North Carolina, was home to some Booths. Whether they were related to Margaret was not clear. So Maggie made up her mind that her trip to Drunken Hills would reveal something to help her solve the mystery. Even if it was only for her own peace of mind. And maybe she'd figure out something about her marriage as well.

Since her feelings for Mac were far from clear, Maggie had a sinking feeling that she couldn't drag Dwight to Drunken Hills without some kind of explanation. If they were going to put their differences behind them, she had to be completely honest. In the past, though, complete honesty hadn't worked all that well. Dwight liked things his way and he wasn't good at compromise. Besides telling him about Mac, she knew she would have to let him in on her plans for her future. And he wasn't going to like it. That was for sure.

CHAPTER
Nineteen

The Days of DJ and Beer

Maggie had never believed in love at first sight. Maybe she still didn't. But when DJ waltzed into her dorm her freshman year of college and flipped his thick brown mop of hair out of his eyes, her heart hit a speed bump and she was gone. She was an English lit major struggling through the required chemistry class and DJ was an upperclassman and lab assistant. Doctor Mahamet, the chemistry professor, unknowingly acted as Cupid when he assigned DJ to tutor Maggie. By the end of the semester not only was Maggie in heart-pounding, sweaty-palmed, chills-down-the-spine love with DJ, but she also pulled a B+ in chemistry. DJ and Maggie forever after referred to Doctor Mahamet as their fairy godfather -- only partly because of his sexual persuasion.

Maggie and DJ went from late nights at the library to late nights at his apartment. After he drilled her on her chemistry, he taught her about sex. Not just sex, though. Maggie wasn't entirely new to the game. But about sex with someone whose merest touch sent shock waves through her body. Someone who only had to look at her to make her heart race and desire pound through her like a raging flood. And, to Maggie's overwhelming surprise, DJ appeared to feel the same. He'd had an entire stable of girlfriends before her, but she was the one who had reached inside and touched his core. They were inseparable.

Over beers at the *Blue Note Bar,* they exchanged life histories and wishes for the future. Soon it became apparent that their futures would be intertwined.

Maggie loved the time she spent with DJ. He was the wild child to her conservative self. DJ was spontaneous and unrestrained in his approach to life. Maggie hopped on the ride and, hanging on for dear life, threw her hands in the air and enjoyed the heck out of it.

Fall turned into winter and then into spring. Maggie kept waiting for the moment when DJ would look at her and realize that he had made a huge mistake. But it didn't happen. He told her over and over that he loved her, adored her, wouldn't want to be with anyone other than her. Finally, she believed it.

The summer after Maggie's freshman year was glorious. Rather than returning to their separate hometowns, they found jobs working at a camp for diabetic kids. The camp was in the rolling hills of Pennsylvania on an inland lake. They spent their days chasing the boisterous crew of diabetic children who were savoring their sameness. Instead of being odd kids with a "disability", they were a gang on an adventure.

Maggie thought of the camp as an adventure for her as well. She loved the children. Loved helping them be just kids. Loved learning about diabetes. But she also loved spending every night in DJ's arms. It was heaven. If summer had never ended, she would have been fine.

But, of course, it did. Fall came and Maggie and DJ returned to school, but in his senior year, DJ was restless. His engineering classes bored him, he said. He drank more beer. He bought a motorcycle. He spent whole days without calling her. Maggie was lost. She couldn't get DJ to open up to her. She didn't know what was going on with him. She tried to keep busy with classes and pledging a sorority and cheering the football team on to an occasional victory, but she was confused and sad.

Until …

The phone was ringing as Maggie opened the door to her room. She dumped her stack of books on the bed and lunged for the phone. Cradling the receiver between her chin and the crook of her neck, she shrugged out of her jacket and sagged onto her bed. "Hello?" She was sweaty and breathless from running up the stairs.

"Maggie May?"

DJ! Her stomach did a slow forward roll at the sound of his voice. "Hi," she said unable to think of something clever to say to him, something to let him know that she did not appreciate being ignored.

"I need to see you." He sounded excited.

"Oh-h-kay. When?"

"Now. I can pick you up in fifteen minutes."

"But," Maggie said, "you have a math class." She knew his schedule by heart.

"I'm cutting it."

"DJ, you can't. Your scholarship. You need an A in that class."

"Maybe. Maybe not." He sounded impatient. "Are you coming or aren't you?"

When had she ever turned down an opportunity to spend time with DJ? Never, she guessed, and now didn't seem like the time to start. "Okay, DJ, I'll be out front."

Maggie wondered what it was that he had to tell her. He hadn't sounded this enthusiastic about anything since they'd returned to campus. A thought struck like a kick in the ribs. Was he going to break up with her? Was this the end she'd been dreading?

Maggie was pacing up and down the sidewalk when DJ roared up on his motorcycle. He screeched to a stop, gravel spitting in his wake. In one fluid movement he kicked down the kickstand and got off the bike. He swept Maggie into his arms, lifted her off her feet and twirled her around. Okay, so maybe he wasn't going for the breakup. But what then?

She wasn't in suspense for much longer. She climbed on the bike behind DJ and clung to his waist as he restarted the engine and shifted into gear and pulled onto the road. A few minutes later he'd reached his destination and Maggie was relieved to find that they were in "their" spot —- a secluded patch of grass on the bank of the river. The exact spot where they'd first made love. Maggie laughed with sheer exultation. Whatever he had to say, it couldn't be terrible. Not here.

DJ pulled off his helmet and tugged her down in the grass and was kissing her before she could remove her own helmet or even catch her breath. Her body responded and she was kissing him, running her hands down his back and arching her spine to get closer to him when suddenly her brain kicked in and she pushed him off of her. "DJ," she protested. "Give me a chance to take off my helmet. What's going on?"

DJ rolled onto his back and stared at the red and yellow umbrella of fall leaves above their heads. He propped himself on one elbow and a huge grin split his face. He was so obviously delighted with himself that Maggie could do nothing but grin back at him. "Are you going to tell me what's on your mind?" she asked. "Or am I going to slowly and surely lose my own?"

"It's so simple," he said. "I don't know what took me so long to figure it out."

"Figure out what?"

"I'm dropping out of school."

And just like that the bottom of Maggie's world fell out. Her eyes burned and a single tear slid down her cheek. She brushed at it with an angry gesture. Dropping out of school? That's what this was all about. He took her to their place to tell her. Men are imbeciles.

"Hey," he said peering at her face, "don't look like that."

"How would you expect me to look? Thrilled? Over the moon? Doing handsprings? The man I love is leaving me. Honestly, DJ, you are such a dolt."

He burst out laughing. Not the response she had expected at all. She jumped to her feet and paced to the edge of the river and stood with her back to him staring at the water. The nerve.

"Maggie, come back here," DJ said.

She refused to turn around. "Why should I?"

"Because," he said, "I have something to say and you need to look at me while I say it."

Maggie hesitated for a moment before she swung her head so she could see him and then whirled around like a top. She had lost the capacity to breath or to speak. She couldn't take her eyes off him. Because – DJ was on one knee, holding a tiny velvet box. She gulped.

"Maggie May, my love," DJ said, "will you run away with me and marry me and make me the happiest man on earth?"

Maggie burst into tears and threw herself at him, knocking him over and ending up lying on top of him. She kissed his eyes, his nose, his cheeks, his lips. She cried and laughed and hiccupped and DJ laughed along with her. Finally, he said, "Does that mean yes you will marry me?"

"Oh, God, yes. Yes, yes, a thousand times yes." She was a blithering idiot but this adorable, handsome, hunk of a man had just asked her to spend her life with him. Blithering seemed like an appropriate response.

Then she slowly came back to earth —- her balloon of joy had sprung a leak. "You said that you were dropping out of school," she said.

His face lit up. "Let me amend that. We are dropping out of school. To go to Europe and backpack and I'll take pictures and you can write and we can see the Eiffel Tower and The Tower of London and The Leaning Tower of Pisa and, oh, we'll see it all."

"Oh." Maggie couldn't breathe. She'd been given the toy she'd been begging for only to find out it was broken. "But we can't just -- "

"Yes, we can, Mags. I can't stand school anymore. I hate Engineering. I need time to figure out what I do want. Besides you. I want you. I want this for us. For us."

"My parents." Maggie was in tears, mascara running in streaks down her cheeks.

"Mine too. But I'm doing it. I'd rather do it with you ..." He let his words trail off, but Maggie knew. She knew he would leave. And she knew without a single doubt that she would follow wherever he led.

So Maggie and DJ made their plans. They dropped out of school. DJ sold his motorcycle and Maggie cashed in the savings bonds her Nana Belle had given her the day she was born. They made reservations on a flight leaving New York for Paris. They made plans to be married. Not the big, traditional wedding that she had always dreamed of. Her mother would kill her, but if she was with DJ they could start their own traditions. They would find a justice of the peace in New York before they left and then they'd say their own private vows to each other at Notre Dame in Paris. All very romantic. And hush hush. They planned to call their parents once they were safely married and in Paris. No point in upsetting them before that.

They almost made it. Only a few more hours and they would have been aboard the Paris-bound flight. Maybe it would have ended the same way no matter what, but she'd never know that for sure. To this very day it remained the single biggest "shoulda", "coulda,""woulda" in Maggie's life. How would life have been different if... If only.

Maggie and DJ were lying tangled in the bed sheets and each other when the call came that changed everything. Maggie wore only DJ's T-shirt and a blissful smile, while DJ wore only the smile. They had arrived in New York a day before their scheduled flight. The plan had been to find a justice of the peace and get married before they left for Europe, but they hadn't reckoned on an unexpected and little noted legal holiday. Maggie and DJ spent an entire day in a fruitless search for one single justice of the peace who might be working in spite of the holiday. Finally, exhausted and discouraged they gave up.

Maggie was close to tears as they stood on a corner in Times Square being buffeted by the crowds of pedestrians. Traffic surged around the corner and street noise made it difficult to hear. DJ looped his arms around her and pulled her close. "Don't cry," he said, "we'll have to go to Plan B."

Maggie sniffled, but kept her face buried in his navy peacoat. Her voice was muffled. "Plan B?"

"We'll get married in Paris. Much more romantic anyway."

Her face tearstained and her expression woebegone, Maggie raised her head so that she could see his face. Hope streaked across it. "Paris." She considered it for a moment. "It is more romantic. But we'd need papers and stuff."

DJ handed her a tissue. "Where there's a will, there's a way. But let's not worry about it tonight. Let's rearrange things a tiny bit. Instead of getting married first, we'll honeymoon first and get married later."

Maggie nodded and blew her nose. "Honeymoon, it is."

And that's why they were in their airport hotel room a few hours later, sweaty and intoxicated with love and anticipation of their adventure. "Honeymoon" sex, it turned out, was more spectacular than anything before. Maggie felt more alive than she ever had, her body sizzled with the afterglow. Tightening DJ's shirt around her she floated over to the dresser and poured two glasses of champagne from the bottle chilling in the ice bucket. Returning to the bed, she handed one glass to DJ and propped herself up on the pillows as she sipped from her own glass. She dipped a finger in her glass and licked the champagne from it. "Hmm-m," she murmured. "To honeymoons whenever they happen."

DJ sat up and raised his glass. "To my not quite wife." He tilted his head back and took a long swallow. Then he set his glass on the bedside table and took Maggie's from her hand and set her glass next to his. He pulled the pillows from under her head and shoved her gently back onto the bed and rolled on top of her. His kisses were deepening and Maggie's breath was coming in short bursts, her heart beating like a revving car motor and then the phone rang.

DJ ignored it and ran his hands down her body. Maggie tried to stay focused on DJ, but there was something about a ringing phone. It stopped after about ten rings. She sighed and focused on DJ and his lips and hands and -- damn -- it started its persistent clanging again. She pushed DJ away and tried to sit up. "DJ! Honey! The phone."

DJ gave her a wicked leer. "It will stop if we ignore it."

"It might be important."

"No one knows we're here. It's nothing." He pushed her down and she sank under his weight.

Maggie nearly succeeded in turning a deaf ear to the phone, but it wouldn't stop. She shoved DJ off and reached for the phone. "We have to get it. Maybe it's something about the flight tomorrow."

DJ heaved a huge sigh and rolled toward the phone. "Don't forget where we were." He hauled the receiver up and pressed it against his ear and said with an aggravated groan, "Ye-ah."

As Maggie watched his face, butterflies attacked her stomach with a vengeance. She knew. She knew before he said a word. It was the end. His face lost all its color and his body became as stiff as a steel girder. He nodded and nodded and said, "When?" And then. "What was it?" And. "How long?" And finally, "I'll be there as soon as I can." He replaced the receiver in its cradle as if it was made of spun glass and it might break and then he turned toward Maggie. And her heart broke into a thousand pieces.

He stared at her as if he didn't know where he was. "DJ?" Maggie said.

"It's my dad," he said and he was in her arms, crying. She held him until he pulled away and used the sheet to wipe his eyes.

Maggie waited. She didn't know what to say or how to comfort him.

"My dad died." His voice broke. "He had a massive heart attack yesterday morning and they've been trying to reach me. He was asking for me." His voice cracked and he struggled to control himself. "They couldn't find me. He died and I never got the chance to say good-bye."

"Oh, DJ," Maggie began, but he shoved her away.

"I have to go."

Of course, he did. Maggie knew that. But that tiny drumbeat of "if only" pounded in her heart. If only we'd gotten away. Things would be different. If only we'd gotten married. They didn't say much as they got dressed and packed their things, but Maggie knew it was over. Oh, it took awhile. She went to the funeral with him, went back to school and held his hand while he begged to be readmitted. Tried to comfort him and love him. But Maggie knew that he held it against her. That if he hadn't been running away with her, he'd have been at his father's deathbed. That he couldn't forgive himself or her.

DJ vanished as surely as if he had been the one who died and not his father. Where there had been love and excitement and a future of unending possibilities, now there was emptiness. With DJ the sun had been brighter, the rain wetter, the sky bluer, the fog foggier. Without DJ everything was another shade of pale.

If DJ blamed Maggie, she blamed herself more, although she also could count to her credit that she'd shared their secret with her room-mate. She had been so excited about Paris and getting married that she couldn't keep her plans to herself. The night before she and DJ left for New York, her roommate, Denise, came home early from her date and found Maggie packing her bag. And Maggie told her everything. It was through Denise that DJ's family was able to track him down.

If only --

At first DJ avoided her, didn't return her calls, wasn't home when she knocked on his door. Then at last he told her he needed some time. He needed to adjust. He needed to help his mother and his sisters mourn his father. This, then, was the end. Oh, Maggie caught a glimpse of him occasionally -- laughing with a friend or eating a burger at the Student Union -- but it was never the same.

Through all of this, there was Dwight. Solid and reliable and comfortable Dwight. Soon Maggie came to depend on him, but it was never the same as the days of DJ and beer. None of the magic, the heart-stopping thrill of being with someone or the mind-blowing sex. And, in fact, Maggie could never drink a beer again. It was too much like swallowing regret.

In Dwight's senior year of college, they got engaged, and after he graduated they were married in the traditional ceremony Maggie had always dreamed about. And they lived happily ever after. Or almost. It was a successful marriage. They had raised two wonderful kids, taken trips to amazing places, lived in a house they both loved. More than twenty years later, though, the excitement, if it ever existed, had subsided into a ho-hum coexistence. She had her interests. Dwight had his business. So, one fine morning Maggie ran away.

And now -- she was going to see Dwight for the first time in months. Looking forward to it with massive butterflies. How would she feel when she saw him? How would he feel when he saw her? Why was she thinking about DJ again after all these years? Was it Mac who brought back those old feelings she'd had for DJ? Maggie was baffled by her feelings, but one thing for sure, she decided that she'd have to tell Dwight about Mac and her other plans before they saw each other again.

CHAPTER
Twenty

Maggie paced around the bungalow, straightening the pillows on the couch, rearranging the few books on the bookshelves. She cleaned the kitchen sink and rinsed out the sponges. *Okay, quit stalling. Call him. Before you come face to face with him, tell him about Mac and the other things. Tell him.* Still she found tasks that couldn't wait to be completed. When she ran out of chores to do she curled up on the couch with her back supported by a stack of throw pillows. Her cell phone and a glass of wine sat side by side on the coffee table. Okay, she took a deep breath and picked up her glass for a fortifying sip. *I'll just call him and talk about the weekend and see how it goes. I don't have to tell him anything unless I feel like the timing is right.* And her cell phone rang. Startled, she jumped, sloshing wine out of the glass and onto her hand. She grabbed for a wad of napkins and was sopping up the spill as she clutched the phone to her ear. "Hello?"

"Maggie?" Dwight's voice reverberated with uncharacteristic enthusiasm.

At the sound of his voice Maggie realized that she couldn't do it. She couldn't burst this bubble of possibility right before the nervously anticipated reunion. She could always tell him later. *In person. Definitely better in person.*

"Hi," she said as she slugged wine. Did he know? Had he guessed?

"Babe." He sounded happy.

"Hi," she said again. She squeezed the soggy wad of napkins and wine dripped down her sleeve. "Damn."

"Babe?" The joy was oozing out of his voice the same way the wine was oozing down her sleeve.

"Wait a sec," she said and took the mess into the kitchen. She returned with a refreshed glass of wine and plopped down on the couch. "Sorry. I spilled my wine."

"Oh? Well, anyway, I just called to tell you that I'm really looking forward to our weekend. In fact -- " *Drum roll please.* " -- I'm gonna take Friday off so I can be there Thursday night. That way we'll have plenty of time to -- um — figure things out?" He sounded unsure.

Maggie swallowed wine, stalling for time before she answered. Her original plan had been to spend Thursday night with Sarah in Charleston. Sarah was excited to have her and to maybe track down Nancy Beth. Then drive to Drunken Hills and spend Friday hunting for clues to Margaret's death. But now? She was aware that when Dwight heard her plans for the future he would be upset and possibly angry. She couldn't make things worse before she absolutely had to.

She forced enthusiasm she didn't feel into her voice. "Honey! That's awesome. You never take time away from the business." She did realize that this was unusual for him and meant he was taking her seriously. For once.

"You're worth it." He gave a short uncertain laugh. He sounded as nervous as she was.

"It will be fantastic. I'll call and book an extra night at the inn as soon as we hang up."

They talked a bit longer about the weekend and then as they were saying their good-byes, Dwight said, "Oh, Mags, I can't wait to show you the surprise I have for you."

She tried but she couldn't pry it out of him. After they hung up she racked her brain trying to figure out what big surprise he might have. Well, she sure had one for him too. Why was she so nervous about being with Dwight? She guessed she was afraid of his reaction. Well, time would tell.

Back in the days of DJ and beer, Maggie had dropped out of school to elope with him. When that didn't happen, she talked her way back into college, but her heart was never in it. Her grades dropped precipitously and her interest level was even lower. It was impossible to read novels in her Romance Novel class without thinking about what she and DJ had just missed. She saw them as characters in an F. Scott Fitzgerald novel coming to a sad end. Finally, she dropped that class and anything else that reminded her of DJ. And when Dwight asked her to marry him, it was the perfect excuse to abandon the pretense of caring about her classes and quit school. She had finished her junior year, squeaking by, but she never earned her degree. It had eaten away at her for all the years since. The missed opportunity. The failure of it all.

Life with Dwight had been fulfilling at first and raising the kids was all-consuming, but as time went on, she knew that there was a single piece missing in the puzzle. She wanted her degree. But things interfered. Trips planned. Money spent on a new car when the old one died. College tuition for the kids. It was always something. And Maggie had talked herself out of it. The wanting. The needing. Until Sweet River. She learned that she no longer had to put herself last. She could do things to satisfy her needs. Now she was going to have to tell her husband that she wasn't coming back to Ohio with him. Nope. She was enrolling for the fall semester at Sweet River University. Classes began in September. Dwight was going to pitch a fit.

CHAPTER
Twenty-One

Drunken Hills, North Carolina, was a quaint whitewashed village nestled in the rolling hills not far north of Wilmington. The roads leading to the village meandered through forests and rolled over hills providing spectacular views. Maggie opened the sunroof on the Bug and pumped up the volume on the CD player. The sun beating on her head through the open roof gave her a feeling of wellbeing and she sang at the top of her lungs. It felt good to be freewheeling along with only her thoughts and her music for company. The closer she got to Drunken Hills, though, the more the little nugget of apprehension grew, and by the time she pulled into the driveway of the Drunken Hills Inn, the butterflies were in full flight.

Maggie climbed out of the Bug and stretched. Her hands at the small of her back, she turned in a circle to take inventory of her surroundings. The inn was a two-story colonial style building, sided with white clapboard, and featuring a porch that spread across the entire front. White wicker rocking chairs and glass-topped tables were scattered over the porch. It sat at the top of a rise overlooking the Drunken River below. Maggie blew out a sigh. This was amazing. Perfect for a romantic weekend. If that's what this was. Who knew?

The inside was equally inviting and when the pleasant young clerk at the desk showed Maggie her room, she knew this was meant for romance. The king-sized bed was topped with a fluffy white comforter embroidered with flowers and the bathroom was a huge tiled space with not only a shower, but also a hot tub. Best of all, though, was that French doors opened onto a private balcony with the spectacular view of the forest and the river sparkling below.

Maggie tossed her purse on the dresser, dropped her bags and sank onto the bed. She gazed around at the room with all its tiny perfect details —- the coffeemaker, the array of snacks on a tray on the desk, fresh flowers in a vase, the comfy terry cloth robes hanging in the closet. If she'd been filming a movie about a couple's magical reunion, this would have been the room she would choose. She put her head in her hands and thought about crying. Dwight was not going to like what she had to tell him.

Maggie brushed her hair back and stood up. First things first. She'd have some lunch and then check out the village. She'd figure out what to say to Dwight later.

Maggie grabbed a sandwich at the tranquil hotel dining room and then ambled into town. The inn was located at the very edge of the village and it was a bit of a hike. The day was glorious, though, and Maggie was drunk on the clear blue sky and the brilliant sunshine. Ha. Drunken Hills no doubt got its name on a day like today.

Maggie wandered down Main Street checking out the souvenir shops with racks of postcards out front and shops featuring displays of local crafts – hand-painted pottery and watercolor paintings. She read the menus posted in front of cute restaurants featuring outdoor dining before she reached the end of the street. It didn't take long. Drunken Hills made Sweet River seem like a booming metropolis.

A signpost at the corner pointed the way to the Historical Society. Maggie checked the address she had scribbled in her notebook and then set out to find the location. No time like the present to see what she could find out about her ghost.

Over the few months that Maggie had lived in the yellow bungalow, she had become very possessive of Margaret, her ghost. She had stopped confiding in her friends about Margaret's comings and goings. For one thing, she was afraid they would think she'd totally lost it. More important, Maggie wanted to hug Margaret's presence to herself. It was her secret and Margaret had grown to be Maggie's guardian angel.

At first Maggie had believed that she had gone over the edge, completely fruit loops, because after that night when she was so drunk and Margaret put her to bed, she heard Margaret talk to her on many occasions. It could have been explained as a drunken hallucination if it had only been once, but Maggie heard her again when she was sober. And then again and again. Usually it was late at night and the squeak of the rocker would wake Maggie and she would peer from her sleeping loft into the shadowy living room below. There would be Margaret in her white dress, her arms cradling an invisible baby, rocking back and forth. Margaret would look up and smile at Maggie. Maggie would smile back and after a while Maggie started to talk to Margaret. Talking to a ghost? Not a sane thing to do which is why she couldn't let her friends in on the secret. They'd think she'd suffered a nervous breakdown over her separation from her husband and her former life.

And, if they'd think talking to a ghost was crazy, they would definitely think hearing the ghost talk back was evidence that the men with the nets should be on speed dial. So, Maggie kept quiet.

Margaret didn't say much. A few words. Answers to questions Maggie was struggling with. And Maggie was aware that Margaret was quite possibly a figment of her imagination. Her subconscious giving her a way to deal with her problems. That was a logical answer. But Maggie had never been a logical person and she much preferred magic and mystery to science. So shoot her -- she had conversations with a ghost.

The night before Maggie left to meet Dwight at Drunken Hills, she had been tossing and turning unable to fall asleep when she heard the telltale squeak and pulled herself out of bed. Margaret was in the rocker, but this time she eased herself out of it and glided to the bottom of the stairs. Maggie leaned toward her and Margaret took a few steps upward, reaching her hand out to Maggie. "Are you real?" Maggie whispered.

"As real as you want me to be," the apparition replied. "I'm here for you as long as you need me."

"Are you leaving me?'

"Not until you tell me to go."

Maggie shook her head, trying to clear her mind. This could not be happening. It was obvious that she'd lost her marbles and was hallucinating. "I'm nuts," she said half to herself and half to Margaret.

Margaret smiled at her and drifted down the steps and through the closed front door saying, "Follow your dreams, Maggie. Follow your dreams."

Maggie whacked her head with her hand. Then she fell into bed, giggling like a lunatic. As ghosts go, she thought, that Margaret is sure uplifting. Mawkish, perhaps, but an upper for sure. God, Maggie loved Margaret. She could not possibly let her go no matter what anyone else thought about it. Dwight in particular.

The women at the Drunken Hills Institute for Historical Preservation (known locally simply as DRIP) tried to help, but there weren't many records that dated back to the early 20th century. They gave Maggie access to the archives and dusty historical record books, but they provided very little information about the Booth family. After a couple of hours of poring over ancient tomes, Maggie was dirty and discouraged. She had been able to ascertain that a Booth family had resided in Drunken Hills in the late 1890's and early 1900's. In fact, the DRIP women told her that some Booths still lived in an old estate outside of town. Perhaps they were related to Margaret Booth Edison. One of the women scribbled an address on a piece of paper and handed it to Maggie. "Here's the address. The old woman who lives there is Willa Mae Booth Crocker Snidely. I believe her mama was a Booth. Maybe she can help you find your Margaret."

Maggie thanked the women for their assistance and tucked the piece of paper in her purse. She and Dwight could pay a visit to Mrs. Willa Mae Booth Crocker Snidely in the morning. Oops. She checked her watch. Dwight. He would be arriving soon and she was filthy and desperately in need of a shower. Her nerves threatened to render her useless if she couldn't rein them in. Perhaps a valium and a stiff drink would be in order. Only if she wanted to be unconscious when he arrived. She hurried back to the inn her thoughts ricocheting from one thing to another like kernels bursting in a popcorn popper. Her heart came thudding to a near stop when she reached the inn and saw Dwight's red SUV parked in the drive. No time for that shower, after all. Or the drink or the valium. *Time to face the music, Maggie,* she thought and she sucked in a breath and marched into the inn.

To her relief, Dwight wasn't waiting in the lobby. She peered into the dining room and the bar. No Dwight. That meant he must have gone up to their room —- the one with all the romantic accouterments. *Calm down, Maggie,* she told herself. *This is Dwight, for God's sake. Your husband. Not George Clooney or Bradley Cooper.* She wasn't quite ready. She needed a bit more time to prepare herself mentally, if not physically. Damn it, she wanted that shower.

She sighed and pulled out her cell phone. "Honey, it's me. I'm in the lobby. Why don't you come on down and join me for a drink?" As stalling tactics went, this one wasn't bad. And she needed something to settle her nerves.

"Babe," he said. "Why don't you come on up here? I've got wine on ice. Pinot Grigio. Your favorite brand." Low and throaty, he was using his seductive voice.

Maggie nearly gave in, but then played for time. "Sounds wonderful. It's just that...." Her voice trailed off.

Suddenly gruff, Dwight said, "Got it. Be down in a sec." Crap, now she'd done it. Made him mad. Hurt his feelings. Whatever.

But she'd misjudged him. Maggie had taken a seat in a winged chair facing the stairs leading to the second floor so that she could see him before he saw her. Sure enough, within a minute of disconnecting her cell phone, he appeared and her throat closed. He was so handsome in his favorite leather jacket and jeans -- it was like looking at her past. He took the steps two at a time and raced toward her. He swept across the lobby and pulled her to her feet and into his arms. She smelled the familiar smells of his after-shave and leather and allowed herself to luxuriate in the feel of his arms around her. Finally she stepped out of the crushing hug and backed away so she could see his face. "Hey," she said.

"Hey, yourself." Dwight seemed to be devouring her with his eyes. "Long time no see."

Maggie grabbed his hand and dragged him toward the wood-paneled bar just off the lobby. "I think this calls for a drink."

"Doesn't everything?" Dwight said dryly. "Maybe several. But I want to talk."

"We'll talk," Maggie told him. "We've got plenty of time for that."

Dwight pulled her to a halt and stared into her face. "The rest of our lives," he said. "Right?"

Oh, no. There it was already. The thing she was avoiding thinking about. The rest of their lives. Too soon to have this discussion. Way too soon.

Maggie couldn't look at him and she couldn't answer his question. They had some serious talking to do. First she just wanted to be with him. To remember everything that they had been to each other, once upon a time. It was too soon to have any serious discussion of their future. "We have a lot of catching up to do," Maggie said —- ignoring the fact that they had spoken on the phone nearly every day since she'd run away. There, she'd said it again. She'd run away. And that was what they needed to talk about. When they were ready. Not before.

They slid into a booth in the bar and sat side by side. Maggie leaned her head on his shoulder and Dwight draped an arm around her. He ordered wine for her and a beer for himself and they sat in comfortable silence as they waited for the drinks. "So-o-o," he said at last.

"So-o-o," she said. She didn't know where to begin.

But they'd been married a long time and they fell into the easy conversation of the long married. Talk about the kids. Their parents. His business. Friends at home who'd been asking about her. Maggie was careful to steer the conversation away from the future, but she talked about the bungalow, her job, about Gladdie and Jewel and Azalea. About Agnes and her café. And Maggie spun tales about the friendly ghost with whom she shared her bungalow. Dwight listened without a single word of scorn or teasing. He never took his eyes from her face as she told him about Margaret and how she would appear almost every night.

When she finally took a breath, he smiled. "So, I've been replaced by a ghost?"

"Replaced? I wouldn't say that. It's more like she's my roommate."

"Better a ghost, I guess, than some guy." He stared at her for so long that her nerves kicked into high gear again. Did he think she had a boyfriend? He knew better, didn't he? Well, there was Mac, but nothing happened there. Hadn't she wanted it to, though? Oh, God.

"There's no guy, if that's what you're asking," Maggie said. She felt defensive even if she had nothing to be ashamed of.

"Then," Dwight said, his eyes dark with passion, "let's go upstairs, Maggie May."

The silence grew longer and more awkward as Maggie hesitated. Then she made a decision, drained her glass, set it on the table and stood up. She reached her hand out to him and he took it. "I'm ready if you are," she said. And she was. Finally, finally, she was.

CHAPTER
Twenty-Two

Dwight unlocked the door to their room and stood aside so Maggie could go in ahead of him. She took a few steps into the darkened room and turned to flip on the light switch. Dwight hung the "Do Not Disturb" sign on the doorknob and locked and dead-bolted the door behind them. Maggie's mouth was as dry as if she had swallowed sand and her heart hammered.

Dwight maneuvered her toward the bed and pressed her down on it. He ran a finger down her cheek and to her neck and dipped it inside her shirt to place a single finger on her breast. Then he sighed and moved his hand to a more neutral location on her thigh. He wrapped an arm around her and rolled her toward him, kissing her lightly and playfully nipping her lip with his teeth. A bolt of longing shot through Maggie, short-circuiting her brain and making thinking almost impossible. She nestled against him and ran her fingers through his dark hair. *Why had she ever left him?* He was so warm, so familiar, so comfortable, so Dwight!

Fear snaked into her at that moment –- of what she couldn't have said -- and she pulled away. "God, I'm a mess. I need a shower." She leapt up and fled into the bathroom leaving him stunned and alone on the bed.

The shower helped. Maggie scrubbed off the griminess she'd incurred at DRIP and washed her hair until it squeaked. She shaved her legs and armpits and spritzed on perfume after she dried off with one of the soft thick towels. She brushed her teeth, dried her hair and stared at her reflection in the mirror – blonde hair, green eyes, troubled expression. But by the time she stepped back into the bedroom wrapped in one of the comfy white robes, she was under control although her heart jittered with anticipation.

Dwight had turned the covers down and was reclining on the bed wrapped in the other inn robe. Instead of watching television or being immersed in his cell phone as she expected, he was lying with his hands locked behind his head. Waiting. But he'd been busy while Maggie lingered in the shower. Candles twinkled from all over the room and the ice bucket had a bottle of champagne chilling in it. As Maggie got closer to the bed, she could see a lavish display of rose petals sprinkled over the snow white sheet. Her breath caught in her chest. Romance was so not Dwight's thing and yet he'd done all this. For her.

Before she could crawl into bed with him, he rolled over to the bedside table and flicked the switch to turn on his iPod player. And Rod Stewart growled the strains of "Maggie May." *Their song.*

Dwight leaned on one elbow and propped his head in his hand. *"Hey there, Maggie, I want to play with you. The kids are in bed and I got nothin' else to do."*

Maggie started to laugh. She stared down at him for a moment. "You big goof, you never did know the words."

Dwight reached up to pull her down into the bed. She snuggled next to him, her head on his chest. "Remind me again why this was our song."

Dwight winked. " Duh. Because you're name is Maggie."

"It's not the most flattering song I've ever heard. From Maggie's point of view anyway. Have you ever really listened to the lyrics?"

Dwight's expression turned serious. "Lately, Mags, that's all I've done. It's kind of been my theme song."

Maggie felt her face heat up. She knew most of the lyrics by heart. They'd played the song over and over again back when they were first married. Neither of them could ever remember the exact lyrics so they made them up to suit them.

"What did Rod say? He felt like he was being used?" Maggie said. "You think I'm using you?"

"Of course, not." But his face said otherwise. And maybe she was after all. Was she really afraid of being alone? Or was she even more afraid that she actually wanted to be alone? Was she prepared to lose everything in order to take back her life? Stupid as that might sound. Now was not the time for those thoughts, though.

She poked him in the ribs. "So, how do you explain the part where

he essentially calls her old? Something about the morning sun show-
ing her age."

Dwight pulled her closer. "He overlooked all her flaws, that's all I
can say."

Maggie punched his shoulder. "Flaws? Seriously? He laughed at her
jokes. She was funny. And fun."

"How did that line go?" Dwight ran a hand over her shoulder and
crooned. *"We ran away from home so we never had to be alone. You
turned into my lover and totally wore me out."*

Maggie put a finger to his lips. "Close enough."

He fumbled with the tie on her robe and loosened it. He reached
inside and stroked her naked body until she was shaking.

Maggie reached for him and tugged his robe loose and climbed
on top of him. She trickled kisses down to his toes and back up and
he moaned. After that, Rod Stewart dimmed into white noise as they
fell into the black whirling tunnel where nothing and no one else
could enter. But just before Maggie disappeared into the blackness,
she sensed a ghost climb into bed with them. Margaret? No. When she
glanced back over her shoulder, she saw DJ grinning his old wicked
grin at her. He gave her a broad wink and faded away. Damn him
anyway. Maggie squeezed her eyes closed and let herself spin out of
control. Making love to Dwight was like riding a bicycle –- she hadn't
been out for a ride for a long time, but she still knew how.

Each knew where the other wanted to be touched. They had a
special rhythm born of hundreds of nights together in bed. It was
always comfortable and often predictable. This time, though, perhaps
because it had been so long, it was different. This time the sex was
magical. Maggie lost all sense of time and place and was aware only
of physical sensation. She whirled in a misty landscape where images
floated in and out. The river where DJ asked her to marry him. The
little hotel where she and Dwight had honeymooned. The beach. All
the while a voice in her head chanted, "Touch me. Touch me. Touch
me." And, "There. Yes. There." She was hands and lips and touch. She
and Dwight were one being. She heard his harsh breathing and his
whispered words. "I love you, my Maggie." And she whispered the
words back to him. She swirled, feeling nothing but desire and need,
until the world exploded into a million tiny points of light and she
soared into them. And Dwight soared with her.

Afterwards Maggie and Dwight lay side-by-side holding hands. When she caught her breath, Maggie murmured, "Wow."

Maggie could feel Dwight smiling. "You got that right," he murmured, his breath warm on her cheek. He propped himself on one elbow so that he could look at her. "You're beautiful, you know."

Maggie's body was still humming happily after their lovemaking and all she could manage was a feeble, "Hm-m-m."

Still staring at her, Dwight said, "I think we…"

Maggie put her finger on his lips. "Sh-h," she said. "Don't talk now. It will just spoil things. Later is fine." She pulled him back down and fit herself against him spoon style. He curved his arms around her and held her and they drifted off to sleep wrapped in each other.

When Maggie woke up she found herself on the edge of the bed. She rolled over and saw that Dwight was lying on his stomach at the other edge. So typical, she thought, always finding ourselves on the opposite side. Well, I can fix that. She lifted the sheet and scooched closer to Dwight's backside and started to giggle when she discovered one of the rose petals stuck to his butt. She peeled it off and reached over to dangle it in front of his nose.

He opened one eye. "Whassat?"

"Rose petal stuck to your tush," she told him with a giggle. "Cute."

Dwight turned over so that he was facing Maggie. "Oops," he said, "you have one on your cheek." He pried it off her face and flicked it at her.

"Jerk," she said. She peeled one off his chest.

"Careful." A mock warning. And he plucked a petal from her left breast and let his hand linger there.

Before they knew it one petal led to another and they were making love again. This time it was slower but no less magical. Time seemed to be suspended as they found their way back to the place where they both felt safe and protected and, at the same time, more aroused than they had been since they were newlyweds. The second climax was even more intense than the first and they fell asleep again tangled in the covers and each other.

When they woke again the sun was shining through the French doors and they could see blue sky. Maggie made coffee and they took their mugs out to the balcony. Wrapped in the cozy robes, they lounged in wicker chairs and enjoyed the view of the forest and the

Drunken River winding through it.

"God, this is gorgeous," Maggie said. She stretched and threw her head back to see the cloudless sky. "I could do this all day."

"Then let's," Dwight said.

They ordered room service breakfast and ate outside. The day held the promise of warm temperatures and Dwight suggested a picnic by the river. Maggie shot him a quick, startled look, but his face seemed innocent of innuendo.

"First thing," Maggie said, "is to go to the old Booth Estate and talk to Mrs. Willa Mae Booth Crocker Snidely. I want to find out what she might know about Margaret and Rose Dawn."

If Maggie expected resistance, she didn't get it. Instead Dwight appeared to be interested. Seriously. He hopped to his feet. "I'll take the first shower while you finish your coffee." He was halfway through the door when he turned back. "Unless you want to join me." His eyes sparkled with mischief.

Maggie drained her coffee mug. *What the heck.* "Don't mind if I do. Always good to go green."

Dwight leered at her as he tugged her inside. "So that's what they're calling it these days."

Maggie laughed and let him lead her into the shower.

CHAPTER
Twenty-Three

The Booth Estate was located a mile outside Drunken Hills. The house, a two story gray stone building, sat on a hill and the long driveway leading to it was flanked by overgrown and tangled shrubs and browned patches of grass.

"Whew," Dwight said as he maneuvered the Bug up the steep incline, "I'd say no one has been doing any grounds-keeping for at least a decade." He gestured at a massive Blue Spruce sagging over the porch -- branches cantilevered at a precarious angle. "A good wind will topple that thing onto the house."

"The women at the historical society said Mrs. Snidely lives here alone. Refuses any help. Apparently no family either."

Dwight shook his head. "This place is too big for a — what did they say — 90-year old woman to take care of by herself."

Maggie agreed. She and Dwight had stopped at DRIP earlier to get directions to the Booth place and to ask the women there to phone Mrs. Willa Mae Snidely to find out if it was convenient for Dwight and Maggie to stop by. Maggie decided that surprising her was not a good idea. She didn't want to frighten the poor thing into a heart attack. And she didn't want Mrs. Snidely to turn a pack of vicious dogs loose on them either. In this case, forewarned was the only way to go.

Dwight parked the Bug in front of what appeared to be an old carriage house and they made their way up the front walk to the door. Maggie reached for the old brass doorknocker, but before she touched it the front door flew open and a white-haired elf of a woman inspected them with piercing blue eyes. Then her face lit up in a wide smile. "Ah, you must be Maggie." She eyeballed Dwight. "And who might this handsome young fellow be?"

Maggie smiled in delight. "Indeed I am Maggie Murphy, Mrs. Snidely. And this is my husband, Dwight."

Mrs. Snidely opened the door wider and gestured for them to enter. "Where are my manners?" she said. "Please come in. I can't have you just standing on the doorstep, now can I?"

Maggie and Dwight stepped through the doorway into a sunlit room filled with well-worn but comfortable appearing furniture. White lace curtains fluttered in the breeze from the open windows and an old console television was tucked into a corner. A tea set occupied the place of honor on the coffee table and Mrs. Snidely motioned for Dwight and Maggie to sit on the couch. She pulled an old wing chair up and placed it opposite the couch.

"Thank you for seeing us, Mrs. Snidely," Maggie began.

"Oh, my dear. It's my pleasure. I don't get much company out here these days. Please call me Willa Mae. I never did like the name Snidely." She paused and seemed for a second to have forgotten them.

"Mrs. Snidely. I mean, Willa Mae?" Maggie prompted her. "Are you okay?"

Willa Mae gave a quick exasperated shake of her head. "Oh, dear. I drifted off, didn't I? I do that these days. What was I saying? Oh, yes. The Snidely name. Never cared for it. If my Earl hadn't been such a handsome fellow, I would never have taken the name." She paused again to arrange the tea things on the table and then looked at them as if she just remembered they were there. "Would you care for tea?" she asked.

Dwight cut his eyes to Maggie and shrugged. Was she all there? Then he said as perky as could be. "I'd love tea, Willa Mae. Just the thing for a day like this."

Willa Mae patted his hand. "You remind me of my Earl, young man. He loved his tea." Then she grinned. "Course he put a shot of whiskey in it to make it palatable, he said. The devil."

Dwight chuckled. "I think he had something there, Willa Mae."

At that moment, Maggie loved Dwight more than she ever had. This was a side of him that she hadn't seen before. Flirting with an old woman and making her feel desirable? She would never have believed it if she wasn't seeing it for herself.

Willa Mae poured tea into three cups and handed one to each of them. She offered sugar and cream and then got up and left the room.

Maggie and Dwight looked at each other in consternation. Was she coming back? They needn't have worried. A minute later Willa Mae returned with a dusty bottle of Old Irish Whisky in her hand. She passed it to Dwight and he whooped with pleasure.

"Now that's what I'm talkin' about, Willa Mae."

A fat strawberry blonde cat strolled out from behind the television set where it had been napping. After much sniffing and deliberation, it concluded that Dwight met its stringent standards and jumped into his lap. Dwight stroked its back and the animal purred like a lawnmower.

Willa Mae beamed her approval. "That's Riesling. She likes you." She patted the cat's head. "Don't you girl?"

Maggie rolled her eyes. She wasn't sure she could control this interview the way things were going. Willa Mae was plying Dwight with tea laced with whiskey and he was guzzling it as if it was Gatorade and he'd just scored the winning touchdown. Even the black looks Maggie cast his way didn't slow him down. After 20 minutes of idle chit chat and tea swilling her patience was exhausted and she removed the cup from his hands and set it down with a thump on the table. "Enough, Dwight," she said. "You won't be able to walk out of here."

"But it's good," he protested. His crooked grin was adorable -- if a bit loopy.

Maggie scowled at him and he tipped his head to rest it on the back of the couch and closed his eyes. If he started to snore, she'd kill him. But Willa Mae was smiling at him as if he had brought home an all A report card, so Maggie made an effort to ignore him. Anyway, she was outnumbered. The cat's purrs announced that she was taken with him as well.

Maggie focused on Willa Mae. "I don't know what the DRIP ladies told you, but I'm looking for any information about a Margaret Booth Edison. I thought you might know something that could help."

Willa Mae fingered her teacup and cast a longing look at the bottle of whiskey. Was she going to sweeten her tea with a shot? This sweet little old lady was really something. She reminded Maggie of Helen, the sex-crazed octogenarian from the *Get Your Groove On Conference* – the one who wanted to know about birth control and bikini waxes. Honestly, Maggie thought, I wouldn't be a bit surprised if Willa Mae knew a lot about those things. Maybe she even sported a bikini wax under her conservative blue slacks. Maggie realized that her thoughts had gone far astray and dragged her attention back to the subject at hand. Margaret.

"I live in Sweet River, South Carolina," Maggie told her, "in a little house that was once part of the Edison estate. After I moved in, I learned that it was haunted."

Willa Mae clasped her hands in her lap and leaned forward as she listened -- her eyes never leaving Maggie's face. "Please go on," Willa Mae said. "Haunted you say. Who is haunting your house?"

"I know this sounds crazy, but I've seen her. My ghost. I think it's Margaret Booth Edison herself."

Willa Mae chuckled. "I would be the last one to call anyone crazy. Folks around here would tell you that I'm several turnips short of a barrel. Tell me about the ghost."

Maggie told Willa Mae what she knew about Margaret's life and her maid Birdie Byrne who was allegedly murdered in Margaret's bed in the bungalow. She explained about the diary she had found and what Margaret had written about Daniel and Connor. Willa Mae never moved a muscle as Maggie talked. Finally, Maggie said, "I really don't know why this matters so much to me. I guess I want to know about the ghost who shares my house with me."

The tick-tock of the cuckoo clock was the only sound as Willa Mae digested Maggie's tale. "My granny was named Margaret, but her last name wasn't Edison. She was Margaret Booth Preston. And she didn't die until years after you say this Birdie Byrne person was murdered in her bed and your Margaret vanished."

That was unexpected. Was this the proof she was looking for that Margaret had escaped alive that awful night at the bungalow? Excited by this tidbit, Maggie pursued it. "According to Sweet River public records, Margaret gave birth to a daughter, Rose Dawn Booth. Margaret's husband, Daniel, wasn't the father. If her diary is correct, then the father was someone named Connor."

Now it was Willa Mae's turn to look surprised. "My mama was Rose Dawn. Rose Dawn Preston." Suddenly, she leaped to her feet and scurried out of the room. She returned with a Bible in her hand and opened it to a page in the front where the family tree was written in scratchy script. Rose Dawn Preston, born 1900, daughter of Margaret and Conrad Preston.

Maggie and Willa Mae stared at each other in shock and disbelief. Could Conrad Preston be the same person as Margaret's Connor? Maggie would have bet her life on it. She turned to Dwight to get his opinion and found that he had fallen asleep. Big help he turned out to be. Drunk on tea. Honestly.

"I think," Maggie said, "that the Connor who Margaret said was the father of her baby girl was none other than your grandfather Conrad. I'm betting that the two of them ran away from Sweet River together."

Willa Mae tapped a finger on the Bible. "What about my mama? Did Margaret and Connor? Or maybe Conrad? Run off and leave the baby girl behind?"

"I think that's exactly what happened. I found a newspaper clipping that said that the baby's grandmother, Margaret's mother, had custody and was going to take her to be raised in Drunken Hills."

"They didn't cover their tracks very well, now did they?" Willa Mae heaved a huge sigh. "It's romantic, isn't it? I do love a good love story."

"Me too." Maggie cut her eyes to Dwight, dozing next to her. "Now the only thing left to figure out is who was it that murdered Birdie Byrne in the bed in my house? And why? Could it have been Daniel?"

Maggie and Willa Mae tossed around possible scenarios for a little longer and then Maggie nudged Dwight with her elbow. "Wake up, Sleeping Beauty. Willa Mae and I think we can make a pretty good guess what happened to Margaret and Connor and Rose Dawn. Time for us to go."

Dwight struggled to a sitting position looking groggy and disoriented. He knuckled his eyes and groaned. "What was in that tea anyway?"

Willa Mae batted her eyes. She couldn't quite pull off the innocent look she was going for. "Besides the whiskey? That's my secret recipe."

Dwight gave his head a shake. "Whoa. It sure packs a punch." He started to stand up and then sank back onto the cushions. "What did you learn about Margaret?" he asked Maggie.

"Tell you later," Maggie said, "when you're in shape to listen."

She hauled him to his feet and supported him as he stumbled toward the door. At the door they said good-bye to Willa Mae and promised to keep in touch.

"I can't thank you enough for your time and for the tea," Maggie said. She laughed and nodded at Dwight. "I'm sure some of us will never forget it."

"I enjoyed having visitors," Willa Mae said. "Please let me know when you figure it all out." She stepped outside and watched as they made their way to the Bug. "Tell my grandmother next time you see her that Willa Mae says howdy," she called after them.

Maggie poured Dwight into the passenger seat and climbed into the Bug. As she drove down the steep driveway, she looked in the rearview mirror and saw Willa Mae still standing on her front porch holding Riesling and waving.

Maggie drove a couple of miles down the road and then pulled into a scenic turnout. She shut off the engine and turned sideways so that she could see Dwight. He was slumped in the passenger seat, his baseball cap pulled low and his eyes shaded by his sunglasses. Maggie waited. Finally he struggled to a sitting position and removed his sunglasses so she could see his eyes. He was so pathetic that she started to giggle. Her giggles escalated into peels of merriment and she pounded the steering wheel in glee. Every time she thought she had herself under control, she'd look at Dwight and it would start all over. At last she gulped and hiccupped. "Sorry," she said. "I couldn't help it."

Dwight groaned. "I'm an idiot."

Maggie agreed. "You are, but you're a cute idiot." She smiled at him.

"I cannot believe I let a little old lady drink me under the table," he said. "What was in that tea anyway?"

"Beats me."

"Well, if word of this episode gets out, I'll be the laughing stock of Winslow."

Maggie started to giggle again, wiping tears from her eyes. "Oh, babe, I won't tell a soul. I promise."

Dwight leaned across the console to take her hand. "I'm a moron. And I love you."

Maggie squeezed his hand and stared out the front window seeing nothing of the landscape. How was she going to tell him about her plans when he was being so sweet? She let the silence linger so long that Dwight cleared his throat. "Ahem. Maggie? Where are you?"

Maggie faced him. Let her gaze rest on his dark eyes and worried expression and then said, "I'm right here. I love you too. No matter what." Okay, now that was stupid. Being cryptic wasn't going to cut it here, but she was in luck. Dwight was still addled enough from his teatime that he let the comment slide.

"Where to now?" he asked. "Picnic time?"

"Definitely," Maggie said turning the key in the ignition and firing up the Bug. "This day is too gorgeous to waste."

They spread their blanket in a clearing on the bank of the Drunken River and spent the afternoon drinking sodas and polishing off the sandwiches and cookies they bought at the Drunken Market. It was a beautiful warm day and they waded in the icy river getting soaked and then lying on the blanket in the sun to dry out. Dwight was playful and relaxed – any thoughts of business relegated to another time and another place. And Maggie responded. This was the Dwight she loved. What was she thinking? She should just go home with him and forget all the other nonsense. Maybe….

When he stretched out next to her and played with a lock of her hair and drew a finger down her cheek, she sighed. She ran her fingers through his thick dark hair and pulled his face down to kiss him. Even as desire curled its way from her toes to her heart, she knew that she was going to have to tell him. Her dreams had been on hold for too long. He'd understand wouldn't he? The image of DJ floated over his head. Damn DJ anyway.

With an effort she ejected DJ from her thoughts and focused all of her attention on Dwight and his breath warm on the back of her neck. She shivered as he kissed her in that special place. No, she didn't have to tell him anything yet. Really, it was such a beautiful day and they were getting along so well. Why spoil their romantic weekend before she absolutely had to? There was plenty of time for that. Maggie rolled over into Dwight's arms and traced his face with her fingers. Today was for magic and remembering the good times. Today was for Dwight and Maggie. Everything else could darn well wait.

They lingered by the river until a late afternoon breeze came up and the chill in the air drove them away. Taking her time Maggie folded up the blanket with care and stuffed the remains of their picnic lunch into the back seat of her Bug. Dwight wrapped his leather jacket around Maggie's shoulders and she breathed in the special aroma of old leather and Dwight. She sighed and leaned into him. It was the perfect moment to tell him her plans. "Dwight," she began, "I need to tell you something."

He turned so he could look her in the eye. "So, tell me," he said

-- his face as open and relaxed as she had seen it in a very long time. "I'm ready."

She couldn't do it. Coward, she chastised herself. She wasn't ready to have this end. So, she took the coward's way out. "I love you."

He grinned and pulled her into his arms and kissed the top of her head. "Aw, Maggie May, I love you too."

As they drove away from the clearing by the river, Maggie looked back. The trees were swaying in the breeze and ripples crisscrossed the river. A bird swooped down to pluck his dinner from the water. Peaceful. She sighed with contentment and wanted to freeze this moment forever.

Dwight unlocked and opened the door to their room at the inn and as he closed and bolted it behind them they fell on each other -- their kisses unrestrained and frantic as they ripped at their clothing. He pushed Maggie against the wall and slid his arms under the leather jacket she still wore. He lifted her shirt and ran his hands from her waist up to her breasts. She shivered -- whether from passion or because his hands were cold and slightly rough she wasn't sure. Her face burned and she knew it wasn't just sunburn. She hadn't been this turned on since -- well -- since the days of DJ and beer. But she wasn't going to go there. That was DJ and that was then. This was now and all about Dwight. DJ was long gone. She had to quit thinking about him.

Maggie wriggled out of the jacket and let it fall to the floor while Dwight steered her in the direction of the king-sized bed. With one hand he tugged off the comforter and with other he toyed with the clasp of her bra. She reached behind her to unhook it and gasped as Dwight circled her nipple with his thumb. Maggie pulled her shirt off over her head and tossed it and then her bra aside. Half-naked she stared at Dwight and saw his eyes darken. Hmmm.

She unzipped her jeans and Dwight tugged them down until they caught around her knees. As he kissed her she tried to get the jeans off but only succeeded in tangling them around her legs and tumbling in an ungainly heap onto the bed. She watched Dwight pull off his own shirt and then struggle with the zipper on his jeans. Then she wrecked things. Maybe it was nerves. She knew her timing was horrible, but she couldn't help herself. She started to giggle. The more she tried to stop the harder she laughed. This was bad. She knew Dwight didn't like to be laughed at. He would be furious with her.

As he stared down at her a variety of expressions crossed Dwight's face. Surprise and confusion first, followed by a storm cloud. Then he shocked her as a tiny smile lifted the corners of his mouth. "Maggie May, you're killing me here. I've been thinking about this moment all day and -- you think it's amusing?"

Maggie hauled in a deep breath and wiped her eyes on the sheet. "It's not you. It's us." A giggle bubbled up around her clenched lips. The look on his face was so comical that she burst out laughing again. She couldn't seem to stop.

Dwight sank onto the bed next to her and bent to pull off his jeans. Clad only in his boxer briefs he propped himself on one elbow and watched her, a quizzical expression on his face. "Let me know when you're finished," he said.

Maggie choked back her giggles and said, "I'm sorry, babe, but I couldn't help it. We're acting like a pair of sex-crazed actors in a bad X-rated flick."

Dwight rolled onto his back and stared at the ceiling. "Hmm. The United Parcel man huh?"

Back when the kids were little Dwight and Maggie went through a period of renting X-rated movies and watching them in bed behind their locked bedroom door. Dwight hoped that the movies would ignite something between them and lead to a more adventurous sex life. Maggie never exactly objected but she thought the movies were kind of ridiculous and she couldn't help making fun of them. The UPS man was a classic.

Maggie giggled and propped herself up on the pillows. "Here's your package, Ma'am, and let's go to bed where we can do kinky things to each other."

Maggie snuck a look at her husband. He had his eyes closed. She nudged him. "Hey. Wake up. We're not through here."

His eyes popped open and he gave her a practiced seductive look. "We're not?"

She snaked a finger inside the elastic waistband of his boxer briefs and wiggled it. "Uh uh. Not by a long shot."

He rolled on top of her -- his hands on either side of her head. She could feel how aroused he was and Maggie's giggles trailed away. Her mouth was dry and her heart started to race just a little. He brushed his lips over hers. "Show me what you've got," he said.

Maggie took a breath. "Wel-l-l," she whispered. "As they say in those cheesy romance novels, you show me your -- um -- manhood and I'll show you what you can do with it?"

Dwight hooted. "Manhood? Seriously? Is that what they're calling it?" He pulled off his boxers. "I'll show you manhood, my Maggie May."

He was as good as his word. Better, Maggie thought. Way better. She couldn't think of a thing to add as her husband made love to her as if it was the first time and they were young and wildly in love.

Earlier on their way to interview Willa Mae they noticed a run-down, grey vinyl sided building just off the highway. A sign identifying it as *The Drunken Roadhouse* hung lopsidedly over the front door. "Now that's my kind of a place," Dwight commented as they drove by.

So later when Dwight and Maggie discussed where to have dinner it seemed like an obvious choice. As Dwight wheeled the Bug into the huge gravel parking lot, Maggie began to have doubts. Trucks -- small, large and in between -- most dirty and sporting huge tires were the predominant vehicle. Half the lights in the sign over the door were burned out so only the words "Drunk House" were spelled out in red and blue bulbs -- flashing on and off in an erratic pattern.

Dwight chuckled. "I'm thinking we've come to exactly the right place."

The trees surrounding the roadhouse on three sides swayed as a gust of wind blew through them. The sound of rushing water came from somewhere nearby. Maggie shivered. "I hope we don't get stabbed."

Dwight took her arm and guided her toward the front door. "Don't be silly. I've got your back."

He heaved the heavy splintery door open and urged Maggie inside. They stood at the entrance and surveyed their surroundings -- a spacious room with an open fireplace in the center. A large wood bar lined with heavy barstools stretched along one side. It was crowded -- most of the tables occupied by families or older couples. A tall, gangly man in perhaps his late twenties with a guitar slung over his shoulder ambled over to greet them. He shoved a shock of dark wavy hair out of his eyes and said with a welcoming smile, "Hey. Welcome to *The*

Drunken Roadhouse. I'm Zach. Are you here for dinner or drinks? Or both?"

"Both, please," Dwight said with a grin.

Zach swept his arm to include the entire room. "Plenty of tables. Sit wherever you like."

Dwight led Maggie across the room to a table located between the fireplace and the huge windows. Maggie shrugged off her lightweight leather jacket and hung it on the back of a chair but before she sat down she walked over to the bank of windows and peered out. The forest outside was thick and dark and she observed the Drunken River burbling along at the edge. It gleamed silver in the waning light.

"That's the river right below us," she said. "How cool is that?"

"I told you this was a good place," Dwight said.

"It just might become my new favorite restaurant," Maggie said as she perched on the scarred seat of her chair, "if the food is good."

"It's a bit of a drive from Winslow," Dwight said.

And a bit of a drive from Sweet River, Maggie thought with a sigh.

Zach appeared at their table, guitar still slung across his back, and handed them menus. "Christa, over there." He pointed across the room at a tiny blonde in tight jeans. "Will be your server. I'll get you started with drinks, if you like."

"I'll have a beer. What do you have on draft?" Dwight asked.

Zach listed the selections and Dwight ordered. Then he said, "And, my wife will have a glass of ...." He paused and turned to Maggie with a grin. "What do you want, Mags? The usual?"

Will wonders never cease? Her take-charge, I know-what- you-want-before-you-do husband was actually asking her what she wanted to drink. He really was trying hard. Maggie smiled at him. "A glass of pinot grigio," she said to Zach. And to Dwight she said, "The usual, but thanks for asking."

"Are you the entertainment tonight?" Dwight asked Zach.

"Sure am. Every Friday and Saturday night from nine 'til whenever the place closes. Helps pay for tuition in law school. I'll play after the family crowd heads out and the bar crowd moves in."

Zach gestured at a sprightly white-haired gentlemen in a plaid shirt and worn jeans who circulated from table to table chatting and laughing with the guests. "My great grampa, Zeke, owns the place."

Maggie turned to check Zeke out. With his white beard curling from his chin, he reminded her of Santa Claus -- if Santa had joined WeightWatchers and lost 50 pounds. "Family business?" she asked Zach. "How old is your great-grandfather anyway?"

"Gramps will be 90 on Christmas Eve."

"He's amazing," Maggie said.

As Zach headed to the bar to put in their drink orders, Maggie and Dwight settled back to people watch. It was a lively crowd. Small children dodged between tables and older couples called out to each other. Everyone seemed to know everyone else.

Over burgers and fries Maggie and Dwight settled into a desultory conversation about trivial things relaxed by their day together and the sex earlier. Neither was eager to spoil the mood.

As the family groups finished their dinner and drifted toward the door, the bar began to fill with a younger crowd who gathered in groups around large round tables or broke off to play pool. Music from the jukebox blared and a few remaining little girls danced together on the large dance floor. At precisely nine o'clock, Zach took a seat next to the fireplace and began to tune his guitar. The bar patrons settled into their seats and waited for him to begin to play. The room grew silent in anticipation and then he struck the first note and his silvery voice lilted over the room.

Maggie sipped her wine and listened. "He's really good," she whispered to Dwight.

Zach's music was a mellow combination of blues and country with a touch of pop and rock thrown in -- perfect for a blustery wine-soaked evening. Maggie smiled at Dwight and twined her fingers through his. The music floated over them.

When Zach finished his first set and took a break, Dwight excused himself to use the restroom. When he returned he was beaming a cat-who-swallowed-the-canary, self-satisfied smile. Maggie stared at him. What was he so smug about? "What's so funny?" Maggie began and then the song on the jukebox ended and a new one began.

The strains of Rod Stewart's raspy voice singing *"their"* song, drifted across the dance floor. Dwight leaned down and whispered, "May I have this dance, Maggie May?"

Maggie pushed her chair away from the table and stood up. She folded herself into her husband's arms and leaned her head on his shoulder. "I'd be delighted to dance with you."

Maggie was dumbfounded. Dwight hated to dance. He was a natural athlete but preferred sports that had rules and instruction books. Dancing didn't come with a rule book and made him feel like a moron. Oh, sure they'd done a polite box step or swayed to the music at a wedding -- but nothing more adventurous.

Now, though, he held her tightly against his chest and twirled her around like a pro. She relaxed and let him lead. Dwight sang the lyrics along with Rod under his breath. When Rod finished singing Maggie May, the song on the jukebox changed to another of Maggie's favorites from another time, Van Morrison's Brown Eyed Girl. Dwight swung her away from him and broke into a sexy, silly solo. Maggie giggled and followed his moves. Then they danced to Rod's Sweet Little Rock and Roller and finally stopped to catch their breath.

Sweaty and disheveled, her cheeks flushed from exertion, Maggie laughed. She hadn't danced like this -- free and loose and unrestrained since -- well -- since the Days of DJ and Beer. DJ loved to dance and never missed an opportunity to drag Maggie out onto the floor and show off his moves. She never tired of trying to keep up with him. Damn it. Why couldn't she get DJ out of her head? This was sweet, solid Dwight -- her husband of many years. *DJ was long gone. And forgotten. Yes, absolutely forgotten.*

Maggie grinned up at Dwight as he led her back to their table. She dragged one hand across her sweaty forehead. "Wow, you're full of surprises tonight."

Dwight pulled her chair out for her and sank bonelessly into the one next to hers. "Maggie May, darlin', you ain't seen nothin' yet."

At the end of Zach's second set a redhead wearing cowboy boots and a tight denim mini-skirt wandered over to the jukebox and plugged in quarters. As she walked back to her table, the sounds of Garth Brooks boomed out. Maggie leaned over the table toward Dwight as another country tune followed. "I love country music. Wanna dance?"

Dwight shook his head. "I draw the line at that. Songs about cowboys loving their trucks and kissing their cows don't do it for me. Sorry, babe."

Disappointed, but not surprised, Maggie took a long drink of wine and concentrated on the dance floor. She tapped her fingers on the table in time to the music and one foot bounced of its own volition. She was so absorbed that she nearly jumped out of her seat when she felt a tap on her shoulder. She whirled around to see Great-Grampa Zeke hovering behind her.

"Would you do me the honor of this dance?" he said to her.

Flustered she stammered, "Oh, no. I - I couldn't. I mean. I shouldn't. I'm not."

"Oh, go on Maggie," Dwight urged her. "You know you want to."

"Please," Zeke said. "Do an old man a favor."

"In that case," Maggie said. "I would love to." She pushed back her chair and followed Zeke onto the dance floor.

Great-Grampa Zeke was a fantastic dancer for a man of nearly 90. Heck, he was a fantastic dancer for a man of any age. He whirled and twirled and stomped his boot-shod feet to the music. Hands around her waist he led Maggie into his version of the Texas Two-Step and, after a few stumbles, Maggie caught on. The two of them spun around the dance floor as country song followed country song. By the time Zach returned from his break and Zeke escorted her back to Dwight, Maggie was breathless and laughing.

"Thank you, little lady," Zeke said.

Maggie reached up to kiss his wrinkled cheek. "No. Thank you. It was my pleasure."

She sank into her chair and guzzled the Diet Coke that Dwight had thoughtfully gotten for her. "Whew. He's really something."

Dwight's eyes gleamed and he rubbed his forefinger over his lips. "Depends on your point of view, I s'pose, as to who is really somethin'."

Maggie stared at him without speaking and then pushed aside the Diet Coke and gulped her wine. "And your point is?"

"Ah, Maggie. All in good time." Dwight chuckled. "Listen to the music."

They stayed at the *Drunken Roadhouse* listening to Zach and drinking until he played his final song and the bar emptied. They were so caught up in each other that they almost missed the fact that they were the last to leave the bar and wander out into the chilly night air.

Dwight hesitated and then turned back to press two twenties into Zach's hand. "It's been awesome. You're very talented. Thank you so much."

The musician beamed at them. "Y'all come back, hear. You're always welcome."

Tipsy from the wine and the dancing, Maggie stumbled as they walked toward the Bug. Her thoughts flashed back to the night she almost went to bed with Mac thinking in her fuzzy mind that he was

Dwight. She gave herself a mental head slap. Mac was hot, no doubt, but this was Dwight, real and in person. No need to pretend. Or was there? She was too tired to debate the issue.

Back at the Inn Maggie, too exhausted to even undress, curled up on the bed with her head on Dwight's shoulder. He turned on the television and scrolled through the channels until he discovered one of their favorite movies, "When Harry Met Sally." He tugged the covers over them and pulled Maggie closer. "This is perfect," Maggie murmured. The last thing she remembered was the classic scene when Meg Ryan exhibited orgasmic delight in her meal and the woman customer told the waitress, "I'll have what she's having."

Sunlight slanted through the gap in the blinds as Maggie stretched and forced her eyes to open. Muzzy and just a bit hung-over, Maggie struggled to figure out where she was. Her mouth tasted like ashes and her eyes were gritty. Then she saw Dwight sitting in the chair by the window and it all came back. Clad in his pajama bottoms and a faded Cleveland Browns T-shirt he was bent over his laptop -- dark hair mussed and falling over his eyes. She studied him through half open eyes for a few minutes. He looked sexy.

"Hey," she said -- trying for seductive.

He looked up and smiled. "Hey."

"I missed the end of the movie."

"You went out like fog rolling in off the lake," he said. "I didn't have the heart to wake you."

Maggie threw back the covers and realized that she was still wearing the sweater she'd worn to the bar and her lacy panties, but her jeans and boots were missing. Dwight had obviously undressed her. Her thoughts again drifted back to the night with Mac -- the night that Margaret, her favorite ghost, supposedly undressed her and tucked her in. She shook her head. Obviously, she was several cupcakes short of a dozen.

"Hey, Mags," Dwight said. "Where did you go?"

"Oh, um, you wouldn't believe it if I told you," Maggie said. "What got you up so early?"

Dwight chuckled. "It's not that early. It's nearly eight thirty. I already called DRIP."

"You did? Why?"

He climbed into bed next to her and propped two puffy pillows behind his head. "I had a hunch. I was thinking about how Margaret ran away with Connor and left the baby behind. And that Margaret's mother left town with the baby to live with family in Drunken Hills."

"Go on."

"Here we are in Drunken Hills and I wondered if any of that family was still around so I called DRIP and asked if any Prestons lived in the area."

Maggie studied his face. He was enjoying this. "Don't keep me hanging. Are there any Prestons?"

Dwight gave her a thumbs up and a huge smile lit up his face. "There are. I got an address and a nice lady at DRIP offered to call them and see if we could make an appointment to visit. I'm expecting a call from Mrs. Lantry at any moment to let us know." There was a knock at the door and he bounced off the bed. "In the meantime, let's have breakfast." He opened the door and ushered in a shy teenager wearing a white jacket and bearing a tray laden with breakfast goodies.

"Right over here, my man," Dwight said and pressed some bills into the boy's hand.

Maggie rolled her eyes. "You really are full of surprises." She clambered out of bed and stumbled into the bathroom. "I'll be back in a second."

When she came out wrapped in one of the white fuzzy robes, Dwight handed her a champagne glass. "Mimosa?"

She took the glass from him and looked him in the eye. "Incredible."

They clinked their glasses and then sipped. "Mmm." Maggie sighed. "I could get used to this."

Dwight concentrated on uncovering the various dishes to reveal fresh fruit, fluffy scrambled eggs, biscuits and toast with jam and butter, crispy bacon and waffles with syrup. He poured each of them a cup of coffee from the carafe on the tray. "Help yourself, Mags, while it's still hot."

Maggie gazed up at him from under her lids and batted her eyes. She sipped her mimosa and said, "Talk about hot."

He set his glass down and reached for her, but his cell phone rang just at that moment. He glared at it. "Talk about timing." He checked the caller ID. "Mrs. Lantry at DRIP." He swiped at the phone. "Oh, yes. Thank you so much. That would be perfect. My wife and I will be there. Yes, I've got it." He scrawled a number on a napkin. "We appreciate it. Yes, I will."

He disconnected and turned to Maggie. "We have an 11 o'clock appointment at The Singing Winds Estate, the old Preston place." He leered at Maggie. "Eat up. If we hurry we can squeeze in some exercise before we have to leave."

She slowly slathered a biscuit with butter and piled fresh fruit onto a plate. She blinked with mock innocence. "Oh, land sakes, Mr. Butler. You do turn a girl's head."

Dwight took the biscuit out of her hand. "I promise you, Scarlet. You will think about this tomorrow."

And he was as good as his word.

CHAPTER
Twenty-Four

At precisely five minutes before 11 o'clock, Dwight pulled the Bug into a long gravel lane winding up a small slope to a stately mansion with white pillars guarding the massive front door. On either side of the lane horses frolicked in grassy fields bordered by white picket fences. Peaceful and pastoral, Maggie couldn't help but compare it to Tara and Gone With the Wind.

"Wow," she murmured.

Simple gold lettering on the mailbox at the foot of the lane said, "Preston." Nothing more formal to identify it.

As they got closer to the mansion, though, they could see that the paint was peeling in spots. The lawn was spotted with weeds and the shrubbery was overgrown. Still, the Preston place had a stately dignity that even disrepair couldn't spoil.

"It looks deserted," Maggie whispered. "Do you think anyone is here?" She pointed at a ramshackle barn located a short distance away.

Dwight parked the car and they climbed out and looked around. Big old trees surrounded the house and on the porch a swing dangled from a rusty chain as the morning breeze blew it back and forth. From inside the house they heard a dog's frenzied yipping.

"I don't think the dog lives here alone," Dwight answered. "Let's go find out."

His hand on her elbow, he guided her up the rickety steps. The porch was dilapidated and several boards were broken. Nail heads stuck up through the cracks. They picked their way over the rotting wood and pressed the tarnished brass doorbell to announce their arrival. Maggie glanced at her watch -- right on time. From inside a voice called to them. "Just a second. I'll be right there." Odd, but Maggie thought the voice was familiar.

There was a scrabbling sound of locks turning and then the door opened. Maggie's eyes widened and her mouth opened and closed in surprise. "Grandpa Zeke," she cried. "We didn't know that you're a Preston."

He grinned. "And I didn't know that you are my grannie's Maggie either." He stepped back and motioned them inside. "But here we are. I made coffee. Would you like a cup?"

His grannie's Maggie? Who was his grannie and what on earth did he mean by that? Maggie couldn't wait to find out.

"Yes, please, I'd love coffee," she said as she checked out the huge foyer. A massive staircase opened onto the space with a large empty sitting room to the right and a dining room -- also devoid of furniture -- to the left. A dusty chandelier hung in the center of the room and the sunlight caught on dust motes floating in the air.

Zeke followed her gaze and smiled an apology. "It's only me lives here. I don't need all this space so I sold everything 'cept what I really need." He ushered them into a large kitchen area and pointed at two chairs tucked around a round oak table. Along one wall of the room was a stone fireplace and across the back windows opened to a pasture where horses galloped playfully from one fence to the other. The table was set with cheery red woven placemats and heavy pottery mugs.

"I spend most of my time in here these days," Zeke explained. "The kids want me to sell the place, but I haven't lived anyplace else in my life. Where would I go? Some home where I'd play checkers with a bunch of drooling idiots? No thank you."

Zeke busied himself at the counter for a couple of minutes while Maggie and Dwight watched. Then he placed a platter of cookies in the center of the table and poured coffee into the mugs from a big tin pot. He sat down across from them and put his elbows on the table and leaned toward them. "Now then. What can I do for the pair of you?"

Today, Maggie noted, Zeke looked even more mischievous than the night before. He wore tattered overalls over a bright plaid shirt and his eyes sparkled behind wire-rimmed glasses. A rust colored puppy galoophed into the kitchen and skidded to a stop to eye the strangers warily. Then, apparently deciding they were harmless, it trotted over -- toenails clicking on the hardwood floor -- to sniff them out.

"Be nice, Merlot," Zeke said. He turned to his guests. "Do you mind him being here while we talk? We don't get much company these days and he's curious."

Dwight patted the dog's head. "Don't mind a bit, do we, Mags?"

Maggie shook her head and then blurted the question that had been troubling her since they first arrived. "When you first opened the door, you said you didn't know I was your grannie's Maggie. What did you mean by that?"

Zeke chuckled. "Oh, that. My sister, Willa Mae, told me that an attractive young couple paid her a visit and she told me --"

"Whoa, wait a minute," Maggie interrupted him, "Willa Mae is your sister? She never said a thing about having a brother in town." She poked Dwight. "Did she?'

Dwight's grin was rueful. "You're asking me? I don't remember much after that first cup of tea."

Zeke burst out laughing. "She got you with her special recipe, did she? That Willa Mae is full of tricks. You gotta watch her all the time." He wiped his eyes with his napkin and then said to Maggie, "She never mentions me. I think maybe I'm an embarrassment to her." He shrugged. "We haven't been real close lately. Fact is we haven't been close since Mama died and left me this place. Willa Mae thought it shoulda gone to her -- her being the oldest and all. But Willa was married to that no good Bud Crocker at the time and Mama was afraid he'd get his hands on the place and do heaven knows what with it. So she left it all to me in her will. I think that if Willa had been married to good ole Earl at the time, things woulda been different."

"She told you about our visit," Maggie insisted. "What did she say? Why did she call you?"

Zeke took off his glasses, polished them on his napkin and then put them back on. He frowned. "I guess maybe she wanted to talk to someone who knew about Mama and Margaret and all of that. You must of stirred up some memories. So when Mavis Lantry down at the historical society called this morning, I figured I'd find out more from you myself." He chuckled. "Bit of a surprise to see my dancing partner standing on my doorstep. A dandy one though."

Maggie poured cream into her mug and stirred. "Did she tell you about my ghost? Margaret?"

"Yep. Sure did. I don't remember Granny Margaret much. Willa Mae is older so she recalls more than I do. I have heard the stories. Mama used to tell us about how Margaret and my grandfather, Conrad, had this true life romance. They were meant to be and all that. Ran away together. I guess if anyone was going to be doing some haunting, it would be Granny Margaret. She sounds like that kind of a gal."

"Your mama was Rose Dawn, right?"

Zeke nodded. "Yep."

"Did Willa Mae tell you about how Margaret vanished from Sweet River?'

"Nah, she didn't give me details."

"There's a lot more to the story," Maggie said and filled Zeke in on the mysterious disappearance -- the bloodstained sheets, the murder of Birdie Byrne and the baby left behind. He never took his eyes off her face as he listened with his head cocked to one side.

"Well, now," he said. "That's some story, but how can I help?"

Maggie scratched her chin with one finger. "I don't know Zeke. I guess I wanted to try to fill in the gaps in the story. See where Margaret might have gone. I hoped she found some peace and happiness in the end."

Zeke got up and went to the stove to get the coffee pot. He refilled their mugs and sat down. Merlot laid his head on Zeke's knee and Zeke stroked him lost in thought. Then he smiled at Maggie. "Well, maybe she had some happiness for a while, but as Mama tells it, it wasn't a fairy tale ending."

"Go on."

"Granny Margaret and Old Conrad did live here in this very house for a bit. My mama grew up here too. Seems that my grandfather wasn't meant for the peaceful country life. Raising horses and tending the crops wasn't enough excitement for him and he upped and enlisted in the army and went to war. He never came back."

Maggie stared out the window at the horses and the green fields. Sad. A lump in her throat, she asked, "He died in the war then?"

Zeke shook his head. "I guess maybe he did, but Margaret never got an official notification from the army. No body or anything like that. He just never came back. Margaret tried to find out what had become of him. Went to Washington and all. Never found a trace. She and Mama took over the horses and the mansion and she died waiting for him to come home."

"Oh, no," Maggie said. "That's not fair."

"Life isn't fair, Maggie," Dwight murmured as he took her hand and rubbed his thumb over her fingers.

"She never married again?" Maggie asked.

"Not that I know of," Zeke said. "I'm guessing that since she wasn't an official widow woman, she would have thought it was wrong. I do recall a beau or two that she kept company with, but nothing official. My mama ran away, herself, when she was really young. Married my daddy before she was 17 years old. Had Willa just a mite later. Margaret was right miffed at Mama but when Mama and Daddy moved home and took up living in the old Booth place where Willa still lives, Margaret forgave her. Left her the mansion when she died. So I grew up here too."

"Poor Margaret," Maggie whispered.

Zeke laughed. "You have that wrong, Missy. Margaret was one feisty old woman. She might not have been lucky at love, but she sure enjoyed the heck out of her life. I'm not sure what would have happened if Conrad had come home after all. She might have met him at the end of the lane and had him at the wrong end of a shotgun. Or, on the other hand, she might have fallen into his arms and lived a long and happy life with him. Family legend has it that about once a year or more old Margaret went on what she called 'a lark'. Up and disappeared for days at a time. Then she came home and carried on as if she'd never been away. I guess some of the family wondered about her but we'll never know what she was up to, now will we?"

Zeke didn't have much to add so Dwight and Maggie finished their coffee and cookies, thanked him, and left. As they piled into the Bug and drove down the gravel driveway, they could see Zeke waving and Merlot standing beside him between the pillars on the rundown porch.

Neither of them said a word as Singing Winds faded into the distance. They passed a sign that read "Scenic Turnout" and Dwight did a U-turn and pulled in. Spread below them were rolling hills and the Drunken River twisting among them. They got out of the car and stood arm in arm gazing out over the magnificent view.

Finally, Maggie pivoted to face Dwight. "I've been thinking that maybe Margaret is still looking for her lost love. Still looking for Connor. Or Conrad. Maybe that's what she's been doing -- um -- haunting my house."

Dwight pulled her closer and rested his chin on the top of her head. "Ah, Maggie May. Always the romantic, aren't you?"

"Hmm. Not really. If you ask me, it's sad and terrible. The found love and then lost it."

Suddenly a vision of DJ crying in her arms in that hotel room long ago flashed into her mind. Her beautiful DJ. Her first love. Lost. Just like Connor. DJ abandoned her as much as Connor had Margaret, hadn't he?

Dwight traced the line of her face with his finger and bent to kiss the back of her neck. "Let's stop thinking about Margaret. Let's concentrate on us. What do you want to do with the rest of the day?"

She leaned back against his chest and let him wrap his arms around her. *Go away, DJ. You didn't want me then, so stop bugging me now. Poor Margaret. Maybe, though, she ended up with her own Dwight.* Maggie hoped so.

"I'd like to explore the village," Maggie said. "So many shops, so little time."

Dwight gave a short laugh. "Some things never change. When in doubt, let's go shopping."

CHAPTER
Twenty-Five

It was a gorgeous summer day and they spent the afternoon exploring the quaint village of Drunken Hills. They wandered along Main Street ducking into any shop that appealed to them. As they lunched on tuna sandwiches and chips at an outdoor bistro just off the main street, they people-watched and made up stories about the pedestrians passing by.

A large woman wearing an unfortunate outfit of tight flower print leggings and a voluminous T-shirt top scurried past. "That's Hilda," Dwight whispered. "She's hurrying to the No-Tell Motel for a secret sexual encounter with her lover, Herb."

Maggie giggled. As "Hilda" rounded the corner, a skinny guy with wispy hair wearing baggy Bermuda shorts, black sneakers and a Hawaiian print shirt came into view. "Oh, there's Herb now. He's late and he knows Hilda will kill him if she has to wait."

Dwight chewed on a bite of his sandwich as he surveyed the activity on the sidewalk. "What's her story?" He gestured with the sandwich at a frazzled-looking young woman pushing a stroller bearing identical twin infant girls and holding the hand of a toddler who strained to escape her grip.

Maggie closed her eyes and leaned back in her chair. "Hmm. Let me think. I've got it. She's obviously a foreign agent in the witness protection plan."

"Why do you say that?"

Maggie pointed at the woman's shoes. "Her shoes are a dead giveaway. What average American mother of three toddlers schleps around town in red stiletto sandals? She's not believable."

"Uh huh," Dwight said.

As the young woman and her charges struggled past their table, she paused to tie the sneaker of the intransigent toddler. When she noticed Dwight and Maggie watching her, she shrugged as if to say "caught me" and sighed. "Beautiful day, y'all." She patted the head of the toddler. "Isn't it, Sweetums?"

She pointed at the frozen yogurt stand down the block. "Y'all should try some of our newest treat." And she let her toddler drag her toward the stand.

"Or not," Dwight said. They both laughed.

Over Maggie's objections Dwight bought matching Drunken Hills T-shirts -- his charcoal grey, hers lime green -- at a tiny souvenir shop. "I want us to have something to remember this weekend," he said. "You can wear yours to bed." He leered at her. "Or not."

Maggie cursed herself under her breath. Oh, yeah. After she told him about her plans, he certainly wouldn't forget this weekend. She could only pray that he'd understand and not be too angry. Things were going so well. She pulled the lime T-shirt over her camisole and pirouetted to model it for him.

He gave her a provocative stare. "Babe."

The knot in Maggie's stomach expanded to the size of a third world nation. He would never understand. Never.

The maitre d' led them across the quaint dining room to what Maggie thought was the best spot in the house -- a heavy wooden table for two nestled next to the huge fieldstone fireplace. It was covered with a white linen tablecloth and set with heavy silver dinnerware. A vase of tiny red flowers rested in the center of the table. As a cozy fire crackled behind them they toasted each other with glasses of red wine.

"Very romantic," Dwight said as he swirled wine in his glass.

"Says Mr. Romance," Maggie teased with a smile.

"Hey, I'm romantic. Who was it who sprinkled your bed with rose petals?"

"Oh, was that you?" Maggie chuckled. "I thought it was part of the turn down service."

"Service with a smile." He grinned. "But I'm not through yet."

"I should hope not. What have you got up your sleeve now?"

"All in good time, my dear. Meanwhile, let's enjoy this delicious French wine."

The smug look on his face made Maggie suspicious but she was determined to keep the mood light and romantic. She knew she was going to have to spoil everything very soon. Dwight was leaving tomorrow to go back to Winslow and he expected her to follow. She couldn't postpone telling him any longer, but neither one of them seemed eager to discuss anything heavy so they slipped into the comfortable conversation of the long married.

Maggie picked at her dinner as she tried to find the best words to broach the subject. Dwight didn't seem to notice. He cleaned his plate and then ordered dessert and coffee for both of them. Finally, with dessert finished, Maggie cleared her throat. "Dwight, I -- um -- I have something I have to tell you."

Dwight gave no indication that he'd heard her. He was busy reaching into his jacket pocket. Too keyed up to listen, he pulled out a thick folder and dropped it on the table in front of her. Then he sat back and beamed at her.

"What is this?" Maggie asked.

Dwight's smile broadened. "I told you I had a surprise. Open it."

"First I should tell you something," she protested.

But Dwight wasn't about to be deterred. "Later, babe. Open it. I can't wait."

Maggie picked up the folder and turned it over in her hands. Embossed on one side was the insignia of the Winslow Travel Agency. A gold cord held the folder shut. Her breath caught in her throat as she slowly unwound the cord and removed the contents -- a printed itinerary and two replicas of airline tickets. To Paris.

"Oh, Dwight," she said. "Is this..."

His smile said it all. "It is. Two first class tickets to Paris. Look at this too." He spread a page in front of her -- reservations at the little hotel they'd honeymooned in.

Maggie gulped and tears formed in her eyes. He'd done all this. Turned himself into a romantic. Made reservations. All for her. Typical Dwight, of course. He fully expected her to be overcome with delight. When -- she was going to break his heart.

He stared at her. His hopeful expression made her want to cry. "Say something, Maggie. Are you surprised?"

"Surprised? Of course, I am. Shocked even. But Dwight ...."

His face was registering doubt now as she continued to look at the papers in the folder as if they might explode in her face. "Maggie?"

Maggie took a deep breath. "Dwight. Honey. I can't."

He looked confused. "You can't? Can't what? Can't believe how awesome a surprise this is?" His lips tightened. "Or something else?"

Maggie reached for his hand but he jerked it away and picked up his coffee cup. He settled back in his chair and glowered at her. So, that's how this was going to go. She knew it.

"I'm so sorry. It's a wonderful surprise -- a trip we've talked about for years. You are so sweet to do all this, but ..." She hesitated at his grim expression and then rushed on. "I enrolled at Sweet River University for next term beginning in September. I signed a lease on the yellow bungalow."

Relief washed over his face. "Oh, well then. I thought this might come up and I have the solution."

He again stuck his hand into his jacket pocket and this time he pulled out a folded booklet that he opened and spread in front of her. What had he done now? She hesitated -- her stomach churning -- before she picked up the booklet and saw that it was a listing of fall classes at Winslow College, the small local college near their Ohio home. She thumbed through it as Dwight watched. Finally, she looked up and met his eyes. "Sweetie, this is great, but Winslow doesn't have the program I want and Sweet River does. You know I never finished my degree when we got married and I've always regretted it. Over the years I decided that I wanted -- no, needed -- to go back and get my degree in Creative Writing."

Never one to give up when he wanted something Dwight insisted, "Winslow has that. I checked."

Maggie sighed. "I know. But Sweet River has a combined writing and history degree that I got accepted into. I'm so excited. Especially with all of this Margaret stuff. I can't wait to learn more of the history of the south and ..." She broke off at the look on his face.

"Let me get this straight. You'd give up a romantic trip to Paris with your husband to stay in a boring little town and go to a one horse college?" His words were harsh.

"Couldn't we do it some other time?" Maggie hated the pleading note in her voice. "You know how much I've wanted to go back to school and this is perfect."

He glared at her. "You could have asked me before you went and did all this."

Ah, so that was the problem. Again typical Dwight. She should have asked his permission?

Now Maggie was angry. She slammed her cup on the table and glared back at him. "Asked? Asked? I should have asked? I wasn't aware that I needed your permission. Besides what would you have said anyway?"

Dwight scooped up the travel folder and the college catalog and crammed them in his pocket. He tossed the gold cord into his empty coffee cup -- his face a storm cloud.

Maggie tried one last time at offering an olive branch. "Please, honey. Try to see it my way. I'm excited about this. Can't you be happy for me?"

Obviously not. He signaled the waiter to bring their check and signed it with their room number before Maggie had a chance to say another word. He shoved back his chair and stood up. "I guess we don't have anything more to say," he said and started to walk away. He stopped and turned back. "Coming?"

Maggie followed him across the room, her cheeks flushed with anger and her heart racing. She had rejected his gift and, therefore him. He was crushed. But he'd get over it in time. Wouldn't he?

It didn't appear that he would get over it any time soon. As soon as they were back in their room he pulled out his bag and began tossing his clothes into it. When he started for the bathroom to get his shaving kit, Maggie put a hand on his sleeve to stop him. "Please, be reasonable. We need to talk about this."

He snatched his arm out of her grip and disappeared into the bathroom. He returned with his toiletries in his hand and shoved them into the open bag. "Talk? Don't you think it's a little late for that?"

"You can't leave this way," Maggie pleaded with him. "It's late. At least stay until morning. Don't be stubborn."

He gave her a helpless look and relented. "Okay, I'll stay until morning but I don't know what we have to say to each other at this point."

"Thank you," Maggie murmured. "We can figure this out."

He sank onto the bed, his head in his hands. Finally he looked up at her. The look on his face broke her heart. "I tried, Maggie. I really tried."

They talked all night but it was useless. Maggie couldn't convince him that she needed to take this opportunity. That it would be better for both of them and their marriage for her to do it. That she needed to reach out for her dreams. In her head, Maggie heard Margaret encouraging her to go for her dreams. Why couldn't Dwight do the same? His feelings were hurt. Yes. But it had been such a wonderful weekend. Couldn't he forgive her a little bit? Think about putting her first for once? Apparently not.

After a sleepless night Maggie finally drifted off just as the sun was rising. She woke when she heard the door creak open and she saw Dwight hauling his suitcase into the hall. He tiptoed over to the side of the bed and stood looking down at her while she pretended to be asleep. Then he bent and kissed her cheek and she opened her eyes. His voice sad and heavy, he said to her, "I'm going now. We need some time apart to think about all this. I'll be in touch."

Maggie caught his sleeve. "Don't go this way. It isn't fair. There's more to talk about."

Dwight sighed. "Life isn't fair, Maggie May. And frankly, I don't give a damn."

He slipped out the door letting it close behind him with a soft thump. Maggie burst into tears. Who knew following her dreams would be this hard?

Maggie's Journal

Once upon a time I went off to college because it was the thing to do. And everything was more important to me than school. DJ especially. I put DJ first and I lost him. Now I'm going back to college because I really want to. And nothing is more important to me. Even Dwight, I guess. So I'm putting school first and I'm losing my husband. I can't win. He just won't hear me.

CHAPTER
Twenty-Six

A couple of hours later Maggie jammed the last of her stuff in the Bug and said a bittersweet goodbye to the Drunken Hills Inn. She'd cried until she couldn't cry anymore. It felt the same as when she lost DJ. Her tears tasted of salt and remorse. What could she have done differently? He'd tried. He had. She'd give him that. But still the same old thing drove them apart. This time, by God, she wasn't giving in. She drank a gallon of coffee and then packed. Before she left she called Sarah and arranged to stay overnight with her before she went back to Sweet River and her new life. Alone.

Sarah greeted her at the door with a hug and a margarita. "Come on in, Maggie. You look like you need this." She pressed the margarita into Maggie's hand and led her to a soft upholstered chair in the tiny living room.

Maggie gulped the frozen cure all and gazed around her. "Cute place, Sarah. But something's missing."

Sarah grinned. "Ah, yes. The bebe. I took Annabelle to my mom's after you called this morning. I figured we needed some serious girl time and adorable as my angel is, she does interfere with girl time."

Maggie set her glass on the table next to her. "I needed that. I'm worn out."

Sarah sat on the couch opposite Maggie's chair with her feet tucked underneath her. "Tell me all about it. What can I do to help?"

Maggie smiled woefully. "You're helping just by being here. Oh, and by giving me this." She took a swallow of her margarita and sighed.

"I've got all day. And all night. Mom's keeping the baby until tomorrow morning."

A tear leaked out of Maggie's eye and slid down her cheek. "I'm an idiot. First I killed him off. Then I had the sexiest weekend imaginable and ended it by killing him off again -- this time with words. Everything was going so well and then, bam, I ruined it."

"Tell me."

So Maggie poured out everything -- well, almost everything -- that had happened over the magical weekend. She even told Sarah about what she and Dwight found out about her ghost, Margaret, and her lover, Connor. Maggie finished her second -- or was it third? -- margarita and concluded, "That's enough about me and the mess I made. I've wallowed long enough. What's new with you?"

Sarah blushed. "Um, well, um, I met this guy."

Maggie shrieked and bounced out of her chair. She plopped on the couch next to Sarah and hugged her. "That's totally the best news I've heard in a long time. Tell me about him."

Sarah giggled and launched into a description of her Mr. Wonderful. Maggie listened to Sarah with part of her attention while the rest was preoccupied with wondering about Dwight. And Margaret.

Maggie had called Big Sugar's daughter, Nancy Beth, from the car and arranged to meet her later. Now she and Sarah were approaching the coffee shop near the college campus where they were supposed find Nancy Beth. As they entered the shop they scanned their surroundings looking for a girl in her late teens or early twenties who might be Nancy Beth. Sitting alone by the window was a petite darkhaired girl with her head bent over her laptop. Could this tiny waif be Big Sugar's daughter? Maggie edged over to the table and cleared her throat. The girl looked up and smiled. "You must be Maggie."

"Nancy Beth?"

The girl smiled. "I know. My dad is a giant. And I'm not. Go figure."

"I'm Maggie Murphy and this is my friend, Sarah."

"Please sit down. I'll get us some coffee and we can talk. I love to talk about the lady. She saved my life."

Over coffee Maggie got to know Nancy Beth well enough to believe that she wasn't making up her story about Margaret and the fall into the well. Nancy Beth appeared levelheaded and self-confident. Surely not one to conjure up a ghost -- even a friendly one.

"Your dad told me Margaret saved your life. He believes it. And after talking to you, I do too."

"I thought of her as my guardian angel. I really miss her."

"I know I sound like an investigative reporter," Maggie said, "but when was the last time you saw Margaret -- your lady?"

Nancy Beth shoved her dark hair behind her ears and leaned forward with her elbows on the table. "It was right before I left for school. I had a huge fight with my boyfriend over my leaving. He thought I should stay in Sweet River and go to college there with him, but I had my heart set on coming here to Charleston. I was so upset after Donnie went home that I took Frizzles and went for a walk. Frizzles always heads right for the yellow bungalow if you let him lead."

Maggie nodded and waited for Nancy Beth to continue.

"Anyway, we went to the yellow cottage and Frizzles ran into the backyard. I chased him and that's when I saw her."

"Where was she?"

"She was in that old porch swing. Just swinging. She was wearing the same dress. The white one with the puffy sleeves. So, I sat down next to her."

Maggie didn't say a word.

"I know it's hard to believe, but it's true," Nancy Beth said. "Swinging with a ghost is fairly unbelievable."

"I believe you," Maggie said. "So what happened next?"

"We just sat there for a while and then she kind of got up and drifted toward the edge of the yard. She turned around and I could see the tree branches through her skirt."

Maggie shivered. "And then?"

"Call me nuts, but she talked to me. She said, 'Follow your dreams, Nancy Beth. Follow your dreams.'"

Maggie gasped. "She said that to me too. Exactly. Wow."

They talked a bit longer before Nancy Beth excused herself to go back to her dorm to study. "It was great to meet you, Maggie. I'd love to hear whatever you find out about your Margaret. I know she's real." She shrugged. "Or at least as real as a ghost can be."

"We Southerners believe in all this ghost stuff," Sarah interjected. "It's programmed into our genes."

"Then I must have some Southern ancestors because I'm totally a believer," Maggie said. She turned to Nancy Beth. "I promise I'll call you if I learn anything new."

During the long drive back to Sweet River the next morning Maggie's thoughts were tangled -- worries about Dwight, fears about going back to school, curiosity about Margaret all raced through her mind. It was a far less peaceful drive than the one to Drunken Hills had been just a few days before. By the time she pulled up in front of her yellow bungalow and unloaded the car, she was more than ready for a nap. She unlocked the door and shoved it open and stopped. Someone had been in her place. She could feel it. The air seemed disturbed in some way. Maggie dropped her bags on the floor and walked through the living room to the kitchen. She climbed the spiral staircase to the loft and even peered under the bed. Nothing was obviously out of place and nothing was missing. But Maggie felt it. Someone had intruded here.

She kicked off her sandals and barefooted went into the kitchen and turned on the burner under the teakettle. A hot cup of tea might chase away a serious case of heebie jeebies. Sure enough, in the time it took to make the tea and take the steaming cup into the living room, Maggie convinced herself that she was imagining things. Margaret was here is all, she told herself. I'm nuts. Yet there was something indefinable. The aura wasn't the comforting one that Margaret provided. This was different. More threatening.

"I'm a crazy person," Maggie said aloud. "Oh, god, now I'm talking to myself. I have to get out of here."

She set the tea cup on the coffee table, stuffed her feet into her sandals, grabbed her purse and bolted out the door toward Gladdie's B&B. If anyone could talk her out of this insanity it would be Gladdie.

She banged on Gladdie's front door and her friend opened it. When she saw Maggie standing on the step, she yanked her inside and hugged her. "Maggie, you're home. I'm so glad to see you. Tell me all about the weekend. Was it great?" She stepped away from her and gave her friend a suspicious look. "What? Something isn't right. Spill."

"I don't know," Maggie moaned. "It was great at first. Then it wasn't. And then I got home and someone has been inside. I think."

Gladdie reached for the phone. "I'm calling the police."

Maggie gently took the phone out of her hand. "No. Not yet. Nothing is missing or damaged. And I don't think my intruder was human. Or not a living human. You know?"

"Are you sure we shouldn't call the police? You could be in danger."

Maggie shook her head. "No. I don't think so. Besides the Sweet River police aren't ghostbusters, are they?"

Gladdie gave a short laugh. "Excellent point."

The smell of apple pie hung in the air and Maggie sniffed. "Pie?"

Gladdie dashed for the kitchen. "Oh, no. I forgot. I hope I haven't burned up dessert."

Maggie followed and sat at the kitchen table while Gladdie rescued the pies and set them on the counter to cool. "I told Dwight about enrolling at Sweet River U," she confided to her friend. "He's furious."

"What are you going to do?"

"I thought about giving it up and going back to Winslow with Dwight. He was so sweet and funny and romantic all weekend. He even tried to help me find out about Margaret and Connor. It was better than it's ever been between us. I kind of hoped he'd understand about my degree, but I was wrong. Really wrong. When he went all bossy and, um, Dwight on me, I got mad and dug in my heels and here I am. Alone." She started to cry again. She hadn't known she could cry this much.

Gladdie wiped her hands on her apron and handed Maggie a tissue. "He'll come around in time."

Maggie blew her nose. "I'm not so sure. This might be the end. I know I ran away but I guess I always thought I could go back whenever I felt like it. Now I'm not sure he'd have me. He said," she blubbered, "that he didn't give a damn."

Gladdie patted Maggie's shoulder. "I have the solution. After I feed my guests, we'll go out and get a few drinks and you'll feel better."

"Alcohol might not be the answer," Maggie agreed, "but it's worth a try. I'll go home and shower and change and meet you at *The Book Store* in an hour." She paused. "I'm sure the unfriendly ghost has gone back to his ghostly pursuits."

Gladdie shook her head. " I notice you're saying this ghost is male. I'm not sure I like this at all."

"Don't worry, I'll be fine. Are you meeting me or not?"

"I'll be there."

After more than a few drinks with Gladdie, Maggie wobbled home. Her good mood wasn't restored one hundred per cent, but her determination was. Dwight couldn't dictate how she lived her life and she

wasn't going to give up Sweet River and school and her yellow bungalow just because he wanted her to. She stabbed the key in the general
direction of the lock a few times before she managed to get it in and
turn it. The door swung open and as she stepped over the threshold,
Maggie was greeted with a blast of chilly air. She shivered and then realization worked its way through her alcohol muddled brain. Someone
was inside. She hesitated and then drew in a huge breath and walked
into her living room. Silence. The chill permeated the room, though,
and suddenly Maggie was sober. "Who's there?" she called into the
darkness.

Of course, there was no answer. The room was empty. I'm drunk,
Maggie scolded herself. And insane. She stumbled into the bathroom,
brushed her teeth and pulled her lime green Drunken Hills T-shirt
over her head. Then she tiptoed to the staircase and dragged herself
up to the loft and fell into bed. She closed her eyes and the room
whirled around her and she dropped off a cliff into darkness. She
didn't know how long she'd been asleep when she heard the telltale
creak of the rocking chair in the living room below. She rolled to the
edge of the bed and tried to see into the darkness. She couldn't make
out a thing so she crawled out of bed and peered over the edge of the
sleeping platform expecting to see Margaret. But it wasn't the warm
presence of Margaret that stared up at her. No. It was a man. Tall,
dressed in clothes of the early 20th century, he stalked about the
room looking at the shelves and picking up books and replacing them.
A damp cold enveloped the room and Maggie felt goose bumps prickle
her arms. As she stared at him, the ghostly figure turned and looked
right at her. She took an involuntary step backwards but couldn't bring
herself to look away. While she stood frozen to the floor, the ghostly
figure raised one hand in a salute and turned his back and sauntered
through her front wall leaving Maggie staring into the empty room
with her heart racing.

She whirled around and fell into her bed and pulled the covers
over her head. Was that even possible? Was it who she thought -- and
feared -- it was? Connor? Come back for Margaret after all this time?
Or Daniel? Returning to the scene of his crime? I need to call Dwight
to tell him. Then she realized that she couldn't call him. He didn't give
a damn. Maggie burrowed under her covers and stayed there until she
finally drifted off into a nightmare in which Dwight and Connor and

Daniel were threatening to take away her cottage. They glared at each other with cold, treacherous eyes.

When she woke up sunlight streamed through the high windows and the smell of coffee wafted in the air. Maggie rolled over onto her back and took stock. Head throbbing. Stomach feeling yucky. Wearing her Drunken Hills T-shirt that made her think of Dwight. Wait a second. Dwight. She'd dreamed about him. Now she remembered. She'd had a nightmare about Dwight and Connor. What else was there? Oh, God. The ghost. Connor's ghost stalking through her living room and scaring her half to death. Or was it Daniel? What she wouldn't give for Margaret right now. And speaking of Margaret, she heard noises in the kitchen below. Had Margaret returned? Maggie sniffed. Coffee. Margaret was in the kitchen making coffee? Oh, no. She really was seriously insane. Even in her muddled state she knew that ghosts do not make coffee. She scrambled out of bed and tugging her T-shirt down, she edged down the spiral staircase careful not to lose her balance and tumble to her death. Although the way her head felt that might not be the worst option.

"Oh, there you are," Gladdie trilled as she popped out of the kitchen.

Maggie jumped. "What on earth are you doing here? You scared me to death?"

Gladdie handed her a cup of coffee and a hot sweet roll dripping with butter. Maggie's stomach rolled at the sight of the food, but she was more than grateful for the hot coffee.

"After last night," Gladdie said, "I figured you might need some coffee first thing. I used my key."

Moaning, Maggie drooped onto the couch. "I guess I had a few too many, huh?"

Gladdie's smile was wise. "I'd say that was the truth. Last I saw you, you were mumbling about Dwight and someone called DJ and Connor or Conrad, you used both names. And how you messed up your life over and over."

"Oh, no. I'm sorry. I'm a jerk. Thanks for being there. I needed that, I guess."

Gladdie winked. "No problem, but I would like details when you aren't under the influence of a great deal of booze. Sounds like a great story."

Maggie slugged coffee. "That explains the nightmare at least. The thing is when I got home, I really thought I saw a ghost. Not Margaret, though, but a man. And he saluted me. It was creepy."

"You were, dare we say, buzzed. That's all."

"I suppose." But Maggie wasn't convinced. That cold air and that salute were real. She knew it. Even if no one else believed her. Dwight would have loved to hear about all of this if she hadn't driven him away. Oh, crap.

CHAPTER
Twenty-Seven

Maggie easily fell back into her Sweet River routine. She worked four days a week with Jewel at Jewelicious and spent the other days reading and researching at the library and the historical society. Most nights she curled up on her couch and read books she'd always meant to read or watched mindless television on the new set she'd finally relented and bought. Occasionally, she'd entertain her friends at home or go out with them to different local spots. It was a peaceful life, she guessed, marking time to the beginning of the fall semester at Sweet River U.

She spoke to Dwight maybe once a week if she was lucky. When she called him, it usually went to voicemail and she pictured him drinking a beer and pointedly ignoring the call from his rebellious wife. When she was in a more melancholy mood, she even pictured him with some hot little chick and not even hearing the annoying ring of his cell phone.

Dwight did call from time to time, but the calls were short and perfunctory, usually concerning some problem with one of the kids or one of their parents. She couldn't confide in him, as she had before, about Margaret and Connor and the visions -- or hallucinations -- she had. He wouldn't have been interested and she didn't want to hear that scornful tone in his voice so she just didn't tell him.

She tried to entertain him with anecdotes about Chloe and April that she learned in her weekly conversation with Molly. But Dwight didn't seem to care about the girls either. *What did he care about? Getting his own way, that's what.*

It was pretty much the same with James and Julie. When she talked to them on the phone they were happy to share some of what was going on in their lives. The censored version, of course. Parents don't need to know everything. But both kids were determined to solve the mystery of their parents' marriage.

"What's up with you and Dad?" James asked. "He won't tell us a thing."

"When are you going back to Ohio?" Julie demanded. "The house seems funny without you there."

And so it went.

The summer rolled on. Maggie was alternately sad and content, depending on the day. She was counting the days until the semester began at the university when Gladdie called.

"Hey, Maggie," Gladdie said, "Chad and I are going out to the fair tonight. We wondered if you'd like to go with us."

"The fair?" Maggie had been reading about the county fair for weeks now and she had to admit it sounded like the prescription to cure her blues.

"Yep," Gladdie said. "The Sweet River August Fair. It's a tradition around here."

"Well, let me check my calendar and see if I'm free," Maggie said. "Oh, good, as it happens I do seem to have a vacancy."

"Great," Gladdie said. "We'll be by to pick you up around six-thirty. Okay?"

"Perfect. I'll be home from work by then."

"Oh, maybe I should mention," Gladdie said, "that Mac is coming along with us too."

"Gladdie." Maggie's voice rose an octave in warning. "I'm not going on a date. I'm married in case you have forgotten."

"I haven't forgotten," Gladdie said, "but it seems that perhaps your husband might have. When did you last hear from him?"

Maggie sank onto the floor, phone in hand. "You had to remind me." She conducted a brief inner debate that concluded when she pictured Mac -- hot and sexy and smart. Damn Dwight anyway. He made it hard to resist. "Oh, okay. But it's definitely not a date. Got it?"

"Sure, Maggie, anything you say. See you later." And Gladdie hung up.

Maggie spent an inordinate amount of time figuring out what to wear on her "definitely not a date." With the picture of Dwight's hypothetical hot blonde chick lodged in her mind, Maggie took out and rejected most of her wardrobe. Finally, she chose a pair of jeans that Dwight thought made her butt look good and a camisole top that was appropriate for the warm weather and still covered her -- um -- assets. With cute sandals, she had an outfit that worked. Now to figure out why she cared.

At six-thirty Maggie was waiting on her front porch when Chad's pickup pulled up in front. She checked out her image in the window of the house before she hurried out to climb into the backseat of the truck next to Mac. "Hi." Her voice came out a high-pitched squeak. *Oh, brilliant. Sound like a dummy much?*

Mac grinned at her and gave her a hand to haul her into the seat. "Glad you decided to come. The fair is always fun. Even if we senior citizens are a little long in tooth for the rides."

Gladdie leaned over the backseat. "Speak for yourself, Mac. I happen to love the rides. Bring them on."

Maggie shuddered. "Not for me, thanks. I'd much rather tour the livestock barns."

Mac burst out laughing. "A girl after my own heart."

Maggie enjoyed the fair in spite of herself. Mac and Chad were easygoing and fun to be with. Gladdie was so head over heels for Chad that she was giddy. It was a happy group that explored the fair.

They rode the rides, ate popcorn, checked out the 4H barns, tried out a greasy elephant ear and pigged out on pizza and beer at the Road Warriors Tent. Finally, they ended the evening at a rollicking country music concert. Cowboy-booted ranchers stomped along with mini-skirted teens and older couples as the denim-clad musicians twanged their guitars and the piano player's fingers flew over the keys. Maggie hooted and hollered along with the rest of the crowd.

As they walked toward Chad's truck at the end of the evening, Mac looped his arm around Maggie and pulled her closer. She stiffened at first but then relaxed. What the heck? A man showed some interest in her and why should she resist? Where was Dwight after all? Or, for that matter, stupid DJ? Both gone and forgotten.

Mac helped her into the back of the truck and tucked her under his arm. She could smell his cologne and the beer on his breath. When he kissed her, she responded without a single thought. He deepened the kiss and she clung to his shirt as the world spun. Then she sat up straight. "I'm married," she announced.

"Oh, for God's sake, get over it," Gladdie said from the front seat. "You're no more married than I am."

Maggie started to protest but thought better of it. Gladdie was right. When had she heard from Dwight? She couldn't remember. It wasn't like she was going to hop into bed with Mac, was it? He was a sweet guy who happened to find her attractive. Go with it.

Unfortunately, Maggie's words had struck a target with Mac. He eased away from her and fixed her with a laser gaze. "Let me know when you're ready, Maggie. Just don't take too long."

As Maggie got ready for bed that night she replayed Mac's words over and over. He was cute and sweet and available. What was she waiting for? Dwight? Divorce papers? Okay, she would have to have it out with him and soon. This limbo had gone on too long and cute guys like Mac wouldn't wait forever.

Somehow, though, Maggie could never quite dredge up the courage to confront Dwight. She knew she was a coward, but after all the years of marriage she wasn't quite ready to walk away. Well, correct that, to be fair she had already run away and now she wasn't sure why. For a stupid degree. Or was it something else? Maybe Dwight was just letting her stew by herself. Maybe. More likely, he'd had enough and was already hiring a lawyer and preparing to ask her for a divorce.

The summer staggered to a hot and sweaty close without Maggie having made a decision one way or another. The first day of the semester at Sweet River U loomed close and she was attacked by the same jitters she suffered when she was a coed off to her freshman year of college. The very year, it occurred to her with a jolt, that she met and fell in love with DJ. God, that was so long ago. A lifetime ago. Several lifetimes.

CHAPTER
Twenty-Eight

With each passing day Maggie lived in the little yellow bungalow she grew more uncomfortable with the lie she was living. Each time someone greeted the poor young "widow" with special kindness and solicitude she was swamped with guilt. She didn't believe she deserved the sympathy and concern directed her way. Scorn and condemnation for abandoning her husband would be much more appropriate.

If it hadn't been for Maribelle Mitchell, Maggie might have left Dwight resting in peace much longer than she did. It happened one beautiful Saturday morning. Maggie and her friends, Gladdie, Jewel, and Azalea took an early Jazzercise class each Saturday at the Sweet River Community Center and gathered afterwards for coffee at Agnes' Café. The sky was a brilliant cloudless blue and the temperature hovered just below a comfortable 80 so they took their mugs outside to sit at one of Agnes' marble-topped sidewalk tables. From their vantage point they could see everything that was happening on the village green. Friends and acquaintances stopped to talk before they continued on their way.

Mirabelle Mitchell, owner of the upscale Mirabelle's Restaurant, a fellow Jazzerciser and a volunteer at the Sweet River Playhouse, stopped at their table to invite them to the latest production at the Playhouse.

"What play are you doing?" Jewel asked. "And who's got the lead? Anyone I know?"

"Probably," Mirabelle said. "The play we're doing is a new one for us. Called Black Widow. Honey Barber is the lead -- you know her, don't you? -- but honest to goodness, she knows absolutely nothing about playing a widow. For Pete's sake, any one of us could do a better job, I'm telling you."

Silence dropped like a dark cloud over the table. Jewel, Azalea and Gladdie feigned a fascination with the contents of their coffee mugs while Maggie just squirmed in her seat. Mirabelle looked at them and gasped. "Oh, God. Oh, Maggie. I didn't mean. I'm so sorry. I just. I don't."

Mirabelle glanced at her watch. "Oh, look at the time. I have to go." She jumped up and raced away before any of the others had a chance to speak.

Azalea tugged on the hem of her hot pink sweatshirt. "Awkward much. That Mirabelle puts her foot in her mouth as often as she serves Lobster Thermidor, the specialty at her restaurant." Azalea patted Maggie's hand. "Are you okay?"

Maggie gulped. "Of course. I know she didn't mean anything by it, but I must say I feel awful when people are so nice to me."

"Why on earth?" Jewel asked. "People are being kind."

"Yeah, Maggie," Gladdie said with a knowing smile. "Why on earth would you be upset?"

Maggie frowned at Gladdie. "I guess it's time for the big confession, huh?"

Gladdie nodded. "Way past time if you ask me."

"I didn't ask you, Gladdie."

They're going to hate me, Maggie thought. I've lied to them all this time. They'll never forgive me.

"What are the two of you talking about?" Jewel asked.

"Yeah, is one of y'all going to clue us in?" Azalea asked.

Maggie placed the coffee mug she was clutching on the table and, without looking at anyone, said, "Here's the thing. I'm not actually a widow."

There, she'd done it. Brought Dwight back from the dead.

"What do you mean?" Azalea asked -- her dark eyes wide and curious.

"I'm a bad person. I invented the whole widow thing. It all started at the *Get Your Groove On Conference* and ...." Maggie went on to tell her friends the whole sad story of how she had murdered Dwight again and again and again.

No one spoke for a few seconds after Maggie concluded her confession. Then Jewel looked Maggie in the eye. "For heavens sake, girl, why did you wait so long to tell us?"

"I was embarrassed I guess. Who makes up a story like that? I was ashamed of myself."

"Oh, Good Lord, girl," Azalea said. "You don't have a single thing to be embarrassed about. So he left you did he? For someone younger?"

"Oh, 'Zalea. No. He didn't run off with some hot chick. *I* was the one who ran away. From a perfectly good husband and a perfectly good life in a perfectly nice town. And then I killed him."

"It's not like you shot him or something. You did give him a hero's death," Gladdie said. "At least there's that."

Maggie smiled a sad smile. "Shut up, Gladdie."

Azalea drained her mug and stood up. "Well, y'all, I'm going for more coffee and when I come back we're going to talk about something way more interesting than Dwight's return from the other side." And she marched inside.

Jewel nodded. "We love you, Maggie. Widow or not. It's your story to tell and we'll keep it that way. No one will hear a word about it from us. Not until you are good and ready. " And, mug in hand, she followed Azalea inside.

Gladdie grinned. "Now that wasn't so bad, was it?"

"Oh, no," Maggie said. "Piece of cake. Nothing makes a girl prouder than telling her friends she's been lying to them for months." She peered into her empty mug. "Do you think Agnes would have a shot of Kahlua to put in my coffee?"

"Don't be silly." Gladdie grinned again. "Of course she does. But it will be fine. Your secret is safe with us."

And it was. For a while.

Maggie could have let her friends leak her secret to the population of Sweet River, but she thought it would be better to admit to it herself. But how?

The longer it went the more awkward it became. She was about at the point of marching into Agnes' Café one morning and making an announcement to all the gathered patrons. She was confident the news would spread rapidly in a town as small as Sweet River. Fortunately, or unfortunately, the matter was taken out of Maggie's hands and she was outed by – of course -- Verdie Cranford.

"That Verdie Cranford is a force of nature." "If you want to know what's going on in Sweet River, ask Verdie." "There isn't any gossip that Verdie hasn't heard. Or started." The citizens of Sweet River recognized power when they saw it. And Verdie had power.

Verdie was the Post Mistress of the Sweet River Post Office and had been since mail was delivered on horseback. Or so went the local legend. And while it was probably an exaggeration, Verdie had ruled over the Sweet River PO for so long that no one could remember a time when she hadn't. Verdie and her husband, Frank, were childless. A long and painful story was behind that fact. One that only a few folks knew. But if Verdie couldn't have children of her own she could turn her considerable maternal instincts loose on the population of Sweet River. She adopted each of them as her own special child and looked out for them whether they needed (or wanted) her to or not.

Verdie thrived on gossip. She lived for it. And for passing it along. Which is why, when she thought about it later, Maggie should not have been surprised that it was finally to Verdie that she revealed her guilty secret.

When she encountered Verdie Cranford at Agnes' Cafe on her very first afternoon in Sweet River, Maggie remembered that Agnes told her — or was that a warning? — that Verdie knew everything about everyone in town. And that she loved to share her knowledge. She hadn't known then, though, that she would become grist for Verdie's rumor mill.

Maggie arrived home one afternoon to find her mail carrier, Verdie's husband, Frank, had stuck an "Unable to Deliver Package" notice in her mailbox. The notice informed Maggie that she had to sign for a package. Since she wasn't expecting anything -- she had been consciously avoiding online shopping -- Maggie was a little confused until she remembered that she had asked Dwight to send her some of her treasured classic books. Rather than go out and buy new ones for her novel course at Sweet River University she pleaded with Dwight to send them to her. Feeling the way he did about her attending SRU, it took a bit of cajoling before he agreed with an epic lack of enthusiasm. This package must be the books. But why would Dwight have decided that she needed to sign for them? A bunch of old books certainly could have been left on her doorstep, but she chalked it up to Dwight's engineering mentality and set out for the Sweet River P.O to claim her box.

It was a brilliant late summer morning and everyone, it seemed, was outdoors enjoying the last of the warm days. Maggie waved at her neighbors as she steered the Bug through the quiet streets. At the Post Office she found Verdie Cranford waiting on Sukie Hamilton. The pair were engaged in a spirited discussion and hardly noticed Maggie as she lingered in the back of the lobby pretending to be mesmerized by the display of stamps.

Finally Verdie and Sukie concluded their business and Sukie brushed by Maggie on her way out the door. She gave Maggie an airy wave of her hand. "Nice to see you, Maggie. Beautiful weather."

Without waiting for a response Sukie floated out the door leaving a cloud of lilac scented perfume in her wake. Bemused, Maggie shook her head and edged toward Verdie.

Verdie grinned at her. "That Sukie is a piece of work. The old biddie insists that she deserves a large post office box for the cost of the small one. Claims she keeps me in business." Verdie ran a hand through her short, grey curls dislodging the glasses she had tucked there. "Oh, my."

Then she focused on Maggie. "So what can I do for you today, Miss Maggie?"

Maggie dug in her bag and pulled out the notice. "Package came that I needed to sign for." She wrinkled her nose. "Can't imagine what it could be."

Verdie took the notice from Maggie and disappeared into the back of the post office. "I'll be right back."

She returned carrying a large box. She put it down on the counter and put on her glasses to read the label pasted to the front. "Yes, the sender did request a signature," she said. She bent closer and squinted. "That would be a certain Dwight Murphy. Sent from Winslow, Ohio. I believe that's where you come from."

Maggie gulped and felt her cheeks grow hot. "Oh, yes. I, er, will sign whatever you need." And get the heck out away from Verdie's avid scrutiny.

Verdie gave Maggie an inquisitive look. "Dwight Murphy? Any relation? Your son? Your father?"

Maggie swallowed. The jig was up. She could stammer out some answer. She could lie to Verdie and say it was from her son. Or she could woman up. And stop the prevarication and the pretending. Good old Dwight was risen from the dead. Hallelujah.

"No, not exactly, Dwight Murphy is my husband."

Verdie's eyebrows shot up. "Your dead husband?"

Maggie wanted to grab her package and bolt out the door, but she'd begun this confession and she was darned well going to get it all out there. "He isn't dead. And I'm not a widow." There she'd done it.

Verdie was looking at her with something akin to glee. "I knew it," she said. "I just knew it."

Maggie picked at the tape on the edge of the package refusing to meet Verdie's eyes. Then she sucked in a breath and blurted, "I know. I'm sorry. I didn't mean to lie to everyone. It just kind of happened. I met Mary Lou at the *Get Your Groove On Conference* and the women thought I was a widow and I -- um -- let them. It didn't seem like that big a deal at the time. Then when I moved here I liked the idea of starting fresh so much that I just let sleeping husbands die. Or stay dead, I guess." Maggie sighed. "I really am sorry."

Verdie patted her hand and started to laugh. "It's okay, dearie. I'm sure that a lot of us have lied about something at one time or another."

Maggie let out the breath she had been holding. "Thank you, Verdie, but this was a big lie. Dwight is in perfect health -- although he's really upset with me. I didn't feel up to big explanations is all."

"Don't you worry your pretty little head about it, Miss Maggie. Take your package and head on home. The world will not come to end whether or not your hubby is dead. Or miraculously alive." Verdie guffawed.

A few minutes later, Maggie left both Verdie and the burden of her guilty conscience behind at the post office. As the door closed behind her, she realized that she wouldn't need to plan a confession. Verdie would take care of that for her.

When Maggie got home she tore open the package anticipating nothing more than a stack of worn paperbacks. Her breath caught in her throat as she ripped off the last piece of wrapping and opened the box. Sitting on top of her books was a brand new iPad decorated with a single red bow. No note. Nothing. Maggie carefully removed the iPad and stared at it. What was Dwight thinking? Had he relented at least a tiny bit from his stand against Sweet River? A new iPad? To help her with school? Was this a peace offering? Maggie was almost afraid to believe that he'd changed his mind and joined Team Maggie, but she allowed herself to hope.

She picked up her phone and punched in Dwight's number. She wanted to thank him for the gift. And, just hear his voice. But her hopes were dashed when he didn't answer and voicemail picked up instead. She left a message. "Thanks for the iPad. I love it. Call me."

But, of course, he didn't.

For the next few days every place that Maggie went, conversation would stop. She figured that Verdie had spread the word and was relieved. Uncomfortable silences were a small price to pay for deceiving the good and kind people of Sweet River. She could suck it up if she had to. So, she smiled a tiny smile and admitted her perfidy to those bold enough to question her. She was the center of Sweet River gossip until Pastor Kitchens out-of-control youngest daughter, Sindy, dropped out of school and roared off on the back of a black Harley with none other than bad boy Chance Lavendar. Maggie was left behind as the wheels of gossip churned elsewhere.

Whew.

CHAPTER
Twenty-Nine

Her first class was History of the Civil War South. The professor was Steven Marlow -- by reputation one of the better profs at Sweet River. Maggie was eager to take his class. She walked into the assigned classroom dressed in jeans and a T-shirt and looking like any other coed, except two decades or so older. She found a seat near the front and pulled out her brand new notebook and a fresh pen. Ready to dive in, she settled back to observe the other students file into the room.

The professor was at the front of the room, his back to the class. He scrawled something on the board and then turned to face the class. Maggie gulped and flushed, she knew, bright red. Her face was hot and she believed every student in the room was focused on her. After all, she had nearly slept with this professor while she was drunk and kissed him quite thoroughly when she was most assuredly totally sober. Mac MacDougal in the flesh. Oh no. Could she walk out? Drop the class? Have the floor open and swallow her?

Before she had a chance to exercise any of those options, Mac began. "I'm Professor MacDougal. Y'all can call me Mac. I know you were expecting Professor Marlow, but unfortunately, he broke his leg while skiing in Chile and is quite incapacitated. He's taking this semester off to recuperate and I'm taking over this class and a couple of others. Now, if you are in any way disappointed enough to want to get out of this class, it won't be a problem. Go to your advisor and request a drop or a transfer and it will be done in record time. But those of you..." He paused and singled out Maggie -- she thought. "...who decide to stick with me, I promise it will be an interesting ride."

A couple of students applauded -- suck-ups, Maggie decided -- and Mac grinned. "So, let's get started ... "

Well, Maggie thought, the gauntlet has been thrown down. She was sure Mac was a good professor and the class was one she had been excited about. What the heck. She wasn't a quitter no matter how uncomfortable the situation made her. She uncapped her pen. Let the games begin.

It wasn't nearly as problematic as she had feared. Mac was indeed an excellent instructor -- charismatic and interesting and challenging. His classes flew by -- always too short for the discussion he engendered. His assignments were tough but fascinating and Maggie grew to love them. Mac never so much as cast a suggestive look in her direction, but with Dwight's continued coldness, she began to entertain thoughts of a liaison with Mac.

She hadn't acted on these thoughts and, as the semester neared its end, Maggie conducted a daily debate with herself over what to do. Her other classes were fascinating as well. She adored writing and her professors were both talented and inspirational. She began to envision a career for herself perhaps writing historical fiction.

Margaret hadn't abandoned her either. She made an appearance almost every night and Maggie looked forward to seeing her. Margaret was mostly silent, rocking in the chair or flittering about the house, but sometimes she spoke to Maggie. Her voice was pitched low and it was hard to distinguish her words, but Maggie heard her. "Believe in yourself. Follow your dreams. Never give up."

Was she speaking to Maggie or to herself? Maggie couldn't be sure.

Connor or Conrad hadn't shown up again which was a relief. Maggie wasn't sure how to interpret his ghostly presence. She told herself he had come back for Margaret. That was the ending she wanted to write. And so, one day, she decided to do exactly that. Her creative writing professor assigned them a project in historical writing. Since the particular program in which Maggie was enrolled combined history and writing, the professor wanted them to merge the two fields in a work of fiction. Maggie had no problem deciding that her story would be that of Margaret and Connor (or was it Conrad?). The day the project was assigned, Maggie rushed home and tossed her books on the couch. She carefully removed the loose brick in the fireplace and slid her hand inside to extract Margaret's diary secreted there. She opened it to the first page and read over the words...."Daniel is coming home tomorrow and I am not sure whether I am excited or frightened."

Maggie booted up her laptop and began to type.

CHAPTER
Thirty

Life is what happens when you're busy doing something else. Maggie had heard that old adage in a hundred different versions. It turned out to be true. At least partly. The days sped by. Maggie was either in class or studying or working at Jewelicious. It was oblivion, but a delicious sort of oblivion. She buried herself in the past and the present, and tried not to look too far into the future. No matter how hard she tried, though, she was haunted by thoughts of Dwight every bit as much as she was haunted by Margaret. Where was he? What was he doing? Did he miss her? Did she miss him? This way lay madness.

Six weeks into the semester Jewel decided to close the shop for a day so that she could work on increasing her inventory before the holidays and so that Maggie could have an uninterrupted day to study. Maggie argued, of course, but Jewel was adamant. "Take the day off," she said. "You deserve it. And if you don't want to study, go shopping. Get a massage."

Maggie planned to spend the morning at the university library researching the history paper Mac had assigned them. And, after lunch with another student in his class, she thought she might stop by Mavis Burdick's *Nail Tips* nail salon for a mani/pedi. She was, she thought, in need of some serious personal maintenance and repair.

She was stuffing her laptop and history notes into her backpack when her cell phone rang -- the old-fashioned telephone ring that meant James was calling. Maggie had to admit that her smart phone did offer some perks.

Maggie smiled to herself as she dug the phone out of her bag and swiped it on. James never called. Unless, that is, he had a problem. A tiny nugget of concern wormed its way into her head – what could his problem be? Turned out – she was the problem.

They had no more than covered the basic hellos than James launched into a lecture. Sounding frighteningly like his father he said, "Mom. Seriously. When are you going to give up this nonsense and come home?"

Maggie gasped. Nonsense? Really? He was sounding more like Dwight by the minute.

James continued, swept along by his own momentum, "Poor Dad is all alone in that big house. Lonely and alone while you are out gallivanting –"

Maggie's patience was gone and she interrupted, "Gallivanting? That's what you think I'm doing? Listen to me, young man, whatever I am doing is one, none of your business and two, definitely not gallivanting." Maggie had to stop to catch her breath. She was hyperventilating.

"But Julie said," James interjected.

"Julie? What does your sister have to do with this?" And then the light went on. James was doing his sister's bidding. "I'll have you know, James, that your sister hasn't a clue. Do you know where your poor lonely father is right now?"

"Um, no, I guess not. At work?"

"He happens to be at a golf outing in Florida sponsored by a client. Yes, he's definitely suffering there. That's after he was in Paris for two weeks on business. And then he has another trip scheduled for the week after the golf thing."

James sounded sheepish. "I didn't know. Julie told me –"

"And just when have you ever listened to the drama queen anyway? And I presume that you and Julie think I should go home to an empty house. And do what? Clean and can jam, perhaps? Or, wait, I know. I can knit an afghan and plant a truck garden or –"

"Okay. Okay, Mom. I get it. I'm sorry."

Maggie sighed. This was her much-loved older child. And if he sounded like Dwight, was it his fault? Probably not. "James," she said. "Listen. Dad and I will be fine. We will figure this out. For the first time in a long time, I'm doing something that excites me. I love school. Now what about you?"

Maggie and he chatted for a few more minutes about classes and the cute girl in his chem lab before they hung up. Maggie threw herself backward onto the bed and flung an arm over her eyes. She loved her family. She did. But sometimes they were a lot to handle. Good old Mom had gone off the rails and they couldn't understand it. Honestly.

So, when Dwight called one evening a few days after James' call to ask about her plans for Thanksgiving, Maggie was surprised and relieved.

"Thanksgiving?" she exclaimed.

"Yeah," Dwight replied with a touch of the old Dwight in his voice. "You know the holiday with the big bird and too much food and football?"

Maggie snorted. "And me in the kitchen all day? Yeah, I do remember that."

There was silence at the other end of the line. It stretched out so long that Maggie finally said, "Hey, Dwight, are you still there?"

"Hmm? Oh, yeah. I'm still here." He cleared his throat. "I was just thinking. Anyway, I called to find out what your plans are."

"Plans? I hadn't given it any thought. Why? Did you have something in mind?"

"I guess I figured you would come home -- I mean -- come here for Thanksgiving. Julie called and wanted to know. James has a week off so he's coming home. And, well, you know."

Maggie hesitated. The truth was she missed them all. The kids and, oh damn it, Dwight too. She had always loved Thanksgiving -- Dwight was right about that at least. Maybe she should take a break. She hadn't been back in Ohio since May. But it was the middle of the semester. School was overwhelming her and she'd already promised Jewel that she would work on the dreaded Black Friday shift.

"Umm." She hedged. "I don't know, Dwight. I've got a lot of work to do and --"

"Never mind." His voice was gruff. "I'm sorry to intrude."

"Wait," Maggie protested. "I didn't say -- "

"You didn't have to." The bitterness in his voice made Maggie's stomach ache.

"I could maybe," she began.

"No problem," he interrupted her. "We'll be fine. Don't worry about us." He paused and Maggie thought he'd hung up. Then he said, "I miss you, Mags. I really do." And he was gone.

Maggie sat staring at her phone for a long time after that. The pain in Dwight's voice was killing her. Maybe this whole thing was selfish of her. She loved her family. Maybe she should just give up this college craziness and go home where she belonged. Too upset to do anything meaningful, Maggie tried to distract herself with frivolous television. She was listening to some inept singer massacre a classic rock song when she gave it up and crawled into bed. A few hours later she was awakened by the now-familiar creaking of the rocker. Margaret. Maggie rolled out of bed and crawled to the edge of the loft and peered down. Margaret looked up and smiled. "Follow your dreams, Maggie. Follow your dreams."

Maggie scowled. *Thanks a lot, Margaret. How am I supposed to follow my dreams when I'm making everyone else miserable? I never wanted my dreams to exclude my family. To exclude Dwight. But apparently that's exactly what has happened.* Suddenly Maggie had an idea. She could fix this. If she couldn't go home again, home could just come here. Dwight and the kids could come to Sweet River for Thanksgiving. It would be crowded but fun. She had the new television so James and Dwight could watch the football games while she and Julie cooked. It was an inspired idea. Maggie was too excited to go back to sleep. She picked up the phone to call Dwight. He wouldn't mind if she woke him, she knew he wouldn't. As it turned out, she didn't wake him after all. She listened to the phone ring until it went to voicemail and hung up. She pictured Dwight alone in some bar drinking away the pain she was causing him. Or, more likely, drinking in some bar with the hot chick who was nursing him through the pain she was causing him. Really? She didn't really think that, did she? Still...

Maggie got up and made coffee and curled into the rocking chair that Margaret vacated a short time ago. She sipped and rocked until the sun came up and then she pulled on her running clothes and went out for a run. As she ran through the tree-lined streets near the yellow bungalow she'd grown to love, she waved to another early bird out for a stroll and nodded to the boy delivering the Sweet River Press. It was peaceful and the chill in the air was refreshing. Maggie felt at home here in this small welcoming town. Sweet River had become her home. By the time she got back to her yellow bungalow, she knew exactly what she had to do.

Maggie let herself in the house and before she could change her mind she picked up her cell phone and called Dwight again. Damn it, she thought, as the phone rang, be there. Please be there. On the fifth ring she heard Dwight's sleep numbed voice. "Hullo. Uh. Whosis? Maggie? Are you okay?"

"Never better," Maggie said. "I've been thinking. What if you and the kids came here for Thanksgiving? You've never seen the place and I'd love it if we did the family thing here this year." She didn't want to sound pathetic, but she'd beg if she had to. "Please, Dwight. Think about it."

He chuckled the old Dwight chuckle. "You don't have to work so hard at it, Mags. You had me at family." A slight pause and then, "You've never invited me. Us. Before."

That was a punch in the stomach to Maggie. She hadn't invited them, had she? She'd been so busy finding herself -- God, she hated that expression -- that she had nearly lost them. Time to fix that was now.

"Oh, good," she said. "I can't wait. It will be like old times."

Of course, it wasn't like old times. Old times involved a huge meal cooked in the large kitchen in the roomy house in Winslow, not a tiny turkey cooked in a minuscule kitchen in the cramped cottage in Sweet River. From the moment Dwight and the kids arrived early on Thanksgiving morning and piled out of the car and into the cottage it was strained and uncomfortable.

Oh, yes. Julie raved about the sleeping loft as Maggie had been sure she would. She oohed and aahed over the way Maggie had fixed things up. And James? He seemed to like the house, but he grumbled about her internet. Why didn't she have wireless? Had she moved back to, oh my god, the 20th century? The dark days when dinosaurs ruled the world.

After the car was unloaded and the house explored -- that took all of a minute -- they stared at each other unsure what to do or how to relate to one another. Dwight used one finger to set the rocker in motion -- back and forth. "Margaret's chair?" he asked.

"Yes," Maggie replied -- eager to have a conversation without emotional repercussions for them. "And guess what? I think Connor was here too."

Dwight quirked an eyebrow at her. "Seriously? Why am I just hearing this now?"

Maggie frowned. She should have told him. "I'm not sure. You said you didn't give a damn."

To his credit, Dwight let that comment pass. "Well, tell me now. I wondered how long it would be before old Connor, or Conrad, surfaced."

Julie flipped her long blonde hair over her shoulder and looked from one parent to the other. "Are you two going to tell us what you're talking about? Who are Margaret and Connor anyway?"

Dwight laughed. "I'll let your mother explain. She's the original ghostbuster. I just came in for the last act."

Over coffee and sweet rolls, Maggie poured out the story of Margaret and Connor and Daniel and Rose Dawn. She even did something she seldom did. She pulled Margaret's diary from its hiding place and showed it to them. For a moment it felt right. It felt like family again.

Julie fingered the diary -- careful of the ancient pages. "This is cool, Mom. I mean it's really old and her writing is so spidery and old-fashioned."

James was more interested in his mother's ghost. "You really saw a ghost? Seriously? Maybe you just need therapy." He flashed her a dire look. "You know with being separated from Dad and all."

Poof! The mellow feeling vanished.

"Look, kids," Maggie said. "I've tried to explain this to you over the phone. It's something I have wanted for a long time and when the opportunity came along, I had to take it."

"Sure, Mom," Julie said. "You had to leave Dad. Did you want to do that for a long time too? And what about us -- James and me -- did you have to leave us too?"

Maggie wrapped her arms around her daughter and pulled her close. She could smell the scent of coconut shampoo in Julie's hair. She sighed. This was tougher than she'd thought it would be. "Listen to me, Julie. And you too, James. This is not about you. I'm not sure if I can make you understand, but I'll try. When your Dad and I got married, I gave up on getting my degree. I always thought I might go back to school one day, but life interfered with that and I just didn't. I didn't mean for any of this to happen. It wasn't a plan. I found something I really need and want to do. If I wasn't making you guys miserable, I'd say I'm happier than I've been in a long time."

Dwight looked like she'd slapped him. He had heard all this before. Wasn't he listening? Did anyone ever really listen? Maggie felt like she was just white noise. No one ever heard her. Really heard her. Was it too late?

A tiny crease formed on Julie's forehead and she bit her lip. Sure signs she was doing some serious thinking. "I get it, Mom. Really. You don't need to worry about us. We'll be fine. I promise I'll be here for your graduation."

Maggie hugged Julie and kissed the top of her head. "Thanks for that. What about you, James? Will you be here? Dwight?"

James ran a hand through his cropped dark hair and grinned -- a grin so like his father's that it took Maggie's breath away. "Sure, Mom. I'll come to your graduation."

Maggie noticed that Dwight hadn't agreed to attend her graduation, but she wasn't going to make an issue of it. The tension had eased a bit and that was enough for now.

Thanksgiving wasn't perfect, but it was good enough. Maggie and Julie cooked together in the tiny kitchen while the guys watched football on television. Then they switched positions, because they were an equal opportunity family, and Maggie and Julie went for a long walk while Dwight and James made Dwight's famous stuffing and gravy. It was congenial if not totally without strain.

Maggie set the table with her mismatched dishes and flatware and the four of them loaded their plates in the kitchen and brought them into the dining room. Dwight said a basic blessing that seemed to skirt the issues confronting them. "Thank you, Lord, for this meal and for our family. Amen."

They ate and drank and talked and laughed. Maggie was just thankful that the four of them were together and that no one was throwing things -- insults or cutlery. It was enough for now.

As they cleared the table and cleaned up the kitchen, Maggie debated whether to extend to them the invitation to Azalea's house that she had been given. Azalea and her family hosted an annual Thanksgiving evening get-together. Azalea explained it saying, "Just about everyone in Sweet River stops by. We just open the house and have plenty of food and drinks and whatever happens happens. It's Thanksgiving and the county fair rolled into one." She rolled her eyes. "I was going to say without livestock, but I'm pretty sure we have had livestock on occasion. It's an event. Y'all should come."

When Maggie explained that her family -- Dwight and the kids -- were driving down for Thanksgiving Day, Azalea said, "You and y'all's family should come."

Now, Maggie thought, what the heck, we can't just sit around and stare at each other for the rest of the day. "Hey, y'all. My friend Azalea is throwing a Thanksgiving Bash and asked us all to come over."

Julie giggled. "Did you just say y'all, Mom? You have turned Southern. Next thing we know you'll, I mean y'all, will tell us y'all have a serious addiction to grits."

"Guilty." Maggie laughed. " I confess that I do have a hankering for grits from time to time."

"I knew it." Julie punched the air with her fist.

"Does that mean yes, you'll come?" Maggie asked.

"Sure," Julie said. "This place is cute, but it's kinda claustrophobic. I'll go." She winked at Maggie. "Will there be cute boys?"

James caught Julie in a headlock. "Baby sister, you never change. Cute boys?" He eyed his mother. "So, will there be cute girls?"

Maggie laughed. "Plenty of both, I presume. And you, Dwight, can meet my friends."

A look of anguish crossed his face before he erased it. "Love to, Mags. Nothing I'd like more."

Maggie gave him a quick look. That was sarcasm, pure and simple. But his face was devoid of emotion -- bland and innocent. Hmm.

CHAPTER
Thirty-One

Azalea and Jermaine and their two sons lived in a sprawling ranch style home on the edge of Sweet River. The house was surrounded by about an acre of land. Trees and bushes still in flower grew wild in the back of the house and the river burbled in the distance.

Dwight wheeled into the long driveway already crowded with cars and trucks of various ages and makes and parked behind Azalea's Beemer. As they climbed out of the car, 'Zalea bustled out from the house to greet them. She swept Maggie into a hug. "Maggie. I'm so glad y'all made it." She cast a curious eye on Dwight. "So, this is the infamous Dwight, is it?" She hugged him too. "And this must be Julie and James. Your mama has told me so much about y'all."

Azalea led them into the house and waved an arm at the dining room table laden with a platter of turkey and stuffing as well as every other Thanksgiving dish probably ever eaten by human beings since the time of the Pilgrims. "Help yourselves," Azalea said. "There's plenty for everyone and more in the kitchen."

"Wow," Maggie said. "I have never seen that much food in one place in my entire life. Did you cook all this?"

Azalea beamed. "Hardly. Jer and the boys and I cooked the turkeys and stuffing and a duck or two, but most of the rest came from my guests."

"Oh, no, "Zalea," Maggie cried. "I didn't know I should bring something."

Her friend's silvery laughter filled the room. "Don't be ridiculous. What could you bring from that tiny kitchen of yours? You brought yourselves and that's plenty." She shooed them into the living room where a makeshift bar had been set up. "Get drinks and mingle." She looped her arm through Dwight's. "I'm just going to borrow this ole boy of yours for a while. Get to know him a bit."

Dwight cast a pleading look over his shoulder as Azalea led him away, chattering nonstop into his ear. Maggie had to laugh at the expression on his face. She would rescue him soon, but in the meantime, she would, as Azalea directed, mingle. She turned to say something to the kids, but they had disappeared.

Maggie observed the crowd for a few minutes before she spotted Jewel and hurried over to say hello. "Whew, Azalea said she was having a few people over not the entire population of South Carolina. I've seen political conventions with fewer attendees."

Jewel rolled her eyes. "'Zalea and Jer's Thanksgiving Day Bash has become a tradition around here. It gets bigger every year." She scanned the crowded room. "Did you bring your family? I want to meet them."

"They seem to have been sucked away," Maggie told her with a wry smile. "'Zalea kidnapped Dwight. She'll have wangled his total life story out of him by now."

Jewel took Maggie's arm and hauled her toward the bar. "You're gonna need a drink to survive this madness." She turned to the bartender -- a college kid hired from Sweet River University. "Give the nice lady a Magnolia Crush." When Maggie eyed her curiously, she said, "Don't ask. Just drink. It's a tradition. Oh, look there's Dud Lighthouse. I have to talk to him. Be good." And Jewel disappeared.

Drink in hand Maggie slowly circulated through the crowd. She was amazed to find that she knew many of the other guests. She hadn't been in town for long and she felt as if she'd known these people for years. She felt, to be honest, at home.

"Hey, Maggie."

"Glad you came."

"I heard your family was in town."

One sip of the Magnolia Crush was more than enough for Maggie. Strong stuff. She wandered into the kitchen to put it down and then went searching for a glass of wine. As she started for the bar she bumped into Gladdie and Chad coming in the door. They hugged -- the usual Southern greeting, Maggie had discovered. "Hey, Gladdie. Chad. I'm glad to see you. I want you to meet Dwight and the kids."

"Meet the undead Dwight, you mean?" Gladdie nudged Maggie and snickered.

"Oh, no," Maggie said. "How many of these people still think I'm a poor widow woman? How am I going to explain very-much-alive Dwight to them? I have confessed that his death was greatly exaggerated to a lot of people, but I haven't taken out an ad in the newspaper or anything."

"I imagine most of them have heard it through the grapevine. You know how gossip flies around here. If Verdie knows, they all know."

Maggie caught a glimpse across the room of a dazed Dwight holding a beer and sandwiched between Azalea and Jewel. He looked helpless as he turned from first one and then the other while they chattered non-stop. She should rescue him right now before he combusted in front of the entire population of Sweet River. She started to pick her way across the room when she felt a hand on her shoulder. "Hello, Maggie," a deep voice greeted her. She whirled to find Mac MacDougal smiling at her.

Mac swept her into a bear hug just as Dwight spotted her and started across the room toward her. Horrified, Maggie tried to extricate herself from Mac's arms and only succeeded as Dwight reached her side. He stood looking from Mac to Maggie and back for a long, hostile moment and then he shrugged and stuck out his hand. Well-mannered if nothing else. "I'm Dwight Murphy," he said in a mild voice. "Maggie's husband."

Mac took a step back, his face ashen and then he recovered. "Mac MacDougal. I'm Maggie's history professor at Sweet River University."

Dwight's words dripped icicles as he began to understand. "I see. Her professor. Well, isn't that perfect for the two of you?" He turned his back on Maggie and Mac and threaded his way across the room toward the bar. Then a beer in each hand, he slammed out the door into the backyard. Maggie could see him through the kitchen window -- polishing off the first beer and starting the second.

"I'm sorry, Maggie," Mac said, "I had no idea. You should have warned me that he would be here."

Maggie leveled a glance at him. "I'm not entirely sure that I thought you needed a warning that my husband and children would be attending Azalea's party. It's really none of your business." Maggie was well aware that she was taking out her guilty feelings on poor Mac, but she couldn't help it. The look on Dwight's face spoke far more than any words could have. He was hurt and angry and, damn her own stupidity, he felt betrayed. How was she going to fix this?

"Excuse me, Mac," she said. "None of this is your fault. I'm sorry too. More than you can ever realize. I think I'd better find Dwight. Okay?"

Mac stared at her. "Sure. Fine. I get it. I thought maybe we had something going, but -- " He lifted a shoulder Dwight's direction. " -- I guess I was wrong."

"Oh, God, Mac," Maggie said. "I really don't have time for this right now." She reached up to touch his shoulder. "Later. Please."

Mac nodded and Maggie headed to the backyard to find Dwight and see if she could repair the damage. Outside, however, she paused to watch James shooting baskets with a pair of tall, stunningly good looking African-American boys -- Azalea and Jer's sons -- Braxton and Donovan. James was shorter by about a foot at just under six feet but he moved with style and grace and his shot was nothing short of perfection. "Yo! Nothin' but net," he crowed. "Let's see you match that."

One of the other two took the ball and dribbled it with menacing slowness as he eyed James. "You ain't seen nothin' yet."

"Bring it," James called. "Show me what you've got."

Maggie had to smile. James looked so much like Dwight had back in the day. She remembered watching Dwight play during their college days. After the days of DJ and Beer. Oh, no. Where on earth had that come from? She needed to find Dwight. Not reminisce about stupid DJ.

She found him in a pack of guys huddled around the open hood of Azalea's Beemer. One of them held a grease-soaked rag and was twisting something in the engine while the others offered opinions. Maggie didn't speak engine so it sounded like Greek or perhaps Martian to her. "Looks like it's the doozy whatsis," one said.

"Nah," another said. "I think it has to be the dingus leaking ptomaine."

"Let's try to start her up," a tall, gorgeous black man said and dug in his pocket for the key. As he turned to get into the car, he noticed Maggie. "Hey, Maggie," he said as he picked her up in one giant hand and twirled her around.

"Put me down, Jer. You big jerk." Maggie threw her head back and laughed. It honestly felt good to laugh like that. She'd been holding her breath ever since the kids and Dwight arrived.

When he heard her voice, Dwight pivoted with excruciating precision to face her. "Hey, Maggie. What brings you outside? I thought you'd want to stay inside and talk to your friends." His words were mild but his voice was cold enough to freeze ice cubes.

Jer set Maggie on the ground and pushed her toward Dwight. "Looks like you need to spend a little time with your -- not quite deceased -- husband. We can talk later." He slipped his tall frame behind the wheel of Azalea's car and started the engine.

Dwight frowned, confused by Jer's words. "Deceased? Me?"

"How do I explain this? I told you about the *Get Your Groove On Conference,* didn't I?"

He nodded.

"Well, what I didn't tell you was that I kind of got mistaken for a widow and I kind of didn't confess that I wasn't. For quite some time after I moved to Sweet River, most folks thought I was, that you were -- "

"Dead?" Dwight said helpfully.

"Well, I guess you could put it that way. But I think that pretty much everyone knows now that I'm not a widow."

Dwight thought this over for a second and then his sense of humor rescued the situation. He burst out laughing. "Any chance that I died a hero's death?"

Relieved, Maggie giggled. "Oh, yes. I think you were murdered trying to stop a bank robbery."

Dwight threw back his head and laughed. "You do flatter me, Maggie May. Always have."

Maggie heard the words "Maggie May" and sucked in a breath. He hadn't called her that since Drunken Hills. Maybe the ice was thawing after all.

The party was still going strong when Maggie and Dwight decided to leave. Julie had, indeed, found a cute boy to hang out with -- Mayor Chesterfield's son, Ray. They were playing a rowdy game of pool in the basement with a crowd of young people cheering them on. When Julie saw her parents at the foot of the steps, she pleaded with them. "Let me stay. Please. It's early and I'm having fun."

Ray leaned on his pool cue. "I promise I'll have her back at the yellow bungalow by midnight, Miss Maggie."

"I thought we'd drive back to Ohio tonight," Dwight said. "Come on, Julie. It's not too late to start."

Julie gave her head a vigorous shake, blonde hair falling over one eye. "It's way too late to drive back tonight. I can stay with Mom." She turned to her mother. "Can't I? Please?"

Maggie and Dwight exchanged knowing looks. They'd never been able to resist Julie. Probably not a good idea to give in to her all the time but, in this case, Maggie really didn't want them to leave. She needed more time with all of them. So, she said, "Okay, Julie. Midnight, though."

Dwight shrugged his shoulders. "She's a big girl. Let's make it no later than one."

Julie threw herself at Dwight and hugged him. "Oh, thank you, Daddy. Thank you, Mommy. You're the best."

She turned back to the pool table. "Okay, hotshot, cue them up. I'm gonna beat you this time."

Maggie and Dwight climbed the steps to the cluttered kitchen. They surveyed the chaos of dirty dishes and glasses. Plates stacked in the sink. The garbage can overflowing with trash. "We should stay to help," Maggie said.

Dwight rolled up the sleeves of his shirt. "Let's do it."

They had managed to clear away some of the clutter when Azalea, glowing with exertion and excitement, blew into the kitchen. She saw the two of them elbow deep in the mess and exclaimed, "What are you two doing? No, no, no! Jer and the boys and I will get the heavy stuff later after everyone leaves. And I hired some of Agnes' girls to come in tomorrow morning. Seriously. Stop and go enjoy the party."

Maggie dried her hands on the apron she'd filched from the drawer -- a dark apron with an NBA emblem and the words "Players Do It on the Court" embroidered on it. Azalea raised an eyebrow when she saw what Maggie was wearing. "Nice sentiment, but hardly applicable here. Go have fun you two."

"Actually," Maggie said, "we were on our way out when we decided to help clean up."

Azalea flicked her fingers at them. "Even better. Shoo, the pair of you. I believe you have things to discuss. Go on now. I'll make sure James and Julie get home later."

"Thanks, Azalea," Dwight said. "I'll just go say goodbye to James and see if I can get the car out. Meet you outside, Mags."

As the door closed behind him, Azalea admonished Maggie. "He's a good one, girl. Go see if you can mend some fences. He's a keeper."

Maggie removed the apron and handed it to Azalea. "Thanks, 'Zalea. I'll do my best."

"If all else fails, ask Margaret for help." Azalea laughed -- a low throaty sound. She flipped the apron onto the counter and hurried back to her guests. She threw one last comment over her shoulder as she left. "Good ones are hard to find. You know?"

The thing was, Maggie did know, but she wasn't sure what to do about it after all this time.

As they got into Dwight's SUV, Maggie asked, "Did you find James?"

"Yep," Dwight said. "Drinking beers out back with Azalea's boys and some others."

"Beer?" Maggie stopped with her hand on the door. "I don't think he ..."

Dwight opened the door for her and gave her a hand up. "Relax, Maggie. He's almost 21 and he's in college. A beer now and then won't hurt him. I made him promise to only ride home with someone who hasn't been drinking."

"But," Maggie began and stopped. Beer? Beer meant DJ. And she had to admit that beer led to many other things that she wasn't eager to think about James doing. Mostly sex, of course. He was way too young for that. If she was honest, though, she had to admit that she had been younger than James when she and DJ -- well -- when they made love for the first time. Look how well that ended. No wonder she was concerned.

"Hey," Dwight poked her thigh. "Where are you? Stop worrying about the kids. They're good kids. We raised them well. They'll be okay."

Maggie clutched his hand and held it against her thigh. "Will we be okay?"

Dwight pulled his hand away. "Time will tell, I guess." They rode in silence for a few minutes and then he took her hand. "I hope so."

"Me, too." Maggie squeezed his hand and prayed that she had made the right decision. "Me, too."

CHAPTER
Thirty-Two

Back at the yellow bungalow Maggie made them cups of hot chocolate topped with real whipped creme -- the South was creeping into her veins, she guessed -- and lit the pretend fire in her fireplace. They settled themselves on the couch and took tiny sips of chocolate, Dwight leaving just the right distance between them. She wasn't going to be allowed to get the wrong impression that all was forgiven between them.

"Fun party," Dwight said after a while. "Nice people."

Maggie took a breath. "About Mac."

"Stop right there," Dwight interrupted her. "I don't think I need or want to hear about Mac."

"But," Maggie protested, "it's not what you think."

Dwight let his head drop against the back of the couch and heaved a weary sigh. "What do I think?"

Maggie eyed him waiting for the explosion she feared was lurking beneath the surface. "You think that something is going on between us."

Dwight turned so that he could look her in the eye. "There isn't?"

Maggie's cheeks burned. "Not that way, there isn't."

"You're blushing, Maggie May. Either you're lying to me or to yourself. Or both. There is something there. Any moron could see that."

"I don't want him," Maggie said. "I want you."

Dwight shook his head -- the bleak look on his face said more than his words about how he felt. "Are you sure about that, Maggie May? Or are you kidding yourself again about why you really want to stay in Sweet River?"

"I'm not," Maggie said but she knew that if Dwight really had been murdered at that fictional bank robbery, she would turn to Mac in a microsecond. He was sweet and smart and, damn it again, hot. But he wasn't Dwight. And, oh no, he wasn't DJ. But then neither was Dwight and that had always always always been the problem between them. DJ was the wedge. Did Dwight even know that? Maggie couldn't bring that up if he put a gun to her head. Old news and best left alone.

She put her cup on the coffee table and scooched over so she could snuggle next to Dwight. She stroked his thigh with her hand and felt him suck in his breath. "I don't want to talk about Mac anymore. I want to talk about us."

Dwight stiffened and removed her hand from his leg. He moved out of reach and said, "I really don't think you can separate the two. You need to figure out what it is that you want. Sweet River and Mac or Winslow and me. It's as simple as that."

Maggie leaped off the couch and stood with the fire at her back facing him. She glowered at him and then flung the words at him. "It's not that simple, dammit. You don't listen, Dwight. You never listen. I love it here because it's mine. I don't have to be Mrs. Corporate Wife. I don't have to do what I don't want to do. Here in Sweet River I get to be me. Just Maggie. Maggie who loves writing and history and wants the degree she gave up to raise your children and support you through grad school and make a lovely home for you. What about me? When is it my time? Sure I like Mac. He's a nice guy. And he listens. He really listens. How about that?" She stomped her foot in frustration and whirled to watch the fake flames in the fire.

Behind her there was only silence. Maggie wondered if Dwight had snuck out of the room. She turned around and saw him slumped in the corner of the couch head thrown back. Was he asleep? Had he fallen asleep during her tirade? That would just frost her cookies. Honestly. Fortunately, he hadn't fallen asleep. He cracked open one brown eye and a slow smile slid across his face. "Whoa, Maggie May. That was some speech. I didn't know that you felt that way. I guess I really haven't been listening, have I?"

Maggie stared at him. She couldn't have been more shocked if he'd opened his mouth and butterflies had flown out. This was the Drunken Hills version of her husband. Welcome back.

When she didn't say anything, Dwight patted the couch next to him. "Come back here, Maggie May. Sit down and tell me exactly what it is that you want. I promise I'm listening."

Hours later when Julie and James banged in the door, Dwight and Maggie were curled up together on the couch sound asleep. They'd talked and talked and talked until the words trickled dry and they fell asleep. Maggie had tried to explain all of it -- her needs, her desires, her love for her life here -- and Dwight had listened. For the first time, in maybe ever, he actually listened to her. Now it was up to both of them to figure out how to handle the truth. It might take more time than either was willing to give it, but at least, it was all out there. Please, God, Maggie prayed as she hugged her children. Make it all right.

The next afternoon Maggie hugged each of them goodbye as they climbed into Dwight's SUV for the drive back to Ohio. Julie pulled her close to whisper in her ear. "The house is adorable and Sweet River is cute. I'd love to come visit over Christmas break if I won't interfere too much with your school projects."

Maggie held her at arm's length and looked her in the eye. "Julie, you are always welcome, you know that. I am a bit suspicious, though, of this sudden change of heart. I'm thinking it might have something to do with a certain boy you met here."

Julie squirmed away from Maggie and twisted her hair into a ponytail. She flipped it over her shoulder and grinned at Maggie. "Well, there is that too. Ray is a cool guy and we agreed to get together over break."

Maggie smiled at her daughter. "I agree. Ray is exceptional. Good grades and a good family. I couldn't approve more."

Julie climbed into the back seat of the SUV, fastened her seatbelt and plugged her iPod earbuds into her ears. Maggie turned to James. "Hey, dude. Was it super boring at old Mom's house?"

James chuckled -- a Dwight chuckle if she'd ever heard one. "Okay. I'll admit that it was fun. Meeting Jer and Braxton and Donovan was awesome. I never dreamed I'd be on speaking terms with an NBA legend."

"Not quite a legend," Maggie said, "but a very good player. I'm so glad you had fun. Come again. Please."

James pecked her cheek. "Roger, Momster. I will."

That left Dwight. He lifted her off her feet and twirled her around. Laughing, Maggie begged, "Stop, you big jerk."

Dwight deposited her on the curb and, one hand cupping her rear, dipped his head and gave her a long kiss that had the kids hooting from the car. "Get a room, guys."

"Where did that come from?" Maggie asked as she tried to catch her breath.

"Been there all along," Dwight said. "I kind of forgot for a minute."

He kissed her again -- a more sedate kiss this time. "For the first time, I think I know how you feel. I'm not such a Neanderthal that I can't be dragged into this sparkling new world. I promise I'll work on it."

"That's all I ask."

"One other thing I'd like though," Dwight said as he stepped up into the car. "I'd like you to think about coming home. We can't work things out if we aren't together."

"Okay," Maggie agreed. "I promise I'll think about it."

Dwight played his last card. "There is a perfectly good college in Winslow, you know. I wouldn't ever ask you to give up your degree for me again but you could finish it in Winslow. Or even Cleveland if you wanted a bigger college."

A knot began to form in Maggie's stomach. She loved her classes at Sweet River U and she would hate to transfer, but if Dwight was trying this hard, she at least had to meet him halfway.

"Let me get through this semester first," she said hoping that was a big enough concession to buy her some time.

As the car pulled away from the curb and headed toward the highway, Maggie stood on the sidewalk and waved. Long after her family disappeared from view, she was rooted to the ground staring after them. She felt so much better than she had a few days before. Thanksgiving had turned out to be a success -- not an unqualified success, but close. Maggie began to whistle as she went back inside the yellow bungalow. It might be Black Friday for the rest of the world, but, for her it was Sunshine, Lollypops and Comin' Up Roses Friday.

CHAPTER
Thirty-Three

As the days whirled in a frenzy toward the end of the semester and Christmas, Maggie felt as if she was caught up in a whirlwind. School took up most of her energy, but she wanted to at least get a few Christmas gifts. She owed them all that much of her time. So, one Saturday in December she closed her laptop and pulled on her warm coat and boots and went shopping.

Downtown Sweet River was dressed in its best Christmas finery. Tiny white lights were strung everywhere and a giant tree stood guard next to the gazebo in the center of the town green. Santa ambled up and down the street, ho ho ho-ing and offering cutout cookies and lollypops to the children out shopping with their moms and dads. Christmas music enveloped the entire scene, blasting from some unseen speakers.

"Fa la la la," Maggie hummed along with the music.

She was enchanted by the village at any time, but at Christmas it was really something special. She had forgotten, in the rush and crush and mass chaos of the large malls, what it was like to be in small town America. It was festive and merry and Christmas spirit saturated the air. She knew that it was still possible for people to be sad or lonely at this time of year, but it would be more difficult in Sweet River. As Mary Lou Jennings said at the long ago *Get Your Groove On Conference,* "People in Sweet River are the givingest people on earth." True, Maggie thought. All true.

She'd jotted down a few gift ideas so she stuffed the list in her pocket and consulted it as she meandered in and out of the gaily decorated shops on Main Street. The first, and easiest, thing she wanted to do was to go to *Jewelicious* and pick out several pieces of jewelry for Julie.

Julie had inherited Maggie's love of gems and Maggie knew it would be no problem to find just the right thing for her daughter. The problem might be knowing when to stop. She wrested open the heavy door to the shop and stepped over the threshold into a sparkling wonderland. Jewel had decorated a large tree with different pieces of jewelry and trained a spotlight on it. The jewels glittered like stardust.

Jewel looked up from arranging a tray of rings and spotted Maggie. "Hey, you. I didn't think you were coming in today. As you can see, business is slow at the moment."

Maggie shook her head and sauntered over to a display of some of Jewel's newest pieces. "I'm not here to work. I'm here to shop for Julie. And maybe for my mom and my sister."

Jewel removed a few trays from beneath the counter. "This is the newest stuff. Just finished some of it last night. Look it over."

Maggie searched through the trays, pulling out pieces, slipping rings on her fingers and holding earrings up to the light to test the degree of sparkle. "You've outdone yourself, my dear. I would love to buy it all, but I can't afford it on my salary," she joked.

Jewel waggled her fingers in the air. "You do get a discount, you know. And I will accept a payment plan."

Maggie poured herself a cup of coffee and sipped it while she selected gifts for everyone on her list. As Jewel rang up the purchases Maggie leaned over the counter to observe some pieces that Jewel was working on. A pair of earrings with different stones dangling from a larger green hued opal and a necklace of the same stones made a matching set. "Wow," Maggie said. "I love that. How much?"

"Oh, those," Jewel said without looking up. "Special order. Making them for a guy's wife. Some nagging battle-ax he's trying to appease, I think. Who knows?"

"It's a shame," Maggie observed as she took her packages from Jewel. "If she doesn't appreciate them, she's crazy. Right?"

Jewel shrugged. "I guess." She bent to put the tray safely under the counter and walked Maggie to the door. "Will I see you Monday?"

"I'll be in after class."

Maggie stepped out onto the sidewalk and looked up and down. Her stomach rumbled and she decided to go into Agnes' to grab a cup of tomato basil soup to fortify herself for more shopping. Any excuse for tomato basil. As Maggie reached for the door handle she felt a gloved hand close over hers. Startled she glanced up and looked into the brown eyes of Mac MacDougal. "Oh," she said.

"Sorry to scare you," he said with a grin. "I guess we both had the same idea. Tomato basil and a tuna sandwich?"

Maggie tried to sound casual even though her nerves jangled. "Yep. The usual."

Mac held the door for her and followed her inside. *Agnes' Cafe* was jammed with Christmas shoppers. The place was buzzing. Maggie spotted a single table being vacated by an older couple and headed toward it. Then she stopped. It would be rude not to offer, wouldn't it? "There seems to be only one table available. Would you like to join me?"

Mac shook his head. "No, that's not necessary. I'll just get mine to take out."

"No," Maggie insisted. "It's fine. Please join me. I hate to eat alone."

"Okay, then," Mac said and took the seat opposite hers.

One of the cute young coeds who worked as a server during the busy times, hurried over to their table. "Professor MacDougal. What can I get for you? Coffee? Anything."

Maggie murmured to him under her breath, "A small case of hero worship."

He smiled an embarrassed smile. "Angie. Nice to see you. Ms. Murphy and I will both have coffee first. And I'm pretty sure I know what we'll have to eat as well."

Angie looked at Maggie as if seeing her for the first time. "Oh, my gosh. I'm sorry. I didn't see you."

"I get that a lot," Maggie said. "Aren't you in my History of the Civil War class?"

"Oh, gosh," Angie sputtered and dropped her pencil on the floor. She retrieved the pencil and said with a rueful grin, "Of course, Maggie isn't it? I'm sorry. I'm an idiot."

"Don't apologize. We'll both have coffee, a cup of the tomato basil and a tuna sandwich. Right, Mac?"

He nodded agreement. "Thanks, Angie."

She sprinted away to put in the order.

"I think we embarrassed the poor girl," Maggie said. "I can see why she wouldn't notice me when she's in the presence of the great and sexy Professor MacDougal." Oops. Had she really just called him sexy?

What was she thinking?

Mac toyed with the salt shaker centering it on the table. Finally, satisfied with the placement of the shaker, he raised his eyes and caught her staring at him. "Hmm. Did you just call me sexy?"

Maggie couldn't look at him -- her eyes darting around the cafe hoping perhaps for an airplane to land on the table to create a diversion. Or maybe just a total power outage that would send them scurrying back onto the street. When neither of those things happened, she gaped at him. "I did. But I didn't mean it."

He chuckled. "Oh, you didn't mean I was sexy. Thanks a lot."

Flustered, Maggie scrambled for words. "Well. I did mean it. But I didn't mean it that way."

"Well, then what way did you mean it?"

Maggie stammered, trying to think of what to say until Mac took pity on her. "I'm teasing you, Maggie. I know exactly what you're trying to say."

They were interrupted by Angie serving them their coffee so Maggie had time to collect her thoughts. "I apologize for the other day, Mac. At 'Zalea's party. That was really awkward."

Mac tipped his chair back and waited for her to go on.

Finally as the silence became more than awkward, she blurted, "I never told Dwight about you so he was unprepared."

"Ah, you failed to tell him about your sexy history professor. The one who would have slept with you if he wasn't such a complete gentleman." He paused. "And a total ass."

Now it was Maggie's turn to be surprised. "What do you mean by that? A total ass? Why?"

Mac took her hand and looked her in the eye. "Because I had my chance and I will never have it again."

"What?"

"Maggie, darlin'," Mac explained, "I saw the way your husband looked at you. As if he thought you were all that and the sun and moon and stars. I couldn't begin to compete." He added after a moment, "I wouldn't even try. More's the pity."

There didn't seem to be much more to say so they, by mutual agreement, changed the subject and talked about the final projects he had assigned them. Maggie told him about her creative writing project combining history and writing and Mac listened intently firing penetrating and intelligent questions at her. As they were finishing their lunch he said, "Wait until next semester. I have some really fascinating ideas in store for you guys."

Maggie played with the napkin in her lap, afraid to meet his eyes. "I might not be here next semester, Mac. Dwight wants me to move back to Winslow."

Mac placed his hand over hers and gave it a squeeze. "I'm very sorry to hear that."

Maggie and Dwight had begun talking on the phone almost every night after Thanksgiving. If she was too busy with writing or studying, he would let her go without a complaint and she liked that they were sharing again. He seemed intrigued by the ongoing saga of Margaret and Connor. Since she was fictionalizing Margaret's Diary, Maggie allowed herself to create an ending. She had no idea what had become of the star-crossed pair and was also confused by the Connor/Conrad dilemma. It seemed obvious that Connor was in fact Conrad Preston, Margaret's real life husband. Maybe too obvious.

She was struggling with how to resolve this one night when Dwight called. He seemed uneasy at first but Maggie still had her brain wrapped around Connor so she wasn't paying as much attention as she should have been. When Dwight finally blurted his question, Maggie made him repeat it.

"It's almost Christmas, Maggie. Would you consider coming home for the holidays? The kids and I would love it. I have to invite my mom too. She's alone since my brother is taking his family to California this year."

To be honest, Maggie had known this was coming. Dwight had brought the kids to Sweet River for Thanksgiving so now it was her turn. She'd been turning it over in her mind ever since Thanksgiving. There wasn't a good reason not to go back to Winslow. School would be over. Jewel could cover for her at the store. If she said she couldn't go, she'd have to lie. Make up some excuse. Telling him it scared her to go back to the "scene of the crime," so to speak, would stir up things she didn't want to address. Like moving back to Ohio permanently.

So she took a deep breath and plunged in. "I've been thinking it over and, of course, I'll come home for Christmas. I don't want to celebrate without you and the kids and I couldn't ask your mom to come here. So, yes."

"Yes?" He sounded like he couldn't believe he had won without more debate.

"Yes," Maggie said. "I'll be there."

That settled, they quickly agreed on a time and a date. The semester finals would be finished by the 15th but Jewel needed her to work that last pre-Christmas week. So Maggie agreed to drive up on December 23.

"And you'll stay until after New Year's, won't you?" Dwight asked. "There's a party at the club and -- "

"Let's take it one step at a time," Maggie broke in. "Let's see how Christmas goes and then decide about New Year's. Okay?"

He sounded deflated, but he agreed. One step at a time.

On the last day of the semester, Maggie turned in her papers and took a final exam in her required math class. She hadn't been sure about the end of the Margaret Chronicles as she called her creative writing project, until a few days ago when she realized what she had to do. When she finished the story, she jumped up to call Dwight, but then had second thoughts. Would he like the ending? She wanted to know, of course. He'd been such a big part of all of it and, in a large sense, Margaret had brought her back together with Dwight. Now as she parked the Bug in front of the bungalow, she decided to stroll downtown to let the lights sink into her soul. Just as Margaret had been responsible for (maybe) saving her marriage, Sweet River had saved her from an unfulfilling life. Maggie meandered down the street, waving at last minute shoppers and small children on their way to talk to Santa. It was a bittersweet time for her.

She sank onto a park bench with a perfect view of the huge brightly lit spruce and thought about the gift she was giving Dwight. It made her sad, but it was the only thing left that she could do to repair the damage she'd done by running away. She had the papers in her bag but she hadn't had the courage to deliver them to the Admissions Office. She was dropping out of Sweet River University after the semester. She had applied and been accepted, of course, at Winslow College. Dwight would be ecstatic. Maggie not so much. Sweet River felt like home in a way that Winslow never had, but that old adage, Home is Where the Heart Is, struck Maggie as the truth she had to accept. If she wanted Dwight -- and, of course, she did, didn't she? -- she had to give up Sweet River and all it had meant to her. That was the part she was struggling with. Give up the yellow bungalow and Margaret and go home to Dwight and the life they had built together? Yuck. She sounded like a Hallmark Card.

She was tired of mooning over Sweet River, so she eased herself to her feet and dusted off the seat of her jeans. It had started to snow -- just a few flakes dancing in the air -- and Maggie walked back to the yellow bungalow in a snow globe. "There's no place like home for the holidays," she sang under her breath. "For the holidays there's no place like home."

Maggie unlocked the door and slipped inside. She lit the fireplace and cracked open a bottle of red wine. She'd turned down offers to go out and celebrate with Gladdie and Jewel and Azalea, preferring to spend a quiet night alone in her beloved house. When she left Sweet River, she wouldn't have nights like this. Time all to herself. She poured herself a glass of wine and curled up on the couch with a comforter over her. The firelight flickered and cast shadows on the walls. Maggie kept the lights off -- reminding herself what the bungalow might have been like when Margaret lived here with Rose Dawn. It was warm and peaceful and after her second glass of wine, Maggie fell asleep. She dreamed she heard a baby cry and woke up with a start. The firelight still played over the walls and the ticking of the clock was the only sound. Except -- a baby was crying. She wasn't imagining it. She rubbed her eyes and half sat up. Then she gasped as she saw the rocker gently rocking back and forth. Sitting in the rocker was the ghostly figure of Margaret and tucked safely in her arms was a baby. Never before had Maggie seen a ghostly baby in Margaret's arms. Only Margaret cradling an empty spot where a baby should be.

Maggie bumped the coffee table as she tried to sit up and her glass tipped over and then shattered as it fell on the floor. The ghost, Margaret, turned then and smiled at Maggie. She bent to kiss the baby she held in her arms. "Don't be afraid, Maggie. It's time. I promise you." Then Margaret floated up from the chair, wrapped her arms around the baby and drifted away through the closed door.

Maggie stared after her until she noticed the red wine in a puddle next to her. She tiptoed into the kitchen and returned with a wad of paper towels to clean up the mess. "Goodbye, Margaret," she whispered into the dark room. "Be safe."

Maggie could only think of one thing to do. Call Dwight. She needed to tell him about this. He'd flip. She snatched her phone and hit the button to call him. No answer. The phone rang and rang and finally went to voicemail. Where was he? She needed him now. Maggie put her phone back on the table. I don't need him she thought. I wanted to share something with him. And that's different. Like with DJ. Only she'd needed DJ like she needed air or water. Look where that got her. This was different. She'd try to tell Dwight about it later.

In the meantime, Maggie decided she needed sleep and she pulled on her green Drunken Hills T-shirt and mounted the spiral staircase and fell into dreamless sleep.

Since she didn't have classes the next morning Maggie had decided to sleep in. She hadn't set an alarm so she was annoyed when the sound of a motorcycle awakened her at just before eight. "Damn it," she mumbled and pulled the covers over her head. "Figures those neighbor kids would be out disturbing the peace when I finally get a chance to sleep."

She buried her head under the pillow but the motorcyclist wasn't giving up. Plus, she had to pee. She rolled out of bed and staggered down the steps, cursing the inconsiderate moron who was ruining her chance to sleep in. She used the bathroom, started the coffee and still clad only in her T-shirt stumbled to the window and peered out. The stupid motorcycle was parked in front of her house. Great. Not only did he wake her up, but he also had the nerve to park on her grass. Well, on her weeds, but the point was the same. She got her coffee and then went back to the window. The motorcyclist was standing in her front yard, hands on hips, staring at her house his face hidden under his helmet. Maggie backed away from the window. Was he here to rob her? Murder her? Kidnap her? Where had she left her phone?

She scrambled around the house searching for it. Damn it all. She had to call the police. Where was the stupid phone? Her hands shook.

Suddenly she heard pounding on her front door and she froze. Her voice trembled as she called, "Go away. I've got a gun. I've got a pitbull in here. Down, Buster."

The intruder had the unmitigated gall to laugh. Then he called, "Relax, Maggie May. It's just me. Don't shoot."

Maggie's heart slowed a bit as she stomped over to the door and yanked it open. A blast of cold air made goosebumps break out on her bare legs. "You scared me to death," she began and then she felt her mouth fall open and her heart start to pound as she saw who was standing on her doorstep. "DJ?" she squeaked. "Is it really you?"

The "intruder" tugged off his helmet and a shock of dark hair fell over his eyes. "In the flesh," he said and swept her off her feet.

Maggie was laughing and crying at the same time as she felt his familiar arms pull her tight. Where had this man been all these years? DJ was laughing and crying too. "Maggie May, I've missed you," he said with a husky voice.

He set her down and she stepped back to drink him in. Beat up leather jacket, worn jeans, dark hair flopping into his deep brown eyes, but most of all that old devil-may-care DJ smile tugging at his lips. The smile that said life is to live to the fullest. A smile that begged her to take a chance with him. A smile she hadn't seen in years.

When she could form words, Maggie said, "Where did you come from? I thought you were dead."

DJ grinned. "I thought I was, too, but as I've learned recently rumors of my death have been greatly exaggerated."

Maggie chuckled. "Dwight James Murphy. I could kill you right now, but I think it's been done."

"Is there another option?" he asked.

"I'm open to suggestions," Maggie answered.

He reached for the hem of her T-shirt and pulled it over her head as he guided her toward the couch. "Will this do for now?"

Maggie opened her arms and pulled him down on top of her. "It's a good beginning."

After that Maggie lost track of time. It could have been minutes or hours later when she floated to consciousness. A tiny smile of satisfaction played over her lips as she watched the snowflakes flutter outside the front window. Had that just happened or was she dreaming? Carefully, so that she wouldn't disturb him -- even if he was just a hallucination -- Maggie rolled onto her side. DJ. His cheek resting on her bare shoulder, he was sound asleep, his breathing deep and even. She watched him sleep a while -- finally allowing herself to believe that he was really here on her couch. With her. With her fingertips she brushed his hair off his forehead and he stirred and opened his eyes.

"Hey," he said.

"Hey, yourself. I can't believe you're really here. Where have you been for the last 20 years?"

"That's a very good question. I'm not sure I know." DJ raised himself on one elbow and stared at her with an unblinking gaze. "I got lost."

"You vanished. One minute we were running away to Paris and the next you were gone."

He rolled off the couch taking the comforter with him and scooped up his leather jacket off the floor. He tossed it to her and she shoved her arms into the sleeves and folded them across her chest. He pulled his jeans on and paced back and forth in front of the fireplace. Finally he sank into the chair across from the couch and leaned his elbows on his knees. Maggie waited. She could wait forever, if that's what it took, to hear the answer.

Finally, he raised his head. "I know. When my dad died I felt like I let him down. I was running away from all his grand expectations for me and then I wasn't even there. He died asking for me. The guilt about killed me."

Maggie gazed at him afraid to utter a sound. He was finally talking to her and she wouldn't interrupt -- even if she had to bite her tongue off to stop herself. The look on his face made tears come to her eyes.

"I blamed myself. I should have been there. And, what's even worse, I blamed you."

"Me?" Maggie couldn't help herself from crying. "I didn't even want to run away. You did. I only went with you because I was afraid I'd lose you if I didn't." She paused and swiped at her eyes. "And I lost you anyway."

DJ crossed to the couch, sat next to her and put his arm around her. "I was a stupid kid. What can I say? I've thought about this a lot. Really I've done nothing but think since you ran away."

"I didn't -- " Maggie began, but DJ held up a hand to stop her.

"Don't deny it," he said. "But now I think I get it."

"After my dad died," he continued, "the only way I could make it up to him was to live the life he had planned for me. Somewhere in my muddled brain I thought it would ease my guilt. So I went back to school and got my degree and I took you with me. I didn't think about it, I just did it."

Maggie pulled his jacket more snugly around her and tucked her feet under her. "And?"

"And we got married and lived happily ever after? Or at least I thought we did. Until you left. Then I woke up. At first I was pissed. How dare you run away? This was not the plan." He grinned a rueful grin. "Blah, blah, blah. I thought I could order you to come back and you would surrender."

At this Maggie lost her patience. "Order? Order! What on earth would make you think you could order me to do anything? Dwight James Murphy you are a complete and total idiot."

He took her hand and stroked her palm. "I'll give you that." He shrugged. "Worth a try?"

She took a deep calming Yoga breath. Ohm. "So what changed?"

"First we talked and then we had the weekend at Drunken Hills. I missed you. I missed us. For the first time in years I missed DJ, damn him, the little coward."

"Uh huh."

"I found us again and I thought my big surprise would make you come running back to me."

"And I said no to Paris and no to Winslow College and you left in a huff and didn't call me for weeks," Maggie said. "Very helpful."

He nuzzled her neck. "I'm a dolt. I just didn't get it. Until Thanksgiving."

Maggie shifted away from him. He wasn't getting off this easily. "Thanksgiving was wonderful."

"It was. I met your friends and I saw the town and I could see why you love it here." He scowled. "And I met your professor. That hunky Mac that you are always on about."

Maggie had to giggle. "Jealous, huh?"

He sighed. "I was. I still am, but when we talked that night, I listened to you for the first time. I mean, really listened. And it dawned on me that I wasn't the only one who gave up dreams."

Maggie slid down so that her head was on the back of the couch and propped her bare feet on the rickety coffee table. "I'm listening."

"I went home and realized that I wasn't any happier with our life than you were. I mean, I love you and all that, but we weren't doing what we thought we'd be doing. So when I got it figured out, I took a drastic step."

"What was that?"

DJ sat up and faced her, his eyes sparkling with excitement. "I quit my job. And, if you agree, we can put the house on the market. I thought we could live in Sweet River while you finish your degree." He waited -- his body tense with anticipation -- for her response and at her continued silence, his face fell. "You aren't saying anything, Mags. Was I wrong? Isn't that what you want?"

Oh, God. Just when she thought she knew the ending to the story everything changed. He quit his job? Seriously? How many of these surprise twists could she endure? If Dwight, um, DJ, thought he had the last word, he was wrong. She had a pretty big shocker of her own.

Maggie jumped off the couch and found her book bag on the floor. She rummaged in it until she found the sheaf of papers she wanted. She dropped it in his lap. "I got you a Christmas present."

He looked confused. "What is this?" Then he opened the folder that contained her formal resignation from the Creative Writing Program and her letter informing the administration that she was dropping out of Sweet River University. His eyes widened and his eyebrows shot up into his hairline. "Maggie?"

She smiled at him. "Yes, dear?"

Neither of them said a word as DJ read Maggie's letters. The only sound was ice pellets plinking against the window. Maggie held her breath. Finally, Dj struggled to his feet and marched over to the fire-place. He tore the letters into pieces and tossed the scraps into the fireplace. "I fear we have become a cliché."

Those were not the words Maggie was expecting to hear. "Cliché?"

DJ stared at her, a contrite smile tugging at his lips. "Like in that story where the wife cuts off her hair and sells it so she can buy her husband a fob for his special watch. And he sells his watch so he can buy her fancy hairclips for her beautiful long hair. You know the one I'm talking about?"

Maggie punched his shoulder. "Duh. I'm an English major. O'Henry's *Gift of the Magi*."

"Yeah. That's the one. I never really liked the ending. Fortunately, I can change the ending of our *Gift of the Magi* story."

Maggie smiled at him. "Dude. You realize you threw those letters into a fake fire. Right?"

DJ shook his head and shrugged. "So much for my grand gesture, huh? But I can fix that."

He retrieved his bike pack from where it had fallen when he came in the door. He rooted around in it until he found what he wanted and knelt in front of Maggie with one hand behind his back. "I was going to wait, but now seems like the time to give you my Christmas present." He pressed a business folder into her hands.

Maggie stared at him, confused. Then with trembling fingers she opened the folder, pulled out a thick sheaf of papers and began to read. Suddenly, she stopped and choked back a sob as she held up a single sheet of paper. Wide-eyed, she said, in a shaky voice, "Is that what I think it is?"

DJ grinned. "Depends on what you think it is."

"This says that you made an offer to buy the bungalow. My bungalow. The little yellow bungalow." Maggie was babbling and she knew it, but it was hard to comprehend.

"Not quite," DJ said as he pulled another page from the stack and handed it to her.

Maggie's mouth fell open. At that moment she couldn't have managed a word if her life depended on it. Eventually she found her voice and croaked, "And the big house too? You made an offer on the big house and the bungalow?"

DJ beamed. "I know you love this place." His glance took in the tiny living area and the winding stairway to the sleeping loft. "But I figured it would be too small for the two of us and the kids when they visit. I thought we could convert it into a studio for you and we could live in the big house."

Tears trickled down her cheeks and dripped off her chin. "You did all this for me? Quit your job? Placed an offer on the Edison estate?"

A concerned look crossed DJ's face. "I did. You're crying. Aren't you happy? I told Azalea that it was all subject to your approval. I can call her and bail on the deal. Our offer hasn't been accepted and we can still get out of it."

Maggie started to laugh. "Don't you dare. I'm overwhelmed is all. You are amazing. And here I thought you were dead."

"I take it that's a yes."

Maggie threw her arms around DJ and buried her face on his shoulder. Her voice muffled she said, "Yes. A million times yes."

CHAPTER
Thirty-Four

"I'm going out to get pizza," DJ said as he opened the front door. "After a day like today we shouldn't have to cook."

Maggie sighed. "If we could even find the kitchen."

She sank onto the couch in the living room of the yellow bungalow and propped her feet on one of the packing boxes crowded into the small space. She watched DJ leave and leaned her head against the back of the couch. It had been a very long day and the room was chaos. But it was happy chaos.

Things had moved quickly after DJ's surprising resurrection. Maggie and he had returned to Ohio to celebrate Christmas with the kids. She was in the kitchen with Julie -- up to her elbows in cookie dough -- when the phone rang. One glance at the caller ID told her it was Azalea and she snatched the phone with one flour-covered hand while she dangled a cookie cutter from the other. "Hey, 'Zalea, can I call you back? I'm kind of busy at the moment."

Azalea laughed a low throaty laugh. "Not a chance, girlfriend. You need to hear this right now. Are you sitting down?"

Bad news? Maggie's heart began to pound with apprehension. "Is everything okay? You? Jer? The kids?" She had an awful thought. "Has something happened to Gladdie or Jewel?"

Azalea chuckled. "Relax. Everyone in Sweet River is just fine. Better than fine actually."

Maggie's heartbeat slowed. "Now you're teasing. What's the big news I have to hear right now?"

There was a beat of silence and then 'Zalea's slow drawl. "They accepted y'all's offer."

"Who? What? Offer?" And then Maggie realized what Azalea

was saying and began to scream. "They did? We got it? Really? You wouldn't kid me?"

Julie looked concerned so Maggie put her hand over the mouthpiece. "We got the house. We got the yellow bungalow."

Julie hugged her and the two of them danced around the kitchen while Azalea -- now on the speakerphone -- gave them all the details.

After that life moved at a dizzying pace. Christmas and New Year's and putting the house on the market was a crazy whirlwind, but Maggie and DJ sped through it all energized by the tantalizing thought of moving to Sweet River and starting their new life in the Edison mansion. It was almost too much to believe at times.

They got an offer on the Winslow house the same day that Maggie headed back to Sweet River to begin her second semester at the university. Over Maggie's objections, DJ shooed her out the door and stayed behind to supervise the packing of the last of their furniture and assorted bits and pieces of their Ohio lives. Now, a few short weeks later, they had just finished unloading the moving van. The majority of their belongings were stacked in the rundown garage of the big house, but boxes littered the yellow bungalow. Unpacking was a chore that would have to wait. Maggie dragged herself to her feet and limped stocking-footed into the kitchen to unearth a corkscrew to open the "Welcome to Your New Home" bottle of Pinot Noir that Azalea had left on the counter. She poured wine into a paper cup -- wine glasses were buried goodness knows where -- and wandered back to the couch. She raised her glass and smiled as she looked around the cluttered room. "To us, Margaret. Wherever you might be."

She took a long swallow of wine. Margaret hadn't made a single appearance since Maggie returned from Ohio after Christmas and Maggie missed her. She wondered if Margaret was gone for good. Maggie sighed. She had DJ now. Did she really need Margaret? Really? No, she guessed she didn't but she did miss her comforting presence. Even if she was a hallucination. Good old Margaret had gotten her through some lonely times. Now that DJ had been reincarnated, Maggie had the oddest feeling. She wanted to share that news with Margaret. She shook her head. I'm a crazy person. Here I am dreaming about a conversation with -- what? -- a ghost? The men with the nets will be here soon.

Maggie sipped her wine and waited for DJ to come home with the pizza. Home? Now that was an awesome thought. Home! She and DJ planned to camp out in the yellow bungalow while the construction team he'd hired made some major renovations to the big house. After their offer was accepted, they had driven down to inspect the house and found it was in far worse shape than they'd anticipated. It hadn't been occupied for years and the neglect showed. DJ, though, was excited about the possibilities and since he had "retired" from his job, planned to dedicate his time to making the old Edison place the showplace he believed it could be. In fact, DJ was exploring the possibility of starting his own company to renovate and repair historic homes. Maggie was just happy to have a few more months in the yellow bungalow. And sharing it with DJ would be perfect. Cramped but perfect.

She had dozed off when she was jerked awake by his return. "Mags, wake up. I've got dinner."

The delicious aroma of pizza drifted in the air and Maggie sat up and rubbed her eyes. "You're my hero."

DJ grinned. "If you think I'm a hero because I brought you pizza, I'm going to be king of the world when you see what else I got." He reached behind his back and brought out a thermos with *Agnes' Cafe* stenciled on the side. "Voila."

"Is that what I think it is?" Maggie jumped off the couch to take the thermos from his hand. DJ watched her with a smug expression while she unscrewed the cap and sniffed. Her eyes went wide. "Tomato basil. You are definitely my prince."

She hugged DJ and then scurried into the kitchen to unearth paper plates for the pizza and mugs for the soup. They shoved aside some of the clutter on the rickety coffee table and spread out the food. Maggie took a tiny sip of the still-steaming tomato basil soup and groaned with pleasure. "This is so perfect. But I thought you were going for pizza. You had to make a special trip downtown to get the soup."

"Yep. Nothing is too much trouble for you, Maggie May. Besides I had an ulterior motive."

What else had he done? The look on his face said that he could hardly contain himself. "What was that?"

"Nope. Not telling yet. All in good time, my dear. So eat up and it will become clear soon."

Maggie knew it was useless to try to pry anything out of him so she dug into the pizza and soup. It had been a long day and this supper was the perfect antidote to the bone weary fatigue that was attacking her. So, they ate and drank red wine and made plans for not just the next day but for the future. When she couldn't eat another bite, Maggie leaned back against the sofa cushions and laced her hands behind her head. "This has been amazing, but I'm falling asleep. Maybe we need to head upstairs." She tipped her head in the direction of the sleeping loft. "We can unpack and get organized tomorrow."

"Okay, but first I have something to give you." DJ reached into the pocket of his jacket and pulled out a small package wrapped in silver foil and topped with a red bow. He sat down next to her on the couch and laid it in her lap.

Maggie fingered the package speculatively. "What have you done? Christmas is over." She shook the package and stared at him.

"Christmas is **not** over," DJ said. "With everything that happened over the holidays I never really got you a gift."

"We bought a house. The yellow bungalow is the best gift I could ever get," Maggie protested.

DJ plucked the box out of her lap. "Okay, then. If you don't want this, I'll find someone else who does."

Maggie giggled and snatched the box back. "Well, if you put it that way ..."

Maggie slid a fingernail under one taped edge and wiggled it to loosen it. Then she turned the package to work on the other end. With both ends undone she tugged the silver foil. But DJ had had enough. He plucked the package from her hand and ripped off the wrapping. "Open it already. We don't have all night."

Maggie had to laugh at his impatience. "We don't?"

Then she relented and pulled the lid of the box off -- revealing a pair of earrings fashioned of multi-colored gems dangling from a single brilliant turquoise colored opal. A matching necklace nestled beside the earrings. Maggie gasped. She'd seen these before. She flashed back to the snowy afternoon before Christmas when she'd made the difficult decision to leave Sweet River. Jewel had been working on them that day and said some old guy had commissioned them for his bitchy wife.

"You? You're the old guy who commissioned these?"

The huge grin on his face told her the answer.

"But that was before. We hadn't even talked about anything. You didn't even know if I'd come back to Ohio for Christmas."

"Some things you just have to take on faith. Besides I wanted you to have them no matter what happened with the two of us. Do you like them?"

Maggie stared at him as tears rolled unchecked down her cheeks. "I love them. And I love you."

DJ pulled her into his arms and kissed the top of her head. "And I love you. I can't believe I almost allowed that moron, Dwight, to let you get away."

Maggie used her shirttail to dry her eyes. Her face buried against DJ she murmured, "He wasn't a totally bad guy. Just sort of unenlightened."

"Sure. But fun DJ is here now and he's quite the party boy. Remember?"

"I do. But right now this girl is too pooped to party. I think we need to call it a night."

"Agreed."

But neither of them moved, either too tired or too comfortable to make the effort to climb the stairs. Finally, Maggie sat up and poured the last of the wine into their cups. She took a tiny sip and then set her cup on the coffee table. She turned toward DJ and then looped her arms around his neck and snuggled against him. "Thank you for the jewelry. I feel bad that I didn't get anything for you."

DJ pulled her closer and rested his chin on her hair. He smelled like wine and pizza and heat. Maggie shivered as he ran a finger down her cheek and hooked it in the neck of her rumpled sweatshirt. "I'm sure we can figure out something to remedy that."

Maggie blushed. Blushed? After all these years of marriage? Really? "Well, then..." She squirmed out from under DJ's arm and stood up. "I'll see you upstairs."

Unfortunately for whatever plans he might have had, Maggie couldn't manage to keep her eyes open until DJ locked up and turned out the lights. He was breathing deeply beside her when Maggie was startled awake a couple of hours later. She rubbed her eyes and rolled onto her back. What was that noise? Then, as she emerged from her sleepy oblivion, she knew. The rocking chair. Which meant Margaret was back for the first time in weeks. Maggie rolled toward her snoring husband and poked him gently. "Honey. Wake up." He responded by rolling away from her taking most of the covers with him.

"DJ. Deej," she hissed in his ear. Then, "Dwight. Wake up." She nudged him harder.

"Hmm. What? Huh? Mags?"

"Margaret's here. You need to see her. Then you'll know I wasn't making her up."

Reluctant to abandon the warm covers DJ sat up and swung his long legs over the edge of the bed. He rubbed his eyes. "Okay, where is she?"

Maggie tilted her chin in the direction of the railing. "Down there. I hear the rocker squeaking."

She took his hand and they tiptoed to the edge of the sleeping platform and peered into the dusky living room. A single lamp glowing from the end table next to the couch cast shadows on the wall. It took a moment for her eyes to adjust, but then Maggie squeezed DJ's hand and pointed. "In the rocker," she whispered.

She heard DJ's sharp intake of breath. "Whoa," he whispered back.

Maggie stared at the rocker and then gasped. "That isn't Margaret." She clutched her husband's hand. "Look. Margaret is over there. Next to the fireplace."

Sure enough, a shadowy form hovered next to the faux fireplace, her back to Maggie and DJ. She appeared to be looking out the window.

"Then who?" DJ began.

And it hit her. Could it be possible? Was it? Then the figure rose from the chair and they knew. Conrad? Or was it Connor? It didn't matter what he was called. It was a tall, male figure. Then there was another shock as he glided toward Margaret and handed her the bundle he was cradling in his arms.

"Rose Dawn," Maggie breathed. "It has to be Rose Dawn."

DJ was silent -- every ounce of his attention focused on the tableau below.

The three luminous figures turned toward them as they crouched on the edge of the sleeping platform. With the baby in her arms, Margaret gazed upwards. Then a smile passed over her face. She gave brief nod in their direction, took Connor's arm and the pair of them drifted through the front door and disappeared.

"I have to quit drinking," DJ said. "Those hallucinations are incredible."

"That wasn't a hallucination. I've been telling you. Now maybe you'll believe me. That was Margaret and Connor and the baby. I know it."

DJ shook his head and tugged Maggie back into bed. When they were snuggled under the covers he said, "Mags. I don't believe in ghosts. Seriously? That was a figment of our imagination."

"Oh, right," Maggie said. "A mutual figment? That's more unbelievable than ghosts."

He plumped the pillow behind his head. "I guess." Then he brightened. "We own a haunted house. We could sell tickets and have tours."

Maggie laughed and tucked herself under his arm. "I doubt it. I kind of think that was a farewell performance. She was here to help me when I was alone and trying to figure things out. Now I have you back and we can figure things out together. I don't think Margaret -- or Connor -- will haunt us again. I'm kind of sad about it, though. I'll miss her."

DJ lifted the edge of the Drunken Hills T-shirt that Maggie was wearing. "I'll have to try to take your mind off her then won't I?"

She ran her hand over his chest and murmured. "You can try."

And DJ was as good as his word.

CHAPTER
Thirty-Five

Several weeks later Maggie wheeled the red bug into the driveway next to the yellow bungalow and threw open the car door. The pickup truck DJ had bought a short time after the move to Sweet River was parked off to the side so she knew he was around somewhere. Good. She had something she had to show him.

Maggie burst into the bungalow and was greeted by the sound of hammering coming from the back of the house. She tossed her book bag into a corner and followed the noise into the kitchen. As she poked her head through the door she started to laugh. The only part of DJ visible was a pair of denim-clad legs balanced precariously on the top rung of a stepladder. Plaster dust drifted down like a snowstorm from a gigantic hole in the ceiling.

Maggie tiptoed across the room and tapped DJ on the knee. "Hi, Honey, I'm home."

The pounding stopped and he sneezed as he picked his way down the steps to the floor. He removed his baseball cap to reveal dust particles sprinkled like dandruff in his messy dark hair. He brushed dust off his shoulders and grinned at her. "Hey, Mags."

"What's going on?" Maggie gestured at the gaping hole in the ceiling. "I don't recall the kitchen being in this shape when I left."

"Oh, this." DJ shrugged. "I wanted to see about that leak over the sink. I got carried away."

Maggie snorted. "I see a trip to Home Depot in your future."

DJ nodded. "Many trips, I fear, before this place is finished."

"Before you go anywhere," Maggie said, "I have something to show you."

She opened the refrigerator and removed a can of TAB for herself and a beer for DJ. Then she led the way into the dining room. He popped the tab on the can of beer and dropped into one of the rickety chairs as she foraged through her book bag. Then she straightened with a folder in her hand. With a flourish she placed in on the table in front of him. "Ta da."

DJ fingered the folder with curiousity and then looked her in the eye as he realized what it was. "Babe?"

"Yep. It's my final project from last semester. My creative writing project. The one that Margaret inspired. Historical fiction."

"An A Plus? Wow. Fantastic."

"Read what the professor said," Maggie urged him. "I couldn't believe it."

"'Maggie, this is amazing. You have true talent and I expect we will see much more of it in the future. Perhaps on the New York Times Best Seller list. Keep up the good work. I look forward to seeing you in class next semester,'" Dwight read.

He dropped the folder on the table and pulled her down into his lap. "That is awesome, Maggie. I am so proud of you. Can I read the whole thing?"

She snuggled into his arms. "I want you to read it all. But first you just need to read the last chapter of the book."

"Now?"

"Yes, now."

Maggie paced around the room, tidying and rearranging as DJ opened the folder and started reading. The ticking clock and the swish of an occasional car passing on Cranberry Lane were the only sounds other than the pages turning. Just when Maggie didn't think she could stand the suspense another second, DJ closed the folder and leaned back in his chair.

"Well?" Maggie thought she might explode with impatience.

DJ took a long sip of his beer and then grinned at her. "Babe."

"What? The suspense is killing me here."

"It's awesome. It all makes perfect sense. I love it."

Maggie blew out the breath she had been holding in. "I gave it the ending I wanted."

When DJ didn't say anything, Maggie asked, "Um. Did you happen to notice the date of Margaret's last diary entry?"

He shook his head and then shuffled the papers until he found the page. He stared at her with understanding beginning to dawn and a broad smile broke across his face. "You little mystic. The date is the year you were born." He looked at the page again. "Not just the year, but your birthday. Are you implying what I think you are?"

Maggie grinned. "It's fiction, of course, so I took some poetic license."

"Are you suggesting that Margaret died on the day you were born? And that in some mysterious way you are her reincarnation?"

"I keep telling you it's fiction, but why not? I've always had this weird connection to her. Sooo...."

"You have a great imagination, babe." DJ set the pages he had just read on the table and neatened them so all the edges were aligned. "Margaret would have been proud. She started the story and you gave it the best ending."

DJ set his beer on the table and pulled her into his lap. He nuzzled her neck and she shivered. His words were muffled. "Does that mean I'm Connor?"

Maggie shrugged. "Could be. Maybe we're star-crossed lovers."

DJ chuckled and stood up with Maggie in his arms. "Time cannot diminish the power of love."

Maggie wound her arms around his neck. "Good things come to those who wait."

He set Maggie down and put his hands on her shoulders to turn her around. He gave her a nudge in the direction of the door. "Let's just see about that, shall we?"

The Margaret Chronicles
As compiled by Maggie Murphy
The final entry

September 12, 1965

I am so happy to be back home in my little yellow bungalow on Cranberry Lane. Of course, this isn't my first visit. I've been back many, many times over the years since that awful night when my darling Connor and I fled Sweet River. This time, though, is different. I feel it. There is something in the air. I don't know how to describe it. Waiting. It's as if the house is waiting.

The air is still. Silent. But there is an electricity. A current. Can this be the time? After all these years, can this finally be the end of my long vigil?

The awful night was a lifetime ago, but I remember it as if it was yesterday. The cold night air. Daniel standing over my bed. The knife in his hand. The smell of the blood.

But I'm getting ahead of myself. I must include everything and not allow myself to skip ahead.

I was furious when I found my letters to Connor secreted in Daniel's desk. All along I had believed that Connor had abandoned me and left me to live a lonely life in Daniel's home. When I discovered that he never received my letters declaring my undying love for him and could only assume that I no longer cared for him, I was both overjoyed and angry. I decided to confront Daniel.

When Daniel arrived home from his business trip I was waiting for him. I took the packet of letters from my pocket and flung them at him. At first he denied knowing what they were, but ultimately he broke down and confessed that he had prevented my letters from being sent. He claimed it was to protect me from an unscrupulous gold digger who could only have wanted me for my money. Of course, I never believed him. His eyes were cold and his face composed and calm. He was consumed with jealousy.

I told him that I was leaving him. He didn't know that I had written to Connor and that Connor was waiting for me in the yellow bungalow. It didn't matter. I would have left without Connor. I could not tolerate any longer the cruel manipulation of my life and happiness.

My mistake was in telling him that I would no longer allow him to live in the manor. I told him he had to pack his things and be gone before the dawn of the next day. Then I turned my back and hurried back to the yellow bungalow and Connor's sweet embrace.

Connor and I had discussed the situation long into the previous night and decided that we could not stay in Sweet River. I feared that the town ladies would shun me and my dear baby and I could not condemn Rose Dawn to that life of scorn. My mama, Eliza, had family who lived in Drunken Hills, North Carolina, and we decided to move there. That awful night I was packed and ready to leave. I had only to take baby Rose Dawn to the safety of my mother's house where she would stay until Connor and I were settled in Drunken Hills.

When I returned to Connor from my confrontation with Daniel we gathered up my trunks and a few household treasures and loaded them into the carriage he had rented for our journey. My serving girl, Birdie Byrne, was left behind to clean the bungalow. I offered her the use of the house until she could secure employment elsewhere and she accepted gratefully.

After our tearful goodbyes with Birdie (who I forgave for not mailing my letters in spite of all the pain that resulted. I know how afraid she was of Daniel and his temper.), Connor and I took Rose Dawn to Mother's. It was there I discovered that I had left Rose's beloved stuffed lamb behind. I knew that she would be inconsolable without it and told Connor I must go back to the bungalow to retrieve it. He argued with me and told me I should not go, but I insisted. It was difficult enough to leave my baby, but I couldn't leave her without her favorite toy.

When Connor and I opened the door to the yellow bungalow and stepped inside. I knew immediately that something was amiss. I called Birdie's name repeatedly, but there was no answer. I tiptoed across the living room and peered up into the sleeping loft. Was she so soundly asleep that she didn't hear my calls? I started up the circular steps and halted as the scene at the top became clear. A single lantern was throwing an eerie light and it cast a glow on a man standing over the bed. I squinted and he half turned toward me. Daniel. In his hand a knife. There was blood everywhere. I froze with fear and loathing. Then I stumbled back a step and fell into Connor's arms. Haltingly I told him what I'd seen and he carried me to the couch and set me down. Then he mounted the steps himself.

Mere moments later he was back at my side. "We must leave," he whispered to me. "Daniel has killed Birdie. I'm sure he was after you. He will kill you next if he sees you. We can call the police when we escape."

"No, Connor. We can't." I protested but I knew we had to leave.

Connor half-carried me outside and threw me up onto the seat of the carriage and climbed aboard himself. He whipped the horses into action and we galloped away down the street leaving the scene of blood and murder behind us.

That was the last I saw of Daniel or Sweet River for many years. Even though we did call the police and reported what we believed to have happened, we learned from my mother that no one was ever charged in Birdie's death. Since she had no family there was no one to insist that the murderer be brought to justice. It would seem that Daniel got away with his crime. But he lost something important to him as well. I made good on my promise to evict him from the manor house and I kept him from inheriting the money we had saved over the length of our short marriage. I owe my bar-

rister a great deal for that.

Connor and I settled happily in Drunken Hills. Mother brought baby Rose to us shortly after that awful night and the three of us found a large old home on acres of land. We were so content. I thought it would be that way forever. Until the Great War.

Connor could not ignore the call to duty. I pleaded with him to stay at home. We had a small child and a large farm. I couldn't handle all of that on my own. But try as I might I could not persuade him to stay with us. The saddest day of my life was that crisp fall day when Connor kissed us goodbye and left to join his Army unit. I could not stop weeping for hours.

Connor promised me that he would return. I pressed my gold pocket watch -- the one my father gave me on the day of my wedding to Daniel -- into his hand and told him to keep it to remind him of me. On the back Father had engraved the words, "Time cannot diminish the power of love." He swore he would be back to return it after the forces of evil were defeated.

Alas, that is the one promise he made me that he hasn't kept. Yet.

The officers who came to the door at the farm some months later told me that my beloved had died in battle in Germany. His unit was sent in to rescue some school children who were cornered in their tiny school building. It was a trap the officers said. When the soldiers entered the school, the Germans were hidden inside and fired their weapons at them. Then they set fire to the school. No bodies were ever found. No trace of my beloved.

I told the officers who brought the horrible news that I could not accept that Connor was gone. I know in my heart that he survived. Somehow my beloved --- the most clever of men --- hid out and was not killed that day. I told them he was alive. I would not believe otherwise. The officers left me shaking their heads and whispering to each other. I don't care. They were wrong. Somewhere Connor is still alive. He will come to me. I know it as sure as anything.

Today the house is waiting. Waiting for Connor. I know it.

Over the years I have made many visits to the yellow bungalow. When I have felt the need to be close to Connor, I have escaped from the obligations of the farm and my family and come home. I never sold the bungalow. I couldn't bear to do so. So it has sat mostly empty over all these years. When I return I tie back my hair and put on my apron and whisk away the cobwebs so I can leave it clean and ready for my next visit. I have never told anyone where I go on my little larks, but I believe that Rose has her *suspicions. She has never said a word, but her smile when I return tells me she knows. Some things are better left alone, though, so we don't talk about it. Rose has no faith. She believes her father is long dead.*

The girl is living here now. I have seen her many times. It makes me so happy to know that my dear cottage is not sitting empty waiting for me. She is so young. Reminds me of when I was a girl and so terribly in love with my dear Connor. There is something about her. Maggie. Something that speaks to me. Whatever it is, I feel at peace.

This last lark has been taxing for me. I am not as young as I would like to be. My old bones are weary. I have cleaned and dusted and even baked an apple crumb cake -- Connor's favorite.

Now, dear diary, I will rest for a while in my rocker. Then I will gather up my bags and return to the farm. Perhaps, it is time for me to give up my larks. Perhaps I should let Connor go after all.

The air is stirring now. Something is happening. Oh, my dear diary, what is this? Can it be? Oh, yes, I see him. Oh, Connor. Oh ....

A Final Word
By Rose Dawn Booth Preston
As compiled by Maggie Murphy

I don't know exactly when Mama died. All I can do is guess. Mama disappeared on one of her "larks" and had been gone longer than usual. I never really worried when she disappeared since I'd known for years where she went on her "larks." I was in my twenties when my curiosity overwhelmed me and I decided to follow her. She climbed into her old Model T and set out with me following in my car a safe distance behind. I have to admit that I wasn't surprised when she ended up in Sweet River, South Carolina, and parked on Cranberry Lane in front of the old yellow bungalow. The very bungalow where the two of us lived when I was just a baby. Until then I hadn't realized that the place was still unoccupied. As I watched from down the street, I saw Mama unlock the front door and vanish inside. I waited to see if she would come out and when she failed to do so after an hour, I drove off and left her to her own devices. I never mentioned to Mama that I knew where she went but I suspect she knew that I knew.

Mama would return from her larks and attack whatever chores needed to be done with renewed energy. She always seemed refreshed and cheerful after a lark.

Since we never discussed it I could only guess why she kept returning to the yellow bungalow. Mama never accepted that Papa died in the Great War. She claimed that she would feel it in her heart if he was gone and I believe that she never quit looking for him. What better spot than the bungalow?

271

So, when she was away longer than I expected I drove to Sweet River and the yellow bungalow on Cranberry Lane. I wasn't surprised to see her car in the driveway and I pulled in behind Mama's Model T. My heart pounded as I opened the car door and slid out. I stood hands on hips staring at the door enveloped in unnatural silence for a few seconds before I stepped onto the porch and reached for the doorknob. My hands were shaking as I tested it. Unlocked. I turned the knob and slipped inside.

It was cool and quiet. The sun from the open front door slanted off the hardwood floors casting rainbow shadows on the walls. I squinted into the gloom as my eyes adjusted to the dimness. "Mama," I called. "Mama are you here? It's Rosie."

I half-expected Mama to appear wiping her floury hands on her apron. But there was only silence.

Somehow, though, the silence wasn't creepy. Rather I felt as if the house had put its arms around me in a warm embrace. "Mama," I called again, venturing further into the living space.

And then I saw her. Sound asleep in the rocking chair facing the fireplace, her head resting against the back of the chair. As I tiptoed closer I saw that there was an open book -- was it her diary? -- lying in her lap. "Mama? Wake up. It's Rosie."

I knew before I touched her. I kissed her cheek and it was chilly. I shook her shoulder gently and her hands fell to her sides, the pen she'd been clutching dropped to the floor and rolled under the couch. Tears rolled down my own hot cheeks. She was gone. Mama was gone.

I carefully replaced her hands in her lap and sat back on my heels to observe her. Her face was blurry through my tears. I scrubbed at my eyes with my fists and tried to think what to do next. I had to call someone. I had to get help. But first I needed to spend a few quiet moments to say goodbye. I took one of her cold hands in mine and discovered that she had a gold watch wound through her fingers. I'd never seen it before. It was scratched and scuffed as if it had been trampled on over and over. I turned over and read the inscription on the back. "Time cannot diminish the power of love." Odd, I thought as I dropped it into my purse. And then I quit thinking and sobbed quietly for a long while.

I called Old Doctor Cardwell's office from a pay phone in the village. The man who answered the phone agreed to meet me at the bungalow when I told him about Mama. It turned out that this was young Doctor Cardwell, the grandson of Old Doctor Cardwell who delivered me. The young doctor *told me he had learned the story of my birth and about the murder of Birdie Byrne and how Mama disappeared the same night Birdie was murdered by reading his grandfather's old journals. I hadn't heard any of this. I only knew that Mama and Papa had a wonderful marriage until Papa went off to the Great War. There was so much more I didn't know.*

I took Mama's diary away to read later. It explained so many things. I knew that Mama would want to be with Papa so I had her cremated and I took her ashes and flew to Germany to the battlefield where Papa died, or, as Mama believed, survived the battle. I sprinkled her ashes over the battlefield and I knew as I did so that she was again safely in the arms of my father.

When I came home I wanted to do one final thing for my mother and father, Margaret and Connor (or Conrad as I knew him). I wrote this one last chapter in her diary. I will hide it in the yellow bungalow for the next generation to find. Or, if not, to be kept in secrecy. Goodbye Dear Mama. Sleep well.

A Year Later

"Ouch, Julie, that hurts. " Maggie flinched. "That's my head not a pin cushion."

Julie removed the last bobbie pin from her mouth. "Stop whining, Mom. I'm almost finished." She stuck the pin in Maggie's hair and stepped back to admire her handiwork.

"There," Julie said. "Perfect." She put her hands on Maggie's shoulders and turned her so that they both faced the full-length mirror leaning against the living room wall. "Just the look for that trendy graduate. Perky yet intelligent." She tipped her chin toward the mirror.

Maggie grimaced. "This is so silly. Women my age shouldn't be wearing a cap and gown and doing the whole graduation ceremony thing. I should have just had them mail me my diploma."

"Uh, uh," Julie said. "And, what? Deny me and James and Dad and everyone else the pleasure of celebrating your accomplishments? I don't think so."

Maggie fiddled with the cap Julie had arranged on her head with such care. "I'm too old for this," she protested. "Wrinkles and muffin top should not be paraded around in a ceremony meant for the genuinely young. Not the young at heart."

"First of all, you don't have wrinkles. And secondly your muffin top is nicely camouflaged by that charming gown."

Maggie swatted her daughter's arm. "Are you trying to tell me I'm fat?"

"If the gown fits …. " Julie giggled. "Seriously Ms Jazzercise fanatic. You look awesome. And you know it."

Maggie sighed and stared into the mirror. "I'm just nervous. Maybe having graduation and a housewarming all on one day is too much. Maybe I should have postponed the housewarming."

"Don't be silly," Julie said. "The good citizens of Sweet River have been dying to see what Dad and you have done to the old Edison place. I think they might stage an actual intervention if you weren't having this party. And by intervention, I mean break-ins. Relax, Mom, we've got it all handled. You just need to let us do our thing and enjoy the day. You've earned it. And stop tugging on that gown. You're going to mess up the look."

"Where's Dad? And James?" Maggie fumed. "We're going to be late if they don't get here soon. There's only one thing worse than wearing this get-up and that's running down the aisle of the auditorium to catch up to my class."

"Don't worry. They'll be back soon."

"Will they have everything we need to bring off our surprise?"

Julie nodded -- her blonde hair swinging. "Trust Dad. He can handle it. It will be perfect. Everyone will be so surprised."

At that moment Gladdie, Azalea and Jewel flung open the front door to the yellow bungalow and tumbled into the living room letting in a gust of cold winter air. "Who will be surprised?" Gladdie asked.

Maggie shot a warning look at Julie and put a finger to her lips. Julie grinned and nodded as she turned her mother to face her three friends. "Mom is the surprise. Look at her. Can you believe how great she looks?'

Maggie's three friends clustered around her. "You do look fabulous," Gladdie said.

"Totally," Jewel agreed.

"But," Azalea added, "there's always room for improvement." She reached into the tote bag she carried and removed three gift boxes wrapped in heavy silver paper and topped with lilac colored bows. "No graduate should march across the stage unadorned."

Maggie stammered, "You, uh, you shouldn't have."

"Of course we should," said Jewel. "You have worked so hard and you deserve a few tokens of our affection."

Gladdie guided Maggie to the couch and pushed her down. "Open these."

"But," Maggie began and then opened the gifts. "Oh, my," she said when she finished, "you shouldn't have, but these are amazing."

She held up each gift in turn -- all made of brilliantly colored stones in shades of blue and turquoise. Earrings from Gladdie. A bracelet from Azalea. And an exquisite two leveled necklace from Jewel.

"You made these," she said to Jewel. "I'd know your work anywhere. And they are beyond beautiful. I love them. You guys are so fantastic. I love you guys."

Maggie hugged her friends and tears formed in her eyes. "I can't believe how lucky I am to have found y'all."

"Mom," Julie scolded. "Do not cry and ruin your make-up. I don't have time to redo it."

"Put on your new jewelry," Jewel said. "Time's awastin! The guys are holding seats for us, but the auditorium is small and we don't want to have to stand in the back."

Julie paced in front of the window as Maggie slipped on the new jewelry. "If Dad doesn't show up soon we'll have to leave without him."

Maggie looked into the mirror and admired her reflection. "He'll be here. I'm not going without him." She turned to her friends. "What about the big house? Is everything set up there for the party this afternoon? DJ wouldn't let me go up to check. He wants it to be a big surprise."

"Agnes has it under control," Gladdie said. "She's got all the food made and ready to set out at the proper time. Believe me, Maggie, she's outdone herself."

"And," Azalea put in, "the house looks gorgeous. DJ did an amazing job of restoring it. Wait until you see."

DJ, Maggie knew, had worked long hours to put the finishing touches on the house before the housewarming party. Putting the house back together after years of neglect had been a much larger job than either Maggie or DJ had anticipated. But, together, they had worked to return both the big house and the bungalow to their former glory.

Maggie was nervous about the unveiling later, but first she had to graduate. Seriously what was she thinking?

A horn sounded in the driveway outside and the women peered through the window. DJ and James threw open the doors of the red pick-up truck and bounded toward the house like a pair of puppies.

DJ hurried across the room and caught Maggie up in a hug. "You look great. Ready to go conquer the world?"

Maggie shook her head. "Not really, but these guys think I am so..." She snuck a look at the other women who were busy getting ready to go outside. "And," she whispered, "Did you get it?"

DJ nodded. "All set for the big reveal."

"You rock," Maggie said. She wound her arms around DJ and breathed in the scent of leather and aftershave. "What did I ever do without you?"

"It must have been a struggle, but now I'm here to take you to face the music."

"I'm so proud of you, Mom." Julie appeared at her side and inserted herself between her parents. "Getting your undergrad and your masters and all in one year. You are seriously outstanding. Now let's get going before you lose your nerve."

"Okay. Let's go graduate."

"We can party afterwards," DJ added.

As Maggie stood in line with her fellow graduates, she fingered her new bracelet and thought back to what had led her here. What if I'd had coffee in the house that day? What if I hadn't stopped at McDonald's and met April and Chloe? What if I hadn't stopped in Stallingsworth and stayed for the *Get Your Groove On Conference* and met Mary Lou and found out about Sweet River? Would I still be in Winslow? Would Dwight and I still be married? No answers to that one, of course, but this past couple of years had been one surprising development after another.

She peeked out at the gathered crowd. Where were her family and friends? She couldn't see them, but she knew they were there. DJ and the kids. Azalea and Jer and their sons. Braxton and Donovan. Gladdie and Chad. Jewel. All there for her. And she had thought she was invisible. Now, she felt entirely too visible. Uncomfortably so.

The girl behind her in line gave her a nudge as the President of

Sweet River University began to call out the names of the graduating class. Her heart pounding Maggie followed as each graduate made his or her way across the stage. And then -- "Margaret Kathleen Murphy. Bachelor of Arts in English and Master of Fine Arts in Historical Fiction and Creative Writing."

Maggie took her time as she crossed the stage and accepted her diploma from the president. Her moment in the sun and she was darned well going to enjoy it. She stopped for a second to stare into the audience. A single long and loud wolf whistle broke the silence and the crowd rustled and some tittered. Then a clear young voice rang out, "Way to go, Mom!" Julie's voice. Followed by a deeper male voice. "You rock." James. Maggie grinned and gave them a thumbs up. She was still smiling as she made her way to her seat to watch the rest of the class be awarded diplomas.

It was a small midyear class and the class speaker did not give a lengthy speech so Maggie and her fellow grads were out in the hallway to greet their families in record time. Maggie was surrounded by DJ and James and Julie when a small figure bolted across the lobby and launched herself at Maggie.

"Woof," Maggie said as the small figure collided with her stomach and almost knocked her down. Startled Maggie looked down. Chloe! And following Chloe at a much more sedate pace, April. How on earth?

"Chloe," Maggie said. "April. How did you two get here?"

"Mr. Murphy asked us to come," Chloe explained. "And Aunt Molly bringed us. Are you surprised?"

Maggie bent to lift Chloe into her arms. "Oh, I'm super surprised."

April asked, "Are you happy to see us? We didn't know. Aunt Molly said it was okay. And Mr. Murphy. But you know -- we didn't want to intrude."

Tears rolled down Maggie's cheeks as she looked over Chloe's head at DJ. "I couldn't be happier. Mr. Murphy is great at surprises." She kissed the top of Chloe's head. "Do you have any more surprises, Mr. Murphy?"

DJ shrugged. "Well, maybe one more." He looked over his shoulder and Maggie saw a slim woman appear from the restroom and hurry toward them. Something familiar about that walk. And as the young woman got closer, Maggie shrieked, "Sarah." She set Chloe down and swept Sarah into a hug. Sobbing, she tried to smile at DJ.

"I can't believe you did this," she said.

He handed her a tissue and wiped a tear that threatened to drip down her chin. "These guys were part of what brought us to right now. I thought you'd want them to be part of today."

Maggie blew her nose. "Look at me. I'm a mess. But this is the best graduation ever. DJ Murphy you made my day."

"I try."

"It's so beautiful," she said as she and DJ and the kids unlocked the big brass lock on the front door and let themselves into the big house. "It came," she said as she indicated the large semi-modern chandelier hanging in the two story foyer. Light from it reflected off the walls making the foyer sparkle.

As the months stretched on since Maggie and DJ bought the old Edison mansion, the population of Sweet River grew increasingly curious. Because the house had been included in the Sweet River registry of historical homes and because it had been such a disaster for so many years before they purchased it, Maggie and DJ knew they would eventually have to open it to the public. They debated allowing the home to be included in the semi-annual historical home tours, but ultimately decided that they preferred their privacy to public scrutiny on a regular basis.

Their alternative plan was to have one giant housewarming party and invite all of Sweet River. They had hoped to do it at Christmas but time-consuming delays in getting various supplies and additional delays in finding competent craftsmen to do the work made that impossible. Finally, they set a date to coincide with Maggie's graduation and crossed their fingers that it would be ready. It had been a race to get it done and Maggie hadn't seen the house complete until the afternoon following her graduation from Sweet River U.

She turned slowly to take it all in. The aroma of floor polish and fresh paint mingled with the delicious smells of Agnes' cooking. The hardwood floors gleamed under their feet. Maggie led the way into the kitchen where Agnes was putting the final touches on platters of appetizers and other snacks. It wasn't as sumptuous as the Thanksgiving spread at Azalea and Jer's but no one was going to go away hungry. For sure. On the stove a pot of tomato basil soup simmered. Maggie lifted the lid and breathed in. "Yum."

"We can't thank you enough, Agnes," Maggie said. "This all looks so wonderful. We need to pay you for doing this."

Agnes waved her hand. "No way. This is my contribution." She leaned closer to Maggie. "Don't tell anyone, but I love doing this. If I had my way, I'd close the café and just cater events."

"I'm going to bet that after this, you'll find lots of takers on the catering idea. But don't close Agnes'. Where will I get my tomato basil fix?"

"Don't worry, Maggie. I'm pretty sure one of the girls would buy the place if I figure out a way to get the catering going."

They wandered into the living room where a bar was set up and a tuxedo-clad college student was organizing glassware. DJ poured two glasses of wine and handed one to Maggie. "Here's to the house. To the bungalow. To our new lives in Sweet River."

Maggie clinked her glass against his. Julie and James poured themselves wine and the four of them toasted each other. James removed a package from under his jacket. "Where shall I put this?"

DJ motioned toward the large room across the hall from the living room. "Put it in my office until after the party," he said. James disappeared into the office that had once belonged to Daniel. The very place where, if Maggie was correct, Margaret had confronted him about the letters that he had confiscated and prevented from being sent to Connor. So much history. But Maggie preferred it as it was today. DJ's office from which he ran his fledgling company M&D Restoration and Design. In working on the old mansion he had discovered that he loved doing construction. In particular he loved old homes with lots of history. He hadn't yet figured out how to do historic restoration exclusively but he would one day soon. Meanwhile, he was increasing his clientele for simple home construction and repair by diligent advertising and word of mouth. A satisfied customer is the best advertising, Maggie said. What mattered most to her was that DJ was happy. Excited about each day and what he could do. And even better bringing that excitement home to her each night and sharing it.

The doorbell pealed. "Must be the gang," Maggie said. "I told them to come over before everyone else. We can give them a private tour before the rest of Sweet River descends."

The Murphy family moved as one into the foyer and DJ tugged

open the heavy front door to reveal Azalea and Jer and Gladdie and Chad on the step loaded with bags and bottles. "Goodies for the party," Azalea explained.

"Really. That is NOT necessary. Agnes has it handled," Maggie said.

"Too late," Azalea said and brushed past Maggie into the house.

Maggie shook her head. There never was any point in arguing with 'Zalea. It was a waste of time and energy. "Well, welcome to our home," she said. She peered past her friends. "I thought Jewel was coming with y'all. We wanted to give y'all the tour at the same time."

"Mom," Julie interjected "What's with this y'all business? I swear you get more Southern by the minute."

"Your mom is totally Southern, Julie," Gladdie said. "Deal with it." She gave Julie a hug and stepped into the foyer and pulled off her damp boots. " Can't ruin these gorgeous new floors," she explained.

"And Jewel?" Maggie persisted.

"Well, that," Gladdie said. "She's right behind us. Caught a ride with someone."

"Oh? Who?" Maggie asked but didn't need an answer since Jewel appeared at the end of the slate sidewalk that wound its way to the front porch. "There she is now with -- " Maggie stopped short. "Is that who I think it is? With Jewel?"

Azalea and Gladdie exchanged glances and Jer and Chad developed a consuming interest in the molding. Maggie stared and then she burst out laughing.

"Did you guys seriously think this would bother me? Really? Oh my goodness, I'm so happy for her I can't tell you."

Relief hung in the air as Jewel, hand in hand with Mac MacDougal, stepped onto the front step. "Hi, Maggie," Jewel said. "Sorry to be a bit late but Mac had to attend to some post-graduation stuff."

"Hi, Maggie," Mac said. "Thanks for asking me."

"Of course, I would have asked you, Mac," Maggie said. "If I'd known about this --" She swung her arm in an arc to indicate the pair of them. "Why am I the last to know?"

Jewel fiddled with the buttons on her jacket. "I, um, don't know. It's still fairly new and um, I wasn't sure how long it would last. And you were so busy."

Maggie tugged Jewel into the house and hugged her. "Never too busy for you. I, personally, couldn't be happier."

DJ shook Mac's hand. "I personally am over the moon about the two of you dating." He grinned at Maggie and she punched his arm. "Just saying," DJ said.

As Maggie and Julie gave Gladdie, Azalea and Jewel the guided tour of the house, the guys tagged behind. Maggie's friends exclaimed over the high ceilings, the arched windows that opened onto the spacious backyard and a yet-to-be-restored gazebo. They admired the wainscoting and the crown molding that bracketed the soft grey walls. They commented on the somewhat eclectic décor -- a blend of furnishings from DJ and Maggie's Ohio home and thrift and antique shop finds that Maggie unearthed over the last year.

As the women snooped in the bedroom closets, Maggie dropped back to eavesdrop on DJ and the guys. "No way the Patriots win again," Chad was saying. "It's got to be time for the Panthers one of these years."

"Where did you find this flooring?" "This grout is amazing." "Who did you get to do the plumbing?"

Plumbing? Grout? Football? Maggie quit listening.

"I've saved the best for last," she said as she stopped at the door to the kitchen.

DJ came up beside her and added, "After two years of cooking in that tiny kitchen in the bungalow I figured we deserved an upgrade. So -- " He stepped aside to let them into the kitchen. "Voila."

"Oh, my," 'Zalea drawled. "This is all that and a biscuit."

The kitchen was a gleaming testimony to the 21st century. Granite countertops, stainless steel appliances, hardwood floors, white-washed oak cabinets and a long island surrounded by comfortable looking bar stools.

"This is not your Margaret's kitchen," Gladdie said. "Wow."

"And we didn't want it to be," Maggie said. "Living in a historic house is one thing, but cooking in a historic kitchen is quite another."

Agnes' turned away from the stove. "I could run my catering business from here. Easily."

"Catering?" Azalea said. "If you're serious I have some clients for you. Have you heard of the ..."

Maggie smiled to herself. Another business was born. And, all of this, she thought was because I was out of coffee. She hugged the thought to herself and escorted her friends into the living room to wait for the arrival of the curious citizens of Sweet River coming to check out the new house and the newest residents. And, of course, to eat and drink and socialize. Home sweet home.

Hours later after what seemed like an endless stream of neighbors had passed through the house to eat and gawk and gossip DJ helped their last guest, Verdie Cranford, to her feet from the armchair where she had been holding court during the entire party and escorted her and her husband, Frank, to the front door.

"It was a lovely party," Frank began. "Thank you so much for inviting us." He stuck out his hand to shake DJ's.

Before he could do that, though, Verdie put her hand on his shoulder. "Wait, Frank. I'm not ready to leave yet. I think I'll just have a bite more of Agnes' delicious guacamole."

"Oh, certainly, Mrs. Cranford," DJ said. "I'll get a plate for you."

Maggie started to rise from the chair that Verdie vacated moments before. "I'll go, DJ. Verdie, come sit down." Maggie rolled her eyes at Gladdie who was sprawled on the couch.

"No, that won't be necessary," Frank said. "Verdie, these young people have been on their feet all day. They need to relax and enjoy their home. They do not need to entertain two old fogies a single second longer. We're leaving."

"No, it's really fine," DJ insisted. But Frank was propelling Verdie out the door.

"Wait a minute," DJ said and hurried into the kitchen and returned with a plastic container. "Here's some of Agnes' guacamole to go." He handed the dish to Verdie.

Verdie glared at Frank and then turned to DJ. "Thank you so much young man. I'm glad you aren't dead after all."

DJ chuckled. "I am too, Mrs. Cranston. I am too."

With that Verdie stormed out the door with a chagrined Frank trailing in her wake. "Sorry," he murmured as the heavy door latched behind him.

DJ leaned against the closed door and burst out laughing.

"You got the Verdie seal of approval," Jewel told him. "Your future in Sweet River is guaranteed."

"We should go too," said Gladdie as she struggled to her feet. "You guys don't want us hanging around."

"Yes, we do," Maggie said. "We have one last surprise but we need to go down to the bungalow to show you. You can't leave yet. None of you."

"More surprises? I don't think I can take the suspense." Azalea pulled Jer to his feet. "We're in."

Jewel looked questioningly at Mac who nodded. "I wouldn't miss this for the world."

Maggie laughed. "Okay, DJ, let's show 'em what we've got." She linked her arm through her husband's and they led the way through the overgrown garden back to the yellow bungalow.

Lights glowed in the window and to Maggie it looked infinitely more welcoming than the big house. She sighed. One last detail and she would leave it behind. Well, except for using it for her studio and guest house. But no more late nights with Margaret.

Maggie fished the key from her pocket and unlocked the door. DJ and she stood back to let their friends enter. The faux fireplace crackled merrily and candles flickered.

"Romantic," said Gladdie as they settled themselves in the somewhat cramped living room.

"Yes," said Azalea. "What do you have up your little sleeve?"

Maggie called, "Julie? Are you ready?"

"Yes," came a muffled voice from the sleeping loft above.

"James? How about you?"

"I'm on it." James voice from the kitchen.

"Good. Let the surprise begin."

James emerged from the kitchen balancing a tray holding a bottle of champagne and a stack of plastic glasses. He was followed by Braxton and Donovan carrying an assortment of bags and bottles and, yes, a trowel. He handed glasses to each of them and then sat cross-legged on the floor in front of the fireplace.

"Next," he said and Julie descended from the loft carrying a backpack.

Maggie went to stand by the bookshelves that bracketed the fireplace. She pulled something from one shelf and held it up. "Remember this?"

"Is that what it looks like it is?" asked Gladdie. "Margaret's diary?"

"I thought you put it back in the secret hiding place," Jewel said.

"And sealed it up," Azlea finished.

The men exchanged baffled looks and waited. The women obviously knew something (or a lot of somethings) they didn't.

"Okay, enough suspense," Maggie said. "Yes, this is Margaret's diary. When it came down to it I just couldn't let it go. Couldn't seal it back up in the wall. I felt like it was a sort of lucky charm for me." She looped an arm around DJ's waist. "For us."

"But," she continued, "I wanted to put something in the hiding place. So I decided on this." She nodded at Julie who opened her backpack and pulled out a stack of books. She handed one to each of the women who began to whoop as they realized what each of them had in her hands.

"You sneaky little thing," Azalea said as she waved her copy in the air and danced around the room.

"Quiet," Maggie said. "I can explain." She set her copy of the book on the rickety coffee table.

The cover of the book was a deep chocolate brown and appeared to be made of leather. On it, in gold letters, it said -- *The Margaret Chronicles. As Compiled by Maggie Murphy.*

"It's my last year's final writing project," Maggie told them. "But new and improved."

Mac grinned. "Steven -- That's her writing professor -- " He explained to the group. "Steven told me how good it was. But how did you get it published?"

"If you want something badly enough, you can find a way," DJ interjected. "It was important to Maggie. To both of us." He picked up a copy of the book from the pile Julie had set on the coffee table and opened it. "Read inside."

"Rose Dawn Press," Gladdie read. "Rose Dawn? Margaret's baby? I don't get it."

"I do," said Chad who had been silent during most of the discussion. "She self-published it. Right?"

Maggie blushed. "I did. I didn't want to wait through the endless process of trying to get it published by a so-called real publisher. I wanted it as quickly as possible. I hope you don't think I was cheating."

A chorus of no's.

"This is so awesome," Jewel said. "I think we all agree."

"But," Maggie continued, "I didn't want to leave the hiding place empty so I decided to put one of these in there and seal it up for future generations to find one day. Or not. I'll still have a piece of Margaret but a piece of both of us will be hidden in the wall of our bungalow."

"That's cool," Jer added. "Now what happens?"

"James," DJ said. "Guys. Proceed with step number two."

James opened the bags and emptied the contents into a large container and added water. The other two knelt in front of the brick wall behind the bookcase and carefully removed the loose brick that hid the secret hiding place. "Voila," James said. "Mom's book goes in here."

Maggie reached into the bookshelves and pulled out another book. She held it up for the rest of them to see. "I had two made with real leather covers. One for us to keep and one for the hiding place. I figured leather would hold up better than paper."

"And it looks more authentic," Jewel said.

Maggie started to place the leather-covered book into the hiding place but DJ stopped her. "Not yet, Maggie." He pulled a pen from his pocket. "Sign it."

She shook her head. "Not just me. All of us. We're all part of it." She took the pen from DJ and using her best penmanship signed her name on the blank page inside of the cover. She passed the pen to Gladdie. And one by one each of them signed.

"There," said James as he scrawled his name and then recapped the pen, "we're all set. Except for one last tiny detail." He picked up the bottle of champagne and gave it to DJ.

DJ uncorked it with a flourish and poured champagne in each glass. As Maggie carefully placed the diary in a metal box and then wedged it into the hole in the brick wall, they raised their glasses. "To Margaret."

James replaced the brick and DJ grasped the trowel and filled the cracks around it. "James researched this and this stuff is supposed to last hundreds of years," he said.

"That's the plan."

Finally, DJ sat back and examined his handiwork. "To Maggie," he said.

Maggie leaned against DJ and sipped her champagne. *Margaret? Are you there Margaret? I think you are.*

Maggie's Journal

Margaret is gone. She hasn't visited in ages. But DJ is here. And Julie and James. And all of our new friends. And we have our new house and our new life here in Sweet River. Together. Still, I kind of miss Margaret. Is that weird? Maybe she will come back to haunt the place if someone else needs her. I hope so.

SOMETIME IN THE FUTURE

The girl stood hands-on-hips assessing the brick wall in the living room of the historical bungalow she and her husband had just purchased. A fake fireplace was centered on the wall. Old and dirty it leaned precariously into the room. The bricks on either side of it were cracked and crusted with white powder. The mortar was falling out in chunks. Maybe it hadn't been such a good idea to remove the wallboard that had covered the brick, but once she learned that the dirty and stained wallboard hid a brick wall she refused to give up on revealing it. And, in as bad shape as it was, she still loved the look of the brick. They could restore it to its original state with enough elbow grease and chemicals. First the fireplace had to go. No problem there.

They'd had a brilliant idea last night that led to her standing now in front of the brick wall. They'd been in the house a week and Derek decided to try to see if the fireplace worked. He'd spent an hour cleaning the knob that turned on the gas. He checked the connections and then called her into the room, "Honey, I'm going to fire this thing up. You need to be here for that."

She'd hurried from the kitchen leaving a pot of tomato basil soup simmering on the stove. "Are you sure we should do this? That thing looks dangerous."

"I am almost positive it will work."

"Almost? I don't think we should be …."

But Derek wasn't listening. He turned the knob slowly and as the fake logs started to turn red there was a loud bang and the fireplace fell forward into the room. Derek jumped back. She screamed. And, fortunately, the fireplace remained standing and nothing exploded.

"That's it," she said. "I'm done. That thing goes."

"I agree," Derek said as he wiped his grimy hands on the leg of his jeans, "but we need a fireplace. With the price of fuel these days, it would be great to be able to have a fire to warm the house on cold South Carolina nights."

And, one thing led to another, and the two of them decided that they would put in a real fireplace in the brick wall. Nothing to it. Ha.

She could hear pounding coming from the back of the bungalow -- Derek pulling the crumbling deck off the house. He was busy. And she could handle this on her own. She wasn't some wimpy woman from way back in the 21st century. Nope. She was a modern woman. She could do stuff.

She crouched in front of the brick wall. Derek said they couldn't put a fireplace in until they knew what was behind the bricks. Wouldn't want to hit wiring or plumbing. Or, god forbid, a dead body.

Okay. Ready. She pulled her latest generation iPhone from her pocket and scrolled to find the x-ray app. Then she pushed the power button on their brand new wireless portable x-ray machine. A miracle. It could see through anything. Probably could see clear through not just the bricks but the outside wall as well. The machine hummed as it warmed up. The green light came on and she aimed her iPhone at the wall and scanned back and forth. The x-ray machine clattered as it spit out pictures of whatever was hidden behind the wall. Finally she turned off the app and sat on the floor to examine the printout from the x-ray machine.

"Derek! Hey. Come in here." She grabbed one of the pages and ran toward the backyard where she could see him hauling the rotting deck boards away.

He lumbered across the yard and stopped when he saw her waving the page. "Are you okay? What's that?"

"Look at this." She held the page in front of his nose. "There's something in the brick wall."

"A skeleton?"

"Don't be stupid. Looks like a box of some kind to me. And, furthermore, it's behind a loose brick. Come help me get it out."

Derek shook his head. He knew better than to argue. "Okay. Let's see what you've found."

Minutes later the pair of them had removed the loose brick and pulled a dusty metal box from its hiding place. She used her shirttail to scrub off some of the accumulated dirt and fingered the latch. "This is exciting," she said.

The girl worked on the latch until it came lose and she pried open the lid. Inside the box a book was tucked -- its leather cover wrapped in a layer of plastic. Careful not to damage it she removed the book and unwound the plastic.

"It's a diary," she said. "Look. It must be really old."

She sat on the floor with the book in her lap and eyed it. A chocolate brown cover -- embossed gold lettering. *The Margaret Chronicles as Compiled by Maggie Murphy.*

"Wow," she said. "Derek this is so cool."

She opened the cover. Published by Rose Dawn Publishing. 2010.

"Oh, it's really old. I mean. 2010! Ancient actually. I wonder who put it there. Someone who lived here back then. All those years ago. The pages are all crumbly and the print is faded but I can read it. I'm going to read it cover to cover."

Derek grinned at her. "Of course, you are. I would expect nothing less."

"Look at all these signatures. They all must have lived here. Or something. I don't know."

She began to read. "The dedication says, *'To Margaret Who Started it all.'*

He peered over her shoulder. "What's written under the dedication?"

She squinted. *"To Maggie Who Finished It. With love, DJ."*

"Something tells me this was meant for me. I've felt something special about this bungalow since we first saw it." The girl handled the book as if it was made of glass.

She turned to the first entry in the diary. *"May 11, 1899. Daniel is coming home tomorrow and I am not sure whether I am excited or frightened."*

She looked up at Derek with shining eyes. "This is so unbelievable. Hundreds of years have passed and I already feel like I know these people. This Maggie and Margaret. I think we have ghosts. Friendly ones."

Derek dropped to the floor and pulled her into his lap. He kissed the top of her head as she bent over the diary. "You always do love a good ghost story, don't you, Meg?"

She leaned against him and began to turn the pages of the diary.

The End (Finally)

More books by Terry Sykes-Bradshaw

The Awful Truth About Dead Men

When five friends schedule a Girls Getaway Cruise in the Florida Keys, they anticipate doing nothing more than escaping the nasty winter weather in Ohio by sailing on a 90-foot sailboat called the Mirage. Their idyllic interlude is interrupted when Kate Kelly, who has always dreamed of solving a crime, stumbles upon the body of the boat's captain, Nigel Fairweather, sprawled on the floor of his cabin. She assumes he is dead.

This horrifying discovery makes a shambles of their carefree vacation. And when the body vanishes the five women decide to take matters into their own hands to solve the mystery. Only then can they return to more important things – like acquiring the perfect tan, wearing flip flops and guzzling little umbrella drinks.

The five learn that aboard the Mirage what you see is not always what you think you've seen.

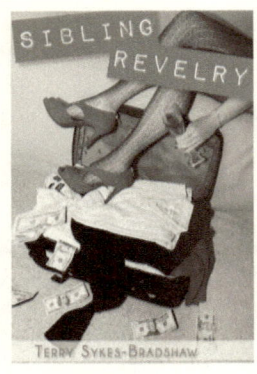

Sibling Revelry

It begins with a margarita and ends with being held hostage by a desperate killer. Not exactly the vacation of their dreams. When twin sisters Kate Kelly and Chrissie Montgomery plan a holiday in Europe to celebrate their Big Birthday, they anticipate shopping, sightseeing and pigging out on gourmet cuisine. Within hours of arriving in Paris, however, their trip goes horribly wrong.

They soon find themselves on a wild journey from the streets and sewers of Paris to the casinos in Nice and the wharf in Barcelona before everything comes to a shocking conclusion in a bullring in Spain.

Find More Online at www.terrysykes-bradshaw.com

www.ingramcontent.com/pod-product-compliance
Lightning Source LLC
Chambersburg PA
CBHW020438270626
47155CB00022B/631